PRASERIAN

KAYDRIE TOLBERT

To the man who constantly gives me butterflies. My best friend. The inspiration for my writing. The one who proved to me fairytale love does exist. To my greatest support. My sweet husband, Chasen. I love you darling.

Kaydrie Tolbert Books
ISBN: 978-1-7350974-0-4 (Paperback)
ISBN: 978-1-7350974-1-1 (Ebook)
ISBN: 978-1-7350974-2-8 (Hardback)
Library of Congress Number: 2020910460
https://kaydrietolbertbook.wixsite.com/website
Copyright © 2020 Kaydrie Tolbert

✿ Created with Vellum

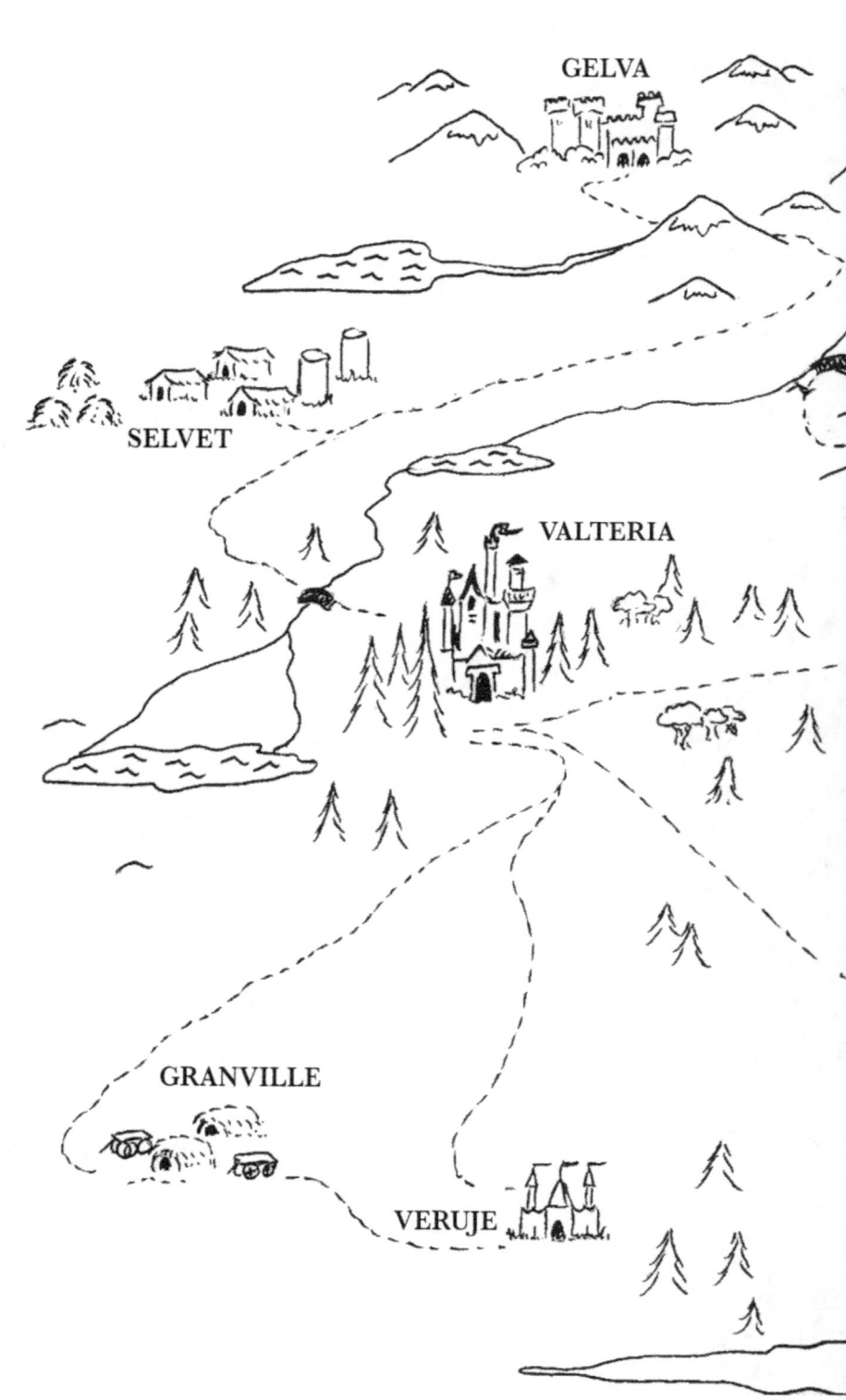

CHAPTER 1

he crimson roses had died quickly. I was in a trance as I stared at the flowers in front of me, the ones I hadn't replaced since that day. The last four weeks since his funeral had been long and plodding. The once soft, vibrant roses from the service were officially wilted, falling onto my writing desk – as if responding to the suffering that was in the deepest corners of my heart.

Grief. Why was it allowed to greet me so soon? What a cruel thief to affect the young. Memory being the only form of overcoming it's forbearance, yet still creating another type of pain. How could I ever win?

I felt as if I would never recover from the shock. Shock was something else I hadn't experienced before, but I quickly became acquainted with its deafening effect. I never expected I would be the only individual to resemble a Praserian in Valteria. It was a heavy realization. I could hear fate placidly laugh, taunting me towards that thin divide between bitter sorrow and complete agony. I wanted to surrender to the pain and cry. I swallowed hard to hold back the onset of tears that I felt building in my throat.

The days couldn't pass by fast enough. Everyone had returned to their normal routines once again, hardly skipping a beat. The only exception was me.

I could feel inside my empty, unsettled heart the deep pressing urge to react the same way, hopeful that if I behaved like everything was normal then I could somehow convince myself that it was. Yet a part of me felt that by moving on and getting back to normal, I was betraying his memory. It was like pretending it never happened. Life without him would never be normal, so why act as such?

I knew the answer to that question, and it ate me up inside. *He would want more for me.* With this in mind, I promised myself when I woke up that I would try my hardest to let go, to end my mourning.

Over the last month, it had been a constant battle to get back into my routine, to go on living as he would want. I knew that I couldn't drag on with death's bags at my feet any longer than I already had. No power in this world could relinquish or prevent the binding chords of fate that besets every soul who has ever been fortunate enough to taste a play on living.

"Life has unexpected turns. You keep moving forward until you get back where you began. Innocent, humble, pure. No one should leave the world worse than they entered its beautiful sphere. Anyone can achieve that splendor of innocence again." I could hear his voice echo in my ears, as he would quote it daily. He insisted

it gave us reason to be better. Even while battling his illness, he still found reason to say it.

I knew it was time – I needed to do something more than wallow. In an attempt to bring back some sense of normalcy, I decided to go visit the garden. I slowly made my way to the garden, walking aimlessly through the castle, trying to ignore the servants around me as I passed by. I was nervous, realizing enough gossip was probably circulating around the castle about me and my family, adding the sight of me probably wasn't wise.

I stood out wherever I was. I looked completely different from my family. My hair was distinctly black as night and landed just beneath my shoulder blades. My cerulean blue eyes reflected the majority of my thoughts for those who dare to look at me directly, which fortunately was few and far between. My heavy, dark eyelashes encircled and accentuated my already noticeable eyes, making them even more vibrant. I was very petite and many in Valteria considered that a weak characteristic; they see powerful women to be slender and tall. I liked to think they were mistaken. *I am courageous and strong willed in my own eyes, although I haven't had much opportunity to prove it. People can only pretend for so long before I see how they truly feel.*

I didn't like the idea of being a topic of conversation, although I should probably be used to it by now. *It's okay Allene, don't pay attention to them and they won't pay attention to you.* I kept my eyes on the ground as I walked, trying to keep the courage I had to go outside. I was determined to do this for myself.

I hadn't been exposed to direct sunlight since the funeral.

It was something that always brought me joy, which I had purposefully robbed myself of over the last month to mourn in my own way.

I took a deep breath as I stepped through the door frame that led to my goal. The sun instantaneously warmed my skin, making me dizzy from the sudden flash of harsh light. I did it; I was finally outside. It took only a few moments to adjust to the brightness of the summer day, and I yearned to see the garden again.

Flowers that were in the early stages of blossoming before his funeral were now in full bloom, showing off the best versions of themselves. I smiled as I came to the cherry tree, picking the largest cherry I could see. In that moment, I felt my sorrows ease just a little; just enough to give me hope.

However, my hope didn't last long. I was quickly reminded why it had taken me so long to venture outside of the safety of my room in the first place. As much as I tried to ignore them as I walked by, it was hard to dismiss the eyes of the servants that surrounded me. I felt like I was on display for everyone and the realization made me uncomfortable. People's stares were beating down on me harder than the sun itself, ruining any bliss I could pry from the garden's liveliness. I found myself chewing on the pit of the cherry I had picked to calm my nerves. I could practically hear the gossip starting to form and my goal for the day quickly faded. *This was a mistake.*

As swiftly as I had left and visited the garden, I found myself returning to my room. The failure of my outing brought feelings of regret to what was supposed to be a happy accomplishment. Cowardly running from the servants stares,

I returned to sit in my pale, dull, and tedious bedroom. The unfortunate room hadn't been changed for a few centuries. It was almost like it was created before color ever existed.

The ash stone walls were accented with ivory and pewter gray rugs on the floor. The bedding was thick and heavy, weighed down by its magnolia coloring like a large cloud. The only addition of color was a handful of poppies on my desk that I had picked from the garden earlier that morning. They were displayed next to the wilted roses from the funeral, leaving a stark contrast in vibrancy. Well, that and the ruby ring he had given me, that was proudly dancing with light. I closed my eyes, hoping it was a dream, wishing it all away.

I was trying to write songs in my journal to keep my mind distracted. Words and rhymes would come to my mind and I would write them down, then scribbling them out quickly after. The combinations I would create rarely made much sense, as the words and rhymes came from what emotions I was currently feeling. It was a secret escape that I had discovered a few years ago. It was an opportunity to channel all my inner feelings into something productive. Singing and writing songs, it was my hidden hobby that I shared with him. He genuinely thought I was the best singer that he had ever heard. I knew my range was limited and my creativity for song lyrics mediocre, but he made me believe that I possessed a special talent when it came to music. *I miss him.*

I was intently focused on the start of a new verse to a song I had been writing when a knock on the door startled me.

"Come in," I said softly, readjusting my posture to its appropriate expectancy, imitating being tall and proper. The door scraped open as I saw the color of shady russet hair and amber eyes peek in.

"Good morning Princess Allene, how did you sleep?" asked Damien. I instantly slouched and turned away, trying to gain focus again. Damien chuckled and continued, unoffended by my nonverbal reply. "Oh, just fine Damien. I am so glad you stopped by for a visit. It's been too long! How are you doing?" Damien attempted to speak in a sing – song voice that I assume was his imitation of myself.

"You interrupted my train of thought," I accused, trying to turn back to my writing.

"I think you are ready for a break from thinking, princess," Damien encouraged.

"Why would you say that?" I asked, acting surprised. I turned to see Damien folding his arms, raising his eyebrows in disbelief of my ignorance.

"News spreads too fast around here." I huffed under my breath, pushing my papers to the side.

"It got out as soon as your bedroom door opened this morning. *The princess finally emerged from her room.* It has been quite the gossip." Damien laughed, making it hard for me to hold back one of my own. Damien always was good company and it was refreshing to see his face.

Damien was the herald of the knight Ajax. He was around the age of seventeen, with poker straight hair that went to his ears. Damien took pride in his 5'11" height, which happened to be 9 inches taller than me. However, it was considered average for a Valterian. Nonetheless, he tended to comment on our difference in height frequently. I guess I shouldn't complain; matters could have been much worse.

The list of things to tease me about seemed tremendously long.

Damien had told me on numerous occasions that I was impossible not to tease, even if I was a full Valterian. I didn't display elegance and poise very frequently, so I could understand where he was coming from. Luckily, I was more than all right with the teasing coming from Damien.

We had a slight age difference of two years, me being older. He had been my best friend for the last thirteen years. One of my only ones. He was like a brother to me. Any amount of teasing didn't threaten our friendship.

"Damien, you did it again," I mentioned.

"Did what?" he asked innocently.

"You don't have to be so proper when you see me. I wish you would just call me Allene. Stop bowing and asking silly questions that you already know the answers to." I repeated this to him exasperatingly, yet he never seemed to understand. I couldn't tell if he did it just to get a rise out of me, or if it was because he was raised to treat any royal with the utmost respect. He claimed it was the second reason, but I stubbornly thought it was the first.

"I apologize, Allene, it's a habit. Everyone else around here talks like that. It's hard to shut it off sometimes."

"I don't talk like that. You never see me conversing with Risa in that way."

"That's royal to royal. Plus, no offense, but you don't get out enough to hear how the rest of the staff converses about you and your family. Despite what you think, everyone in the castle speaks with complete respect for you."

I huffed under my breath. He was right. I didn't believe it.

"Why do you get sick of it anyway? I would love being treated like everyone treats you. People bow at your feet! They ask how they can help. They're always at your beck and call. Instead, *I'm* the help! All I'm good for is assisting the mighty, *Sir Ajax*," he said with sarcasm and then continued, "Trust me when I say, I would do anything to be in your shoes one day." He spoke with a repulsed tone regarding his current situation and shook his head, unpleased, while sticking out his tongue.

I held back my laughter, desperately trying to be sympathetic with his frustration. He displayed his notorious pout that made him look like a child who was forced to eat a bug under peer pressure, the one he always got when he was in an offended mood.

Realizing the door was still open, a panicked look shot across his face. He almost slammed it shut but barely caught the handle in time to make it a quiet transition. He leaned against the wall and looked behind his shoulder as if someone was there. I could tell he was praying that no one had heard him gossiping about Ajax.

I nodded my head at Damien, unsure of what to say. I thought about what he asked. *Why do I get sick of it? Simple. I hate people being fake.*

I got up from my chair and stalked swiftly toward Damien. I took a step back and cleared my throat. His eyes widened, knowing I would try to match his dramatic performance. Mine were terribly sloppy in comparison, so he always was preparing for the worst.

"Prince Damien, how did you sleep? How are you feeling? Do I need to get you anything? Take a seat; you must be more comfortable. Please sit! Oh, yes, the king? Dead? How tragic. Did you see his hair? Valterians have much better hair than Praserians. Probably why he wore that hat instead of a crown for most of his rule, or maybe he shaved it to hide his true nature. Also, I hear anyone with even a dash of Praserian blood has a blackened heart and that when they die they bleed black too! Must be why they chose a closed casket for his viewing. Evil things they are, much like a disease, or even a plague for heaven's sakes. God save us all from these despicable creatures that infiltrated the crown! Oh, but surely we mourn the king!" I announced with pure dry enthusiasm. I took it one step further and bounced around my room like the ladies in the courtyard I had overheard gossiping about such things just yesterday.

Damien's eyebrows went up in shock from my sarcastic acting. He soon recovered from the lingering bitterness of my act and held an indiscernible look.

"Do people really ask that many questions? Are they really that obviously rude?" he asked doubtfully, but he took a seat anyway as if my offer had been sincere from earlier.

I laughed and sat on the floor, picking at the floral strands of the prime pressed rug.

"The rude comments I can handle. It's the questions that really bother me. Not to mention *you* just asked three," I pointed out.

"My apologies." He clamped his hand over his mouth, trying to prove that he learned his lesson. However, we both knew he would have to be reminded once again tomorrow. I chuckled with pleasure at how sedate his voice sounded. If only everyone could be like Damien.

"Well, don't be angry, because I have another question for you," Damien said softly.

"What's that?" I invited him to continue.

"How are you holding up?" he asked timidly. I knew what he probably wanted me to answer, and part of me wanted to give him the answer he expected. Another part of me didn't want to answer at all.

I sighed and stared out my massive window. Sapphire sky stretched on for miles with no shapes or color disturbing its purity. At that moment I had a secret desire to vault out of my window, sprout wings, and fly away from all my problems and leave them far behind. I was itching to start over, to see if life could exist outside of Valteria. I always wondered what beauty lies beyond the mountains near the sea, just a day journey away.

I knew the answer to my question. *Praseria.* It claimed the ocean and beaches in its mainland. I had only heard rumors of its beauty. The different exotic fish that existed in the sea, the smells of salt, the birds that sang songs so beautiful that it felt like angels spoke through them. I remember my father saying the sunset is what made it the most special and was what he yearned for. I often questioned what it would be like to live a Praserian's life. What may have changed since my father was young? Questions and thoughts came plundering into my mind.

"It's getting easier every day," was the best answer I could give. Damien could sense I didn't desire to talk about it. It was sweet of him to ask and I knew he genuinely cared and would be there for me, but if I was going to properly get back to normal I had to start acting like nothing was wrong in the first place.

Damien put his hand on my arm and squeezed it softly. He was always intuitive on my moods and swiftly took the liberty to change the subject.

"Are you going to be attending tomorrow?" Damien asked.

"Tomorrow?" I tried to appear to have a tad bit of interest. However, he saw right through my façade. My hesitant eyebrow raise wasn't very convincing but I stood behind it anyway, hoping it would be enough. He smiled with delectation.

"The Gala festival?" *Now he had my attention.* Hope and prospect filled his eyes, like a child asking for another slice of cake after he already had a third forbidden piece that he happened to sneak past watchful eyes.

A short sigh escaped my lips. I couldn't believe that it was already that time again. The Gala festival was the most distinguished and significant day of the year in Valteria. Everyone gathers in the pine meadow and watches performances by those who want to sing while dressing up like someone they are not. Most everyone would cover their hair with outrageous hats and buy new clothes for the festival. It gave the sense of a masquerade, just much less formal and silly.

I had only gone once when I was six, so the memory was hard to recall perfectly. It was a festival my father had created in his attempt to bring new traditions to Valteria. I vaguely remember it. I do remember that food was everywhere, with the smell of rich liquid honey and warm mazurek and danishes in everyone's hands. Everyone was laughing and smiling, talking and dancing, and songs would glean in the background.

I had gotten lost and it took a couple of hours until my father found me crying in the grass behind an old oak tree. My mother was completely overcome with anxiety over the matter. She was terrified I had been kidnapped by a commoner, denying the natural curiosity of a six year old as the reason for the mistake. Placing blame and fear on the common people had been too easy for her. Her safety net, her comfort, was and always would be her power over decisions. When she felt afraid, that is what she would do, she would exercise control. She would make absurd demands – a testament to herself of the power she had. Ever since the incident, my mother had made the rash decision to forbid me or Risa to go to the Gala, referring to it as a day "asking for a disaster." She found it easier to require me to stay in the castle while we let the people enjoy their one day of time off to be with their loved ones.

I had always wanted to go again. Each year the urge kept growing. I believe the reason it was so intriguing was because it was an opportunity. An opportunity to be free and to allow me to be the person that I wanted to be. It was a celebration of equality that my father hoped would bring fairness for all, including himself and I. Every citizen could socialize and not many would know who you truly were because of the encouragement to dress in outrageous fashion. For that night, you could be whoever you wanted to be. It didn't matter if you were a merchant or magistrate. It was a special festival to bring together the people and to remind them that we are more alike than it may seem.

Every Gala festival I had found myself reading books or writing songs alone in the castle. The way Damien proposed the question made me think, *why waste another chance to go and enjoy the festivities with my one true friend?* However, it was a huge risk to go. If I got caught, my mother would never forgive me and I couldn't even fathom the repercussions it could have. My mother was not someone to displease.

I put my head in my hands and peeked through my fingers just a bit to see Damien's face. The hope still remained in his expression.

"Damien, I wish I could, but you know what my mother would do if she found out. I wouldn't be able to even consider leaving the castle, probably ever again!" I exclaimed.

Damien sighed and nodded in a dampening manner, his arms falling to his sides, his confidence wiped clean.

"I had a feeling you'd say that. None of the other heralds want to go! This is one of the only times I'm free from Ajax," he murmured.

"Then go. Cherish it!" I tried to encourage him. "At least you'll be enjoying yourself. I'll be sitting here with sorrow and envy."

"You're suggesting I go alone?" He scrunched up his shoulders and squinted his eyes like I was joking.

"What's wrong with that?" I wondered out loud. *I would rather go alone than not go at all.*

"Everyone has someone to talk to there. I would be the only one who doesn't."

"Isn't the point of the festival to socialize with new people anyway? To meet and enjoy other people's company?"

Damien let out a quick, "Ha! It's supposed to be. But

everyone knows you don't go to the Gala alone. It's unsettling not having a friend there to help you through the conversations. Especially if you are there to meet. . ." his sentence trailed off.

"Meet. . . who?"

"You know. . ."

"No. . . I actually don't," I said bluntly.

"Women of course! It's the only way I ever will. It is my one day away to mingle with women that aren't here at the castle," he exclaimed with slight embarrassment and red checks breaking through his freckles. I held back a smile.

"How could I have helped in that aspect?"

"You could help introduce me in conversation. I am not the most skilled at speaking to women."

"You seem to be doing fine right now," I shot back.

"Women that aren't you. . . no offense," he said assuredly. "You're like my sister. I don't think twice when I speak with you. When I am around other women, it makes me nervous to say the wrong thing."

"Well, if you want me to tag along in an attempt to draw women to speak to you, I think you would actually be better off on your own. I am not regarded as the friendliest or the most liked individual people meet. Why don't you ask Garren?" I suggested.

Garren was the porter of the castle. In the castle, everyone treated him kindly. Everyone smiled whenever they caught sight of him, *especially* the ladies. He would be Damien's perfect chance of meeting beautiful women. He was like a royal who wasn't in the royal family, respected and looked up to. The people highly valued him. *Too bad he couldn't be of royal blood and take my place,* I thought to myself.

Damien was quick to respond.

"Absolutely not! He doesn't like me. Plus, isn't he. . .old?"

I hadn't thought about his age in comparison to Damien's. Now that he mentioned it, there was a big difference, probably by 10 years or so.

"Well, what about. . ." I started imagining faces that I had seen around the castle and tried to match them with names.

"What about, Kyros?" I announced, matching up a pale white face with deep brown eyes and reddish hair.

"The Marshal? He's off getting some goods down in Granville. He won't be back for a couple of days."

I sighed in defeat. "I don't know Damien, I don't have a lot of friends or associates to suggest. I wish I could help, truly I do."

Damien stared blankly at my wall. Then his eyes sparked with excitement, beaming proudly.

"At six o'clock sharp tomorrow, be waiting by your window. Make sure to bring a bag of coins." He said it so happily that the joy seemed to move his muscles as he jumped off my bed and scampered to the door in a hustle.

"Wait, Damien, do not get ahead of yourself! What are you planning?" I inquired.

"You'll see! Trust me, you won't regret it!"

Then Damien was gone just like that, giving me no time for a proper response. For some reason, despite the mischief I felt he was brewing my way, I wanted to see what would happen. Succumbing to a quick decision and with curiosity getting the best of me, I promised myself that I would be waiting for Damien at six o'clock.

~

*M*any moments after Damien left, I got tired of sitting in my room alone so I decided to go see what my sister was doing. She had been kind to give me space, and had only come to visit me once a week since our father's funeral. But I was beginning to miss her cheerful demeanor. It seemed annoying the last few weeks but now I really longed to feel her happiness with the hopes that it would rub off on me.

I walked through the castle hall, admiring the details it held. The castle's main hallways and foyers were not dull like my room. The castle was modeled with stone flooring that paired with grand walls, tapestries, pictures, beautiful paintings, vases, arches and pillars. All my father's suggestions. His additions brought an artistic soul to the otherwise lifeless castle.

I turned at a corner and followed a floral rug up to my sister's door. I knocked gently on the wood, afraid if I knocked harder my fist would turn red from the firm surface.

Modesta, Risa's lady's maid, opened the door silently. Her curly, long, beige hair was pulled tightly back. Her heart shaped face and hazel eyes held a small white grin.

I had never had a lady's maid, only because I refused to. Who wanted someone doing their hair everyday and writing letters for them, basically catering to your needs like a child? I felt I needed to learn the things they did and fend for myself.

Independence was the one lesson my father had taught me well, and I excelled at it.

I enjoyed learning how to do things on my own. If anyone offered a hand I would never reply lightly. Always wanting to be self sufficient, I did not want others to treat me like I couldn't comprehend the same tasks they could.

"Good morning, Princess Allene, do you need help with something?" Modesta asked with a brief hint of a smile.

"I am looking for Risa, is she here?" I queried.

"I believe she went to your father's study to gather some things."

"Thank you." I turned away from Modesta with an appreciative nod and headed toward my father's study.

"Wait, Princess Allene! Can you please deliver this to Risa for me?" Modesta placed a small black box in my hand.

"What is it?" I questioned.

"I do not know. Someone left it for her. According to the servants, they expressed urgency in getting it to her. I was on my way to give it to her now but if you wouldn't mind passing it along to her since you are already on your way. . ." Modesta trailed off, questioning if asking me to do a job of hers was appropriate. I could see her starting to fret over the statement and I quickly stopped her.

"Not a problem at all, I'll be sure to give it to her right away." I promised, the anxiety leaving Modesta's face from my reassurance and understanding.

I turned back in the direction I was going, cupping the box to show Modesta that I would keep it safe.

As soon as I heard the door shut, I examined the box as I walked. It was made with a green velvet casing. The box was very small. I contemplated what the contents of the box could be. Maybe a ring, as a gift? Or a brooch perhaps? I shook the box, trying to see if it could give any hints. No sound, none at all, just a little mystery.

I walked up the stairs to the study, receiving many greetings from maids and guards. I nodded back in reply as I continued to study the box.

I arrived at my father's study and opened the door. Risa was sitting in Father's chair looking at a book. Her cascading dandelion locks brushed along her petite pixie nose, her smile briefly showing off her dimples. Risa towered in my father's chair, her tall slim stature obvious. She gazed up at me with her almond eyes, startled by my presence.

"Allene, what a surprise! What are you doing here?" She took her eyes away from her novel, setting it aside and beckoning me in, giving me her undivided attention.

I slowly made my way to Risa, holding the box tightly. I wanted to open it but I held back, waiting.

"Looking for you actually. What are *you* doing here?" I retorted suspiciously. Risa had never set foot in our father's study before. When he was alive she found it mundane and rather boring being surrounded by old books and literature and made a conscious effort to avoid the study at all costs.

"Just looking at some of Father's old things. Mother has asked me to help sort through his belongings, see what we want to keep and what we want to. . ." her thoughts trailed off, a sense of sorrow in her voice which she quickly replaced with a small grin. Classic Risa, always putting on a proper face. A trait she inherited from our father. She believed with her entire being that everyone had a fairytale ending. The characteristic of her positive attitude radiated warmth and comfort to all who had the privilege of being near her.

"Anyway, I was hoping I could find a journal or something special to hold onto, but I have found nothing of the sort. I don't know how you could find anything in this disarrangement." She threw her hands up, exaggerating the mess of his study. Risa chuckled at the suggestion.

"Well father wasn't the neatest person. You should speak with Mother. I am sure if he did have any journals she would know where to find them."

"I thought so too, but it didn't seem that she knew much of where to look. This was the last suggestion on her list. I will come back and continue searching later, I need a break from the dust in this room; I can feel it starting to give me allergies," she said, shaking her head.

Rising from the chair, she viewed the room and then me, taking a quick look over my wrinkled blue gown. It was another moment where it was hard to contemplate that we were even sisters. To no surprise, Risa's dress was the most current in fashion. White being the new choice of color, it managed to shine in the dingey room from its perfectly pressed seams.

It was difficult to compete with Risa for the affection of the people. She was a role model for many of the women in our kingdom, possibly even lands beyond our own. She had quite a reputation, the gossip about her being nothing but positive. Comments about her gracious character, how eloquently she spoke, how mature she had always been, all just a few of the constant compliments I heard surrounding my sister. There wasn't a part of her that you couldn't look at

19

and not beam. She couldn't comprehend how amazing she was and that is exactly *why* she was amazing.

Moving on from observing my clothes, Risa caught sight of the green velvet box poking out through my fingers.

"What's that?" she inquired curiously.

"It's for you. Modesta asked me to bring it to you."

Risa beamed with excitement.

"For me! Who is it from?" She instantly swiped the box out of my tightly grasped hand, smoothly skipping to the other side of the room.

"Didn't have a name attached." I told her, stretching my notably sore fingers.

She opened the box eagerly, revealing a small note. Not what I expected, and by the looks of it, not what Risa expected either.

She unfolded the sides of the paper with her fingertips as if it would shatter like a thin piece of glass. The crippled paper weaved down in a wave. All I could see was unclear black ink in a very messy form of cursive.

Risa quickly started reading, not offering for me to indulge in her surprise. Her face kept lighting up every time her eyes crossed the page. All I could do was attempt to read the smudges from the other side of the paper as she laughed with enjoyment.

"Well, who is it from?" I implored for a hint, tired of the mystery.

"I would say, but they didn't leave a name." She dropped her eyes, searching across the page for some evidence of the writer.

"Not even a signature? Here, let me see the letter, maybe

I'll see something." I stretched out my hand for the rippled paper. Risa shot her hand back with her long and delicate arm so it was out of my reach. Another benefit of her Valterian genes being rubbed in my face.

"I apologize Allene, this is personal. I don't mean to cut our conversation short but I must go. I will see you at dinner. Thank you for bringing this to me."

She grabbed the box, crumpled the paper again and put it back the same way it looked before. She swiftly got up, kissed me lightly on the cheek and skipped out of the room.

I knew she apologized, but it didn't make me feel any better. I was offended that my own sister would not share this with me. She had shared countless thoughts and feelings with me before, in fact her personality made it impossible for her not to overshare. What would be stopping her now? My impatience and offense got the better of me. I looked in the direction she went, and followed.

CHAPTER 2

I persistently followed Risa up staircases and through winding hallways. I stayed behind her and hid around corners or in doorways to avoid being seen. She was oblivious to anything else around her, and had complete tunnel vision getting to her next destination. I relaxed a bit when I realized she probably wouldn't notice me even if I wasn't being discreet. After many minutes of tumbling after her, I was inquisitive of where she was going.

I followed her through the grand hall which arrogantly presented every bold piece of memorabilia passed on through the generations of the royal family. There was an aging knight's armor, glass encased crowns, sashes and badges bragging about God – given talent that led our land to freedom many times over and various other old antiques.

I refocused on Risa as I tore my eyes away from an eye-capturing emerald. My eyes filled with water as I held back a laugh. Risa was single handedly the most amusing person to watch. As she made her way through the castle, she twirled on the stairs, danced up steps and sang while she walked. I was silently laughing at the interesting show when it came to a sudden impede as Risa halted at her destination. I was surprised to see she was standing in front of my mother's bedroom door.

Without permission to proceed, she quietly entered the room. What was she doing? No one ever went near my mother's room, including Risa and me. It was acknowledged as a way to disrespect her duties as queen; she wasn't supposed to be bothered except by invitation.

I waited until Risa silently closed the door before continuing forward. I ran up the colossal wooden stairs. Gently, with all the force I was capable of, I pressed my ear against the door. The timbers' thickness hid conversation extremely well. I assumed that was the point.

Despite my ears' best efforts, the words from their discussion vibrated through the hinges but refused to go much farther. Many minutes passed and I continued to be unwavered and patiently waited in hopes of discerning something. My optimism diminished rapidly. Every word the door hid from me tested my patience and it eventually ran out.

I said a silent prayer, asking to hear my mother and Risa, assuming God would help me hear as he can. If I would have thought of this earlier I could've saved myself a substantial amount of time because my prayer was ironically answered.

I heard the first sound that actually made sense. I heard my sister start to laugh as she came a bit closer in proximity to the door. What I heard next made me regret eavesdropping in the first place. I bet God was laughing now.

"Mother, I want you to read this."

I heard a rustle of paper followed by a surprised gasp. After a few moments the rustling stopped.

"I know it is not my place to ask this Mother, but–" Risa was immediately interrupted.

"Nonsense child, don't waste another breath. I understand. It only makes sense that you go, given the circumstances of course. I will allow it just this once."

Silence stretched on and I found myself wishing I could see the facial expressions being exchanged to understand what the silence meant. Was she happy? Shocked? Sad? Then finally I heard Risa give a faint whisper that cracked from what sounded like tears of joy.

"I am very grateful. This could change my life."

"Which is exactly why you must go to the festival. I ask that you keep quiet about this to your sister, I don't want her to be envious of you."

Festival? As in the Gala festival? Envious? My eyes widened in shock, my jaw dropped as low as it could go. She knew I wouldn't ever be jealous of Risa. I had been overshadowed by Risa my entire life and never felt envious! I didn't mind Risa soaking up the attention of others, it meant less attention on me. Mother knew that wasn't how our relationship worked, we were always supportive of one another. It was an excuse so I wouldn't find out that Risa received permission to go to the festival.

My mind started racing. What could I possibly be envious

about? I sucked in a quick breath of air so the silence I had maintained wouldn't break.

"I appreciate your generosity and your trust in me. I won't tell a soul!" Then I heard her feet skidding to the door.

I shoved myself away from the door and ran as fast as I could down the hallway to avoid being seen.

Once out of sight of my mother's room, I walked briskly as servants greeted me, although I didn't even glance. The force of my speed made me out of breath, sweat accumulating on my scalp. I could feel people's distressed stares burn into my skin as I passed by.

I tripped many times over my long dress, the hem being torn gradually with every move. I stopped for a quick breath. I didn't give my mind time to ponder as I gathered the heels from off my feet and ran for a place to be alone.

I got to my room and grabbed the handle earnestly. I slammed the door loud enough for everyone to hear but I didn't care. I locked it with as much force as I could muster, enough that I thought it would break.

I scanned my room and slumped to the floor, letting my back rest against the wall. My head collapsed to my chest and an apace breath came out of my mouth in a hurry.

My rage was building every second. The betrayal I felt was so deep that I couldn't even speak. I sobbed until I was sore but I didn't feel the pain. The pain I felt was inside, a throbbing ache that was drumming in my finger and only one thing was journeying through my mind. *Why?*

Why was she allowing Risa to go? Keeping it a forbidden secret from me, keeping me from freedom and merriment!

What did Risa have that I didn't? As sisters my father made

us feel equal in every possible way, but through my mother's eyes we were completely different. Differently judged, treated, respected, and loved.

I felt like I couldn't ever please my mother. No matter what I did, her perspective of me would never change. I was invisible to her. Never seen or heard. Never looked at or questioned. Ignored and never thought of, a breeze in the night.

The reason for this was simple: I wasn't Risa. I wasn't considered a proper representation of the Valterians. Risa brought my mother the respect of the people that I knew I couldn't accomplish, no matter how hard I *tried*. *Appearances, all mother cares about is appearances.*

It's been this way ever since we were children. My grasp on what I had as the first born slipped through my fingers, letting it be caught by Risa. People would comment about Risa getting her looks from my mother. My mom saw a reflection of herself in Risa, it made them connect more and it made her proud. If we had conversations with other important ambassadors or families, my mother would brag about Risa first, leaving very little room to speak about me. Any positive attribute of mine was taken away by the judgements of our people, clouding my mother's opinion of me along with it. When comparing the two of us, Risa had more to offer Valteria. My mother would act as if I didn't exist and Risa was the heir, I know she wished for it.

I could then see where she may misinterpret my anger as envy for my sister. But I hadn't been experiencing envy or anger towards Risa. I was angry with my mother.

I let my body lay on the floor as I took deep breaths. My

eyes closed and didn't reopen as I tried to get rid of my headache. Before it could go away, I heard a hushed tap on my door.

I sat up and cleared the tears from my face and went to stand in the middle of my room. I straightened my dress, trying to hide the torn hem from my heel catching it earlier.

"Come in." My voice was shaky and nothing could be done about it. Risa came through the door.

"Dinner is ready. I thought I would let you know."

"Anything else you want to tell me?" I whispered.

"What?"

"Nothing. Thank you but I'm not hungry," I said. Risa could sense the tension and immediately began being her caring self, trying to offer me support.

"Are you all right?" she asked.

"I'm fine, I'm just tired." I lied but my voice gave it away.

"Are you sure? I can bring you up something to eat if you don't want to join us."

"No. I'm fine Risa, I just need some rest."

Risa wasn't convinced, but she knew an attempt of pushing the conversation further would do no good.

"All right. If you insist, I'll tell mother that you won't be attending dinner."

Risa turned for the door until I felt an emptiness in my stomach. All that crying had made me hungry. I gave into the hunger pang and her offer.

"Wait, Risa?"

"Yes?" She turned, happy to see me acknowledging her efforts.

"Could you bring me up some soup and bread?"

She smiled slightly, her dimple caving in.

"Of course, I will be right back." Risa left, the door slowly closing behind her.

I had been waiting for a couple of minutes when Risa returned with a tray that had two bowls of soup and two slices of bread. She set the tray on the floor.

"Risa, I'm not going to eat that much," I declared.

"I know, the seconds are for me."

She crossed her legs on the rug and laid a cloth across her lap.

"Thank you," I said.

"My pleasure. Mother wasn't at the dinner table and I didn't feel like eating alone. I hope you don't mind."

I shook my head and seized my slice of bread. I swallowed a couple pieces and then stared at Risa who had a pondering look on her face.

"It's too bad that mother won't let us go to the festival," I mentioned. I looked to see her reaction, if she would really hide her secret from me.

Risa's expression didn't change; she just sipped another spoonful of soup.

"Indeed it is." She added no other reply.

I was hoping she would tell me the truth. We didn't lie to each other. Well, as far as I knew. When I wanted to bring it up again she looked like she wouldn't say more.

I finished my soup just as Risa was finishing off her bread.

"Allene, I've been worried about you. I wanted to give you space to grieve on your own, the burden of father's death is one we are all carrying. I need you to know that I am here for you. What good is a sister if she isn't there for support?

Maybe the day after next we could meet for a game of croquet? Take our minds off of things." It was a kind – hearted suggestion and I appreciated her effort to make me feel better.

"That sounds lovely. I am free tomorrow, we might as well do something the day of the Gala. Why don't we play then? No reason we should be cooped up when everyone else is having a good time." I tried pressing her further, hoping she would confide in me and allow me to be a support to her.

"What a pleasant idea. However, I am not feeling very well. I have been fighting a cold all week and it seems to finally be catching up with me. It would be best that tomorrow I rest. Actually, I should get some sleep now, it's been a long day. Thank you for letting me eat with you, Allene." She stood up and brushed off her dress with a swift flick of her hand. She picked up the remains of the dishes, walked into the hall and didn't look back.

"You're welcome," I whispered after her, disappointed in how our conversation ended. *Support each other? If only we could be honest with each other too.*

I stood up and went to my closet searching for my night-gown, trying to set aside my anger. I undid my tight dress and pulled in a breath of air. My sides were sore from the close-ness it demanded of me. Changing into my light weight silk gown was the best thing to happen to me all day. I brushed my thick hair and stared out my window until the sunset turned into night. The stars were glittering brightly and the moon hid behind the mountain nearest to me. I staggered to my bed and tucked myself under the blanket.

I blew out my candle quietly and closed my eyes. I tried

praying, digging deeper into my subconscious to discover my desires. I was hoping that my dreams would seek better things and possibly some answers to finding myself once again. Hoping that whatever those answers were would come sooner rather than later.

CHAPTER 3

I packed the last of my coins into a tiny silver purse and placed it in my bag. I patiently waited at my window, wondering where Damien could be.

I twirled my bag in my hands and up my arms, letting it rub against my wrist until it throbbed. I looked out of my window and to the ground. There was no sight of Damien, just patches of grass and rocks.

I sighed. It was long after six and I didn't like being kept waiting.

After a couple of paces around my room and checking in the mirror repeatedly, I heard a loud tap on the side of my window.

I rushed over to open it as another rock barely missed my ear.

Damien was underneath the window; grabbing stones and chucking them wherever he could.

"Damien!" I silently hissed.

He looked up with rosy cheeks and panting like a dog, cleared his dry throat to speak.

"What are you wearing Allene?"

I looked myself over, perplexed. I was wearing a traditional evening dress, my favorite, in fact. A baby blue gown that was tight until it hit my waist, letting it flare at my legs and down to my feet. A soft lavender lining peeked through the slits of the puffy sleeves. The neckline came in a deep V and the lining covered my chest.

I looked back at Damien with a confused and offended look.

"What do you mean?" I asked.

He shook his head in amazement and chuckled.

"If we are going to the festival I think you want to be disguised." He had pointed out what he thought was obvious.

My eyes lit up. He was sneaking me out! I *was* going to the festival! The bells of freedom vibrated in my head. The feeling of not being princess Allene for a couple of hours felt like a prison break.

"Disguised! Right! Damien you're brilliant. Hold tight, I will be right back." I skipped to my closet.

I surveyed multiple dresses and clothing from my wardrobe last year. Nothing seemed right. I finally decided that to fit in with the people, I would need to wear my most comfortable clothes and not my most elegant. I tried on an older tea gown that was loose fitting and flowed nicely. The bold teal color popped nicely with my eyes and was a more classic style among the people. Then I slipped on some old summer boots that were quite worn. I pulled the pin out of my hair, letting it fall to my shoulders in a black curly ripple. I quickly looked myself over and then ran to the window in a dash.

"Better?"

Damien smirked.

"Allene, you look better in this attire than you do in your fancy royal gowns."

I raised an eyebrow

"Not that you don't always look nice! It's just these clothes fit your personality better. But that's just my opinion," he said in embarrassment.

I smiled in amusement, "You're fine Damien, I understand. You're off the hook."

Damien also had downplayed his appearance. He wore a lightweight tunic and tight green trousers. His high boots made him look taller than he was and his hat of choice had multicolored feathers sticking up on one side. He looked quite handsome.

"Now what do I do?" I was dying to get out of my room and feel the air on my skin. I was still in disbelief that I would finally get a second chance to attend the festival. I felt greatly indebted to Damien.

"I hooked a rope to your window sill last night. It should be toward your right."

I hesitantly looked for the rope when I stopped and stepped back. Reality had taken away all the excitement.

"What about my mother? And Risa? They might catch me," I persisted.

Damien nodded, acting like he was already aware of the problem.

"I heard from Ajax that your mother was visiting a cousin

in Veruje, she left last night." That would explain her absence at dinner, I thought to myself. She was probably visiting cousin Lidia. Mother had few relatives she was close with; however, she would visit Lidia from time to time.

"Risa is being watched over right now by a friend of mine at the festival. I should receive word of when she plans to return. As for the servants, the majority of them are at the festival. No one will notice your absence, especially if you don't exit through the castle doors." He smiled smugly, proud of his preparation.

"Damien, I am in debt to you." I grinned with pure satisfaction.

My hands quickly searched the rough stone wall when a stiff, itchy fabric found my fingers. I wove them through the thick rope and cautiously swung my leg out of the window to hang loose in the air.

"Be careful, Allene! Go down very slowly, just like at the treehouse!"

Three summers ago Damien found a treehouse on the grounds. No one had any idea where it had come from and we were pretty certain that no one else knew it existed. It had a rope to get up and down. We went almost once a week to get away from it all. It hadn't been too long ago. I had a strong feeling I would be all right.

I swung my other leg over the side, placing my waist and stomach over the window. The sill was piercing my gut and I tightened my hands on the rope. I took a big breath of air in and gently lifted my waist off the edge.

I let my feet dangle around the rope as I slowly slid down. I moved my hands opposite of my feet. As I was moving my left hand and right foot, I felt a slight feeling of falling. I tensed my grip.

My whole body wrapped around the rope like a child would their mother. I gripped it harder to the point where the touch of it burned my skin and my stomach felt like it was going to drop.

I heard Damien call out to me but I wasn't listening. Panic shot through my body, securing myself safely to the rope.

I tried loosening my body and got little success. I already got this far, there was no turning back. After a couple of moments I took one more breath and dared myself to slide down an inch.

I moved my feet first and left one hand on the rope as I moved the other down. I was finally getting the hang of it, but sooner than I thought I had reached the bottom. Damien grabbed my arm when he had the chance.

"Are you all right?" he asked earnestly. I brushed my hands together and saw blisters starting to form. My hands were burning with a gritty sting but I was grateful to be in one piece.

"Yes, I'm all right." I was so happy to be out of the castle that I completely ignored the fact that I should have been terrified of getting caught.

"Damien, what are we waiting for? Let's go to the festival! I can barely keep my feet from moving." I was running in place, waiting for him to say the words.

"Then let's run, Amelia! I want to get good seats for the festival and we are already fashionably late!" He started running north and I ran with him. He was much faster than I thought. His legs were full of power to run the distance and I was struggling to keep up with his pace.

"Wait, Damien! Who's Amelia?" I called out to him once I was a few steps behind.

"You are! You can't have your name at the festival or everyone else will know who you are. Silly girl," he mocked.

I smiled. Amelia. I loved that name. More than anything I liked how I *really* was going to be someone completely different for one day.

"I almost forgot!" He stopped dead in his tracks, I barely dodged the sudden halt.

"Put this on to cover your hair, make sure none of it is showing," he concluded.

He threw me a red scarf made out of fine silk. I draped it over my hair and tucked it under, making sure there wasn't even a strand to be seen. I knotted it tight and hoped no one would mention my eyes, but even so, it was a risk I was willing to take.

"Perfect. And lastly, if you are to fit in properly at the Gala festival you need a funky hat. No worries, we can get one there. Let's go."

Damien took off again but at a much slower pace now that we were finally off of royal grounds. I pondered my new name some more, trying to embrace my new character. I could imagine Amelia being someone everyone was friends with, someone they could relate to. Damien was getting farther ahead so I pushed my legs faster in the same direction.

After many minutes of fast walking and my mouth watering for nourishment, we found a large crowd of dancing people in a wide clearing. The Gala festival was always in the forest, allowing people to escape the city for the event. Vendors and booths formed a circle, their tables up against the surrounding mass of trees. There was hardly any empty space in the center of the clearing, where a wooden stage had been set up for performances. People had blankets laid outside the clearing where they could chat and eat the assortment of foods offered by the vendors. Music filled my ears in mere seconds and I welcomed it. Damien followed the music as I trailed on from behind.

I studied the sound. It was a soft beautiful song with trumpets and violins. Such an odd combination that I hadn't heard before. I listened to the flutes and other elegant instruments at dances and ceremonies but never had I thought this would be considered good music.Hearing this type of music changed my perspective and sparked the yearning to be creative with my own music and song writing. The change from traditional music was addicting.

I felt my feet shuffle against the ground lightly and my body moving with the music as we made our way closer to the sound.

"What do you think of it Al–I mean Amelia?" Damien whispered.

I swayed toward him and let out a small sigh.

"It's all too great. The freedom, the music, the dancing. I've been missing out on so much. Why didn't you sneak me out for the Gala festival years ago?" I instantly accused him.

"You never really mentioned your desire to attend," he replied calmly, doing a shuffle with his feet. He had a point, so I let it go.

Then the music slowly came to an end as a man stepped

up with a large yellow hat that favored the right side of his head and started a more upbeat song. Everyone started jumping up and down, twirling and laughing, holding onto their colorful array of hats. I couldn't help but join in, the atmosphere being absolutely captivating and contagious. I spotted a hat vendor just a ways away and pulled Damien over to help me pick a suitable one.

The tradition of hats for the Gala festival came from the commoners. They wanted to create their own sillier version of a masquerade. Like picking a mask, the hats were a way to outwardly express themselves. Vendors worked on their hat designs all year, anticipating the day of the Gala to showcase their newest creations for people to wear and enjoy.

After scanning the vendor's options, I had narrowed it down to two hats. Holding them both up and giving Damien a mini fashion show, I asked which he preferred.

"Hmm, I don't think I am the person to ask. . ."

"The turquoise one. It brings out your eyes and matches your dress. Plus, you can't go wrong with the lace detail," the older lady tending to the booth said so matter of factly, eavesdropping on the conversation and answering my question.

"Turquoise it is." I paid her with some of the coins I had brought and proudly placed the hat on my head as Damien walked back to the crowd of dancing festival goers.

My feet wouldn't stop pounding the ground. I could feel my heart racing with the vibrations from the instruments. This song made me picture a group of children playing a game. An energetic game, laughing and smiling.

It brought back memories of when my father used to play games with Risa and I as children. A smile came over my lips.

I hadn't smiled an *honest* smile in weeks and the feel of it was refreshing. I wasn't the only one with a wide grin on my face, everyone there was smiling grand too.

The dancing stretched on for at least an hour but no one grew weary. Damien had to lug me away with all the strength he had to convince me to take a break to eat. We sat on the grass and Damien went to fetch some refreshments from one of the festival vendors. He came back and placed an apple in my hand with a small cup of honey, charred bread, and water to wash it down.

We ate silently, letting the music still hold our ears. Then Damien chuckled and looked around me.

"Hey! Over here!" Damien waved his hand in the air. I looked to see who he was talking to and my eyes fell on two younger individuals. They waved back and made way to sit down next to us.

"I thought you said you had no one to go with," I accused him, turning my head his way.

He shrugged and replied, "I didn't think they would make it." He smiled with delight. "But I think you'll like them."

A young girl with cinnamon hair and dark eyes to match plopped down next to me, wearing a bright red floppy hat that met her shoulders. A man, probably slightly older than myself, gave a huff and took a seat next to the girl, wearing a plain brown cap, not seeming enthused with the idea of a more bold color choice like the rest of the townsfolk. The girl, who seemed near my age, embraced Damien.

My eyebrows went up. Damien never told me he had a specific girl in mind to meet up with at the festival. Then the man patted Damien's back.

Damien glanced at me. Noticing his gaze had turned, the girl looked at me.

"Damien, who is this? You never told us you had a *friend*." Her face had the same expression as mine, perplexed and lost.

Damien cleared his throat and gave introductions.

"This is Amelia. She is a friend of mine in the castle. Amelia, I'd like you to meet my brother and sister."

The girl giggled as she bobbed her head up and down.

"How lovely to meet one of Damien's friends! My name is Freira, Freira Durand." She spoke quickly and wildly, a blur to my ears.

"You are very pretty. How long have you and Damien been friends?" she continued. Her eccentric personality made me pause. She had called me *pretty*. I knew at that point my disguise must have been working well.

"A couple of years," Damien answered for me. I recovered from the awe and properly replied.

"Yes, a few years now. It's a pleasure to meet you." I looked at his brother and he stared at me with a faint expression, like he had never seen a girl. Damien cleared his throat as his brother shot up straight and his cheeks went pink.

"I'm Hassan Durand, Damien's older brother." He offered a bow and I nodded back without hesitation. Hassan had only some similarities to Damien, their smiles resembling one another as well as the shape of their eyes. However, they were opposites in a lot of ways. Hassan was muscular and fit, tall and slim. His eyes were fascinating, almost an olive green, with wavy light brown locks that hung from his head.

"It's a pleasure to meet you as well, Hassan. Damien never mentioned having siblings."

"Damien, how rude! Not a single mention of your beloved sister and elder brother to your closest friend?" Freira continued.

He shrugged. "I guess it never really came up." Damien looked at me. "I never wanted to bother you with too much. You already have everyone else to worry about," he said shyly.

At that moment I realized I was a horrible friend. Not even asking my best friend about his family? I knew Damien was from Selvet, a small farming town slightly east of the kingdom. It was about half a day's journey by foot. We hadn't really discussed much else past that.

Damien always felt like a part of the castle, a part of my own family. We practically grew up together. His family had dedicated him to the knight training program ever since he was young, so it was hard to imagine he had a life outside of the castle. I felt ignorant that I was oblivious to his situation. I didn't understand why he tolerated my selfishness all that time. I wished he would have said something, but I wished more that I would have been thoughtful enough to ask.

"Damien, is there more food for us? I am starving!" Freira exclaimed.

"Uh . . ." Damien looked around and sheepishly smiled at his sister. She sighed and got up.

"Come on, Hassan. Luckily Ma warned us to bring extra coins. You haven't changed one bit! I was hoping while you were gone you would take on *some* responsibility, and manners. *'No Freira, trust him, he will be prepared!'* Ma said. Unlikely! Let's go get some food." Then she stomped in the direction of the food cart. I could see where Damien got his slightly dramatic nature; it must've been in the family. I loved it, and a smirk instantly came to my lips at her reaction.

Hassan got up silently, smiled, and followed his agitated sister.

Hassan turned back multiple times to look at us as they waited in line for their food. It took me a moment to realize he wasn't necessarily looking at us, he was looking at *me*. I wasn't used to men showing interest of any kind and it took me a moment to realize how to react. He stared at me like I was a diamond in the desert. I felt valuable. I grinned and he turned his head away with embarrassment.

"You're right, Damien. I do like them," I admitted, still staring at his brother. Damien's smirk burned my skin. Even though I couldn't see it, I felt it.

"Like them? Or Hassan?" He almost laughed. I whipped my head around to stare down his smug facial expression.

"How dare you make such accusations.First of all, he's your brother, which basically makes him my brother. Second, we just met so that would be absurd. Third, he looks like a man that has no issues with women pursuing his charm. He probably doesn't even have the same appeal for someone that is . . . Praserian," I whispered toward the end.

"Ah–ha! So you do like him," he laughed.

"What on earth makes you say that? I said no such thing," I argued back.

"You said he probably doesn't have the same appeal. The *same* appeal. You like him. Just admit it." I could tell he would hold this over me. I wasn't going to give in that easily, no matter if a slight interest in Hassan was there from his handsome first impression.

I turned my head away from him, remaining silent on the matter. Damien sighed.

"Well that's too bad, it sure takes a lot to get a man to blush like that." I could hear the hinting in Damien's voice, in his words.

My eyes widened but I didn't let him see. I looked at Hassan again. The vendor had issued out their order. Hassan was strategically placing their food on top of each other, cradling it in his arms to retain the greatest amount of food possible. He concentrated on the ground while he walked, as Freira skipped ahead and jumped to her seat.

Hassan sat down with a slight grin and placed the food by Freira, letting it tumble to the ground. She quickly snatched the honey and bread.

"I am starving! Next time Damien, please have food prepared. The journey is quite long as you know and it stirs up quite an appetite," she uttered, placing the bread in her mouth.

"I didn't know if you would make it or not. What is the point of buying food and not having anyone there to eat it?" he queried.

She shrugged, dismissing his point. "You should *always* be prepared."

Hassan had picked up his slice of bread and chewed it slowly, taking his time to examine every piece he bit off. I tried not to glance at him. I didn't want to give anything away seeing as I probably already gave away too much.

"Freira, how old are you? You look taller than Damien, hard to imagine you as the younger sibling," I mocked, getting back at Damien for all his height jokes toward me.

"Fourteen years. Thank you. Damien, you need to remember that," she laughed.

"She is only saying that to get back at me for all the short jokes I give to her," Damien scoffed.

Hassan seemed shocked. "You mock her for her height? I don't see how it's hindering her physical features in any way. Shame on you, brother. I apologize for him Amelia, not all the Durands share the same view of you," Hassan stated.

My stomach clenched with butterflies, but to my ears it caused a ringing as my pulse echoed. What was that feeling? The feeling kept churning and didn't seem to ease. I had never experienced it before I didn't know what to think of the feeling so I stopped thinking of it entirely.

"I never meant it like that Hassan. Don't mistake my intentions, it is only friendly banter," Damien replied.

"Nonetheless, I would do anything to pay her a compliment. You set it up too perfectly, I couldn't resist," Hassan said firmly, locking eyes with me on every word. I tried very hard not to blush. I had to change the subject before it became obvious.

"Freira, tell me what you do back at home. Are you training for a profession?"

"Only the best. I am to become a florist. Our mother tends to our garden and I have always had a passion for plants and flowers," she said excitedly.

"That is wonderful! I quite enjoy flowers myself. I always pick a fresh bouquet in the mornings from our garden," I said.

"Do you tend to the garden by yourself? I would love to hear any advice you might have for me," she asked. I tried to think quickly for a response that wouldn't suggest my identity, but I was having trouble finding the words. Damien luckily came to my rescue.

"Amelia comes from a line of ambassadors."

"You do? That explains how you two met at the castle. I have always been fascinated with politics. You are so lucky to be brought up in a manner where you are required to be informed. Knowledge and schooling are beyond anything I can imagine. Maybe you could share what it is like?" Freria asked urgently. Damien once again answered in my place.

"Freria, she is here to think about anything else but work," Damien stated. Freria quickly apologized.

"I am awfully sorry, you're right. Perhaps another time? I do hope you will come and visit us now that we have been acquainted," Freria said.

"I would like that very much." I smiled reassuring her that I was not offended.

The conversation had ended there as we all focused on the music and eating our food. Freria had finished her food without stopping to take one breath. Hassan had gradually swallowed; staring at the ground like it was demanding his attention.

Freira got up and took the food from Hassan. He shot her with a glare.

"What are you doing with my food?" He extended his arm for it but she pulled back.

"Either eat it or don't. Many people are hungry and don't have food, you're lucky you do! So, if you won't eat it, I will give it to someone else." She started walking away with the tray of food in hand.

"Freira! I was eating it. I was taking my time to enjoy it!"

he defended himself. She ignored him and began jogging. He sighed and ran after her, yelling her name. Damien shook his head.

"I apologize, Freira is a strange one. She adores antagonizing Hassan. You might hear her name more than you'd like," he laughed.

I looked back at them to see the progress they had made. Freira had weaved through dancing people, leaving Hassan alone and unable to get through without running everyone over.

"Why did they come anyway?" I questioned him.

He had a look that I was not familiar with seeing. Guilt maybe? Lines creased his forehead, leaving marks of wrinkles.

"Do you want to know the truth?"

I glared with uncertainty. He threw up his hands.

"It's not bad! It's just, well, you see . . . I invited them." He looked down, avoiding eye contact.

"That's obvious. But what's wrong with that?" My eyebrows creased with misunderstanding.

"I had originally invited Hassan, but Freira insisted she tag along."

"Again, what's wrong with that?"

"I was hoping maybe Hassan and you might find each other . . ." He stopped talking, waiting for me to fill in the rest.

"You mean to tell me that you invited them so that Hassan and I would what? Become infatuated with one another?" My voice wasn't exactly angry, it sounded more astonished. But my feelings were different than my tone. I didn't know if I should be happy or furious. I let him speak again before I would decide.

He stared at the grass without blinking, a distinct urgency in his eyes.

"Not exactly? I don't know! You're never around people, aside from myself, and I felt if I provided you with company that was more than just a friend, that it might be good for you. Love makes people happy, right? You have been miserable these last few weeks. Allene . . . Amelia, you are older than I and still haven't thought of potential suitors yet. It is only a matter of time until your mother forces you to. I thought Hassan would be a suitable match. He has been requested by Ajax to begin training in the royal army. In time, with his rise in station, he may be an option. Given his age, he will likely achieve knighthood within the year, and a commander roll soon after, he could be an eligible choice, even given our families background. Just look at your parents love story, it should have never worked, but it happened anyway, because they were happy! If happiness is a determining factor for your future husband and finding love, I thought Hassan would be a worthy candidate for you to consider. I apologize I involved myself in your personal affairs. I thought I would bring him here for the innocent chance that you may fancy one another."

I sighed. He was right. I never did have anyone to spend my extra time with, aside from Damien. It wasn't that I didn't want to, I just hadn't found the right person to spend it with. I never knew if it was because I was afraid, didn't care or didn't search hard enough. At any royal gatherings I attended, my sister would be the center of attention, and I didn't fight hard for the limelight. I felt I stood out enough already given my appearance that I didn't dare draw any more unwanted attention. No one showed any interest in me before. Hassan would be the first.

I let my feelings wander aside and let new ones fill in their place. Feelings of hesitation, excitement, curiosity, apprehension, loss and many others filled my body to the point I couldn't take on anymore.

I pondered the idea of love, of having a soulmate. Someone who would laugh with you, be there when you needed them, comfort you, help you, and most importantly *love* you when no one else would. Someone who knows everything there is to know about you, knows your life better than their own, knows your likes and dislikes, and can always be what you need.

All the wonderful things that I had heard, read, or seen about love poured into my mind like a rushing waterfall and nothing could hold it back. My heart was telling me to take a chance, to go out on a limb and refuse to let anything get in the way. What could it hurt?

My eyes hunted for Hassan, but I was no sign of him.

Damien was still looking at the ground with a firm and stationary expression.

"What should I say to him? I have never been in a situation like this before." I pleaded for suggestions.

He looked up with a marveled expression, surprised by the direction of the conversation and relieved by my reaction.

"Well, at the festival every year they have one official Branle. Be his partner." He suggested. The Branle. It was the most anticipated dance of the festival, according to the rumors I had heard, at least.

"What happens if everything goes perfectly and then he

realizes I am not Amelia? That in fact, I'm Allene." My heart grew heavy. How could a relationship start from a lie?

"Allene, you *are* Amelia. Love is not about appearances. Your parents are a testament to that! He will not judge you like others have. I can promise you that."

My heart grew happy again, anxious and full of nerves.

"I trust you Damien. That being said, how exactly do you dance the Branle?"

"You have *never* learned the Branle?" His mouth gaped in shock.

"I was taught how when I was very young. I never use the Branle because mother doesn't let me attend events that practice it. She says it's not for royals, that it's too suggestive and . . . sensual . . ." I confessed sheepishly.

"Get up Amelia, darling. Your mother has it all wrong. It's time you learn the meaning of an official Branle."

CHAPTER 4

*D*amien had tugged me up and led me a couple yards away from where we were sitting. He made sure that everything was quiet and that we couldn't be seen. After another sweep around some bushes, Damien stopped and declared in a broad voice, "We are clear."

He walked quietly over and instructed me in a fatherly tone.

"Now, dancing can be difficult or it can be simple. It all depends on your attitude." I raised my eyebrows. He fumbled his words after that, embarrassed at his attempt to sound superior.

"Here are the basics when you are dancing. First, don't talk, you'll ruin the moment."

"What do you mean?" I interrupted.

Damien eyed me but I didn't show that I regretted speaking.

"I *mean* when you dance with someone that you have feelings for and if they have those same feelings about you, it feels like sparks are jolting out of your stomach and that the love that you feel can't be held inside. Like the world has become perfect and not one thing could ruin the moment that you shared. It is a delight that only you and the person you're with can feel and describe. No words are necessary." Damien's eyes glowed with satisfaction as he continued. "You can look back on that memory and feel that same feeling over and over again. *Unless* you talk of course."

The abrupt change of tone he had displayed was surprising.

"Damien, I happen to be curious about how you know this feeling." I smiled, waiting for another passionate response. His cheeks went pink as he stuttered for the words. He tried desperately to conceal his emotions.

"I don't! My mother tells us stories. Stories that taught me how to dance. She told me once that it's how she knew she and my father were meant to be together," he concluded. I just shook my head and decided he would tell me the real reason eventually.

"Second, don't look at the ground. It's not the ground you want to watch, it's your partner. If you can look into their eyes. . ." he got another melting expression and sighed again.

"Damien, do you want to get something off your chest or should I ignore your sighing outbursts?"

"Ignore them please. Now shall we begin?" He went to the middle of the clearing.

"But you haven't even taught me *how* to dance yet," I informed him.

"I don't need to."

"You promised to teach me," I pointed out.

"Will you please just *trust* me?"

I started walking toward him as he placed his left hand on my waist and took my other hand in his.

"What do I do?" I asked.

"Place your right hand on my shoulder." I did as instructed without hesitating. I tried to display an unspoken confidence.

"Now place your feet so they are in line with mine."

I parted my feet to match his position.

"Lift up your neck, don't look down! Keep your shoulders up and breathe." I took in a gust of moist air, the taste of rain on my tongue. The clouds had started to creep in over us, but that wouldn't stop the festival.

"Now, we dance," he spoke with assurance.

"Bu–"

"Just listen to the music. It will guide you." We were out of range from being able to hear any music.

"What– ,"Damien interrupted me once again.

"*I* will hum. Remember don't talk and look up."

I looked at Damien's cheek, since it was the only thing directly in my vision. I pressed my lips together and listened to his hum that vibrated through my arms.

He was humming nonsense, but it was a sweet, soft tune going low to high. My feet stayed put and he didn't seem to mind. The hum got a little faster and yet somehow the soft-ness still lingered in place. My feet moved a tad to the right. Then his feet stepped back and I followed in the same direction.

We moved side to side in a rotating motion, until the hum changed to a very low deep sound. I slowly raised my hand from his shoulder and turned out from his body in the other direction. I went up on my right foot and Damien spun me very slowly as I did my best to balance. I came down from my foot and gently placed my hand back on his shoulder as our feet and bodies turned in every direction possible. I managed pretty well for the most part, my experience with dancing shining through as I did my best to follow his lead. I grasped Damien tightly as I stumbled over my feet, and Damiens, to keep me from falling. It only happened a few times and my recovery got more gracious with each trip or misstep, the harmony in our footwork was increasing by the minute.

My head wanted to fall but I kept it raised, keeping my body at an appropriate distance from his. His hum went up a little higher, then lower and then held out a note for the finish. My feet were where they had begun, right in line with his.

I smiled and closed my eyes. It was a delight dancing with Damien. I had never thought something could be so exhilarating and peaceful at the same time. I very carefully opened my eyes to see Damien smile too.

"You are one of the best dancers I have ever had the pleasure to perform the Branle with. Splendid job, Allene."

"You mean . . ." I started and he finished.

"Amelia. Yes. Hassan will be quite impressed with how coordinated you are when you dance." I laughed.

"I am sure the girl that you have been daydreaming about all day will be satisfied to dance with you as well," I mocked him with a smile.

"I surely hope so," he replied, fear crossing his face.

"Thank you for teaching me. I haven't ever highly favored

dancing, you may have changed my mind," I said, trying to lighten the mood.

"You'd be crazy if you didn't. Remember though, the Branle switches partners. You will be facing each other just as we were and at the conclusion of your dancing with Hassan, you'll be passed along to another man until you make your way back to each other."

I nodded in reply. "Again, thank you."

We walked back to the blanket to find Hassan munching on his food and Freira with an annoyed look on her face.

"There you two are! We couldn't find you anywhere. Where have you been?" Freira asked.

"Well we . . ." I began to think of a clever response when Damien cut me off, once again.

"Rose actually came and asked if we would like to dance with her," Damien said, finishing my lie.

"You mean the girl you want to dance with?" Hassan asked. Damien nodded.

"Not *want* to dance with. She is the girl I am *going* to dance with!" Damien looked at me. That was who he was daydreaming about. I nodded along, pretending I knew the little secret all along.

"You better, then maybe you'll stop talking about it. Wait, what if it gets worse?" Freira shouted dramatically. Damien rolled his eyes, ignoring her passionate outburst.

I sat down by Damien, not sure if I should talk to Hassan or not. I decided to keep to myself, waiting for the conversation to start more naturally.

A couple of minutes had passed and the sky changed its shade of color. It was a dim flaming orange, with pink stripes and specks of light yellow. The clouds blended with the colors, leaving a large glow in the horizon that lit up the forest trees, any sign of rain having disappeared.

"It's so beautiful," Freira had announced aloud.

"I couldn't agree more," I responded.

Not much later than that, the moment we had all been waiting for had come. The music had changed from tapping your feet to a quiet lullaby. The mood shifted quickly as nervous smiles became wider on everyone's faces. Mumbles came here and there, asking people to dance.

Damien arose immediately, fixated on his goal and walked away. I followed his feet to a young girl, with dark brown hair that shaped her chin and soft golden eyes. She was slightly taller than Damien, but a warming glow from her facial expression indicated that height didn't seem to matter.

I saw her take Damien's eager hand as they approached the assembling group of people. I heard a soft pound as a man, quite large, with buzzed hair and chocolate eyes stepped in front of Freira.

"Would you, pretty lady, like to dance?" he asked shyly.

Without any hesitation of his size, she responded with much enthusiasm.

"Well, thank you for asking! I would be delighted," she spoke as a child would, which was fitting considering she still basically was one. She was considered barely old enough to be out on her own in public. The burly man carried Freira away, taking her to dance near Damien.

Sitting awkwardly, I was left with Hassan. I didn't know how to ask him to dance. That was the man's responsibility anyway, wasn't it? Men traditionally brought women to the floor, but Hassan wasn't saying anything. I really did want to ask, but my lips seemed to be sealed shut. I forced my body to turn to Hassan and to my surprise he was standing.

"Amelia, I know you don't know me very well, I don't even know if you like to dance . . ." he trailed off for a moment to then add, "would you dance with me?"

My lips finally parted and words slipped out.

"Yes, I would like that very much."

He offered his hand and I took it grandly, letting him support all my body weight as he lifted me off the grass. I fully appreciated the gesture he had made to me. I was having my first Branle. Most of the dances I attended at the castle were more upbeat or styled for solo performances of couples. They usually involved boring old men or princes that still hadn't hit puberty. This would be my first dance with someone who seemed interested in me. The *real* me.

Hassan was intimidating in the best way possible. He had such an ease about him. I could already feel an immense amount of comfort from being with him.

Hassan placed his hand on my hip as Damien had and took my hand. Hassan was much taller than Damien and his hands fit with mine perfectly. I remembered to lift my neck and I looked down to place my feet with his. I placed my hand on his shoulder, shut my lips, and without trying to be intimidated by his mesmerizing eyes, I let mine look into his. The olive green was ringed with black and I felt like I couldn't look away. They were so different from anything I'd ever seen.

Hassan broke Damien's rule by talking, breaking me from my trance.

"Amelia, you have very unique eyes. I haven't met a single person in Valteria with blue eyes before. They are captivating beyond measure."

I blushed and tried to break my gaze from him but I couldn't. I worried that other people had noticed my eyes as well. I wondered if he was actually mocking me. I could feel my stomach twist. Did he really find them captivating or did he know who I was?

"You are completely different from anyone I have met, and I do not mean that in a demeaning way," he added.

His eyes searched mine for signs of comfort. I immediately felt myself let go of my fear.

"I apologize for seeming offended. I am not very good at this. No one has complimented my eyes before . . . or me necessarily. I don't really know how to respond. I suppose a thank you would be a wise response. Thank you, Hassan."

"My pleasure. I would like to make it a common occurrence. If you prove you can dance, of course." He gave me a friendly wink and continued to dance.

I regained my focus and concentrated on what I was doing. I listened to the music very carefully, trying to understand the rhythm. I began to sense when I was going to move my foot and I would anticipate when he moved first. His hand tightened on mine and he turned me around with him. With every turn he held back without hesitation. He was a talented dancer. I wanted to appreciate his fluid movements but I couldn't. I was distracted, concentrating on the feelings and my feet.

An intense reaction began in me. My feet went numb, almost paralyzed to move. But I somehow managed to keep in constant motion from the fuel that I felt coming from the adrenaline.

Hassan did the same basic moves as Damien, moving side to side, letting me loose and catching me for fun. I wanted to laugh but remembered the moment. His eyes seemed to dig deeper and deeper into mine, almost paining me to look.

I didn't quite understand why my mother had kept me from this. *Sensual* was her way of describing a type of dance that actually provided innocent feelings, feelings of comfort and safety. The joy in dancing and experiencing the feeling of something special I had been robbed of. Envy flooded my mind as I thought about Risa being allowed to attend freely, able to have such an experience without any repercussions.

The thought of Risa made me glance around at all the dancing people. I hadn't seen her. Although, that was probably a good thing. If she found out that I stepped foot out of the castle, she would run to mother and tell. I let out a sigh to forget about my family problems and enjoy the feelings Hassan had so easily placed in my heart.

"Damien mentioned that you have a permanent residence in the castle. Being related to ambassadors, I am sure you have seen many places. Do you prefer being here in Valteria?" Hassan had started up the conversation again, taking me by surprise. Damien and I had not discussed my "background" before coming and I wasn't quite sure how to respond without conflicting our stories. I decided to try answers that were somewhat open ended.

"My family has relationships with many kingdoms, but I haven't had the opportunity to visit many of them. Valteria is all I know, therefore I am required to prefer it."

"Even so, coming from an established line of successful individuals must be reassuring. It has been an ambition of mine to work alongside Damien. I feel ashamed being older and being . . . less accomplished," Hassan admitted.

I was taken off guard by his honesty, a humble side of him shining through, luring me to adore him even more.

"Why would you say such a thing? You must have your reasons for staying in Selvet all this time. Aside from that, Damien mentioned that you would soon be making your way to the castle to train in the army."

"I do have my reasons. Our father is a farmer. His job required heavy labor from the time he was a young boy. Around the time that Damien was born, my father realized his body wasn't keeping up with the demands of the profession. My mother grew increasingly concerned and had my father retire from being a farmer to become a craftsman. The labor was still intense, as you can imagine, and the responsibilities of his new property fell upon my shoulders. He wanted the farm as a legacy, something that our family could pass on for generations and generations. However, my mother wanted more. She hoped that giving Damien to the kingdom to train as a knight would bring our family the necessary funds we would need, much more than the farm could. My mother needed me to help my father fulfill the duties on the farm, while Damien pursued a different path."

I could feel tears starting to well in my eyes as Hassan illuminated a new side to Damien's life that I didn't know existed. Damien wasn't a knight because he wanted to be, he wasn't in the castle to be my best friend, he was there to bring his family a better life.

"I had no idea that Damien and your family were sacrificing so much," I whispered, regaining my composure.

"Don't feel sorry for us, every family has their duties. I am positive your family has sacrificed in their own ways too."

I felt guilt overtake me as I realized how fortunate I had been. Talking to Hassan had given me an entirely new respect for the Durand family and more respect for all the Valterians that were secretly sacrificing to try and live a better life for the ones they love.

"Amelia, I can see you are fretting over this. Don't. As each year passes, the need for our farm seems to decline and the money from Damien's service has left my family with a comfortable amount. I may have a chance to leave my tiny town and officially enlist as a member of the royal army." Hassan's voice had a new sense of curiosity and excitement. I so badly wanted to promise him a place in the castle, promise to let him live the life he wanted to live. I held back.

"That is wonderful Hassan. I am truly happy for you. It would be an honor to have you in the castle," I assured him.

"You flatter me. That is another reason I came to the festival, to get acquainted with what the duty would demand of me. I plan to be here for a few days while I finalize my decision. However, I do have one thing that is making me slightly hesitant already." I was perplexed by his comment; his hopeful tone had turned into concern.

"What may that be?" I asked, trying to read his face to give me some hint as to what he was feeling.

"You work in the castle. In your personal opinion, don't you find it rather odd that the greatest enemies to our land are relatives of our royalty? Why would there not be peace? I fear defending a kingdom that cannot resolve even simple family issues.It makes me concerned about their ability to handle even larger issues that our kingdom could face in the future."

Hassan's words took me by surprise. I processed the comment that should have offended me but I merely laughed at his uninformed conclusion.

"Related? Why would you think that?" I asked.

"Wasn't Faris Amena Praserian royalty before he married Queen Laerina? Would that not make the current Praserian royal family related to the Valterian royal family by marriage?" Hassan was confused, obviously not aware of the history of my father and his family.

"Hassan, you need a history lesson before you work for the kingdom," I laughed at him, his smile acknowledging that he agreed with his lack of information.

"Teach me," he stated softly, our dancing slowing down to be almost standing, inching closer to me to hear me clearly over the loud music. Little did Hassan know that there was no better person to ask to share Valteria's royal history. I was anxious to share the story, to talk about my father. It was an opportunity to discuss just one of the many amazing things he accomplished in his life. I couldn't hold back at his request.

"When Faris left Praseria, he had been in line for the throne. He had no siblings, and his mother had passed away, leaving his father as the only person left to carry out their duties. His father began to age and the public viewed him as a weak ruler. Once Faris had become king of Valteria, the people of Praseria saw it as a conflict of interest to have their king be the father of their enemy. The possibility of war with

Valteria was always on their mind and what if their king wouldn't have the strength to harm his own son if it came down to it? A man, Vincent, had worked closely alongside the royal family for years as an advisor. The public adored his blunt approach to politics. He saw it as an opportunity to cause uprisings against the king. Eventually, the chaos became too much as the people fought for a new royal bloodline to take the Amena's place, seeing as there was no heir to the throne. The king stepped down and the Hadways took the responsibility as the new royal line of Praseria. They still rule today."

I recited the history of my family exactly as my father had recalled to me. I had imagined many times what that story must have felt like to be a part of. I was always curious about my grandfather, as he was the only living grandparent I had left. However, for all I knew, he could have passed away. Once my father became king of Valteria, all communication and affiliation with Praseria ceased, leaving me with only my imagination and stories of old to create who I thought my grandfather would be.

"That is quite the history. Why did the queen even consider Faris then if it seemed to cause so much trouble?"

"You want to know more? My history lesson didn't bore you?" I asked, surprised he had more questions.

"Not at all, I love history. So tell me where this odd alliance even came about," he persisted, still dancing slowly.

My parents had the love story that people dream about and it was one that I didn't often share. Hassan seemed genuine with wanting to know more. I nodded, giving him the reply he asked for.

"War hadn't broken out for five centuries, but that duration of peace almost made the tensions between our two kingdoms worse. No matter how long people forcefully willed peace, trust was never developed. The royal families finally broke under the pressure of who could possibly strike first and who could blindside the other. Rumors of war spread through both kingdoms, each one sending threats to provoke the other.

"Despite unresolved feelings toward Valteria, Faris, who was the prince of Praseria, was not intrigued with the women that had been presented as potential wives. He went searching elsewhere, daring enough to venture into enemy territory for the sake of finding true love. The king was a bit of a hopeless romantic, to the point that he thought only with his heart and not with his head.

"Faris had heard the valiant Valterian princess was seeking a husband. Without a second thought, he jumped at the opportunity to meet her at a ball that invited any eligible young man to try to win over the princess's heart. He had lied about his true identity and fought for Laerina. He had skillfully dyed his hair blond with the help of some lemon juice and the sun." I snickered, that part of the story always made me laugh when my father would tell it. He would always emphasize how creative he had been and how difficult it was to keep the lemon juice away from his eyes. Hassan raised his eyebrows, surprised by my added detail. *Too much information, Allene, just get back to the story.*

"He moved to Valteria, deceitfully lying to his parents that he was staying at an extended cousin's house in Lokali to enjoy bachelorhood before he tied himself to a new queen."

I paused for a moment, thinking back to how my father had shared this story with me. He shared with me his fears at that time, that if my mother would've found out his true identity, he instantly would have been killed. He wanted her to see that not all Praserian's were what everyone thought from their grandfathers' stories of war. He had no fear, only love to give.

Not realizing how long I had paused, Hassan interjected.

"You better not leave this history lesson on a cliffhanger. Believe it or not, I enjoy sappy love stories," he smiled, expressing his continued interest in learning.

"I'm sorry, I was just recalling how the story was told to me. I want to do it justice," I nodded back.

"It sounds like whoever told you the story had a lot of detail. I'm happy I asked you to share it. Please, continue," he beckoned me on. I appreciated his sincere interest in my family's history, even if it was only asked to determine the probability of him wanting to be in the royal army.

"Faris worked very hard to place himself in Laerina's path and eventually gained a friendship with her, which soon became more. Upon proving that he could be trusted and what they felt was real, he bravely exposed his identity. As you may have guessed, she refused to care about him being different.

"Soon after they fell in love, the Praserian's wanted war, greedy for more land. She believed Faris was a spy and that he had lied to reveal secret information about Valteria. She was ashamed and hurt; convinced he only intended to win her heart in order to achieve the upper hand for his own family's gain. No reason or word he said could have changed her mind. She had cast him out to protect herself and the people. She strictly ordered if he ever returned to Valeteria again, to have him killed.

"But as any good love story goes, love wins out in the end. After the war, she realized what he said was true. He was different. The cause of the uprising for war had only been from a small group of Praserians. She set off to retrieve him from Praseria. Once she was reunited with him, she apologized and begged for him to return. Without much hesitation and with sincere understanding, they eventually got married. Not only for love, but as a way to reunite and gain back the peace Valteria and Praseria once had. Soon they were the new king and queen of Valteria," I concluded their love story, just as my father had recollected to me.

Little did Hassan know that this was also my story, my reason for being an outsider. I am the product of two people that shouldn't have ever been together and yet fate had another plan. When I was born, some people say it was God's way of cursing such a union, by giving me the appearance of my father. Risa and I, through our veins, pumped an equal mixture of both kingdoms. We were half Praserian, half Valterian. Everyone knew this. I laughed at the efforts people, like my mother, would go to in order to conceal it. It didn't matter what was underneath the surface of our very identities. What mattered to everyone in Valteria was superficial. If that is what mattered to people, I would lose every time.

At first glance, everyone assumes I am a Praserian. Yes, my sister has parts of my father too, but because her appearance relates to Valterian, they find no reason to mock her or be displeased with her as their princess, as all they see is the embodiment of their kingdom in the proper sense. I can't help but feel that they find me as a poor way to represent the first born of the king and queen. The heir to the throne looked like the enemy, and their pride wouldn't accept it.

At the time of my birth, despite the reconciliation made between the two kingdoms, distaste and vengeance still lived in the hearts of our people. It is not nearly what it used to be before my parents got married, but small misunderstandings and revenge sunk into the minds of both sides.

Soon after my birth, my father began to be treated the same. The acceptance and love the people had was from the symbolism of my parent's marriage. The peace it brought the two kingdoms quickly turned to regret and shame. Rather than healing the wounds of both sides and making the unfortunate situation better, as time went on, it slowly got worse. Despite my father's best efforts to prove himself to his new people, their judgement of where he came from clouded their gratitude and reasoning.

I was removed from my trance of self pity as Hassan let out a quiet laugh that seemed to follow along with the music.

"That is a very complex family."

Again, I should have been offended, but I had a hard time being offended when I knew it was the truth. It was complicated; my life was complicated! More complicated than he could ever know.

"Nonetheless, now you know what you are getting yourself into." I gave him a playful wink. I felt Hassan squeeze my hand lightly, his eyes locking onto mine.

"Yes I do. Despite all that, I have never been more certain that right here . . . is exactly the place I was meant to be."

Hassan was exchanging silent words of affirmation that I didn't know were possible to understand if they weren't being said. My heart was soaring, my body felt like air, and my feet were barely discernible as they danced on the ground.

"I am grateful that you came to the festival and I am happy to hear that you might stay," I said shyly, not holding back my thoughts. It would be wonderful to have Hassan in the castle, I knew it was only the start of something incredible. I could see the smile on Hassan's face turned into a full tooth grin.

The dance started coming to an end and Hassan placed his hands on my waist, letting my body inch toward the ground. The breeze hit my face with a light tap and the music stopped.

The time went by too fast. We had gone off in our own patch of grass, away from the group of people. Neither of us realized that we hadn't switched partners the entire duration of the song. I didn't mind though. Proper manners and norms weren't required at the Gala and what I was feeling with Hassan definitely wasn't normal. I wanted to soak in every moment of it.

Suddenly, our attention was drawn to the darkening sky that was being painted with color like a canvas. Large explosions that flickered like stars and left the smell of smoke in the air were surrounding every corner of the night sky. Fireworks.

Hassan had taken his place behind me, wrapping his arms around my shoulders as we watched the magnificence of the show unfold. One by one, each firework made the darkness of night disappear. Children's laughter and the awe of those that stood by could barely be heard under the fireworks roar.

Hassan had squeezed me tightly and I held his arms

closely, embraced in comfort. The show was approaching its finale, the fireworks becoming more grand and frequent. I didn't want the night to come to an end. I was holding onto this blissful moment, not ready to let go. But the moment I was clinging to came to a rushing stop. What replaced it, was a moment I would never have been ready for.

CHAPTER 5

The fireworks sounded different. They were mingled with a large vibration that shook the very ground we stood on, but that was not all that changed. Suddenly the laughter turned to screams and shouts were heard from one direction. I heard feet running and horses in the distance. Children were crying and there was yelling of men in the background.

"Attack!" they yelled proudly, striking fear in us all.

Hassan had clutched me to his body from the surprise and my heart went cold at the realization of our enemies attack. He quickly cradled me in his arms as he tried to understand the scene that was unfolding before us. He grabbed my hand and started to run for the trees. I quickly realized that everyone else had rushed in the same direction. We were about to be part of a stampede if we didn't hurry and follow the crowd.

"What's going on?" I yelled at the top of my lungs, trying

to be heard over all the commotion, but my efforts were drowned out. I didn't understand what was happening. The run to the trees, only a mere twenty seconds, felt like minutes. Hassan pulled me tightly to his body as he pressed himself up behind a tree. Despite the fear I felt, I couldn't help but feel safe in Hassan's arms. I could feel myself fighting back tears as I watched the people of Valteria trying to find a place of refuge.Catching his breath, Hassan silently answered my question by pointing a finger in the other direction.

Massive rocks shot out of the air and peppered the ground. I could feel it shaking the soil beneath our feet. Spears and arrows soared across the sky, pelting whatever was in their way. My entire body felt frozen as I watched the people trying to find safety. To my relief, it seemed most people had found some sort of barrier between them and the destruction. Some people took cover behind trees, others tipped over vendors booths and tables to shield them and their children from the attack.

Hassan tried to duck down and shield me as best he could as the weapons were landing closer. As he moved, I saw a reflection of pain come over his face, grunting as he tried to hold back a wince. Hassan knelt down, holding his arm. I looked down at his arm to see a sharp spear had cut straight through an outer layer of skin. The wound was deep enough to make him bleed. I reached out in an attempt to hold the wound shut but the blood didn't cease.

Panicking, I frantically looked around for help. Everyone was focused on themselves, trying to hide in the shadows that night fall was almost promising us. Squinting my eyes through the darkness, I could see the armed men proudly bearing a coat of arms that was impossible to distinguish from the lack of light. Their faces were covered by helmets, their eyes practically glowing amidst the dimming sun, the darkness nearly upon us. A few of the men held torches to light the way. Catapults were proudly being rolled and displayed in the light of the burning torches. I could see from the corner of my eye one of the catapults being loaded and aimed in our direction.

"Hassan, we have to move! Now!"

An unexpected rush of adrenaline gave me the courage to try and get us to safety. My eyes searched for a close place to move and I caught sight of the stage. It was about 25 feet to our left and I knew it was our best chance.

"The stage! Ready?" I asked. Hassan quickly glanced at the direction I wanted to go and nodded in agreement.

"Now!" I yelled. Pushing against every instinct to stay, I forced my legs to run across the clearing.

An arrow came speeding past my head and caught the edge of my hair covering, my thick black hair falling into my eyes. My hat must've fallen off at some point without my real-ization. I pushed away the fact that my identity was now revealed and tried not to take my mind off the more urgent situation.

The close call with the arrow made me realize the danger of running. I tried to change tactics, bringing myself to the ground and crawling to the stage instead. Hassan was slightly behind me, alert and following my lead.

"Hassan!" I screamed for help as another arrow landed near my foot, fear starting to consume my short lived courage. I heard Hassan groan in reply. I turned toward him to offer help when another hard pound hit the ground, sending my body farther from him.

My arm caught my fall and I hit the dirt hard with a loud cracking sound. I immediately realized the sound came from my fall, and I felt sick. I wanted to scream but the pain hurt so bad I couldn't find my voice. I was perplexed and dazed, the dizziness starting to take over. *Keep going Allene, you are almost there. It's probably not a bad break, it could be worse.*

I tried to get a clear view of what was in front of me and used my other arm to keep crawling. I was praying Hassan was close behind me. The stage was the only object I could clearly see in my hazy vision and I moved as quickly as my body would allow.

With a short moment of relief, I found I was safely behind the stage, gathering my composure. The strong, confident Amelia had been replaced by a terrified Allene. I wanted to search for Hassan, foolishly hoping he would come to my side at any moment.

"Hassan! Are you ok? Can you hear me?" I tried to scream with what little energy I had, but no reply came, and my heart sank in the silence.

I had just lost someone dear to me. The pain of losing someone again made me battle my own worst thoughts about Hassan's fate. I tried not to become overwhelmed, to stay strong.

"Risa! Damien! Freira! Anyone! Help!" I tried to scream out, but only a whisper came through my lips, making my body cringe from the effort. Panic overcame me as I realized I couldn't move, I was a sitting duck. I was terrified for myself and for my friends. Why was this happening? *Please tell me it's all a terrible dream.*

No response came to my shouts, only cries and pleas that weren't meant for me. I looked around once more, my head hurting, as I felt a sharp cut burn into my leg. This time I screamed. A gray veil started to spread over my eyes as I realized an arrow had made its way over the stage, jutting out of my leg.

I let my head roll to the side, resting on the ground. Pain was radiating from every part of my body. I moaned and let my eyes shut, the smell of blood and the echo of screams overwhelming me. My breathing quickened and sobs came pouring out. I could feel myself starting to slip into unconsciousness, ready to give into the taunting idea of peace that slipping into nothing could bring.

"Wait, stop! Hold your fire! I need help! Quickly!" A voice, which sounded like bees buzzing in my ears, was ordering men to help me.

I felt leather hands pick me up and the pain I was trying to ignore gradually became worse. I let out a thunderous cry and tried to kick in protest, but could barely feel anything. My eyes wouldn't re-open and my body wouldn't move.

"Careful! She's hurt enough!" I heard a rough voice rumble over all the chaos. More rocks hit the ground and when they did, it made the arms that were holding me shake. The pain became unbearable.

"Amelia!" I heard a man yelling my name in agony. Hassan? Damien? I wanted to respond but the pain overtook me. The excruciating discomfort came to a halt, the commotion at a standstill, followed by a beautiful dream of silence.

CHAPTER 6

*S*creams? Crying? My ears were trying to identify the noises that were only a couple inches away. With a long period of time trying to interpret the rattlesnake like sounds and fighting for clarity, I finally identified whispers.

I tried to open my eyes but they seemed sealed shut. My lips wanted to move but they couldn't. An invisible force was trapping me inside my own body. I could feel panic building up in my chest, the feeling of what should be tears simply made me exhausted. *Is this what death feels like?*

I needed to use my voice, to know that I was alive. I desperately wished to see Hassan and Risa, but instead I heard a familiar sound. My father.

I had to be dead. It was the only explanation. If I was dead, I must not have made it to heaven. I could feel the same pain that I had before I lost consciousness. Was this some form of torture in the afterlife? I can't imagine father going anywhere but heaven. There needs to be another explanation. Maybe it's a night terror? *Please be a night terror.*

My head throbbed and I felt my irregular pounding pulse. I tried to remember what had happened, to make sense of it all. Little fragments of memory came and went. I remember dancing with Hassan, watching the fireworks show in his warm embrace. Everything had been pleasant. Then there were torches, boulders, and spears. I became wounded and separated from Hassan. My identity was exposed. I remember harsh cries from my people that still stung my heart. *What happened to everyone?*

I felt something surge its way into my gasping and unmoving mouth. My eyes gained a little strength that seemed to radiate to the rest of my body. I knew I could open my eyes but I feared to see what scene may lay before me.

Forcing my eyes open, I saw a faint glow. I saw a large, dark figure standing in a halo. As the figure moved, I saw that it was a man – an old man. Any hope of it being my father was gone.

The man had a patchy gray beard that accented the thick white hair covering his head and ears. He almost seemed familiar to me. His bushy eyebrows, they looked like my fathers, framing his light blue eyes. *Wait, blue eyes? Why does he have blue eyes? I must be imagining it.* The man pursed his lips, holding an empty cup as he looked at me with distaste.

I glanced around and saw that I was not in heaven, but tucked away in a room. The room displayed a floral rug, a set of armor in the corner, two tapestries hung on each wall and a soft wool mattress encased in heavy wood is what I laid on. *Where am I?* The surroundings didn't look Valterian, they were too ostentatious. It wasn't our cousin's kingdom, Veruje, or another ambassador or aristocrat's house. It was a castle. *But who's castle?*

My hair was neatly braided and pinned around my head. The clothing was unfamiliar. My clothes had been changed into a long tunic. It was the same color as a rose, with gold lace around the cuffs. My heart sank, panic coming over me. *The rose color, the same color of the Praserian royal family. The man's blue eyes . . . the decor . . . the castle.* I knew that I wasn't in Valteria any longer.

The shock of realizing where I was left me praying this was a really twisted dream. *Allene, your dreams are never this realistic.* The sooner I accepted my reality, the sooner I could process what was happening. *Am I a prisoner? No, I couldn't be, if I was a prisoner I should be in their prison. Or maybe they want to use me for ransom so they are keeping me in good condition for an exchange?* I felt frozen in place, completely terrified of what they were going to do to me.

The old man sighed and grabbed a wet cloth. He laid it on my forehead and then paced to the other side of the room.

I swallowed, trying to wash down the burning sensation I could feel in my throat. *You have to say something, Allene. There is a small chance that there is an entirely sane explanation for what is going on, but you won't know unless you ask questions and get answers. Don't be afraid, you don't seem to be in danger . . . at least not yet.* I gradually felt my mouth become less dry. Then, with all the courage that I possessed, I managed to ask the man a quiet question.

"Where am I?" My voice released just a small croak, like it hadn't been used for days.

"A place you don't deserve to be. You are lucky to be alive," the old man snapped.

I creased my eyebrows in misapprehension and held an ignorant facial expression. He sighed loudly with vexation.

"You don't remember anything?" he asked with disbelief.

I shook my head, since that was all I could do with the power I had. I didn't know if this was a person I could trust. I wasn't about to say anything until I knew where I was for certain.

"I take no pity, you deserve it," the old man spat. I was stunned by the harshness. Instincts to defend myself wanted to take over. I forced myself to remain quiet as I assessed the situation further. Valterians may not like me, but this extent seemed rather extreme, especially being the princess. This mistreatment just added to the sinking realization that I wasn't in Valteria anymore.

The old man sighed, his demeanor gradually becoming more calm and apologetic.

"I'm sorry, it has been a long few days. I am crabby from lack of sleep and short on patience. They did say you might suffer some memory loss. You are probably confused," he stated.

I nodded, trying to keep up, my head still pounding as I tried to comprehend a response. The fact of the matter was I didn't have memory loss, but should I tell him that? The man took my delayed response as an indicator that what he said must've been true. He interjected before I had the chance to reply.

"I will tell you what happened. But listen up and listen well, I will not repeat myself," the old man said matter of factly. I could see he was expecting some acknowledgment of his statement. I nodded my head, giving him my full attention.

"Good. The prince set out for our attack on Valteria. It was all going as planned. The prince had told and ordered *all women* to stay behind. I knew the protests for women soldiers was a passionate one by your rebel group but not strong enough to actually follow through with your ludicrous threats. Yet some people had to sneak into the wagons of supplies to participate in the raid. People like you." He gave me a disapproving look and paused, waiting to see if I would defend myself or respond to his claims. I remained patient and listened, still very confused with what I was hearing. The man continued.

"Your wagon stopped. You ran into the *middle* of the fight, resulting in your injured right leg and broken arm. Not to mention you bruised most of your body. I honestly don't know how you avoided worse! Luckily for you, the prince stopped the attack. *For you.* He ordered the doctors to take you back and tend to your needs. I am still in disbelief. Weeks of planning and preparation for the assault to be unsuccessful . . . it's very agitating," the old man explained to me with a disappointed and annoyed tone.

I didn't want to cry, I didn't want to yell back, but I wanted the old man to gain a sense of compassion given my circumstances. If only he knew what I had actually just gone through.

I slowly processed his long and ominous story while I felt

his eyes burning into me for answers. At first, I was still lost. Everything was coming back to me in pieces. When I was watching fireworks with Hassan we were attacked and an arrow injured my leg. My satin scarf had fallen off, exposing who I was. I was thrown into the air and caught my fall by breaking my arm. I remember hearing someone yell my name and feeling someone pick me up. Everything had gone black; I passed out.

The old man said that I was supposed to stay home. *What did he mean? That I shouldn't have left the castle? Yes, but who was this prince?* I had no brothers. If this nightmare was real and I was where I thought . . . I should be dead; the only nearby kingdom that has a prince is Praseria. Praserians wouldn't let a Valterian survive. They especially wouldn't stop a raid for one when it was arranged to intentionally target Valterians in the first place. He hadn't given any indication that he knew who I was. *Maybe I'm not in danger after all, maybe I'm not a prisoner? Then what am I? Who do they think I am?*

Then it all made sense. *They think I am Praserian.*

Thanks to my father, I might be able to survive longer than any Valterian would in these circumstances. This was the first time I had been grateful to look like the enemy. But I still had to escape; I had to as quickly as possible before they found out who I was. In this circumstance, being Valterian was bad enough. Being the princess of Valteria, that was entirely worse. I needed to get back home, to know what happened to my friends, to my kingdom.

I remembered the old man sitting in front of me, waiting for my response. I swallowed, taking away the pain from my throat and replacing it with courage to speak, trying to ignore the nerves that I might say something wrong and give away who I was. I had to play the part, I had to in order to survive.

"You're right, it wasn't fair. I wanted to be part of the group, show my bravery. I can fully see the error of my ways. You must believe me when I say that I did not intend for any harm," I lied in a hoarse tone. I cleared my throat again, waiting to see if he bought my apology. He looked me up and down, attempting to see if I would say anymore.

"Humph," he muttered in reply. I ignored his rebuttal and kept my thoughts to myself, which was probably best.

How can I get out of here without being noticed? How can I leave when I can barely move? For a short moment, the discomfort from my injuries slightly faded and strength gradually came over me. I decided I would start by asking questions. It seemed justified since I had suffered memory loss, making it the perfect excuse to learn more information and better understand my situation. I had to find an answer for getting out of here alive.

"When will I be better? What did you pour into my mouth?" I inquired to the old man. He turned his back and was pouring some water into a glass.

"I gave you a pain antidote," he replied.

"I have never heard of such a thing," I objected.

"If you remember, it's because only the Praserian's were intelligent enough to invent one. You should feel well enough to take care of yourself in about a week. Maybe two. But the prince insists on you staying in the palace until your condition is completely *perfect*," he said with sarcasm. At the moment, I could definitely say he was not my friend. *Or maybe this is how all Praserian's are, maybe it's not me he has a problem with.* I wanted to address it either way.

"I can see your discontent with his decision, he could have left me behind and no one would have ever known," I stated. I was surprised that a prince would stop a raid for a commoner that was apparently foolish enough to get involved. I couldn't see anyone in Valteria doing that for me, even as their princess.

"What is his name, the prince?" I asked. Back in Valteria, my mother rarely involved Risa and I in politics, especially politics that involved Praseria. Although it was a kingdom I was born to fear, I knew very little of who I was in fear of. The only name that really was familiar was King Hadway.

"Aleron," the old man huffed.

"Everyone must be enraged with his decision to save me. That was quite a risk," I said more to myself, than to the man.

"On the contrary, there is little that Aleron could do that would strip the respect of his people," the man replied.

Is that so? From the rumors that are spread about how evil Praserian's are, I could hardly see how that statement could be true.

"I have a hard time believing any royal is truly that honorable," I stated. The old man got wide eyes at my reply, an element of shock surfacing.

"You better not speak that way here. You will be quickly rebuked. People do not tolerate ill speaking of their prince. He is highly favored," the old man said sweetly, changing his attitude almost immediately. *So he doesn't have a problem with everyone. Just me. Wonderful.*

It was refreshing to hear him speak so highly of his prince. In my heart, I was slightly jealous of my enemy.

"What makes him so special?" I asked candidly. The old man looked appalled at my bluntness, not sure how to reply.

"Now I see how you got yourself into trouble with the rebel group," he huffed, ignoring my question. The old man paced at the back of the room, placing more rags in a basin of water. The respect he held for his prince however took over, as he wanted to prove where his worth lay. The man turned to me, a very serious expression on his face.

"Aleron has sacrificed a great deal for his family and his people; he has a gentle heart and will help anyone. Even you. To speak as bluntly as you do, none of us could have fathomed a reason to save you in that circumstance."

Ignoring the old man's remarks, I was surprised at all the things he said about his

prince. The way he spoke of him so kindly made me want to meet him. I wondered if I was the princess here, would they say the same things about me? I couldn't even imagine it.

"You mean, if it had been you in his position, you would have let me die?" I croaked, changing my thoughts.

"Of course I would have tried to save you. I'm not a *Valterian*," he stated as he cringed at the word before he continued. "However, I would have at least waited to see if you were alive first. Not call the whole thing off for one girl who we presumed to be dead," he explained.

I felt my jaw open from shock. I was amazed at the generosity Aleron had displayed toward my well being, if what the old man said was true. Why would he stop a planned attack for someone that was probably dead? Attacks like that always had casualties, what made me any different or worth the risk of retreat? I was a complete stranger to the prince. It was a true testament of his character if what the old man said was indeed true. As for the old man, I tried to take comfort in the fact that he would've at least tried to save me.

Hearing all of this made me feel important, almost to the degree of pride. Even though I should pay no attention to the enemy and should be inquiring about the attack on the Valterians, I found I couldn't help myself. Someone I had been indoctrinated to believe was every source of evil was not so evil after all. It left me curious. How could I not want to understand more? I would probably never get a chance to understand my enemy this well ever again. I was taking my situation as a valuable opportunity for learning.

"What did the princess think of his actions? She must be ashamed of his retreat," I said quietly.

"My dear, how hard did you hit your head? I think we need the doctor to come take another look at you." The old man rose, making his way to the door to fetch the doctor. I reached out with my good hand, urging him to stop.

"Wait, I am all right. Like you mentioned, just a little memory loss and I don't want to embarrass myself more than I already have." I was only trying to retrieve more information about the royal family to give me a sense of how to handle my current predicament of being held in the enemy's castle walls. I had to be careful though, being too curious may seem out of place and raise some questions, even if I did have memory loss to blame.

The old man gave in, taking a seat near the foot of my bed.

"Fine, only a few more questions. I don't have all day. Now

that I know you're all right, it's time I go get some sleep. What did you want to know?" he asked.

"The princess," I said.

"Aleron is a young prince, just in his twenties. He hasn't made much progress on securing a wife. He is very specific on what he is looking for in the future queen. Considering he is the only *present* heir to his father's throne, he is being very selective. But believe me, the king and queen were not pleased with his actions of saving you," he assured me of their distaste. *Present? Does that mean there was another prince?* I will need to ask more about that later.

"I will be sure to apologize to his and her majesty. What are the names of the king and queen?" I inquired.

"His majesty Vincent Hadway is the king, and the lovely queen is Eveline Hadway." I nodded my head, ingraining their names in my memory.

"Can you tell me more about the queen?" I asked. I heard a few things about King Hadway, none of them good. All involving his rash decision making, his will for war, his short temper with servants and prisoners, to name just a few. I was terrified to ever meet him face to face. However, I had not learned much about the queen and I was curious.

"She is very humble and soft spoken. Her main choice of company is her garden. She is the first Praserian queen to tend her own garden. She is outside most hours of the day."

"Is it a garden open to the people? I imagine it's lovely if she spends that much time working on it," I said.

"No one has seen the garden except the royal family. Some servants and people say they have seen glimpses of it. It is said to be breathtaking. She will open the garden for everyone upon the wedding of her son, but that is no time soon," he laughed and shook his head.

More questions came and with each one the man became more tranquil. His obvious distaste for me started to subdue and a more friendly attitude had emerged. Once it felt appropriate, I finally asked him questions about himself.

"What is your name sir?" He poured some more medicine into my mouth; surprisingly, it had no flavor, or maybe that was my head injury confusing my senses.

"Ezra," he replied without any expression or indication that he was curious to know mine. I just smiled and turned my head.

"My name is Amelia," I said with confidence, almost convincing myself it was true.

"Do you remember what village you are from?" he asked.

"I wish I could say I do." This was all I could say. I didn't want him snooping around in the city and finding that there was no one I was related to in all of Praseria. I hope he won't search much more into it.

"That's awful. I feel even worse for your folks. If they come looking I'll be sure to bring them to you."

"Thank you," I said. Even if they thought of looking, they are all probably glad to have me gone.

I realized that I had felt more at home with Ezra than I had in Valteria, even with his first moments of discontent toward me. Our conversation had taken a turn. With the same looks and pleasant conversation, it reminded me of my father. To Ezra, I was considered to be part of his people, unless he found out the truth of course.

"What exactly is your duty here in the castle?" I asked.

"I help the doctor, I'm his assistant. Nothing more, nothing less."

I nodded. I noticed my legs were sweating from the wool sheets and they were dying to move.

"Ezra, may I walk around a bit?"

He considered the idea and nodded.

"I wouldn't want to be stuck in a bed all day. But let me at least hold your good arm so you don't have to put pressure on your leg."

He grasped my arm lightly, helping me out of my bed. The sling that had been placed to cradle my arm from moving was tight to my body. I had no fear of it being bumped as Ezra let me circle the large room.

I felt my legs loosen with every nudge and slide forward. My leg didn't hurt as bad as I thought. The bruises seemed to be only yellow shadows now, an indicator that they had been healing for a while. *But wasn't the attack just yesterday?*

"Ezra, how long was I asleep?" I realized my bruises should have been darker.

"A week. As I said, we presumed you were dead, but the doctor noted you were in a comatose-like state. Your body just needed rest."

I nodded, trying to grasp the lapse of time. An entire week had disappeared and yet no one in Valteria had come for me.

I paced the room for so long that Ezra finally released my arm and I let myself wobble around the room on my own, grasping the wall for support. The room must have been a lady's suite, it was larger than what would be seen in a standard servant quarter. It was quaint and I found the accommodations very considerate considering that they assumed I was a commoner and a traitor. After a couple of moments I smiled.

"Could I go out maybe?" The movement from walking was making me feel more lively, I was eager to push my limits. The sooner I could get out, the sooner I could get a feeling for my surroundings, and the sooner I would be able to flee back to Valteria.

"Give yourself another day or two of rest, there is no rush," Ezra insisted. *No rush . . . if only he knew time was not on my side.*

～

"*T*ell me today is the day," I begged, pouncing the question on Ezra as soon as he entered the room.

Two days had passed – two long, *plodding,* days. I loathed being confined when the imminent risk of being caught was always looming. I was on edge whenever Ezra or a servant entered the room, expecting my luck to run out at any moment. I had made no progress in planning an escape and I was eager to see some hope of surviving this. Familiarizing myself with my surroundings was one part of that plan.

"Child, you are persistent," Ezra concluded.

"You said you would take me out after a day or two. Besides, you must be as exhausted of this room as I am," I accused.

"It's not the room that has been exhausting," Ezra shot back in a smart alek tone.

I scoffed, rolling my eyes at my new friend. Ezra had been

significantly kinder towards me as each day passed. He is what I envisioned an older version of Damien to be.

He smirked, trying to hide the fact that he wasn't as discontent with me as he pretended to be. "I think I am going to regret making the offer."

I paused, shook my head and answered, "Lead the way."

CHAPTER 7

*T*he castle in Praseria was extravagant; it beamed with colors. The main color of choice was maroon. The red rugs stood out from the tan tile floors and the drapes popped against the sandstone walls. Maids were dressed in a deep royal blue and didn't hold back any fear of looking at me when I passed them by. The thick carpet that lined the stairs had ornate floral patterns, almost leaving me dizzy at the picture it created. Paintings and vases lined the walls for display, large arches led into every room, fires burned in the main areas and gold candles and decorative accents hung on the halls. The biggest difference was there was no silence; there was chatter.

Valterian's embraced the attitude of doing your work quietly or being chastised for slacking off. Here, it seemed to laugh and be light hearted or someone would judge you for being a grump. It was contagious. It got me laughing at the sweet sounds around me and it quickly rubbed off on Ezra as well, an entirely new side of him being shown.

Ezra had introduced me to many of the maids and servants throughout the castle as we made our way through the tour, but I could remember none. I was never very good at remembering names and I was trying to stay as quiet as possible. I was still afraid to say the wrong thing to expose my true identity. Too much attention would not be good.

I did a decent job at avoiding conversations and hiding my nerves until Ezra took me to the seamstress. She was around my age with long, braided black hair and dark blue eyes, sweet and joyful. Her serene warmth surrounded the room, leaving a feeling of solace that replaced my anxiety.

"Noni, I would like to introduce Amelia. I believe you two could become well acquainted." Ezra lightly sat me down in a chair facing her direction, being careful to avoid bumping my bad arm and leg.

Noni picked up her needle and a piece of cloth while turning around to reveal her glowing face.

"Amelia? Where have I heard your name before? Well come in, come in! Welcome to my sanctuary!" She got up and came over to embrace me. The room was draped in a rainbow of fabrics and string lying all around in a neat mess. The room was bright, which went with her happy spirits. Some dresses were laid on chairs or her desk, leaving piles and piles of fabric to maneuver around.

"Would you like a sweet?" She handed me a box filled with pastries off her side table. The fascinating welcoming took me off guard. I liked the energy she had and gladly accepted a pastry.

"Where did you get those?" Ezra pointed at the box.

"The kitchen staff and I are good friends. They give me special treats quite frequently. So generous they are! Try complimenting the staff every now and then Ezra, I'm sure they will take to being friendly with you too," she encouraged. I imagined Noni having many friends; she was very outgoing.

I picked out something that looked like a dried cake. Hesitantly, I nibbled off a small piece. The inside had a chocolate color and the taste was ecstatic.

"What is this?" I considered grabbing another.

"No one knows. The pastry boy has created many recipes and says the ingredients are his. Selfish little thing, but he's as sweet as his cakes." She waved a hand in the air.

"It's delicious."

Ezra had grabbed a handful, eagerly shoving one down his throat and stashing the others in his coat pocket.

"Thank you, Noni," I replied.

"You are very welcome! Ezra is right. You and I could be close friends. I have a good feeling about you Lia," Noni continued, seeming to be smug after rewarding me with a nickname so quickly.

"I would love to chatter, but the queen has me making her a whole new wardrobe and I am on a strict deadline. Come back in a couple of days and we can get to know each other a little better," she offered.

"That sounds delightful. Goodbye, Noni," I said, placing the cover on the pastry box as I used the chair to stand.

Ezra offered his arm as we made our way out of the room, our mouths full of dessert.

"She seems like an exciting person to be around," I exclaimed.

"Yes, and only slightly crazy." He winked. "I think we should go meet the pastry boy. I could go for more of those .. . whatever they were." He smiled. I nodded in agreement.

Noni's visit was the shortest of them all. The visit to the pastry boy was very different. He had dark brown hair, the first I had seen in Praseria, with pale blue eyes. He was slightly younger than Damien. He had a very tender personality but was very focused on his work. His name was Terris.

He gave us two pastries each, different from the ones he had given Noni. These were filled with fresh apricots and resembled a turnover. They were just as lovely as the first desserts. We talked with Terris for quite some time while he kneaded dough; he seemed to enjoy having company for small talk as he worked.

After talking to Terris, Ezra insisted we continue on to meet the gate guards next. For someone who hadn't enjoyed teaching me things or talking to me, he had become very eager to show a new level of friendship. I was pleasantly surprised to see such a quick turn of events.

Being in enemy territory, I was worried about keeping up the charade of being one of them. I was obviously doing a good job blending in, considering no one had raised any concern upon meeting me. The more people I could refer to as friends here, the higher chance I had at getting the proper information to leave safely.

Ezra had walked past another room that had quickly caught my eye. The large double doors at its entrance framed a perfect wood piano on the opposite end of the room. I stopped, causing Ezra to turn back around to see what had caused my delay. He saw me staring at the piano. Its mahogany wood was polished to reflect nothing but the wood grain and a person's reflection from its undeniable shine.

"Do you play?" he asked. I shook my head.

"Depends what you mean by play," I chuckled. I loved to write songs and to sing. We had a piano at the castle that was seldom played. My mother approved of singing as a hobby for myself but instrument-wise she had always pushed me to learn the flute. Most aristocats played the piano, she considered it lackluster. She wanted Risa and I to be different, to stand out. Risa had been forced to play the harp, an instrument she was naturally talented with. I stubbornly only learned a few songs on the flute, not connecting with wind instruments. Piano, although a repetitive skill of the elite, was repetitive for a reason. It was beautiful to hear and addicting to play. I had tried to teach myself piano whenever my mother was away from the castle to avoid her disapproval or rebukes.

"It's a beautiful instrument," I said. Ezra nodded with a smile.

"I have been dragging you about the castle for a while now, you should probably take a moment to rest. I could use a cup of water. Why don't you stay here in the music room while I go get us some refreshments and we can carry on again with our tour in a little while?" he said softly. I could see he was trying to be polite and conscious about my current physical state. Sitting down did sound like a good idea, since my legs had started to ache around my bruises. I gave Ezra a silent nod as he escorted me into the music room.

We approached the piano and Ezra made the effort to pull the piano seat out far enough for me to slide onto.

"I'll be back," he said as he let go of my arm.

"Are you sure it's ok that I am in here by myself?" I asked curiously. My mother would have not been happy with strangers roaming the castle unattended.

"I will only be a moment. You'll be alright I presume?"

"Of course. I will stay right here," I replied.

With that, Ezra left the room, leaving me with just my thoughts and the large musical instrument.

Now is your chance Allene, it is the perfect opportunity to escape.

I looked around the room, listening intently to the sounds in the hallway. Ezra's steps had disappeared quickly after his exit. No other footsteps sounded in the corridors. No one was around. I was alone.

As appealing as it was to think about making a run for it, it wasn't possible. My legs were already protesting my brief walk around the castle. I couldn't imagine exerting more energy without falling and injuring myself. My best course of action was to take some more time to heal. As risky as it was to stay in enemy territory, I knew I wouldn't make it far in my current condition. If I was going to make it back to Valteria by myself, if I wasn't going to be rescued, my only chance at making it home would be if I was at my best self. And right now, I was far from it.

Accepting my cumbersome reality, I waited patiently for Ezra's return. A few minutes had passed that seemed more like hours. I was never very good at sitting in silence. I listened once more for echoing footsteps. Nothing could be heard apart from my shallow breathing.

Deciding I couldn't bear the silence any longer, I reached up toward the piano with my good arm, placing my hands on the keys nearest to me. My ruby ring was still snug on my finger, the color reflected on the walls as a sharp light crept its way into the room from the far east window.

It took a moment to sink in that my father had once walked through these halls. This used to be his home. It had become difficult to imagine my father's life outside of Valteria, that he had ever had something different. The ring on my finger had been a gift from him, representing his family. Seeing the accents of red throughout the castle, even the ones on my current dress, solidified the realization that Praseria had been his first home. I suddenly felt grateful at the opportunity to see what royal life would have been like here through his eyes. I could see all the locations he had described so adoringly during my childhood. Although this situation seemed pretty glum, I could get a better understanding of him through it. *Look at you Allene, seeking out the positives. You are seeing things more like Father already.*

My pointer finger pushed the heavy keys one at a time. The thought of my father made me recall an old song we used to sing together. In this very room, he could have sung it with his own mother. As comfort washed over me, I began singing quietly.

"Oh my dear, sweet dear, if only you knew
Just knew, how much I love, love you,
My sweet dear, I will gather the stars for you

Sing till you smile your way through
Through this tender lovely life
I will always be by your side
My sweet dear."

A small tear had made its way down my cheek. I paused for a moment, taking in the warmth it gave me to feel like I was sharing a moment with my father, even though he was gone.

A slow clap suddenly overpowered the room, breaking the moment and turning it into a panicked surprise. With my cheeks burning red at the realization that I wasn't alone, I wiped my cheek to hide any tears.

I turned my head around, expecting Ezra, which would have been embarrassing enough. My stomach dropped at the sight of a total stranger.

Ebony hair was the first thing I saw. The man standing so calmly in the doorway appeared to be a couple years older than I. It was impossible not to notice his engaging eyes. They were ice blue that stood out as they were framed by his long black eyelashes.

The man's red lips slightly parted to show a white shine beneath, which was only magnified by his golden skin. He didn't ask permission as he walked through the doorway to stand a few feet in front of me.

"Were you singing?" he asked, smiling mischievously at me.

Caught in the act, I didn't want to respond. What if it became obvious who I was without Ezra to hide behind? I was hoping Ezra would walk in at any moment and save me from my embarrassing predicament. *How had I not heard the man's footsteps?* I could tell he wouldn't be leaving anytime soon if I didn't give him an answer.

"I apologize, I thought I was alone." I tried to keep my response curt, hoping he would see I was not one for small talk. He didn't seem to get the message, as he approached me even closer now.

"You shouldn't be apologizing. You have a beautiful voice. It's what drew me this way." He winked as he proceeded to take a seat on the bench, carefully placing himself on the opposite end to give me a few inches of space.

The man motioned to my arm, a look of concern crossing his face.

"I'm even more impressed considering the condition of your arm."

His enchanting eyes seemed to lock a potent hold on mine as he studied my face. I hadn't noticed until then that my breath struggled with every small intake of air. My body seemed fettered to the solid bench. I didn't shift or move my glance; I was frozen.

"I didn't mean to interrupt you. I was hoping to join in. I thought I heard you singing a song that my mother used to sing to me as a child," he said sweetly. This time, he wasn't going to speak again until I responded. I nervously smiled as I held my bad arm a little closer to my body, trying to provide a barrier between us.

"Dear sweet dear? My father used to sing it to me as well," I said shortly. The man nodded.

"I could play the other hand for you, seeing as your left

hand is tied up," he suggested, placing his smooth hands on the piano, ready to help.

"That is a generous offer. One I am not sure I can take you up on," I chuckled nervously. The man furrowed his brow, perplexed.

"Are you judging my piano capabilities before even giving me a chance?" he asked. I laughed at his concern.

"Of course not. I am sure you are very good; it's my capabilities that I doubt," I replied honestly.

"That is no excuse, you have an extra set of hands remember?" he said, as he held his hands up.

"Well, I also don't sing in front of people." I gave another excuse, hoping he would drop the matter. The man shook his head, making *tsk* sounds as his eyes met mine once again.

"You just sang in front of me," he pointed out.

"Only because I didn't know you were there!" I fired back. The man got a look of disappointment as he turned to face the piano.

"If I would have known that's how you would feel, I would have stayed hidden in the hallway a while longer." He smiled a crooked smile, gauging my reaction from the corner of his eye. I was trying to stay composed when replying to his witty banter.

"So you were spying on me?" I asked candidly. The man turned on the bench once again, his body now facing mine, his hand by his side, lightly touching my thigh. I shivered at the sudden touch. He smiled at my reaction.

"Not so. I was minding my business actually, taking a stroll. You just happened to catch my ear while I was passing by."

"Right," I replied with uncertainty, not believing it for a second. This man was the definition of trouble. I needed to leave before his wit got the best of me.

"I'm actually waiting for someone.I should probably go find him," I said. The man's face changed into disappointment.

"Who are you waiting for?" he bluntly asked.

"Ezra. He's been helping me with, well, this . . ." I motioned to my arm. The man let out a small sigh of relief and a short laugh.

"That would make sense."

I raised my eyebrow, confused. "What makes sense?"

"I thought I knew you," he said matter of factly.

"I don't mean to be rude but you don't know me. You must have me confused with someone else," I assured him, knowing there was no possible way he could have known me. *I have been in your enemy's land my entire life, it is impossible that our paths would have ever crossed.*

"On the contrary I am very certain of it. You're a difficult person to forget actually. You left quite the impression on all of us during that battle at the festival."

My heart stopped. He was there? He was a soldier? Is there any way he would connect that I was actually Valterian? *I need to get out of this situation. Now.*

I tried to stay calm as I responded.

"We should stop the conversation here before you find out more embarrassing things about me." His eyes focused on my lips that I had been biting from my nerves. I tried not to blush by the sudden attention.

"You don't need to be embarrassed. I am glad to see you're

doing better. Aside from me pestering you, of course." He winked. I gave him a pity laugh, not wanting him to catch onto the fact that what he said was true. I tried to change the subject again.

"I can't imagine what's taking Ezra so long, I better be on my way." I supported myself to a standing position, moving away from the bench. The man quickly stood up, noticing my leg slightly limping from my bruises and scrapes.

"I don't think it's wise for you to go by yourself through the castle. That leg doesn't look too reliable right now," he said, grasping my arm lightly as I steadied myself.

"I'll be alright. Thank you for your concern." The man took my good hand and bowed as he kissed the back of my wrist lightly. Chills went up my spine at the unexpected goodbye.

"As you wish, Amelia." He smiled as he turned away, letting my hand go gently.

"I never told you my name," I said quickly and surprised. I heard his smile almost as clearly as if he had laughed.

"Word travels fast around here. I just happen to be good at hearing it first."

The man sat down at the piano, preparing to play, dismissing my presence or further comments. As I walked outside the room I could hear him singing a tune I hadn't heard before.

His voice was like velvet as he hit all the notes perfectly, sending chills up my spine. He knew I was still in hearing range and yet he had no hesitation playing and singing as loud as his heart desired. He was confident and persistent in a magnetizing way. It was a dangerous combination to be around.

I walked as briskly as I was able in the direction I saw Ezra go, leaving the man's voice behind me to echo in my thoughts as I replayed the moment over and over again.

~

I had caught Ezra making his way back to the music room, a cup of water in his hand. He was surprised to see me by myself.

"What made you leave the music room?" he asked as he passed me the cup of water. I took a sip as we paused to talk. I didn't want to tell him what actually happened. I had already lied to him a lot up until this point; what could another lie hurt?

"I was getting worried, it felt like you were gone for a long time. I thought I would go search for you," I said innocently. Ezra didn't seem to believe me but he also didn't seem to want to ask more questions.

"Now that you have had a break, should we continue on?" he asked my permission. I nodded, grasping the cup tightly with my good hand.

We continued on as planned to see the gate guards. To my surprise, they were brothers. Simon and James. They seemed to be in their early thirties. They were bigger than Ezra and I put together. They had a humorous sense about them as they seamlessly finished each other's sentences throughout our conversation. It was quite impressive to watch.

We had finally completed our tour of the castle, or at least the tour of what Ezra was permitted to show me. Our tour still managed to last a few hours, even with the limited areas we could see. I can't imagine seeing all of it. The castle here seemed much larger in size than ours in Valteria. Which made me think if the situation were reversed, a tour like this for a total stranger in our castle would have never been allowed.

"Ezra, we won't get in trouble will we, for roaming the castle?"

"Please," he scoffed, "no one minds. Everyone in the castle is very social. Rumors about you have been circling as is. It was due time everyone met you. I have one last thing to show you. However, keep me in good time. We should head back to your room before dinner."

I nodded in reply. "Where are we going next, haven't we seen it all?" I asked, trying to imagine what else we could possibly cover. I was beginning to feel tired, but I couldn't object, the more of the castle I could see, the better chance I had of a safe escape.

"I saved the best for last. The stables," Ezra said with a smile.

"The stables?"

"Maybe you will like it, maybe you won't, but it's personally my favorite."

We had walked out of the gates and circled to the back of the castle. The grass had bits of sand poking out for me to see, remnants of the nearby beach intermingling with its blades. I gazed around, taking in my surroundings, noting everything I could for my future escape.

"Ezra, what is that?" I pointed at a turret that I spotted out of the corner of my eye. It was gray in color, standing out from the sandstone blocks that formed the rest of the castle. It looked to be a newer addition.

"That is not a place we will be visiting," he stated, not giving a better answer to my question.

I shrugged off his suspicious reply and moved on to observe the rest of my surroundings. The castle was breathtaking. The Praserian red flag blew slowly in the wind, the contrast it made from the light brown castle walls was captivating. I could hear the ocean crashing in the distance. My curiosity to see it up close increased and the hope that I could see it once while I was in Praseria planted its way into my thoughts. My attention was brought back to our current destination as I heard a new sound.

Horses were sprinting wildly everywhere, but within the safety of a wooden fence that stretched for what seemed like miles. Hooves pounding the earth with force and tails whipping in the wind could be heard across the grounds. The beauty of the stallions and mares kept me from blinking; I didn't want to miss a single moment. I hadn't seen so many wild horses at one time. It was very rare to have them kept on the castle grounds in Valteria, as they were notorious for being too time consuming to train properly for riders. One stopped and looked directly at me, and I felt my breath catch for a moment. She looked exactly like Lamis.

Lamis had been my favorite horse. She was a wild white Arabian that displayed such softness when I was with her. Before Damien's arrival to the castle, she was my only friend. Just like me, she was different from all the others that surrounded her, as she was one of the only wild horses we had. To my dismay, the gate to her stall had been left unlocked while I was away with my father and she hadn't been seen again. I had no interest in replacing her. I found myself being frequently bitter when I was around the beautiful beasts, the reminder of Lamis's accidental escape always leaving me resentful. It had been many months since I had ridden any type of steed. The joy it once brought me to ride had diminished a long time ago.

Here, I wasn't afraid of stepping into the chaos of the pasture. It was almost inviting. I was technically being held captive anyway, so why not fully embrace the insanity? Ezra didn't take a moment to see if I was hesitant about approaching the horses, he seemed to assume I wouldn't question the situation. I tried to take the same calm approach he did.

I followed closely behind Ezra into the corral, watching my step to avoid any pressure on my leg. A handful of horses brushed closely past me, making me cringe. The environment was untamed and out of control, but whenever I looked directly at the beasts, the beauty of it made everything seem different. It made my repeated resentment towards riding and horses seem iniquitous.

I pressed on, holding onto Ezra's shoulder, feeling slightly ashamed to be cowering behind the old man as he slowly made his way across. He didn't seem worried about being trampled, so I tried to toughen up, but I could still feel myself panicking on the inside.

We had finally got out of the pasture and into the barn. A young girl in her teens with midnight hair and peacock eyes was brushing a foal.

She didn't look up when she heard our footsteps, but

instead patted the little horse, gently hugged it and sent it running in the opposite direction.

She slowly crept out of her squat and stood still, looking at the horse from afar.

"Beautiful thing, isn't she Ezra? She has progressed so much since I found her." She turned and her eyes became slits toward Ezra's direction. "Your horse, on the other hand, is a completely different story. He is the most stubborn beast I have ever worked with. He is slow – *very* slow – and head-strong, but he's starting to ease up. Did you come to see him?" she questioned, opening her eyes back to a friendly gaze.

"I would love to see him. Come Amelia. I hope you like him."

The girl led us to Ezra's horse. *He's a physician's assistant, why was he allowed to keep his horse in the castle stables?* It seemed odd. Kendra turned to talk directly to me, distracting me from my questioning.

"Yes, I hope so too. I have worked very hard on training him. My name is Kendra. You're the girl the prince saved, correct? Well you are a pretty little thing – very brave to do what you did." I blushed at her words.

"Thank you. I didn't mean to cause such chaos, I feel terribly sorry about it all," I said, trying to play the part.

Kendra smiled. "Don't apologize. Even if you didn't receive the praises of men for your actions, so many of the women here have admired your devotion to the cause," Kendra reassured me. I nodded in response, at a loss of words for something I didn't do. I was hoping my silence would change the subject.

I followed her down a long hallway, horses filling every

stall. Silver name plates were displayed on all of them. We stopped at the one labeled *Dante.*

I peered in to see a large, chestnut stomach, bigger than I could have imagined a horse could have. Then a black eye came up close to my face. I let out a small squeal and backed away to let Kendra take her place at the front. Kendra unlocked the door and quickly grabbed Dante's mane.

Dante objected at her pull and tried to restrain from her hold, but Ezra came into his view and he became silent.

It was fascinating to watch. The horse was keen and rough, yet gentle in his beauty. I wanted to pet the soft fur that had been so well groomed but held back in slight fear after seeing Dante's reaction to Kendra.

"What breed is he?" I whispered, not wanting to frighten him.

"A thoroughbred. One of the best there is." Ezra smiled.

He stroked the horse's mane and whispered in soothing tones. Kendra still grasped the horse, but no fear was in her eyes.

"He's beautiful, Ezra," I said.

"I would let you ride, but he can be quite unpredictable. Kendra, do you think you could lend Amelia a different horse?"

"Of course! I think I have the perfect one for you Amelia. Are you comfortable riding Dante on your own, Ezra?" she asked doubtfully.

"This is my horse, I am not afraid." He stood taller at his words, his slightly hunched shoulders rolling back to give him another inch of height. She sighed and took my hand in worry, not willing to put up a protest.

"Wait, I think we are forgetting that I am in no state to ride." I gestured to my leg and arm, the reminder causing me to focus on the dull throbbing my injuries were emitting, probably a sign for me to take it easy again.

"I'm sorry, that was rather inconsiderate of me to even offer. Maybe when you're healed and feeling better," Ezra encouraged. Kendra nodded.

"Just to motivate you to heal a little quicker, why don't I show you the horse I plan for you to ride once you are up for it?" She led me to the very end of the stables, to a double locked stall. There wasn't a name plate and there wasn't a window.

She put her fingers on the locks and undid a chain at the bottom and top. She could already see my hesitation from the over the top display of security.

"This one isn't dangerous, but we wouldn't want it running away. It's the best horse we have at our disposal." She opened the door and all I could see was licorice black. Black hooves, black hair, black eyes. The hair was groomed poker straight and untangled, long and clean. I stepped back.

I could see all the features as the sun hit the curves of the beautiful black steed that was in front of me. No sound came out of its mouth, just a quiet huff. Its black eyes seemed to be filled with wonder. The hooves clawed the ground, not in an ominous way, but very gently. It was the most ravishing horse anyone could lay their eyes on.

"It's a Friesian. Her name is Beau. Do you think you could handle her?" Kendra asked. I thought about the question for only a moment, even if I didn't think I could, I would want to try.

"I'd like to say so. Is she yours?" I asked.

Kendra paused. "I wish. The prince just purchased her last week. But I believe if we keep it our secret, it would be completely fine." She smiled wryly.

"Oh, I better not. Thank you for the generous offer," I replied, backing away. The last thing I need is another opportunity to be associated with the enemy prince. He already saved my life and I managed to evade being noticed as the Valterian princess. I did not want to test the waters further than I already had. Luck only goes so far.

"I understand. I will pick out another one for you the next time I see you." She smiled.

Ezra interrupted as he came charging our way.

"The time got away from me, it's almost supper! We will be late. Come now Amelia, let's get you back."

I turned in protest, not ready to leave. Ezra spoke before I had a chance.

"I suggest we hurry," Ezra said in a rapid voice.

He started wobbling away, his wisps of hair blowing in the wind. Ezra was not letting me consider any other options. I looked at the horse, sighed, and followed.

"I'll be back!" I yelled over my shoulder to Kendra. She waved and nodded back as we disappeared into the green pasture.

CHAPTER 8

*E*zra helped me back into my bed and waited silently, staring at the door.

"Didn't you say it was time for supper? What are we doing here in my room?" I whispered, sensing the need to be discreet from Ezra's demeanor. We weren't secretive during our outing so I couldn't understand the sudden change. He didn't take his eyes off the door when he spoke.

"What do you mean? You are supposed to be sick, which means supper in bed. Act as if you are tired," he demanded.

"You told me we wouldn't get in trouble," I accused. He cracked a half smile.

"If we do, it will only be a *little* bit of trouble. Now do as I said. Act tired."

I tried to act like my eyes were briefly closing every second, but the seconds passed so long that my eyelids seemed to droop without the thought of doing so.

Without a word or sound, a young maid came in, my eyes

barely looking her way. I hadn't met her on my tour of the castle, she must have not been around when I was out and about.

"Here is some soup and fish," she stated, handing Ezra the tray of food. She paused for a moment and continued in hushed tones, as if she thought I couldn't hear.

"So is this the girl everyone has been talking about? Poor thing. She looks so sick, Ezra. I hope she gets better," she said sympathetically.

"Me too. She is getting stronger by the minute, I think she will be just fine," he nodded in agreement. I wanted to laugh, since I had been feeling much better. I appreciated his acting skills.

She quietly whispered her good-bye, silently shut the door behind her, and was gone.

"Nice performance, Amelia. We make a fine team. Here is your food; you can get out of bed now." I unrolled the covers and sat on the floor.

"Why didn't I meet her? You introduced me to the other servants in the castle. If you didn't want them knowing we were out I don't understand why you would risk showing me the castle." I didn't have much of an appetite so I just nibbled at my fish while he talked.

"Only certain individuals in this castle are trustworthy. There are different levels of the castle and the staff is required to remain on the floor they are assigned. All the places we visited had people I trust, " he said grimly.

"She seems so kind though. How could she not be trusted?"

"It's the ones that seem the sweetest that are the enemies in the end," he stated blatantly.

"Why are you so cynical?" I questioned his reasoning. I stirred the soup with my good hand as I waited for it to cool off, the steam dissipating quickly.

"History," he said simply. I waited for him to give me more of an explanation, but he seemed content with his one word answer. I pressed him for more.

"History in general?" I asked.

"Yes, that too."

My eyebrows raised, still trying to understand his kurt responses.

"In my opinion, that can't be true for every kind person you encounter. Some people are kind because they are simply that, kind," I said.

He sighed, finally giving in to my persistence.

"I am tired and really don't want to keep talking about this. What will it take to drop the subject?"

"Answer the question with more explanation and I will drop it," I quickly stated back, happy to see my stubbornness paying off.

"You have to promise to keep quiet about this. I am the only one who knows." He gave in too easily, or maybe he trusted me more than he even realized. He looked around to see if someone was watching, even though there was no one else present, and continued after I nodded my head in agreement to his terms.

"Many years ago she was very close with the old prince," he said secretively. I didn't understand why that was such a big deal.

"Which old prince?" I inquired.

"He's been labeled a traitor. I personally was very fond of how he ruled. Do not misunderstand, Aleron is magnificent too. Something about Prince Faris, however, was so reassuring. He had such grace about him."

My mouth gaped. I quickly shut it. Faris. My father? He knew about my father! Would he know what he looked like? Like me? If he had known my father, he might know who I really am. Would he betray me or would he help me? I let him keep talking, trying to get all the information I could.

"Did you know him?" I asked hopefully.

"I did. He was one of my closest friends." Ezra's voice held a sense of sorrow. I hoped to understand what was behind his tone. "You actually remind me a lot of him." Ezra added.

I swallowed, giving a faint smile to hide my nerves. Was it my personality that was familiar to Ezra? Could he see the resemblance that I shared with my father?

"What happened between him and the maid?" I asked, diverting away from Ezra's comment and hoped to bury any questions it may cause. I hadn't heard my father mention much about his time in Praseria. I was in awe of the opportunity to learn more about him through a Praserian's eyes, a Praserian who claims to have been his friend.

"Faris was very fond of Lottie," Ezra said quietly.

"Lottie is the maid?" I asked. He nodded.

"Now let me go on, don't interrupt the story." He gave me a glare. I nodded, letting him continue.

"Lottie loved Faris, but Faris disappeared without telling her. I was the only one who knew where he had gone. He had left for Valteria and met another." He looked at me, waiting to see if my expression had some form of shock, probably from the mention of Valteria, so I pretended to be horrified as best I could. He seemed appeased by my reaction and continued.

"She happened to be the princess of Valteria. He planned to come back to Praseria, but he was captivated by her. He relayed to me his secret plan to woo her. He colored his hair to be the same as hers. He tried in every way to get to her, to be with her. Then out of nowhere he came back. He was completely distraught. He told me that he didn't love Lottie, that he loved Laerina. He had lied to Laerina and had been chased out upon her discovery of the truth. He spent weeks trying to gain back her trust. Finally he told me he had planned to get married. I assumed he was referring to Lottie, of course, but I was astonished when he told me he was planning to marry Laerina. The enemy princess, it really couldn't have been a worse decision at that time. I was shocked but I had never seen him so happy. I knew he didn't love Lottie and it pained him to disappoint his parents so."

"But Lottie is a servant, why would that be any better?" I asked, confused.

"It hadn't mattered to his parents that he had fallen in love with a servant; it symbolized a unity between the lower class citizens and the royals. But marrying the enemy meant that their family would no longer carry the crown." He paused for a moment, silent as if he was reliving that time. He shook his head.

"That is how the crown got passed on to the current royal family. Faris was the only child the Amena's had and he followed his heart, instead of his kingdom."

I let the story sink in. I had not realized the risk my father had taken in the eyes of each kingdom. I don't know how he had the courage to do it. I would have been terrified. It's a decision I could not imagine having to make. Love or your family, marriage or your kingdom. There was no way to win.

"It's unfortunate his parents couldn't approve of his choice," I whispered to myself, not realizing I had spoken the thought out loud.

"Despite his parents disapproval, no one was more upset than Lottie. When he told Lottie the news, she got very angry. She planned to hurt Faris from the pain of his betrayal. I do not want to go into detail, but her desire to be the queen was so unassailable, she was willing to go to great measures for it." Ezra's voice went cold.

I shivered at the thought of the small middle-aged woman who just brought my dinner wanting to inflict harm on my father. Anger started to build up inside me. I needed to know everything, not just half the story.

"Please, tell me the rest," I pleaded with Ezra. He could see the seriousness I held in the conversation, and with a sigh, he carried on.

"She admitted she didn't love him either, but insisted on marriage for the crown. She tried to convince him to think of his parents and the kingdom. Faris refused. He had walked away from it all, with problems filling her lap. Faris left with the princess of Valteria after she came back for him and told all the citizens the truth. He was hated and yet respected for following his heart instead of his heritage. That is what I loved about Faris. I was left with Lottie, trying to contain her rather *creative* mind. It was Faris's request that I ensure she was alright. He thanked me and promised to come back, but I haven't seen him since. Lottie, of course, dislikes me, but nonetheless, I hope I helped Faris live a pleasant life by keeping a close watch on her. I still hope for the day Faris will return to see that I have done him proud." He stared into the ground, mouth tightly shut.

I stopped eating completely; trying to take some of the emotional exhaustion the story had inflicted on Ezra. The story had unlocked many answers about my father and many emotions of my own.

It was refreshing to hear about how much Ezra loved my father. Ezra loved my father like I did, he had someone that appreciated him the way he deserved to be appreciated. I could picture my father having a friend like Ezra. I wondered why he didn't tell me all of this. I went my whole life only having half the story.

I wanted to tell him that father was not going to visit, but I still needed to keep this a secret. I happily smiled at my father's best friend. I was no longer afraid that he would discover my identity, unless I willingly shared.

"You are a good man to help someone like that. I know Faris must have appreciated it and likely thought of you often," I said open mindedly.

"I hope that he feels that way. Each day my heart grows a little heavier wondering what I did wrong, why he hasn't been back." His eyes closed and I knew that he had been *very* close to my father. It hurt him to feel and see his best friend go off with the enemy and leave him alone with a crazy woman to take care of.

"I feel my good deed wasn't worthwhile anymore," he whispered.

My lips went into a straight line. I wanted so badly to take away all of this suffering, to comfort him. I knew I could, but I held back.

"He sounds like an honorable man. I am sure he has a very good reason for not visiting. I *know* he is thankful for your deed, I just know it," I promised, giving the only hope I could.

"I wish you were right," he said. There was a long pause before I responded, locking eyes with his, placing a hand on his shoulder.

"I am," I whispered with conviction. He looked at me with red eyes, tears starting to form.

"I believe you. For some reason, I believe you."

~

I sipped the cup of red liquid that Terris had put in my hand.

"I need to know what you think of it, Amelia."

I licked my lips and studied the taste. It was tangy and full of sugar. It smelled fruity. I picked out all the ingredients one by one. Peach, strawberries, raspberries, cherry, and kiwi. It was cold and tickled my lips, staining them a light pink.

"Terris, it's divine. What is it for?"

"No time to talk! I'm sorry; I have to make up a whole new menu selection. Thank you for tasting it!" Then he stumbled out of my guest room.

I just shrugged and turned to Ezra. It had been eight days since I had been awake and I had permission now to roam the castle, at least the levels Ezra approved. I knew every room and who or what was in it and what it was for. My favorite thing in the castle was still the pasture, but the field was lovely too.

Ezra had taken me out to the field two days ago, flaunting wild flowers, trees bigger and older than the castle, surrounded by little ponds with black and white swans and turtles.

I had never seen black swans. Their red beaks gave them a sense of being mischievous. I had a quicker pace as I approached them and was taken aback by the unexpected greeting they gave. A surprising sound escaped the crimson beaks as the swans caught sight of us. Ezra had given me part of a breadstick to feed them. I slowed down; moving the breadstick into their line of sight. The sudden appearance of food had calmed down their alarm. As we approached, I noticed the reason for their defensive nature. Little cygnets were hidden safely beneath their wings.

As for my recovery, Ezra said I was getting better and that I could leave in another two weeks or so. I thought I could leave sooner. Pain was something I no longer felt with me throughout the day and I no longer needed assistance of any kind to get around.

Ezra said they would *let* me go. Meaning I didn't have to escape, I just had to wait for the day I was dismissed. I could maybe steal a horse and some food and find my way back to Valteria.

But a silent force was pushing that idea out of my head and into the wind. Part of me wanted to stay. Ezra was the last connection I had to feeling close to my father and I cherished that feeling. Despite the fact that I should have been high on my guard in this circumstance, I felt safe. I didn't feel like an outsider here. Yes, I *was* technically an outsider, but only because of where I came from. On the inside and outside, I *was* partially Praserian. I never imagined I would find comfort and joy in that fact. A part of me belonged here. A part of my heritage, a part of my family had been kept from me. It was exhilarating to discover missing pieces of myself that I didn't know existed.

Another part of me wanted to go home. My thoughts instantly drifted to Hassan. I could feel the sweet butterflies fill my insides as I pictured his face. Dread and regret flooded my entire body quickly after. I was worried about my friends and Risa, yet I didn't inquire about how much damage the attack had caused. I didn't want to seem sympathetic to the Praserian's enemy, but their enemy was my home. I couldn't risk raising suspicion. I grew increasingly worried as the concern for my well being became less important. I needed to see everyone again, I needed to see Hassan; I needed to know he was all right.

I had time to decide what course of action would be best and I would take all the time I was given, delaying the inevitable as much as possible.

"It's a beautiful day, isn't it, Amelia?" Ezra asked.

I looked out the window. We had been sitting in my guest room, drawing on sketch pads to pass the time. It was a beautiful day. Rose and gold colors mixed in the sky, with a dash of blue. White clouds plotted in the sky and the shoreline could be seen from every point of the castle.

In Valteria there were no oceans, only mountains. The clear ocean water could briefly be seen from my window, the merit of it blinded my eyes.

"Yes it is," I beamed. I turned to Ezra.

"Ezra, how far is the ocean from the castle?" I had only heard stories of the crystal blue water that stretched farther than the eye could see. I knew my time here was limited and the thought of seeing the ocean for myself was tempting. It also would give me a better idea of my surroundings once I did escape.

"Not far at all. About a ten minute walk actually. That path, do you see it right there?" Ezra pointed to the corner of the window, a sandy path leading to the beach. I nodded in reply.

"That takes you right to the shore," he said. I tapped my foot on the ground, anxious as I asked my next question.

"Do you think I could go out for a little while?" I inquired. Ezra yawned while he stretched out of his chair, seeming tired by the proposal. He pushed through it anyway.

"That's a great idea." His response was supportive. He had been thrilled to show me so much of the castle, it formed a unique friendship between us and I know he enjoyed doing something different.

As Ezra and I have become very close the last few days, he had disclosed to me that his joints had become increasingly achy and hard to move, making him quite tired.

"You don't have to be with me all day. I feel bad taking away all your personal time," I admitted.

"It's not a bother. I like being stuck with you. You aren't the most terrible company I've had." He laughed at his joke.

"As much as I appreciate you saying that, we have had quite a few busy days. Why don't you take the afternoon for yourself? I'd love some time to explore," I offered. Ezra sighed as he tried to gauge my sincerity.

"Ezra, I will be fine for a few hours on my own. I promise," I reassured him.

He smiled in reply. "All right, just a few hours. I will meet you back here for supper. If you need anything –" I interrupted him. "I can ask anyone else. I do know quite a few other people now thanks to you." I patted his shoulder.

Ezra chuckled. "That's true. Be safe. Don't get a sunburn," he warned in a mocking tone. Ezra walked out of the room and shut the door quietly behind him.

Taking Ezra's advice, I rummaged through the wardrobe that Noni had lent to me. She had quite colorful taste, with many patterns and dramatic fabrics represented in all the garments.

At the back of the wardrobe I managed to find a white half-sleeve linen dress that looked to be the most casual option available. I think it was intended to be a nightgown but I didn't mind. A pair of sandals were placed on one of the wardrobes shelves that I chose to pair with it. As long as Noni didn't see my unusual outfit, I should be all right. *I wasn't planning on any company anyway.*

I changed as fast as I could with one arm, as my other arm was still in a sling. I made my way out of the castle through a side entrance that Ezra had shown me a few days prior. I could see my guest room window behind my shoulder and the small sand path directly in front of me. The sun felt nice as it covered my face and hands, sending a slight tingling sensation through my body. I could smell and taste the salt in the air as I made my way toward the beach.

The sand quickly made its way into my sandals, making each step harder to take as it buried my feet into the ground. Realizing I would have better luck without the sandals on, I kicked them to the side, holding them in my one good hand as I continued down the path.

It didn't take long for the path to change. The sand was replaced with a mixture of sand and sea shells, with washed up seaweed lying along the sides of the path. Seagulls were circling the sky and the loud waves echoed as they crashed against large rocks in the distance. The waves drowned out the rest of the sounds as I made way closer to the shoreline. I dropped my sandals down by a rock to pick up later. I walked up to the point where the sand met the water, taking it all in.

It was breathtaking. The never ending sight of blue was so serene. Watching the ripple of the waves as they made their way closer to the shore was mesmerizing. The feeling of each wave hitting differently on my feet was an exciting mystery.

By that point, I had pulled my dress up past my knees so the water wouldn't drench the fabric. A small breeze made the hairs on my neck stand up.

I imagined what it would be like being a creature in the ocean. I hadn't seen much marine life and I was hoping to spot something miraculous from the shore. I squinted and searched the blue waters. Nothing disrupted its path aside from the jutting rocks and the wind.

A sense of calm came over me as I envisioned my father enjoying this same beach, looking at this same ocean. While looking at the water, I spotted an unfamiliar movement near one of the rocks to my left. I was hoping it would be an animal or sea creature, but I was quickly left in shock.

I saw a figure climbing their way to the top of one of the rocks. *Are they mad? Do they not realize how dangerous that is? What if they fall?* The rock towered above the waves, almost like a small cliff jutting out of the ocean. Jagged boulders surrounded the larger rock, patiently waiting for disaster to strike and be the first to catch, or kill, whatever came their way.

I frantically looked around to see if anyone else was in sight, seeing what I was seeing. If that person needed help, I would not be suited for the job. Living in Valteria, I had never learned to swim. The lakes in Valteria weren't deep enough to mandate significant swim training.

I didn't know what to do. I felt helpless, motioning my arms in their direction. I tried to signal for them to get down, but they wouldn't turn my way. Yelling would do no good. It was impossible to get their attention over the noise of drowning waves. All I could do was stand and watch, hoping they wouldn't slip, fall, and plunge their way to an untimely death.

Without hesitation, the individual took a step back and jumped forward off the top of the rock, diving into the untamed waters. I felt myself cringe as I waited to see if they would resurface, hoping they missed the smaller rocks surrounding them. Nothing.

I panicked. Pulling my dress up a little higher, I went deeper into the water, looking for any sign of the person. My instincts told me to shout, thinking somehow that would evoke a response, but I held back, listening for a sign of life.

Many moments went by that felt like hours. I was ready to make a run for the castle to get help, unsure what else I could do. Then I noticed a little ways ahead a disrupted motion in the water. It was a man, his head bobbing up for air every few seconds as he swam in my direction.

My nerves settled at the realization that the man was fine. Annoyed that I wasted even a moment worrying, I was ready to give a stern lecture to the reckless figure that approached me. Once the man reached shallower waters, he stood up.

He pushed his long black hair out of his eyes, slicking his curls back to rest on his neck. He was wearing a black pair of swim trunks that had suctioned tightly to his thighs. His muscular figure was soaked by the sun, the water on his body reflecting harshly my way. It took me a moment to register the sight before me, but once I saw his eyes I knew exactly who it was. My stomach dropped and so did my hand, my dress falling into the water.

The familiar face I saw in the musical room only eight days before was grinning at the sight of me, obviously taking note of my nerves. I was trying not to seem shaken by his presence, pretending that my soaked dress didn't bother me.

"Are you spying on *me* now? I am flattered," he laughed as he approached me. I was trying to make it blatantly obvious that I was only looking at his face, trying not to be distracted by his gleaming chest.

"Don't be flattered. I am furious with you!" I yelled over the loud water.

"You don't hold back at all," he stated, smiling again as he shook his wet hair.

"Is this a joke to you? You had me terrified! What kind of sane person willingly throws themselves off boulders into crashing waters?" I accused.

"Are you implying that you think I'm crazy?" he pressed, his eyes filled with twisted delight.

"Not crazy. Dangerous. *That* was dangerous. You're lucky you didn't get hurt," I scoffed back. The man laughed again, looking down at my dress that now clung to my legs in the frigid water.

"You are one to lecture," he pointed to my arm, the sling now sopping wet. *Right, he thinks I risked my life in their attack. I almost forgot.*

"Mine was accidental," I replied in defense.

"Mine was intentional. You should try it sometime. It really takes the danger out of it when you know what's going to happen," he grinned. It was hard to be mad at him when he took the situation so lightly. Maybe I was being uptight; maybe I didn't understand. If I had grown up around the ocean my entire life, maybe I would have dared to do the same thing.

"I will never be able to understand that," I said more to myself than to him.

"Is that a challenge?" he mocked.

"Not in the slightest," I replied quickly, extinguishing any ideas he might be conjuring.

His blue eyes were even more reflective against the ocean water, it was nearly impossible to look away from him.

"That's too bad. I love a good challenge," he smirked, coming closer to me now. The man towered over me, his chest at the height of my sight. I rolled my eyes at his motion for attention, tilting my chin up to look at him. The sun was shadowing him, extenuating his lean physique.

"Well you'll have to find one somewhere else," I said

sternly, turning away from him as I tried to trudge out of the water, going against the current that was effectively keeping me right where I was.

My leg had healed significantly but it was still not at full strength. I had no idea the ocean waves would be so strong. Each step I took, my dress would catch, pulling me right back. My struggle was becoming obvious very fast.

I heard the man mutter under his breath. Without a word, he came up behind me, sweeping my legs out from under me, cradling me to his chest as he took on the current all by himself. He didn't seem even slightly fazed at the weight of us both, something that I would have thought was an impossible feat.

Within seconds he had made it to the shore with ease. My injured arm had been hugged between us, the other arm was resting on his chest as I tried to balance my weight in his hold. Warmth was radiating from him, remotely calming my shivers from the cold water. It had become worse now that the wind was hitting my skin and there was no movement from the waves to circulate a little bit of heat.

He lightly set me down on the sand, his hands holding my waist as he helped me steady my stance. His firm grasp made me shiver even more and he noticed immediately. Thankfully my blushing went unnoticed as it was hidden by my sunburned cheeks.

"Thank you," I whispered my gratitude, too stubborn to acknowledge much of his heroic scene. His hands were now placed on my rib cage. I stared at the ground, trying to avoid further eye contact with him.

"You should get into your change of dry clothes. You don't want to catch a cold," he proposed the obvious.

"I didn't bring a change of clothes. I wasn't planning on getting in the water," I admitted.

"What could have possibly persuaded you to get in then?" he responded with a smart aleck tone, knowing the answer to his question. I rolled my eyes, this time for him to see. He bit his rosy lips, holding back a smirk.

"Follow me," he said. He walked around me and headed in the opposite direction.

I wanted to reply, to say something witty back to continue our banter but something came over me. A sense of curiosity, a sense of a desire. A sense that the trouble he'd cause me was just beginning.

~

The man had led me quite a ways down the beach. He paused when he came to two palm trees situated closely together. A satchel had been thrown at the base of one of the trees. His shoes were placed next to the bag and a long tunic and a spare set of pants were draped over the other tree.

The man snagged the tunic, folding it over his arm. He approached me with a soft smile, a hint of generosity in his ice blue eyes. "Take it. I'll manage without it," he offered, extending his arm for me to take the garment.

My lips twisted to the side, trying to hide my own urge to smile. I grabbed the tunic, holding it to my chest. "There isn't a place for me to change," I pointed out, observing the long shoreline with nothing but sand and water in sight.

He chuckled. "I had a feeling you'd say that. I change out here all the time. No one is around, trust me. That's why I come out here as often as I do," he said assuredly.

I laughed at his comment. "*You* are here. *You* are around," I said, motioning with my good arm the close proximity between us.

He shrugged at my hesitation. "That tree is bigger than you, big enough to change behind." He had a point. I raised my eyebrow, expressing my lack of trust.

"Don't look at me like that. I have to change as well. Who's to say I can trust that you'll give me privacy? After all, you are the one that was spying on me," he winked.

I gawked, shocked at his reply. "You know that's not true," I fired back. The man bit his rosy lips again, a quality that was attracting quite a bit of my attention.

He crossed his arms in front of his chest, his veins slightly bulging at the sudden constriction. "I promise I won't look. We can change at the same time. And I won't come out from behind my tree until you say I can," he promised.

I believed him. He may be reckless and overly confident but he had also proven to be a gentleman. I looked down at my dress, water still dripping off the seams. My lips felt like they were nearly blue, I didn't have many other options. I nodded at his response.

"I'll trust you," I said, making my way behind the tree.

"That's all I ask," he chuckled back.

I waited until I heard him shuffle behind the tree. I quickly glanced around, reassuring myself that no one was in sight. I removed my sling, a pulsing sensation from the movement making me groan.

"Are you all right?" he yelled from behind his tree. I froze, not realizing he was close enough to hear my small expression of pain.

"I'm fine," I yelled back. The man was silent again.

I hurried as fast as I could without hurting my arm, the wet clothes finally peeling away from my body and dropping to the sand. I shoved the tunic over my head and pulled it down immediately, exhaling as my anxiety declined. I noticed a new scent replacing the smell of salt. Searching for the source I took a deep breath and realized it was the tunic. It smelled like cloves.

I slowly placed my arms back through the tunic and rearranged my sling. It was still wet, but the dry tunic was enough to keep me from shivering. Warmth immediately came back to my face.

The tunic was a little short, hitting about mid thigh. At least it was a long sleeve and seemed to cover the rest of me pretty well. My bruises were almost gone and there were only a few scrapes still visible on my legs. I swallowed hard as I got the courage to speak again.

"You can come out now," I finally spoke up. The man was patient as he slowly stepped out in sync with me from behind the tree. His white trousers seemed even brighter against his dark skin. His hair had begun to dry, the curls settling in a perfect halo around his face. His dimpled smile appeared as he intently stared at me. I was praying my sunburn was still capable of hiding my blushing face. I looked around uncomfortably, not knowing how to react.

"Thank you for letting me borrow your clothes," I said, trying to break the silence. He nodded, stepping toward me, closing the gap between us. I was trying to ignore the fact that he was still shirtless, once again forcing me to look up at his handsome face. Without breaking eye contact, he took my hand in his, holding it to his chest.

"You should keep it. It looks better on you anyway," he complimented me. I instinctively shied away to hide my face, moving my glance to look at the ground. The act made me unintentionally place my forehead on his chest, his proximity being closer than I had realized. Despite his plunge in the ocean, his enticing clove scent was still prominent.

Too ashamed to look back up, I felt his head drop down, his lips brushing against my ear.

"I want to show you something," he whispered, the sudden closeness sending goosebumps to my arms. Squeezing my hand he turned my body to follow behind him.

We made our way back toward the castle, grabbing my sandals on the way. The man had held my damp dress in one hand and his satchel in the other.

"I heard you've suffered some memory loss," he stated, making small talk. I almost forgot our conversation from earlier. In the music room he had said my name. He claimed to have seen me during the attack.

"There really are no secrets in this castle are there?" I asked, ignoring the comment. I did not want him asking too many questions, not when I was so close to being able to go back home.

"Very few. Actually, I'm about to show you one right now.

I trust you can keep this between us?" he looked back, a skeptical look on his face.

"I can keep a secret," I replied. *I have recently discovered I am actually very good at it.*

"Good. Just a little farther." The man stepped over some sand mounds and made his way to a small pool of water. He crouched down in front of the one nearest to us, his back muscles clearly defined as he reached into the water in front of him. I came to his side, tucking the short tunic underneath me as we both gazed into the small area of freestanding water.

"It's a tide pool," he said. I could feel him staring at me, waiting to observe my reaction. I saw little fish that looked like they had swords for a nose wisp past one another. A yellow fish that was shaped like a star was clinging to a rock. A variety of creatures dazzled before my eyes and little crabs of different sizes and shells were busy moving about the exciting sea city. I laughed at the sight. I had wished to see marine life and here it was, right in front of me. I would have never found this on my own.

The man leaned his arm in the water, gently picking up a hermit crab. The crab took refuge by sealing himself in his shell. The man held out his hand flat for me to see the details of the crustaceans shell.

"Amazing isn't it? So many creatures in such a tiny space," he spoke quietly as he placed the crab back into the water, letting it scurry away as it reclaimed its freedom.

A loud trumpet suddenly interrupted us. The man's face didn't seem surprised. The unexpected sound made me jump, showing his dimple smile once again as he found humor in my reaction.

"That's my cue. I have to be getting back. Would you like me to escort you to the castle?" he offered, holding out his hand for me to take. I shook my head. The last thing I needed was anyone to see me walking hand in hand with a beautiful shirtless man, in a tunic that was not mine. People were already talking about me in the castle and that would definitely give them even more to gossip about.

"I think I will stay a while longer," I said, not wanting to admit the real reason I was choosing to stay behind.

The man's face seemed mildly disappointed in my reply but he nodded anyway.

"It was nice to see you again, Amelia. I sincerely mean it when I say thank you for spying on me." He winked and stood up as he prepared to leave.

"Wait!" I said, holding him back a little longer.

"I haven't asked you your name," I inquired, hoping to rid another one of the secrets he had. The man took my hand once again, looking down at me as I still sat on the ground. He kissed the back of my wrist, just like he had in the music room; his classic departure.

"I am sure that fate will have our paths cross again. I'll tell you next time." He swooped his satchel into his arms and took off running toward the castle. I stayed seated as I watched him slowly disappear from my sight. *Next time.* I couldn't help but be giddy over the idea of a next time.

CHAPTER 9

*O*n my way back to the castle I stopped near some wild flowers. I picked a handful to place in my room, just like I used to do in Valteria. The flowers were a lovely shade of pink. I picked the best one of the bunch and placed it behind my ear.

When I got back to my room I was relieved to see that Ezra hadn't been waiting for me. I managed to enter the castle without being spotted in my odd display of wearing a man's tunic. I changed as fast as I could upon returning to my room and tucked the man's tunic under my pillow where no one would find it.

Not long after my return, Ezra knocked on the door, supper in hand.

"That's a beautiful flower. Don't show Noni that you put it in your hair, you'll start a new trend throughout the kingdom," Ezra complimented.

I had Ezra ask the maids to bring a glass of water for the

other flowers I had gathered. We sat and ate dinner together quietly, both of us focused on other thoughts it seemed. *I know what my thoughts are but I have no idea what Ezra is pondering about.*

Suddenly a worried and quick thunderous knock came on the door. Ezra and I jumped at the interruption, losing our trains of thought. Ezra got up to open the door for the visitor. The visitor pushed her way past Ezra and I quickly knew who it was. It was Noni, carrying a violet dress that seemed fit for a child.

"Amelia, I love the flower in your hair, I'm going to have to incorporate that into some of my designs." She invited herself in and started to lay the dress on the bed. Ezra and I exchanged looks.

"Ezra guessed you might like it." I chuckled at her comment. Noni turned at the mention of his name.

"Ezra, what are you still doing here?I need to get her dressed!Out, out!" She started to shove him out the door.

"Dressed for what?" we both asked harmoniously.

She turned and sighed. "The prince is coming."

$\sim$

*E*zra was out of the room without a word and Noni helped me into the tiny dress.

"Noni, first of all, this dress will never fit me! Second, why do *I* need to get dressed up for the prince? I am already wearing a dress you made for me and it at least fits!" I acknowledged the yellow fluffy dress I had put on when I got back, implying that it should be enough.

She didn't answer, she had pins in her mouth and she spat them on the floor.

"Do not insult me Amelia, I know exactly your size! This dress is *just* that! It will show your figure more than the others I brought you."

I stared at the dress again, still in disbelief that it could possibly fit me.

"Why is it necessary that I change?"

"Why? Because he wants to meet you silly! The dress you have on now will not do."

My breath caught in my throat. My eyes became the size of the sky and my body was motionless in her arms. The prince . . . meeting *me?* What if he found out who I was? He might know more than everyone else about my family. I wanted to leave on good terms, be able to leave as Ezra mentioned, freely. I wasn't afraid of being in Praseria until now.

"My, my, Lia! You're a mess! Don't be afraid. The prince is impeccably charming," she tried to comfort me. If only she knew why I was actually afraid, then she would understand.

"Amelia, listen to me." She sat me down on the stool in the corner, my body still rigid like stone. "Everyone in Praseria would die to meet him; they would be cheering and skipping out of their minds, not be taken by alarm. Just take a deep breath and let it out. You'll be fine! And beautiful might I add, thanks to me!" She beamed proudly, not minding the arrogant compliment.

Her words eased my quaking and my fear. Or maybe it was the dress that stopped the shaking, as Noni tightly buttoned the back and limited the use of most of my body.

She worked so quickly as she pinned curls and patted powder on my face, handling two tasks at once. She had placed the flower in my hair back in the vase that was now situated on my night stand.

"Did you get sunburned? Don't you know how awful that is for your skin?" she lectured me as she worked.

After moments of primping with methods I had never used before, she undid the curls, letting them fall and shield my now pink and rosy face. I don't think I had ever been done up this fancily, even in Valteria. Or maybe it was my own fault for refusing to have a lady's maid. Sighing with satisfaction of her efforts, she pulled me to the side and let me look in the mirror.

I looked different. A good, new, different. My eyelids were smeared with a lilac oil, my lips had a shiny sheen from the paint like mixture on my lips, and my cheeks were powdered pink. Noni had somehow managed to hide my sunburned forehead. My hair covered the corners of my face and curved into a wave like the midnight sky. My light yellow dress was beautiful as she said. Little sparkles covered most of it. It may have been fitted and difficult to breathe but definitely worth it.

She quickly cleaned up her makeup and supplies and headed to the door, leaving me speechless in the middle of the room.

She turned at the door and grinned. "You are gorgeous! I did splendidly if I do say so myself. Well I must go, the prince cannot see me here, I look *hideous*. I will see you soon." She turned to leave so quickly that I couldn't interject a word of thanks.

"Oh wait! One more thing!" She put her hand deep into her bag and pulled out something swaddled repeatedly in a sheer fabric.

She joyfully unwrapped it and put her hands around my neck, leaving something hard and chilled on my neck. Then she took my wrist and put something smaller, but the same texture and gently creased it.

"Now you look like a princess!" I admired the jewelry and looked at it more carefully. Pearls made up the entire necklace and bracelet. They were marvelous and gleaming. In Valteria, I never got to wear jewelry like this. Pearl jewelry was only worn in seaside kingdoms, I had only seen settings like this a handful of times in meeting people from Lokali or Gree. Pearls, although seeming like an understated choice for jewelry, were breathtaking. The necklace and bracelet made me feel out of place. I was surprised Noni, or anyone, would go to such great lengths to dress me so sumptuously. Was this meeting more important than Noni had implied?

"Ezra, you can come in now!" Noni blew a kiss to each of my cheeks and quickly ran out.

Ezra came in after her and stopped, gaping. He gained composure and cleared his throat.

"The prince will be impressed," was all he said, then looked away, slightly embarrassed. The mention of the prince made my stomach jump. Would he really be as kind as Noni said or would I regret this? Should I try and flee now? The only place I could escape was the door.

I could run, but they might catch me and force me back here anyway. Plus the lack of air in my lungs from this dress would probably make running impossible. I shouldn't fear.

Only one more week of this charade and I would be going home.

My head was spinning, I felt faint. I sat on the floor, unaware that I was wrinkling my perfect dress.

Ezra held a concerned look. "Are you feeling alright, Amelia?"

I nodded. "I'm just feeling a little light-headed. It could just be from this dress, or from my day in the sun . . . or from my injuries. Water?" I implored.

"Of course. Here." He handed me some water and I sank deeper into the floor. I held myself up on one elbow. After the first couple of sips, the spinning seemed to slip away. I handed him the glass.

"Thank you, Ezra."

"Do you need help up?" he asked.

I shook my head.

"Are you still sick?" he asked, very concerned.

"I am all right, really," I assured him.

"Stay on the floor just a bit longer, in case the dizziness comes back. I don't like to chance it. If you fall again your injuries could relapse."

He set the glass on the table and took a seat across the room from me. I tried to focus on the flowers that were sitting in the glass, to see if my eyes could see clearly again. I jumped as I heard an unexpected voice. It was a panicked, winsome, mellow voice that was coming from the other side of the room. A voice that I had only heard a few hours ago.

"Is she all right?" The man asked.

All my fear seemed to disappear. I turned to see the man from the music room, the man from the beach, standing in my doorway. He was no longer wearing only trousers like he had been a few hours before. He was wearing a white tunic like the one he had lent me, with a red velvet coat placed over it. His hair had been brushed, making his curls hang loosely. His black trousers were fitted tightly to his legs, his black boots as shiny as his hair. I didn't dare take my eyes away from him. I didn't want to. *What is he doing here? The last thing I need is to get in trouble with the prince. Was he here to embarrass me?*

My lips opened very slightly, trying to speak, feeling exposed and rather silly considering he had last seen me in a tunic and he was now seeing me in an entirely new light. The whole image I tried to portray of myself being calm and collected for the prince had vanished. I felt like an open book, a yelling secret that refused to be kept quiet. I didn't want Ezra to know about my encounter with him; it was another secret I was hoping to keep.

I knew it was unsafe to be here, but looking at the man stopped my thoughts, emotions, and worries. I couldn't tell if I was puzzled or afraid. I couldn't show any expression or even identify what would be right to show. I wanted to blame the light-headedness for my confusion.

I tried to build an invisible wall between us, to hide the truth. The man stared at me, a twinkle in his eyes, his dimple lightly appearing. He then stepped into the awkward room. Ezra quickly stood up to reply.

"Yes, your majesty. She is doing much better." Ezra interrupted the silent conversation I could feel between the man and myself. Majesty? *Please tell me I just imagined him saying that.*

"When is our guest's expected departure?" the man asked.

"She could leave in a week or two if she continues to heal at the pace she has, your majesty," Ezra responded. There it was again. Majesty. The realization of what was happening came at me fast. I felt myself catching my breath. *He really was good at keeping secrets.* The man I had been annoyed with, bantering with, flirting with, was Aleron. *Prince Aleron.*

It all made sense. How he knew my name, how he knew about my memory loss, his comment about getting away from everyone, why he wouldn't share his name. It all made sense.

"A week or two you say? I insist that she stay until we have located her family. I will not be sending her away until she has a place to go." A sigh came from Aleron's lips. He walked to my side and held out a hand. At first I didn't want to accept the help, but another silent force urged my hand slowly forward. He grasped my hand tightly, not letting go when I got up.

The prince's offer, although generous, was a new predicament. They would never find my Praserian family. They didn't exist. I was counting on Ezra's word for allowing me to leave in a week or two. This would be a problem.

Aleron's eyes looked over me, studying my face and for the second time today, I had felt pain come from my injured arm, leg, and every other part of my body that had sensory function. Aleron slowly let go of my hand. The heat from his skin disappeared and I yearned for him to take my hand once more. Just another reminder that to me he was brilliantly, fascinatingly different. Yet he also infuriated me beyond belief. I can't believe he lied to me.

"It's good to see you moving around. I was frightened

when I saw you in the attack. I was afraid your injuries might be much worse. I am glad you're alive and I am very happy that you proved my worries to be wrong," he proclaimed, winking at me. He wanted me to play along, acting like we hadn't met before this moment. He wanted to keep our secret.

I didn't know what else to do but thank him, what other choice did I have? No matter how much I wanted to call him out for the liar he was. It was a good thing I had gotten great at pretending, as it would take a lot to hide my irritation with him at the moment.

"I couldn't have asked for better care. I cannot thank you enough for being so kind and understanding toward me. It was wrong of me to get involved in the kingdom's affairs without proper permission. I hope you can accept my most sincere apology," I said in my most fabricated sing-song voice I could muster, looking at the ground in order to concentrate enough to have formed the response.

He placed his soft hand on my shoulder. "Your apology is not necessary. I am not concerned with what occurred or how it happened, just that you are doing well. My name is Aleron Hadway, Prince of Praseria, heir to the throne, and knight of the realm. I am humbled to make your acquaintance." He deeply bowed.

I smiled at his exaggerated example of good manners and proper conversation. He was great at pretending too.

"I am Amelia," I lied, curtsying deep. For the first time being here, it was hard to lie, to the point where I was beginning to feel sick.

"Please, do not curtsy. I will have no one treat me like I am better than they are. I am just a man," he said innocently.

"Why did you bow to me then if you weren't expecting a bow in return?" I wondered out loud. I knew I shouldn't have asked that but I couldn't help myself. Our first conversations had forced a habit of such remarks; it was hard to shut off.

He reacted just as I thought. He didn't take the question rudely but smiled, seemingly impressed by my bold manners in front of Ezra.

"I may just be a man, but you are not just a woman." A smirk turned on his rosy lips that made me want to melt into his arms. The comment took me off guard and I felt my cheeks burn. I could not render a response. I just stared at him with a simple expression.

He was like *me*. Hated the questions and being treated like something special. He wanted to feel normal, be normal. That was the only reason I could assume he didn't tell me who he was right away. But that still didn't justify him misleading me.

"Amelia, I was hoping to speak to you for a moment." He turned to Ezra, still holding the smirk on his face. Ezra, understanding the message, left the room silently. Before he shut the door, Ezra smiled at me, his eyes wrinkled with excitement. He then closed the door and left me alone with Aleron.

Aleron was waiting to hear the door meet its hinge to assure we were alone, to make sure Ezra was distant from us. He didn't look back, but was positive the door was closed and then locked his eyes with mine again, holding my gaze.

"As stunning as you look in this dress, I still prefer the tunic." He winked at me once more, making me nervous all over again.

"What are you doing here?" I hissed, ignoring his brash compliment.

"I know I said fate would likely have our paths cross again, but then I thought, why leave it up to fate? I decided to take matters into my own hands. You did a great job acting surprised to see me by the way," Aleron grinned widely.

"It wasn't an act. You lied to me." I immediately addressed the situation, folding my arms as I gave him a stern stare.

"I did not lie," he said in rebuttal, standing his ground.

"Omission is a form of lying," I accused.

He sighed, bringing his hands to my shoulders, pulling me close as he had earlier. Clove. *He always smells like clove.*

"Don't be angry with me. It was refreshing to have a conversation with someone that didn't know who I was," he defended himself. I was mortified. *The things I said to him, the way I acted.* It was completely unsuitable for a prince. I would have done things a lot differently had I known who he was.

"I was outspoken. I was –"

"Yourself. You were yourself. And I admired every minute of it," he assured me. I sighed, not wanting to be mad. I completely understood where he was coming from, more than he could know. Was I being a hypocrite, being angry at him for lying when I was holding back so many secrets of my own?

"I came here to ask you something," he said, holding my hands in his as he continued. "Tomorrow evening my father is hosting a ball in honor of our safe return from Valteria. I was hoping that you might let me escort you to the ball. Do not feel obliged to say yes. I feel however that it would be a shame for you to sit alone in this room when you could be enjoying what should be nothing less than a fantastic evening." He spoke the words shyly, but soon became braver gradually with every word.

Aleron, asking me to a ball? I caught my breath. Confusion swept over me. My true identity conflicted with my façade. Would that be acting against Valteria?

"If you think I would attend a ball with you –"

His chest exhaled and smiled.

"Fantastic. I will come and retrieve you from your room tomorrow after dinner," he promised.

I was surprised he would interrupt me so rudely; he obviously knew that was not where I was leading the conversation. I interjected. "That is not what –"

"Say no more. I look forward to tomorrow," Aleron insisted.

I bit my lip, realizing there was no point in trying to dissuade him from his proposal. He was a stubborn man, and the prince, I shouldn't push it.

We stared at each other for a couple moments longer. He released my gaze as he placed a feather light kiss on the back of my wrist, the sensation of his lips lingering on my skin. Almost as if he could read my mind, he added in his alluring voice, "Goodnight, *Lia*." He winked, obviously having heard Noni's nickname for me. And with that, he left the room smiling, not turning back.

I could barely feel my heart beating any longer. My entire body felt numb after his gentle kiss and his soft touch.

Ezra came in shortly after he had left and came to my side, waiting patiently for me to say something. He tried to snap me out of my daze.

"What did he want?" he asked.

I didn't move my lips, but managed a few mumbles. Finally, actual words formed.

"He asked me to attend the ball tomorrow night." The words didn't seem true when I spoke.

"With?" he queried.

"With? With him." I turned to Ezra.

Ezra looked unsurprised. "Did you say yes?"

I looked at him deeply with regret and happiness. I was surprised to see an old man so ecstatic for a young girl going to a ball, something my father would do.

I wanted to cry and hug Ezra, but he wasn't my father and never could be. But his excitement was enough.

"Yes," I answered.

"We better get you prepared," he said with enthusiasm.

I whispered looking at the door, "I don't think tomorrow night is something I can prepare for."

CHAPTER 10

I awoke to a loud bell. My hands, in reaction, flew to my ears to cover the vexatious noise. I squeezed my eyes tighter together and moaned.

"Get up you indolent girl! We must get you prepared and ensure you are on time!" Ezra shook my shoulder and I decided not to protest. I knew he wouldn't stop until I got up.

I shoved the covers off my hot legs and sat up. I rolled my head and stretched my sore and tired muscles. My arm and leg had finally been getting better. They remained only slightly swollen and bruised. I fluttered my eyes open to see a bright light filling the room with a happy welcome.

Ezra was by my bed holding a plate, waiting impatiently for me to take hold of it.

I grasped the plate lightly and placed it on my lap. I couldn't help but yawn, bringing tears to my eyes.

"Eat quickly. We don't have all day," he insisted.

I took the fork and started to eat the omelet he set before me, though it wasn't appetizing to my stomach.

"I told you, I am confident that I know how to behave. I don't need lessons. Trust me," I objected with a full mouth of fruit.

"I believe you. I am not worried about your behavior." He waved his hand in the air.

"Then what do I need to get ready for?" I asked.

"Noni is coming and she is going to make sure you are dressed appropriately," he said.

I dropped my fork and swallowed.

"I don't want Noni getting me ready," I told him truthfully. It frustrated me, being pampered for events that would only last a few hours. It reminded me of what Aleron had said the day before. I didn't want to be treated like royalty, even if I *was* royalty, and neither did he.

"*Why?* Do you not like how Noni did yesterday?" He seemed shocked.

I shook my head and moved the plate to the other side of the bed. I pushed my weight off the mattress and headed to my vanity, sitting on the cushioned stool.

"It's not that! I am fine with her bringing me a dress, but I want to do my hair and such. I feel like a toddler, being dressed and having my hair and makeup done by someone else. I feel . . . helpless," I said cupping my hand around my neck innocently. I didn't look at Ezra.

"Point taken, but are you sure? It is Noni's job to make sure people are event ready." His voice was full of uncertainty.

I nodded and looked at myself in the mirror. My hair looked like a nest and my face was drained of all color, aside from the uneven sunburn that still remained on parts of my forehead and cheeks. It would be difficult, but not impossible.

"You have been sick, do you have the energy and . . . skill?" He still wasn't convinced. I turned to him and almost rolled my eyes, but stopped myself.

"Have a little faith Ezra. I am more capable than you think. Tell Noni she can bring me a dress and I will take care of the rest. When do I have to be ready?"

"The ball begins at five, but I suggest you should be ready a little earlier, just in case the prince comes needing you sooner. Noni is actually making your dress today." *Noni is making my dress the day of the ball? What can't that woman do?* I had never met a seamstress who could work so quickly.

"That is the perfect amount of time. I can start getting ready after lunch." I got off the stool and glided toward my bed.

"Don't you want to get ready earlier? You know, just in case?" he repeated. I sighed and shook my head, letting all my weight collapse back onto the bed.

"No. I will be ready in time," I promised. I stared at Ezra, waiting to see if I would need to protest more.

"All right," he whispered, turning away in defeat.

"Ezra, I would like to go pick out my dress, if Noni would let me," I suggested.

"I'm sure she would love your input. I will see you tomorrow morning. I'll have a maid bring you up some lunch for you later on." He started to turn the door handle when I stopped him.

"You aren't going to the ball? I thought everyone was invited."

"Yes. Everyone is. I don't have anyone to go with," he said shyly.

"What about your wife?" I asked the question too quickly, regretting it immediately.

He let out a breath, stronger, heavier and more dangerous than one I had ever seen him give. "With all due respect, being my age, I wouldn't be here if I had a wife that I could enjoy my last few years with instead." Everything was silent for a while, but the silence seemed to crawl around the room, growing by every second, making it uncomfortable. Someone had to speak.

"You never got married?" I asked with sorrow. A man like him deserved a loving wife, not being left to tend to people like me.

"I did. She passed away a couple years ago." His body didn't move, but his neck slowly came down to his chest, the horrible memory striking him.

"I am incredibly sorry for your loss," I whispered in regret for bringing up the subject.

He brought his head up and cocked his head to the side, smiling.

"It's all right. I still feel her love every day. She may be gone but she isn't far. You have a good time at the ball." And then he officially turned the handle and left the room.

I stood silent for a moment after the sudden mood swing. Poor Ezra. I felt incredibly sorry for him. I admired how easily he came to terms with his loss. It was inspiring hearing him say that she was still with him. I pray every day that my father is still with me.

I lay back down, tempted to sleep longer, but I forced

myself out of bed and walked down the corridors to find Noni in her sewing room.

The door was shut and nothing could be heard. I knocked loudly, hoping to bring some sound amidst the silence.

"Come in!" she yelled louder than my knock. I turned the cold slim handle and walked into the room.

It was a mess. Fabric was everywhere. Yarn was covering the floor and string was lining the ceiling. I couldn't even see where Noni was.

"Noni?"

"Lia? What can I do for you?" she asked from the corner of the room, popping up with a needle in hand.

I stepped over all the fabric, getting caught in the trap of yarn. I had gotten caught for the third time, gave up, and stood a few feet from her.

"Do you think I could pick out my dress for the ball?"

"Lia darling, I won't let you just pick out a dress, I'll let you have the *first* pick of the best I have to offer! I heard what happened yesterday with the prince. I don't want to take all the credit but I have no doubt the work I did was a small reason he asked you to the ball this evening." She beamed proudly at her self proclaimed accomplishment. I chuckled in reply.

"Back to the dress. Let's see, anything you have in mind?" she asked.

I shrugged, uncertain of what I would prefer. Noni's taste was very different from my own, I wouldn't know what I wanted until I looked at my options. Her range of color preferences was out of my comfort zone and I had a feeling it would be hard to find a more muted dress from her collection. Noni picked up on my uncertainty right away, answering like she could read my thoughts.

"How about you take a moment to look around. Let me know when you find something you like," she said sewing some lavender fabric tightly.

I opened some of the wardrobes throughout the room thumbing through each of them, my eyes seeking and pondering for the dress that spoke to me. Bright yellow, magenta, maroon, teal, amber, ebony, copper – there were so many choices and they all seemed loud. Until I looked in the last wardrobe and found a subtle fabric that still had enough glamour to make the dress stand out.

"Noni, could I take this one?" I grabbed the dress and held it for her to see. It was milky white, like fog. It shimmered when it was turned and the color looked pure and clean. It was something I would find in Valteria, with just an added bit of sparkle.

"Excellent choice! I haven't had anyone prefer that one yet, usually the ladies in the castle ask for a pop of color. I have the perfect shoes to match it as well. This is so exciting!" she clapped and chirped with merriment.

"Thank you, I am looking forward to seeing it on."

"Stay in your room and I will bring it to you in a hurry. You better be on your way to get your hair done!" she instructed.

I nodded. "I've got plenty of time. Are you coming?" I asked.

"Of course! I haven't told you this," she cupped her hands around my ear. "But someone offered to escort me to the ball," she whispered secretly.

"Really?" My eyes widened, reacting with the surprise she was hoping for.

"Yes, but you'll have to wait and see who it is." She waved a hand in the air and got back to her work.

"Not even a hint?" I asked.

She only took a moment to consider my proposal. "One. You have definitely met him! Now off you go!" Noni said in a hurry.

My eyes had become slits as I looked at her. Who had asked her that we would both know? It had to be someone that worked in the castle. Maybe Terris? Simon? I went through the list in my mind of men that I had met since my time here.

"I'll see you soon. And your mystery date." I grinned an occult smile and scurried out of the room before she could say another word, still striking off names in my mind.

~

I twirled, I pranced, I watched the ruffles from my dress leap like frogs while the beams of sun blazed the room with a frightening brightness. I practiced my ballroom dancing with an imaginary figure, stepping back then forward, just as Damien had demonstrated.

Evening was approaching. I spun toward the mirror to get a good look at myself.

Noni was very proud of the dress she had made me. She truly did make a one of a kind dress. She told me it was even better than the one she had made for the queen.

The white colored fabric was layered. Some of the fabric

was pinned in multiple places to form large ruffles, or as Noni called it, drapes. It came to my feet, barely brushing the floor. The top of my dress was plain fabric until it came to my waist, where the drapes started to form. Noni had been very clever, using the same fabric as the dress to create a sling for my injured arm that blended perfectly into the ruffles. It was a half sleeved dress, very formal, simple and enticing.

Noni had lent me some shoes that matched my dress perfectly. The only drawback was that my dress veiled most of the shoe. Except for when I twirled, then my legs and my shoes were completely exposed.

My hair had no chance of falling out; it was pinned so securely it was part of my scalp. I had to admit that it hurt in some places, almost a burn, but when I thought of Aleron and what the pain was for, it was quickly relieved. Dancing with Aleron was enough to take the pain off my mind.

I was surprised that for the first time since I had initially arrived here, I wasn't just nervous, I was *exceptionally* nervous. I wish I could say I was nervous about being exposed for who I really was; it would have made more sense. No, I was nervous to be with Aleron again. *The prince of Praseria.*

No matter how many times I told myself that, it still didn't seem real. Aleron, the unbecoming, exasperating, advantageous man that I had interacted with, was a prince. It completely took me off guard. I have associated with many princes before, but never have they been as plain-spoken as Aleron. I found consolation when people were predictable. Aleron, he left me unprepared, a feeling I loathed.

I couldn't find the reason for my shock at the news of Aleron being the prince. I knew the answer was there, but no matter how long I searched for it, I couldn't find it. Whenever I came close to it, it would run and slip away like it didn't want to be discovered.

Inside, I knew why I didn't want to discover it. Every fiber of my being knew it was wrong. It was risky, all of it. I regretted not considering the consequences of saying yes to tonight. I regretted not thinking with my head. I was frustrated that it was a fight that I even had to have with myself. It was all starting to be confusing. The anticipation and anxiety of what tonight could be was overwhelming my senses. *He's the enemy prince, how could I believe that his attention is genuine? Is he using me somehow? Does he suspect who I am? Is it some twisted way to get information from me? Why do I seem to be drawn to him? Or maybe it's the idea of him that I am infatuated by? The enticing feeling that something so complicated, so wrong, could actually work?*

Aleron couldn't be my friend, we are destined to distrust and hate one another. One day, our parents would pass and it would be him and I ruling our kingdoms. He would be my greatest threat. *What would mother say by all of this? She would never approve, and I doubt Aleron's parents would approve of his date of choice for the ball if they knew who I was. They could never know who I was . . . my life depended on my identity remaining a secret.*

I looked out my window. The sun was still high in the sky, but the light was starting to fade out. He would be coming soon. I fiddled with my dress, tapped my heels and sighed with every second that went by. Trying to keep calm, I sat on the edge of my bed and traced the pattern on the blanket with my finger over and over again.

This is a bad idea, Allene. You shouldn't have agreed to this. I needed to find Ezra. He could make an excuse as to why I couldn't attend the ball, he could be the answer to my mistake.

I didn't allow myself the time to change my mind. I gathered up my dress and ran to the door, opening it with haste. I was stopped in my attempt to flee as I roughly collided with a firm figure in front of me. The sudden impact made me fall hard to the floor. My bad arm was the first to greet the ground, a small cry escaping my lips as my arm throbbed. I stayed on the ground, terrified to look up at who would greet me.

CHAPTER 11

*M*y cheeks flushed red as Aleron looked startled by our clash. He had hardly even faltered at the weight of my body plummeting into his. He reached down, offering a helping hand, again. I grasped his coat sleeve, catching the end. The dark blue velvet around the edge made my hands soften, afraid of ripping the delicate fabric.

Aleron lifted me up and as soon as I was standing securely on my feet I released his sleeve and straightened my wrinkled dress. Noni was going to be furious with me for creasing her masterpiece.

He chuckled, amused by the sight before him. I didn't think it possible but my face became even redder and I glared at the floor in response to his childish laughter.

Finally breathing evenly again, I felt my face cool down to a soft pink. I looked up from the ground and turned my attention to Aleron.

I stopped to see the same breathtaking face I had seen just

a day ago, but even more beautiful than the last time I had seen him. His smile burned a hole in my heart and his voice made my body feel like air.

"Do you always collapse to the floor around the company of men, or am I just special?" he asked, still laughing.

I smiled, but I was afraid to speak. I was afraid to say the wrong thing at the wrong time. I quickly realized I was putting an unrealistic amount of pressure on this evening. *Relax Allene, it's nothing special, it's just a normal evening.*

I wanted to joke with him as he did with me, just as we had before. But this time was different. This time I knew who he was. It wasn't regular behavior for a prince to joke. Every prince that I had met was proper and not fond of humor, but Aleron was quite the opposite. *Nothing has changed.* He is still the same aggravating, endearing man at the beach. *Be yourself Allene, he doesn't seem to mind.*

"You just have impeccable timing. It doesn't mean anything more," I quipped back. Aleron smiled at my frank reply, his blue eyes dancing with fascination.

"I am offended," he claimed, placing his hand over his heart like my words had truly fazed him. I rolled my eyes at his embellished response.

"If only I believed you," I teased back.

"I am relieved to see the news of my royal position hasn't ceased your sharpness toward me," he marveled, offering his arm to assist me. I didn't deny his help, leveraging Aleron to overcome the weight of myself and my dress as I made my way up to standing. It took everything I had to ignore the pulsing sensation in my arm as I gave a response.

"On the contrary, your egocentric self is even more

consuming now that I know who you are," I fired back, concentrating on his clove scent to numb some of the pain.

"Which makes our relationship even more alluring," Aleron said softly as he placed his hand on my cheek, rubbing his thumb against my cheekbone lightly. The sensation left goosebumps on the back of my neck and made my breath shorter with every second that passed. He made me speechless. It left me feeling like every part of this moment was right, yet I knew it should feel wrong. It was a persistent fight with myself that I hoped he couldn't sense.

Aleron picked up on my loss of words, filling in the gaps as he locked his eyes with mine.

"This dress, it just might barely outshine the tunic," Aleron winked.

"I hate to disappoint you but that is the last time you will ever see me in a tunic," I confirmed, putting his fantasy to rest. He squinted, trying to see if I was being serious.

"Dress or tunic, I am honored to have you attend the ball at my side. You are ravishing, Amelia. No matter what you are wearing." I could feel his eyes burning into my skin as he quickly looked me over. I tried not to seem overly flattered, but my heart was soaring.

"You can thank Noni. The dress . . ."

"The dress is only half of it. It's the beautiful girl in the dress that I am talking about." I couldn't concentrate after that compliment. It wasn't fair, I could hardly compete with his quick cleverness.

"And the color blue, it suits you. It brings out the color of your eyes," I mumbled, losing my grip on a good reply. *Very subtle, Allene.* I definitely could use some lessons on flirting. If

I was going to compete with his perfect compliments, I was in dire need of coming up with my own.

"You mean you didn't prefer the shirtless version of me?" he inquired. My cheeks went hot red, the image of his muscular tan chest glistening in the sun flashing to my mind. I took my eyes away from him, looking at the ground as I tried to hide my surprise. I was immediately embarrassed reliving that revealing moment. His attempt to catch me off guard was a success.

Aleron laughed, settling his hand under my chin as he brought my head up to look at him, his face so close that his curls were brushing my face.

"Were you going somewhere?" Aleron changed the subject by referring to our collision at the door. I was hoping he would be too self-absorbed to ask that question. I hoped it hadn't been obvious that I was attempting to avoid this evening – to avoid *him*. *What could one more lie hurt?*

"Ezra said I was supposed to meet you in the drawing room, I was making my way there."

"Did he? It wasn't that you were just eager to see me?" he challenged. I shook my head, not surprised by his arrogant reply. "Don't worry, I'll spare you the embarrassment of admitting it, we are fashionably late for the ball as is," he added.

I nodded, trying not to be distracted by his long eyelashes.

"Lead the way," I encouraged him, taking his offer to move on from his comment. I gently and hesitantly wrapped my arm around his, ready to follow alongside him.

I walked at the same pace he did and kept my mouth quiet, as difficult as it was. I wanted to speak, but reality continued to creep its way into the back of mind and remind me of my situation. *I am the Valterian princess, with the enemy prince. I need to be careful. Feelings, whatever they may seem, don't mean anything.*

I needed to be aware of everything that I said and did, not wanting to jeopardize my chance to go home. I only had to last a few more days and I could be free. In an effort to be extra cautious, I was going to only speak when spoken to. But he didn't speak; he was suddenly serious, like most princes were. His behavior was polarizing, different and quite confusing to keep up with as he was putting up a facade. All the more reason to be cautious and have tonight be led by logic, not emotions.

We walked down the corridors that led to the ballroom. Servants and guests ignored us, like it wasn't a big deal that the prince was taking the girl who had ruined their most recent attack against their enemy to the ball. That was the way I wanted it to be. Not seen or heard.

I hadn't thought about the attack in quite some time. I had become consumed with what was happening currently, my concern for my home diminishing. Maybe it was because Praseria felt like home to me. I felt accepted and loved by every individual I had met thus far. The addition of Aleron's magntizing effects also didn't help my situation. But now thinking of Damien, Hassan, Risa, and Freira, my wonderings grew.

The questions I had thought of the first day I woke up in Praseria were coming back to me, eagerly, impatiently, wanting answers. I would have to wait and ask Ezra when we had time alone. I was finally at a point where I felt it was safe to inquire about the attack on Valteria more in depth.

I had slowed my pace when we came to the doors of the ballroom. I peered in to see everyone dancing. I tried to pick out Noni from the crowd but she was nowhere to be found.

Aleron stopped at the arch at the top of the staircase. A loud horn was blown. I cringed and without even a glance at me, a small smirk came to his face. Everyone stopped dancing and turned to us, all eyes and ears set on Aleron and myself. He grasped my arm tighter and walked lightly down the stairs, barely hopping from each step. I tried to do the same. I was heavy footed in comparison, trying to ground myself so I wouldn't fall, leading with my good leg. My bad arm was wrapped tightly and couldn't be used for counter balance, making me rely on Aleron again to hold me steady.

Even though the people were supposed to be watching *us* it seemed that everyone was watching *me*. The stares made me uncomfortable so I just focused on the wall and pretended to look out at everyone else like I had been told to do in front of crowds.

Once we got to the middle of the floor, everyone cleared a pathway, and I was beginning to shake slightly from my nerves. As I had not spoken to Aleron since we were in my room, hearing his voice was deafening.

"Thank you all for coming! I am so pleased with this warm welcome home party for our dedicated troops and to celebrate comradery and dedication among our people and a common cause of justice," he proclaimed with a strong tone. He paused, showing genuine concentration.

"Please, return to your dancing. Enjoy your evening!"

Then just like that, chatter began and the music started as people swayed across the floor again. I was bewildered; he said very little and quickly made his point. In Valteria we would say much more than just three sentences. Events like this were a publicity statement, moments for speeches and politics. Saying how pleased we were with the land, any public affairs, or how well off our kingdom was doing economically or otherwise. It was much different here, and I liked the difference much more than I thought I would.

The music started out very slow, just like when we had entered. Without notice, Aleron grasped my hand and wrapped his arm around my waist. He placed my hand on his shoulder. Without even a word, we started dancing. My feet followed him without trouble.

He didn't speak, but looked to the side. His touch on my skin left a fiery sensation. I felt my stomach drop, rendering me speechless.

This wasn't the same man from yesterday. He was beginning to come off as any other conventional, entitled prince. He acted as if I was an accessory rather than a date and I could feel irritation erupt inside of me. After half a dance I couldn't resist speaking.

"I could've done that myself-placing my hand on your shoulder, I'm not oblivious to how dancing works," I spoke boldly. My jaw clenched. *Why are you pushing the boundaries? You may have gotten away with speaking this way before but he is the enemy prince. To him, I am a commoner, not a princess. I have to know my place.*

I shut my eyes, wishing I wouldn't have said anything, hoping maybe he didn't hear or wouldn't respond to such a rude comment as that. He didn't turn his head, but continued his dancing and retorted his unexpected response.

"I know, but you were slow, staring off into space. You can lead if you would like," he assured me with a grin, his dimple showing. My mouth gaped. He was back to his antagonizing self. My suspicion of his odd behaviors grew and so did my rudeness.

"I was not being slow," I spat. I took his offer stubbornly, taking the lead.

I started to spin in circles and go under his arm, weaving in and out through the dance floor. Not having my other arm to aid in my dancing was not going to slow me down.

"You're not an awful dancer. I had my doubts that you would be clumsy, given our record of introductions," he spoke loudly and truthfully, letting his thoughts be known.

"There is a lot you don't know about me," I said firmly.

"It is a good thing we have plenty of time for you to teach me then. I am fascinated to learn more about you, Amelia," he said, his eyes full of curiosity as I avoided his glance.

I nodded to his offer, not giving him any satisfaction with his attempt to mend my irritation with his polished intrigues. A few flirtatious conversations didn't mean anything. He was the Praserian prince. I needed to remember that there was a reason he was considered my enemy.

With that thought in my mind, I wanted to put up a strong front and not let him get the best of me again. He didn't seem fazed by my silence. Instead he smiled, and he kept smiling for what seemed like an eternity. We continued dancing with not much chatter, but more movement. We were the most energetic couple on the floor, going around the other couples that made way for us.

The music stayed the same beat, very slow and graceful, but I seemed to be going faster than the music. Every time we turned, his touch became more frequent, more expected, more familiar. The burning subsided and a feeling of attachment set in. *Don't get distracted Allene. Whatever you are feeling, it's not real. Don't let him get into your head.*

The music stopped while Aleron was turning me toward him, the sweet smell of him overwhelming my senses. We both paused and I stuttered backwards. He smiled and looked directly at me for the first time in a while. Then everyone was silent.

"Switch partners for one dance! Come now, everyone, don't be shy!" A man was booming out for the ballroom to hear. Everyone froze and quickly skittered to find someone else. Except Aleron and I.

Aleron hesitated and sighed. He leaned in toward me, resting his chin on my shoulder, his lips barely touching my ear, his hair tickling my neck.

"Meet me outside after this dance. By the pavilion."

His words repeated in my head like an echo. I had seen one pavilion at the palace, not far from the field. I felt that burning inside me return. Suddenly I could feel the pain return to my body. My fingertips went ice cold. I realized I was afraid. I was afraid of what could possibly happen. I was feeling things I had never felt. I knew the tone in Aleron's suggestion to meet at the pavilion was something to fear.

I couldn't turn down his offer, could I? What excuse could

I possibly make? I couldn't think quickly enough to make a decent lie and found myself nodding in agreement.

Allene! Seriously! You have to get it together. You need to say no! You should stay in public, do not find yourself alone with him. I locked my eyes with his, trying to gain the courage to turn down his suggestion.

His eyes were soft and reassuring as he was slowly walking away, making my heart play tricks on my mind that it would be okay, that I should go. The opportunity to say no dissipated quickly as a swarm of well-manicured young ladies were surrounding him, washing away the tension between him and I and replacing it with a callous attitude.

I tried to wait patiently to see if anyone would approach me. I was easily forgotten and left by myself, just another commoner in their eyes. Withering looks from pompous ladies burned into my skin, their disapproval of me being escorted by the prince's being blatantly obvious. I didn't want to suffer the embarrassment of being alone during the dance, no one would ask me, they probably didn't understand even why the *prince* had asked me. Maybe they thought it was out of pity. *Wait, could it be? Was Aleron's request to escort me to the ball because he felt sorry for me?* The thought made me angry, but also relieved. If it was from pity, it means he probably didn't have any inclination of who I was. *I'll take pity if it means my safety.* I decided to search for a familiar face to distract myself from the objective crowd.

As I surveyed the crowd, I began to notice how understated Valterian balls had been. Praseria seemed to flourish in glamour and boisterous conversations. The ladies in Praseria wore valumputious gowns that practically swallowed them whole. I had a hard time understanding how they remained so poised as they carried the weight of the dresses with each energized step they took to follow the loud music. Valterian gowns were muted in colors and sleek in structure - contrast and statement pieces begged for the scorn of onlookers. Valterian balls were much more reserved and at times, painfully dull from the lack of enthusiasm in the air. In Praseria, the chatter of people surrounding those that danced was a fierce competition that almost overpowered the music. The ball was a symphony of chaos and beauty.

After scanning past a group of ladies in vibrant yellow dresses, being blinded by the potent color, I spotted Terris serving little desserts to guests and chose to seek refuge near him. *Well that checks him off my list of Noni's possible mystery escort.* I hurried over as fast as I could in my heels and stopped right in front of his big plate of sugary desserts. Whatever Terris had created was square and lumpy, but it looked appetizing.

"Good evening, Terris. May I?" I asked politely and proceeded to grab one.

"Ah, Amelia, what a pleasure to see you! Help yourself. Not very many folks here are hungry and it's making me quite disheartened that I went to all this trouble for nothing."

"I appreciate your efforts very much. This event wouldn't be nearly as wonderful without your talented hands." I grabbed a couple more, eating away my feelings.

Terris chuckled as I munched on my fourth serving.

"Glad to see you are enjoying them. You made quite an entrance tonight, Amelia. The whole kingdom has been gossiping about you and the prince since yesterday," he laughed. I tried not to seem shocked by his comment.

I came over to Terris to stop thinking about Aleron, just for a moment. Within a few minutes Aleron had still found a way back into my thoughts. I sighed, trying to avoid a response.

"What are these?" I asked, giving a half smile to conceal the dessert remains in my mouth. I held the squares in the palm of my hand; powdered sugar was drizzled over the top, making it look like snow had fallen all around it. I silently bit into one as I tried to discern for myself what the delectable creations were made from. I was hoping he would take the bait.

"It wasn't negative gossip, Amelia. You are giving the people hope," he assured me. My eyes widened, confused.

"Hope for what?" I asked.

"That we might finally be getting a princess." I tried to swallow the rest of the pastry that seemed stuck in my throat after I heard Terris's reply. *I am already a princess, a princess you do not want associated with Praseria.*

"Terris, that's ridiculous. I am a commoner who the prince took pity on and invited to the ball. I am not Praseria's future princess." I tried to laugh at the news that had been circulating throughout the castle.

"Amelia, the extent of your memory loss is slightly concerning. Do you really not understand the importance of you attending the ball?" Terris asked. I shook my head, still confused.

He sighed. "The prince has never asked anyone to attend a

ball. Until you. How does that not give the people hope? How would that not make you different in everyone's eyes?"

Terris's words started to sink in. Aleron had never asked anyone to attend a ball? What could possibly have made him ask me then? My stupefaction grew. Aleron was the first heir to Praseria's brand new dynasty – the start of his family's legacy. The amount of pressure Aleron probably felt in regards to choosing a wife must have been great. I could only assume he hadn't taken anyone to a ball in fear of his parents disapproval of choice. *So why would he ever take me? As a way to make some passive aggressive statement to his parents?* Maybe I had been viewing this situation more lightly than I realized. This much attention on me was not safe. If it was this important to the common people, I didn't want to begin to imagine the stir it would bring to the king and queen. I only hoped I could last a few more days, quiet down the gossip enough to leave unnoticed and be forgotten. I had no intention of starting so much commotion.

"Terris, I can assure you that the prince asking me to the ball did not mean what everyone thinks it means." I made an effort to convince him with the hopes of convincing myself.

He held back a laugh as he shook his head. "It's not me you need to convince. I think that is something you should save for the king and queen." Terris raised his eyebrows, expressing distant concern for my well-being. I cringed slightly, surprised he would address what was already going through my mind. I hadn't met the king or queen yet, and I prayed it would stay that way. I was very close to being able to make my escape. The less interaction with royalty I could have, the better my chances would be at leaving Praseria in freedom. *That is why tonight was a horrible idea, Allene. You foolish girl, you should have declined any invitation from Aleron as soon as you knew who he was.*

"Where are the king and queen tonight? Noni mentioned she was making a dress for the queen, but I haven't seen either of them," I pried, seeing what secrets Terris may divulge. He shrugged, not giving the question much relevance.

"One of the maids said they had other obligations unexpectedly arise."

Odd. What obligations couldn't wait till after the ball to address? Or maybe it wasn't a what, maybe it was a who? I wondered if whatever Aleron's intentions were for bringing me tonight had been spoiled now that his parents weren't in attendance. Did they think Aleron's choice in bringing me was one of pity? Or one of temporary infatuation that they assumed would pass? Did they know more than I realized, was I being baited? *Be grateful Allene, whatever the reason, their absence is in your favor.*

I heard the music slowing down and quickly dusted the pastry off my hands. I checked to make sure no sugar had gotten on me, knowing Noni would not be pleased if she saw I tainted her dress.

"I better be going. It was nice talking with you, Terris. I hope you have a lovely rest of your evening," I said as I hurried away, not letting him interject another comment.

I was trying to process what Terris just said. I was beginning to feel overwhelmed, like I was in over my head in this situation. *Why didn't you say no to Aleron? You knew you should have said no!* While the people of Praseria were gaining hope, my hope of everything working out smoothly was fleeting, and it was fleeting faster than I could catch.

~

*T*he time had come. The opportunity to decline had gone and I was forced to make my way to the pavilion. My pace was slow, my heart and brain still at war with one another, making each step feel like I was dredging on through knee deep water. Despite my leisurely pace, I was wanting to get there first. Part of me was hoping he wouldn't show so my heart could be disappointed and my head could fully take over my decision making.

The pavilion was white with a bench built into it on the north end. Aleron was sitting on the left side, his impeccably built shoulders slumping slightly over the bench as his hands clenched the wood seat. His perfectly laid back hair was shining in a million directions under the retreating sun. His presence immediately stopped me in my tracks.

I was perplexed by Aleron. Very few things had even been spoken between the two of us and yet I felt a fire when I was with him. A passion, a belonging.

I wasn't sure how long I had been standing there before I gained the courage to face him. I approached with caution, my feet still dragging behind me as I sat down next to him, tucking my dress underneath me. The dress was great cushioning for the considerably hard wood I was sitting on. I gazed over to observe the foot distance we had between each other. He didn't seem to hear me approach or maybe he wasn't acknowledging it. I couldn't decide which one I would prefer it to be. I quickly broke the silence.

"The song hasn't come to an end. Why aren't you dancing?" I asked. He looked down at the grass a little ways off of the pavilion, then back up to the sky, obviously aware of my presence. The blue velvet of his jacket was a lighter color in the sun, matching perfectly with his eyes.

"Why aren't *you* dancing?" he questioned back in a derisive tone. His voice was charming. It had just enough of a deep undertone to make it masculine, but it was like a song as his words flowed. A small laugh escaped his gorgeous red lips. I faltered, forgetting what he had said and quickly regained my composure.

I shrugged. "I don't know very many people here."

"Trust me, any man in there would be delighted to dance with a woman like you." He raised his eyebrows at me as I tried to withhold a blush.

"I am not the prized commodity that you are. I was more than aware of the flock of young ladies surrounding you once they had the opportunity." I tried to hide the slight tinge of jealousy in my voice as I rolled my eyes to the side so he couldn't see.

Aleron's eyes were set on the horizon, looking in the direction of the setting sun. The scenery that was created with him by my side felt unreal. He laughed at me again and turned toward me. I searched his face, trying to anticipate what he would do next. I soon realized that trying to stay ahead of him was simply not possible.

Aleron sighed and slowly reached toward my hand, holding it in his.

"I didn't dance with anyone else, Ameila," he chuckled, not fazed by the statement.

I silently reveled in the satisfaction that he didn't give into a single one of the beautiful women that came to his side. There was more to Aleron than he portrayed; maybe he wasn't as self centered as I thought. *What would my family and friends say about all this?* I was giving the enemy prince more credit than I ever thought I would.

The last time I danced was in Valteria. My thoughts fluttered to Hassan and Damien, dancing at the Gala, learning the Branle. My heart became heavy as I felt a tinge of betrayal by even having this conversation with Aleron as I thought back to those moments before I was torn apart from my friends. Aleron's eyes were fixating on my uneasy expression. *Focus Allene.*

"I did hear a rumor that you haven't escorted anyone to a ball before," I said, squeezing his hand lightly on my last word, not realizing his hand was still placed on mine. I was not sure if I should continue letting him hold my hand. It felt right, but I knew it shouldn't. I tried deciphering his thoughts by watching his facial expressions. His eyebrows furrowed, obviously puzzled by my response.

"Now that's not fair. I am the first to hear about anything around here, remember? What else did you hear about me?" he pressed. My thoughts fluttered back to my conversation with Terris just minutes before, trying to reply. I was struggling to find a way to phrase it without mentioning the suggested interest that people assumed Aleron had for me. I decided it would be better to lie to avoid implying anything romantic between us.

"Just that. It was difficult to believe them. You are a prince. Every prince looking for a wife attends balls," I stated the facts.

I watched the fine lines crease around his forehead and noticed him biting his lip, something I noticed he did when he was concentrated. He thought about my statement for a moment and gave an honest response, as he always did.

"In my opinion, balls have been overrated ever since they were invented. It's a foolish way to meet people."

"That's a bold statement. What has caused you to have such a skeptical opinion?" I asked. I hadn't heard another royal speak negatively about balls. Most royals lived for them.

"It's just an opportunity for people to put up a charade. No one is honest about who they are. They put up a front to be the best version of themselves. Their finest clothes, their fake smiles, their best hair, the most enticing conversation topics they can think of, and not to mention the impenetrable gossip. It gives false expectations of individuals. It's not a scene to create true connections." Aleron spoke so calmly as he defended his opinion. His words sunk in. He was right. I had never thought of it that way before. The worst part about his words was how deeply they related to me. I was the largest lie he had probably ever come across. I was an individual he would despise. An enemy and a liar.

"I see your point. That does sound pretty awful," I mocked. The mention of it made me reflect on my own experiences of balls. They really weren't as glamorous as people think, they were more exhausting than anything else.

"It is. How are you supposed to get to know someone over loud music and noisy conversations? Not to mention the added pressure of the watchful eyes of everyone in the kingdom. That's why I escape to the beach as often as I do. I need quiet places to be myself," he declared, looking at me intently.

"Would you consider this a quiet place?" I couldn't resist asking.

"I would." His brilliant, slightly crooked smile was gleaming.

"I did notice a difference in your behavior from last week and yesterday compared to tonight. It was confusing, until now. You're starting to make more sense every minute," I admitted.

"I can understand now why you were frustrated with me earlier. I apologize that you had to think, even for a moment, that I was wanting to leave your side. I hope you know tonight my focus and attention – all of it – is yours." He held a wild grin, full of mystery, as he stroked my fingers with his thumb. I didn't know what to say. I was completely captivated by his confidence and flirtations. I hardly stood a chance at displaying the same effortless demeanor and smooth responses.

We sat in silence for a couple moments as I looked at the white wood underneath our hands. I stroked it delicately with my hand underneath his, thinking of his words.

Given the circumstances, shouldn't I be terrified? This is my enemy. Despite the technicality, I was completely flattered. I could hardly explain this new feeling. He said things no one had ever said to me before. I didn't want to get carried away in words of affection, I wanted to be strong. But I felt my guard completely fall with Aleron.

A deep sigh escaped Aleron's lips, my attention coming back to him.

"Lia, you seem . . . anxious." The words that came out of his mouth had a rich tone, his warm breath mingling with mine as the air around started to chill with the evening approaching.

I took in a deep breath of the warm air, trying to stay concentrated on my words. "It's not my intention. I have some heavy things weighing on my mind." I didn't hold back. It was as if he inflicted me, once again, with the ability of letting my guard down. It was vital I kept it up. I was being incredibly foolish. Just because he was honest with me didn't mean I needed to be honest with him. *Come on Allene, pull it together.*

"What exactly?" he whispered soothingly, pulling me back to the unhinged conversation, a dark curl falling in front of his piercing blue eyes.

I thought of when I first arrived in Praseria, my memories of the last few days skipping through my mind until it ended on right here, right now. All the obstacles getting in my way of what I knew I wanted to say, to do. All the effortless questions bubbling inside, yet hazardous answers awaiting after they are asked.

"Everything," I finally said in a hushed voice.

"Believe it or not, I might be able to help," he joked, trying to get me to laugh. I gave a small smile at his efforts.

Aleron moved closer, sincere and concerned as he placed his hand on my cheek, cradling it in his palm.

"Talk to me," he pleaded. He took the opportunity to close the minute gap between the two of us, his eyes locked on my neck. I could feel his even breaths gently rebound off my skin. I didn't look at him; I looked at the sun which was now disappearing behind the violet mountains. I focused on everything I wanted to say, not allowing myself to be distracted by the new waves of emotions I felt from his closeness. I decided I would try to be honest while still being inconspicuous. *Here it goes, my chance to find out what happened.*

"Ever since I've been here I haven't gotten any answers," I explained.

"What do you want to know?" He said each word carefully and slowly, split apart for an echo effect, his breath leaving chills as it grazed against my ear.

"I want to know what happened with the attack on Valteria. I have no memory of the event. Before or after."

Aleron took a moment, processing my request. I had no idea how much he might try to hold back, but it was worth a try to get some answers. He nodded.

"That's what's troubling you?" he asked. With some hesitation in my voice, I proceeded to voice my thoughts.

"*Why* did it happen? Are you going to attack again? What did Praseria do? Who all was hurt?" My thoughts, clear and controlled in my mind, came pouring out in a rush of panic, the intrigue to get answers flooding my judgement of taking it slow. My goal to not sound suspicious was gone in an instant.

"Those are some heavy questions that come with heavy answers. Why are you wondering about all of that?" he asked, confused. He released my cheek and leaned back on his palms, his head to the sun.

It took me a moment to even notice that he let go of me. I

just nodded, tears almost forming with the thought of home and the injured people awaiting my return. Or maybe it was because of the abrupt change of emotion between the two of us. My questions were a sure way of ending any positive atmosphere between us.

I heard him turn closer to me and his voice became louder; his tone was filled with concern. He didn't press me anymore and went on to answer my questions.

"We are always fighting for our land," he said. "We have valuable property. A fight or two protecting it isn't unheard of, but we've never had our land destroyed by other kingdoms." I turned toward him, the tears suddenly gone. I could see the discontent he held as it furrowed his eyebrows with anger, the memory turning his face cold.

"Destroyed? What do you mean?" I asked bewildered.

"Valteria destroyed half of our land the year before last, in the dead of night. They burned it, ruining all of our farmer's crops and fields. The soil no longer can sustain vegetation. Many of our people were starving for the remainder of that year. Fortunately, we had other farm lands on the opposite side of the mountain, so we endured. We came close to grave hardship, and ever since then I have carried that burden of avenging my people for the suffering they were put through. Although it could have been worse, lives were still lost. Starvation is the last thing our people should be dying from." I could see the pain of that year through Aleron's eyes. I battled showing the confusion in mine.

Destroyed? Valteria had never destroyed anything unless they were in active war. It must've been a lie, or else I would've known about these attempts to destroy Praseria's resources. That isn't something that just slips past Risa and I. We come from peaceful people. Although Valteria and Praseria are enemies by trade, it had been many years since any disputes had emerged.

"With all due respect, I thought the Valterians and the Praserians were at peace," I exclaimed in defense.

Aleron shook his head, the dissatisfaction of the discussion represented on his face. "So did we. They have been stealing and destroying lands in many kingdoms the past several months. We even had messengers sent to us asking for our assistance from neighboring kingdoms. With the commotion they are causing, it was only right to give them what they were asking for."

"What are they asking for?" I inquired, still not believing what he was telling me.

"War." Aleron gave a curt reply. His soft tone I had been enjoying all evening had suddenly become pained. It was a tone that should demand my understanding, my comfort to him. However, all I could feel was rage. I couldn't decipher if it was rage toward Aleron and his lies or toward myself for wanting to believe him.

"They would never do that. There is no reason for it." I held back sobs. Aleron couldn't see how much the news was impacting me, I didn't want him growing suspicious.

"No reason can justify what they have done. Their actions have harmed too many people to not react," he said firmly.

"Did your family speak to the Valterian's king or queen? Are you sure the individuals that did this were Valterian or could it have been disgruntled citizens?" I proposed the alternative possibility. From my conversations with Ezra, Praseria wasn't aware of my father's death, so I had to act like he was still present. It made my heart ache pretending he was still here.

"I'm positive. I know Valterian armor. They came with over a hundred men and burned everything they could. Do you need proof?" he asked. I could feel him studying my face now, puzzled by my onset of questions.

I hesitated, thinking of home. My mother was always saying how we had plenty of land and how it was important to be loyal to the others around us. She wouldn't do this.

Aleron didn't wait for my response. "Come with me, I'll show you." He got up and took my hand. He started walking up a hill that I had never noticed until now. I followed, holding my dress with my free hand while he gripped my arm to help me up the incline. The breeze was stinging my skin but when we got to the top of the hill the stinging stopped. I froze. I couldn't believe my eyes.

"Look to the North. Can you see it?" He pointed in the direction that my eyes had already noticed, taking in every bit of what was before me. A large piece of land was different from all that surrounded it. It seemed like a line had been cut in the earth to show where color began and ended.

The noticeable line showed on one side charred black grass, with no evidence of life. Barns, crops and trees were all burned and bruised black. It was deserted and nothing was green, the inability to grow evident. All of it was gone.

"They did that?" I whispered with unbelief. I tried not to acknowledge it, but it was hard not to when the evidence was in front of me. I turned to Aleron, holding him tightly to try and ease my pain. His face was tristful, like he was living the memory again. He nodded.

"We were lucky it was contained as quickly as it was. If it had escalated any faster, it would have taken the castle and all our resources with it."

I couldn't speak any more. I sat down at the top of the hill, overlooking the ruins that my mother had created. I would've started to apologize for our wrongdoings, but I couldn't. I suddenly felt very understanding of the act of vengeance Aleron displayed. I actually felt gratitude for his courage to be an advocate for those smaller cities and kingdoms that couldn't defend themselves.

What was wrong with me! Was I really falling for this? Did I really want to thank the man who had intentions of hurting my people, intentions of hurting *me* and calling it justice? Aleron came down slowly to sit next to me. I slightly cringed as his sleeve brushed my shoulder.

"Do you understand now? I did what I had to do with the situation that faced us. I did it for Praseria." He said the words as if he were trying to reassure himself that what he did was right. I unintentionally nodded.

"I understand why," I whispered, so quietly that he could barely hear. I meant it. I understood. If what he said was true, then I definitely understood. It didn't mean, however, that what *I* was feeling was necessarily right.

"Aleron, what happened during the attack?" I looked at his disgruntled face, studying it intently. He looked the opposite way and tried to hide his distress from me.

"We attacked Valteria with two of the neighboring kingdoms, Lokali and Gree. They sent some of their men as part of our alliance, to bring representation from each kingdom. It was a small group of us and my father assigned me as the leader. The plan wasn't to overtake anything; it was to send a warning. We needed to prove that we were just as strong as Valteria, that they couldn't come here again without getting a fight in return. We wanted it to be clear that an attack on one of us would be considered an attack on all." He trailed off, locking eyes with mine. His hair had fallen in front of his eyes, light blue coming through slightly as his hair was pushed by the breeze.

"But when I saw you, we stopped. I was secretly grateful. I wanted to do as little damage as possible. Not many people were harmed from what I could see. Overall, the plan has seemed to work. The other kingdoms haven't reported any attacks from Valteria in the last few days. I hope it stays that way."

"As do I," I simply said, the conversation halting. It was all still sinking in. Not only had my mother managed to attack Praseria under my nose, but apparently Lokali and Gree as well. Kingdoms that had never been a threat to us. I couldn't fathom a reason to attack and raid any of their kingdoms, we have always been at peace with them.

I bit my lip numerous times, making it dry the very instant that I stopped. Knowing Aleron's intentions to protect those around him softened my hardened heart. I felt open to him once again, open to venture back into what we were feeling before I had brought up our difficult conversation.

"Can I ask you one last question?" I whispered, attempting to shift the conversation.

"Always," he replied, his dimpled smile returning to his handsome face.

"I am confused about why you asked me to the ball. Like I said, you're a prince. Shouldn't you be taking a princess? Not someone like me?" I implied, waving my hand up and down to show my injuries and pitifulness.

"And what are you exactly?" he asked. I could feel the life drain from my face, fear striking me. I could feel my palms become clammy as I realized it was stupid to ask questions that I wanted to avoid a response too. Luckily, Aleron salvaged the moment.

"We have plenty of time to discover who you are, to find your family, and we will. I promise." I felt myself relax as I realized his question was in regards to my memory loss, not my secret. Aleron had leaned back on one arm as he brought the other under my chin, his fingers grazing under my bottom lip.

"I want to be very clear that my only concern is *who* you are. I am not worried about your status in Praseria. You impress me, Lia. Behind your resounding honesty, stubborn nature, and snide remarks, I see your wit, your humor, your enticing smile and frankly, the more time I spend with you, the harder you are to resist," Aleron said his words proudly, his fingers now tracing my lips.

The feeling gave me chills. I shifted uncomfortably under his touch, unsure how to reply. He was making it increasingly difficult to speak with my head and not my emotions.

"Aleron, why did you save me?" It was the question everyone was wondering but no one had the courage to ask. It was a faint whisper but I could tell he heard me. His concerned expression molded into a new one that I couldn't quite understand. Uncertainty? It was almost like Aleron stopped breathing, like he wanted to avoid that question as he pulled away from me. I floundered from his reaction, trying to grasp why he closed off so suddenly.

"Please tell me," I murmured. "That's the one question that I *need* an answer to." Without holding myself back, I reached for his hand that was placed on his knee, intertwining his fingers with mine. I could feel the calluses underneath his palm, wondering how he had gotten them.

His gaze met mine with a burning blue fire in his eyes. His breath danced with mine as I waited silently. Everything around us seemed to freeze. I waited patiently until he sighed in defeat, his eyes frantically searching for mine to understand.

"I have wanted to answer that question. I am afraid you won't accept the response." He looked deeper into my eyes, the blue flames blazing even brighter in his own. He didn't have to speak anymore. I knew what he was implying.

"You don't have to give me an answer," I whispered gently.

Aleron shook his head, looking down at my hand as he held it in his. "No, I do. I have just been having an unusual time articulating it," he chuckled, amused with the fact that he was struggling with his words for probably the first time in his life.

"I can wait for an answer," I assured him, not wanting to place him on the spot. He shook his head again, resting his head to the side as he stared at me intently.

"When I saw you lying there, I felt my heart nearly plummet to my stomach realizing I had caused you pain.

Looking at you, at that moment, I was struck with a feeling that I couldn't ignore. I know it was impulsive and foolish as a leader to let that get in my way of completing my assignment, but I had to stop the attack. I couldn't live with myself if I had let something happen to you. I felt like I already knew you, that I was responsible for your well-being. I couldn't bear the thought of losing you before even getting to know you." An illustrious side of Aleron was shining through as he reverently spoke of his attempt at protecting me.

Aleron's words made me feel light as air. The initial feeling of awkwardness faded as quickly as it came and a sense of unbelief took its place. A silent force seemed to confess my feelings that my shield had been hiding. Overpowered by emotions, I could finally explain what I felt. I felt a sincere longing for him, a need to be with him.

Not thinking about repercussions, I embraced my feelings. I felt accepted. I felt a mutual understanding. I felt what I imagined love would be. The feeling – it had been there each time I was with Aleron; I just couldn't discern it before. Now it dominated my every fiber and words started to pour out of the deepest places of my heart.

"Aleron, I have tried to hide the feelings I have toward you. I thought it was infatuation from the idea of you, from what I had heard about you. Or that it was an artificial side effect of your charm that I thought would fade with time . . ."

Aleron gave me an eyebrow raise, obviously adoring every second of my emotional confession. "You think I'm charming?" he mocked, settling in even closer to me.

I rolled my eyes, ignoring him. "Don't make me redact that statement," I threatened.

Aleron held his hands up in surrender, leaning back on his arm. "I'm listening," he beamed. Once I was certain he wouldn't interrupt again, I continued.

"I recognize that there is something different between us. It is a completely new feeling. A feeling that I am afraid to feel." My words came at a steady pace but with an earnest tone.

I saw him smile out of the corner of my eye, too afraid to look at him directly. I felt a warm sensation meet my right cheek. I was shocked to realize it was Aleron's tender lips on my burning skin. The fiery sensation moved up my cheek bone, resting on my ear.

"Do you trust me?" he whispered, as his nose nuzzled into my neck as he waited for my reply. He made me nervous with his sudden closeness, my thoughts becoming less clear every second. I tried to hide the effect he had on me, trying to conquer the nerves he had successfully set into place.

"Yes," I said, frozen in place, unable to move.

Aleron brushed his lips along my jawline, leaving me dizzy. His forehead was pressed against mine, our noses touching, his scent overpowering my senses. Aleron's lips hovered in front of mine, almost touching as he spoke.

"Then don't be afraid of this. Don't be afraid of us." Each word he spoke left my skin warm with his breath.

The tension in the air was gone, almost as if it never was there in the first place. It was replaced with complete serenity. Aleron grasped my hand tighter, silent words flowing through his fingertips as I tried to stay calm by his distracting closeness.

I wasn't confused anymore; I was happy. It all came so

quickly but I was too overjoyed to deny it. My mind was trying to gather all that he had said and keep it forever, not wanting to let any of it go.

As happy as I felt, there was something nagging at me. Something still didn't feel right. The moon and stars were signaling that night was officially upon us and my time to discover answers to my uncertainties was running out.

"Anything else you'd like to tell me?" I asked.

Aleron laughed. "Amelia, darling, I think you have gotten more out of my heart tonight than you asked for." He gave me one of his friendly winks.

"About the attack?" I clarified. His cheeks didn't change color like mine do when I'm embarrassed. Instead, his grin became even larger. When the moment didn't happen as hoped, he sighed and turned his gaze to me.

"Why are you so concerned about the attack?" he questioned. *Great job, Allene, you pushed it too far.*

"It's where I lost my memory. It sounds silly but I guess I thought if I talked about it more, maybe my memories would return," I suggested, trying to come up with a convincing reason for my curiosity.

Aleron studied my face, believing my story as his eyes were full of sympathy.

"I apologize, I didn't mean to hesitate at your question. I know you are looking for answers. It's just a difficult conversation for me to have," he said honestly.

"I don't mean to press you for more or make you uncomfortable," I said, feeling awful that he seemed so conflicted by the topic.

"It's not your fault. The attack, it's been hard to process.

Although I led it and wanted it to be just a warning, the chief commander from Lokali presented an additional idea. I wasn't supportive of it. I wouldn't have gone along with it, but we needed to make compromises between all of us to stay united as a whole, to preserve the alliance." He started to frown which made me frown as well, the mood rubbing off.

"What did you do?" my voice croaked. I didn't mean for it to crack under the pressure but his tone had sounded concerned.

"We stole the princess." His hand separated from mine as he put an anxious hand on his forehead.

I slightly gasped, a new shock setting in. At first I thought he meant me, I thought he knew who I was. But then I remembered Risa. I tried to calm down and get all the information I could, keeping a straight face.

"Where is she now?" I inquired.

"She is in our prison. We were hoping to have her tell us why Valtera did what they did, but she hasn't confessed anything. She is stubborn, she won't say a word to us."

"Is she alive?" I asked, frightened. "You're not going to hurt her are you?" I begged. Aleron shook his head quickly, a chuckle escaping his lips.

"Lia, who do you think I am? Don't you remember, I didn't want any of this? Another leader had suggested if we found the reason behind the acts of war that we could better understand how to stop them from attacking us again. I am not a cruel man, Amelia, but she will stay here until she confesses something. I gave my word."

"Why didn't you try and kidnap the king or queen, if they

have all the answers you need?" My mind was racing faster than I could keep up with.

"They never go to the Gala Festival, that is where the attack took place. We knew we couldn't get to them. Instead, one of the troops set up a coup, telling the princess to meet him at our camp." Aleron said the words with distaste, like he could hardly believe it for himself.

My mouth would have hung open wide but I forced it shut. I was angry. Inside, I fought the urge to hit something. Aleron in fact, but it wasn't his fault . . . entirely. He was only doing what he *had* to do. At least he didn't hurt her. I had to get to the dungeon and set her free.

I got up and Aleron rose to his feet at the same time. He noticed my disgruntledness immediately.

"This is why I didn't want to tell you. All that happened, it isn't a representation of who I am," Aleron said in a worried tone.

I shook my head. "Aleron, I don't think of you any differently. You did what you had to for Praseria. I can't fault you for that." I reached out for his arm, squeezing it tightly. I needed to make up a lie.

"You're leaving," he stated the obvious, still concerned the sudden shift of the evening was his fault.

"Ezra has no one with him right now and I feel awful leaving him alone. I hope you don't mind if I depart early to attend to him. After all he's done for me, I feel it's the least I could do," I said the words quickly, Aleron nodding at the end.

"You promise that's the reason?" he questioned. I wrapped my arm around Aleron's neck, his arms effortlessly finding themselves around my waist as he took the invitation to pull me in tightly. Our foreheads pressed together once again. I gained the confidence to give Aleron a taste of the torment he had been causing me. I placed my lips just centimeters away from his, my heart pounding.

"Do you trust me?" I asked, stifling back a laugh. Aleron smiled, his dimple on display.

"Of course," he replied. I pulled away, my arm falling from his neck to his shoulder.

"Then believe me when I say that's the reason," I replied with as much conviction as I could. Aleron nodded, letting out a deep sigh.

"Aleron, thank you for tonight. For inviting me to the ball, for answering all my questions, I couldn't have asked for more," I assured him, the expectation of tonight being far exceeded.

"Thank you for agreeing to come. I will arrange for a time to see you later in the week," he promised, his blue eyes locked on mine with every word.

"I look forward to it."

"Can I escort you back to Ezra's quarters?" he offered.

"I can manage." My eyes fell to meet his lips that had turned up into a smile. He grasped my hand, bent down, twisted to reach the back of my wrist and kissed it lightly. He leaned in close to my ear again. His hand fell on the nap of my back.

"Until then, Lia," he whispered. Aleron dropped his hand to his side and left without another word.

My heart was throbbing from his nearness and my mind was soaring, but I had to regain focus. I headed in the direction of Ezra's room, in case Aleron turned back to see me. I waited till Aleron was inside the castle, his body becoming a shadow in the distance as he walked through the doors.

That was my cue. I started running as fast as I could, kicking off my heels to prevent me from tripping down the hill as I made my way to the base of the castle. I was only focused on one thing. I had to free Risa.

CHAPTER 12

*E*zra hadn't spoken of or shown me the dungeons. I had to find them on my own. Prisons were usually underneath the castle to prevent rescue and maintain secrecy. If this castle had the same general placement, I would be able to find it without much trouble.

I sneaked back inside the castle through the door Ezra used to get to the stables. I was able to avoid the party that was taking place on the opposite end of the castle. Here, away from the party, it was eerily quiet. I ran through the halls toward the bottom of the castle, lifting my dress to avoid tripping on my feet, trying to hold both my dress and heels with a single hand proving to be quite the challenge. I knew I must've been getting closer, as the surroundings were beginning to change. The walls became stone and soon there wasn't any more carpet. I kept an eye out for guards in case I was caught, but to my surprise, the lower corridors were not well watched. Maybe it was because of the ball and their duties were elsewhere for the night. Whatever the reason, I still was on edge. I tried inventing reasonable excuses to be here, should anyone see me.

I could say I was coming down to see if the prince was here, or I was trying to find my way back to my room. I got lost or my memory had been hazy from my concussion and I was confused. The excuses went on and on, but I hoped I wouldn't have to use them.

I finally approached a dead end; I was facing a heavy metal door. This had to be where the prisoners were held. No guard stood by the door and I instantly grew suspicious. I became discouraged with the idea that a guard may be placed on the other side of the door. I didn't have time to fear what may be ahead because my sweet sister was more important. *She is probably so frightened. I need to find her.*

I slowly came to the door and grasped the large handle. I pulled back with effort but the door wouldn't budge. It was locked. *Who needs a guard if you need a key?* I searched around to see if there were any keys hidden in the stone moldings or maybe in any decor but found nothing.

After minutes of meaningless searching, I knew it was time to give up on the idea that I would be entering through this door. I sat down, allowing myself time to think and giving my legs a well needed break after my attempt at running.

I tried to think of other ways to get into the prison. Maybe there were two entrances? What if this was the end of the dungeon and the guards were guarding it from the *other* side? That meant there *had* to be another entrance.

I thought of another place I would put an opening that

would be tucked away somewhere. If there wasn't one inside, then it had to be outside. What had I seen from my ventures with Ezra that could be an entrance? After rummaging through many ideas, I finally recalled a useful memory. I remember briefly passing by a turret as we went to the stables. That was most likely the most promising place to try.

I jerked out of my sitting position and ran to my last hope. I urgently back tracked my way to the gazebo to find that the night sky had fully taken over. Retracing my steps and walks that I had taken with Ezra, I made my way to the east side of the castle. It didn't take me long to find myself at the side of the turret.

The turret had no windows from the front or the back, and no doors that could be seen. I heard a quiet whistle and my heart skipped a beat, scared to turn around. I crouched in the grass as low as I could without making a noise, hoping the shine of my dress wouldn't be noticeable in the dark. My hands met the dampened grass and my eyes saw someone working outside in the moonlight.

A young woman was fetching some water from a pump. She had many buckets, probably for the banquet inside. She quietly whistled to herself, murmuring words I couldn't hear. I didn't find any of it peculiar, just a maid doing her work. Then she did something unexpected.

I thought she would walk around to the front and give the bucket to the other servants that should be located in the kitchen, but she didn't. Instead she looked around to see if anyone was there. I sank deeper into the grass, trying to hide every piece of me, halting my breathing.

She briefly scoped out her surroundings and when satisfied that she was alone, she walked to the other side of the turret. I noticed her push on a stone in the turret. The turret made a soft creaking sound as I watched it move, or at least a part of it anyway. A slab had slid over, just enough to let her in to then quickly seal shut.

I had never seen such a thing before, a device powered by some sort of mechanism. Uncertain of how to go forward, I decided to wait a little longer to see if anyone else would approach or leave. I watched for what seemed to only be a few minutes when another person came out; this time a boy was grabbing a bucket and pumping the water handle. There must've been many servants, because for the next half hour, people were flocking to retrieve water.

I noticed a consistent sight with each one: they were all around the same size and height and they all did the same thing. I watched over and over again until only one bucket was left. But no one came out.

I waited for some time, waiting for someone to return to get the bucket, but no one came. It was very dark now, the stars in the sky, the time when everyone should be going home for the night.

Although I wasn't familiar with the new contraption, after watching it be used multiple times, I was confident I could open the door. It looked fairly simple and I was about the same size as the girl. Aside from my massive dress. I wish I would have gone back to change. There was a reason people didn't spy in outrageous ball gowns, it made being sneaky very difficult. *There wasn't time to change, I don't know how long I have until Ezra or a maid may notice my absence.*

I very slowly got up and cautiously went to the other side

of the turret, crinkling my dress as I pulled all the fabric tightly to one side to reduce the volume of the skirt to help me fit through the door. I took in a small silent breath and felt myself wincing at the sound of an owl.

I stood in front of the door for only a minute, realizing the danger of being caught outside was just as risky as being caught inside. *Courage Allene, you are doing this for your sister.*

I took a deep breath as my fingers fumbled to feel a difference in the stones. One caught my attention as it jutted out from the rest and I pressed on it, hoping it was the right one. Nothing happened at first, but then the door silently opened into a dark corridor.

I felt fear take over me, unsettling my stomach as I was ready to start lying to whatever stranger might confront me. Holding my breath, waiting for the worst, I realized no one was there. All that I could see was holding cells. I stepped over the grass and onto the hard stone floor, no sound or sign of people anywhere.

I jumped when the door rushed itself closed behind me. Panic took over as I realized that I was trapped. I hadn't thought through how to get out. *Well done, Allene.* I was afraid to move. What if there were other things I hadn't seen going forward? I wouldn't be prepared to handle them, especially with no escape.

I regained my composure and decided to take it one moment at a time. I shook out my arm, trying to symbolically rid myself of any fear. *I can do this.*

The prison wasn't very big; in fact it was only one row of barred metal cells. The stone floor and walls were damp and stunk of mold. I laid my heels by the door and forced myself to walk one step forward, my feet numb from being bare on the wet grass outside, making me unaware of the frigid stones now underneath me.

I let out a breath when I realized my footsteps were practically silent. I couldn't see any guards; I couldn't see any lights, so I pressed on. No people were in any of the cells that I had passed. I had made it about half way down the row when I heard something.

I jittered back from the sound, preparing to meet a guard, but it turned out to be someone's distressed sobs. The crying was very close by, booming next to me. I would only have to walk a couple feet to be right up close to it and have it bellowing in my ear.

I listened to the crying more carefully. I had heard it before. I had heard it almost two months ago, the same cry, at my father's funeral.

I tiptoed a couple feet and stood in front of the cell, my heart racing. The wailing stopped and a sniffle came as the individual noticed she was being watched.

"Please, let me go," she whispered. I could see her skin was glossy from crying. Tears fell and curved around her smooth chin, hitting the bare ground. My mouth hung open as I came down to my knees, letting my dress sweep across the firm frozen floor, lifting the hairs on my back.

"Risa, are you all right?" My astonished voice came out in a high, hushed tone. I wanted to shout with joy to see that she was alive but I had to be discreet.

Risa didn't speak but my eyes soon adjusted to the darkness. Risa had been sitting in the corner of her cell, hugging her arms tightly to her chest. She was wearing her favorite baby blue dress, a fitting choice for her outing at the Gala festival. The light blue was now the color of muddy water and I didn"t think any amount of washing could fix the stains. Her normally well kept hair was tangled and knotted in a messy braid. She didn't have any noticeable injuries or wounds, thankfully. The only damper was her appearance, the twinkle normally held in her eyes was gone and the usual glow of her skin was hidden under excess grime and dirt. *Poor, Risa, you don't deserve any of this.*

Risa squinted her eyes, staring in disbelief. She was confused and shocked to see me – just as I was confused and shocked to see her.

"Allene? Is that really you?" Risa rose from the corner, making her way over to me to get a better point of view. I was pleased when a smile emerged in place of her sorrow.

"Oh, goodness Allene, it is you! What are you doing here?" she asked, completely baffled at the sight of me.

"I came to help you," I confirmed.

She clapped her hands together, relief flooding her expression. Risa didn't even question the oddity of me being her rescuer, a job that would more likely be headed by Ajax. Risa was so consumed with having company that she couldn't stop talking, acting like she hadn't talked to anyone in months, letting it all out as fast as she could manage.

"I thought no one would be coming for me, I thought you were dead! Allene, they tricked me. They sent a note . . . remember that note I received the day before the Gala? At first I thought it was just a disgusting joke! I was such a fool! I played right into their hands!" Risa was beginning to hyperventilate, her breathing becoming short.

"Risa, calm down, you need to breathe," I encouraged her, trying to give her comfort.

"Oh Allene, it was horrible. They threw me into a cart, forced me to watch as they attacked our people, threatened me, demanded I tell them everything I knew but I didn't know what they meant! They became furious with me and put me in this dreadful place until I would confess why we destroyed their land. I *don't* know why we would destroy their land or destroy anything for that matter! We have never set foot in their puny kingdom!" she continued, fuming and distressed. Her hands now held the bars, her face right in front of mine.

I put a finger up to my lips. "Shh, Risa, you must be quiet! They don't know I'm here and we need to keep that way." Risa still had tears in her eyes, her breathing now starting to become more controlled. She nodded as she went into complete silence at my reminder.

"Risa, I don't know what to say. I am shocked that this has even happened. I am *so* sorry. Are you all right? They didn't hurt you did they?" I questioned, grabbing the bars to touch her hands. They were freezing and I noticed dirt underneath her well-kept fingernails.

"I'm all right, truly. I can't believe you came for me, I wasn't expecting to see you. I've been here so long, I was starting to lose hope that anyone was coming for me," she said with sorrow. My guilt took over, realizing the suffering she had been through.

"I would've been here sooner but I didn't know you were here," I apologized.

"It's fine, you're here now. I am just relieved that I can finally leave," she whispered with assurance.

"Did you see the keys to your cell?" I asked.

"A guard had them. You might be able to pick the lock," she offered.

"How?" I wondered. I had never picked a lock before. Once again, I hadn't thought through another essential part to all of this.

"I don't –" then she stopped.

We both turned to hear a loud creak. I wasn't surprised that another moment was going wrong in my brilliant plan. The door was beginning to slide open.

CHAPTER 13

The moon was the only light that could be seen, forming a man's shadow in the dark prison. He stepped through the door and it quickly sealed behind him, standing motionless at the sound.

Risa stepped back from the bars and pretended to sleep. I had nowhere to go, nothing to hide behind. The nearest corner was too far out of reach. It was certain he would catch me if I tried to make my way to it. I stopped breathing and hoped that the man couldn't see me amidst the darkness, hoping stillness would be my advantage.

The man proceeded to make his way toward us. I still tried hard to be invisible but it didn't work. It failed with shame, my heart pounding each time I felt his footsteps vibrate the floor. My heart was just as loud as my breathing, maybe even worse.

"Allene!" the harsh voice spat.

I cringed, ready to face the man. Then something dawned

on me. He said Allene, he knew my identity. *This is not going to end well.* I was regretting not running when I had the chance, but what could be done about it now? I sighed and looked up to see my fate.

I was taller than him and his hair was not the color of mine. I looked over the peculiar boy. Fury was in his eyes, concern mixed with betrayal.

"Damien?" I whispered in disbelief. I blinked twice just to make sure that I was seeing correctly.

Risa came to her knees, heart beating as loud as mine.

"Damien? What are you doing here? Did you come with Allene?" Risa asked.

Damien slowly made his way to us, stopping about two feet away from me. He was wearing an expression I wasn't familiar with. Exhaustion maybe? Whatever it was, I couldn't contain my excitement to see him alive and well. I embraced Damien, holding back tears.

"Damien, you frightened us! I can't begin to explain how relieved I am to see you." I whispered to him quietly and waited for his response. No words were reciprocated. Slightly confused, I pulled away. Damien's face was stone cold and his focus was set on me. I felt the hairs on my arms stand up. For the first time ever, I feared Damien.

"Why didn't you just say it was Damien, Allene?" Risa interrupted.

My voice was gone and only mumbles came out. I couldn't answer her question. I was just as perplexed at the situation before us. It was very clear Damien was not happy to see me.

"I. . .well because. . . " I tried to find the words. Damien rolled his eyes, standing still. His hands were clenched in hard fists, his body looking bulkier than ever before, as if he was trying to intimidate me.

"Don't trust her, Risa," he spoke harshly, glaring at me persistently as he spoke. My heart sank.

"Damien, of course I trust her! She's my sister and your best friend. Why would you speak this way?" Risa insisted. Damien scoffed at me in disgust. *My best friend.* I cringed.

I was selfish. I never wanted him to see me this way. I wanted to be there for him. I should've handled things differently. As soon as I woke up I should have fled to Valteria or made more of an effort to make contact with them. They were what was important and I let my twisted idea of freedom get in the way of that. I wanted him to be able to understand, to explain myself, but I was speechless. To add to it all, I wasn't entirely sure what he was implying. Was he wanting me to admit to sneaking out to the Gala? Or admit that I overheard the conversation my mother and Risa had?

"Allene, would you explain to Risa what you have been doing? Or do you prefer to go by Amelia?" Damien had officially pinned me into a corner and subtly hinted that he knew something more.

"Amelia?" Risa asked, confused. My hands were sweating, my mouth felt like cotton. What was I going to say?

"Allene, what on earth is going on!" Risa was almost to the point of raising her soft voice and I panicked.

"Damien gave me that name. He snuck me out to the Gala festival," I pointed out, glaring at him pointedly. But Damien was already impatient as it was and dancing around the problem wasn't going to work.

"I am in shock that you have the audacity to blame any of

this on me. Are you going to continue to play innocent or should I tell her what I saw?" he persisted.

"There's nothing to tell. She knows about the Gala festival," I said, praying the conversation would end.

"This has nothing to do with the Gala festival. It is what you have been doing since then. I saw you and the prince up on the hill, smiling and laughing. What was that about?" Damien bellowed unsatisfied, stepping in a little bit closer to ensure I heard him.

I was infuriated. He spied on me. For how long? What if I had been in trouble and he just sat there watching? What if I had been negotiating?

I felt guilty. None of these "what ifs" had happened. He had every reason to be mad at me. I had made a mistake but I was not humble enough to admit it just yet.

"You spied on me?" I blurted out.

He shook his head back and forth, looking disgusted. "Please, I am not that malicious. I saw you from afar, not up close. I came to save Risa, like you *seem* to be claiming. Allene, I thought you were dead! We all thought you were dead! You disappeared! Do you have the slightest idea of how worried we have all been? Imagine my surprise to find you alive and well, flirting with the prince of Praseria! Can you understand why I'm confused as to whose side you're on?" I could hear the pain in his voice as he spoke. I could feel my heart sinking into my stomach. I could have sent a letter. I could have let him know I was okay. I could have let him know what was going on and I know he would've been there to help. I abandoned him.

Flashbacks of my father passing away instantly filled my

emotions, the pain I'd felt. I put him through those same dreadful feelings. I wouldn't wish that feeling on my worst enemy and I put my best friend through it. I felt tears break through.

"I am on your side, I always have been, I swear it," I promised, reaching for Damien's hand. He quickly moved it away, the action leaving a numb feeling in my empty hand.

"Allene, I am just as confused as Damien. Will you please explain what's going on?" Risa asked again.

I sighed and looked at each of their faces. Damien had seen what happened. I had to be truthful, but now for the first time I felt deep regret. The feeling made my insides ache and my head hurt, my mouth numb. I finally spoke, the words bumping into one another as I tried to hold back my cries.

"I snuck out to the Gala festival and during the attack by the Praserians I was injured. The prince saw me and thought I was Praserian. He brought me here to help me. He stopped the attack, to *protect* me. It was a misunderstanding that saved my life and probably many of our own people's lives as well," I defended Aleron, trying to get them to understand. They both stared at me, waiting to hear more before they spoke again. I sighed, hoping they would put an end to my rambling. It was obvious they wouldn't budge, Damien's glare pushing me to continue on.

"I pretended to be Praserian to blend in. I had no idea you were here or else I would have come sooner. I was waiting to fully heal before returning to Valteria," I paused, hoping they would see the reasoning behind it all. Damien's lip pursed, a frown forming.

"That doesn't explain you and the prince." He said each word slowly, the irritation in his voice being made evident.

"Aleron asked me to the ball and I couldn't say no. He saved my life. Despite who he is, he has been kind to me. I promise that is all that happened, nothing more than that. I had every intention to come back home very soon." I admitted everything, feeling so raw to show my flaws to the people I love the most.

Risa's face was blank, no emotion at all, until I saw a hint of shock. Damien kept his hard face, not surprised at the news. Risa recovered quickly, blurting out her feelings.

"Wait, you've been here this entire time? You went to the ball with that . . . ghastly tyrant!" Risa exclaimed.

"It's not like that! He saved me, Risa. You don't understand the entire situation." I tried to explain to her the best I could without being consumed by my hurt.

Her eyes shut and her body slightly shook. Her first words were a deadly whisper.

"How dare you tell me that I don't understand. I understand perfectly. This Aleron you keep talking about, he captured me for nothing! He's a lying monster, Allene, saying we burned his lands when we didn't! Using that as an excuse to harm our innocent people! Using that excuse to kidnap me! *That* is who saved your life. That is who you've been prancing around with. Do you not see how serious that is?" She said each word with pure fury but never raised her voice, which almost made it hurt worse.

"He was telling the truth. I didn't believe it at first either, Risa, but I saw the burned fields with my own eyes. It wasn't his idea to capture you either. You're wrong, about all of it." I frowned, worried I wouldn't be able to convince her.

Risa's lips creased together, biting her lip, no emotion in her response.

"I can't trust you," she said in disbelief. I shook my head, reaching for her hand again through the bars.

"Don't say that. You know that's not true," I spoke with pleading in my voice, begging her to take back what she said.

Risa pulled her hand away, tears in her eyes. "You're on their side now. I am sitting on the other side of these bars, unable to leave, and you are vouching for their character and actions. If you were on our side, that wouldn't happen," she argued, obviously hurt as she said the words out loud.

I paused; I took a deep breath and exhaled. I didn't know what to say. I didn't want to choose a side, I wanted to be happy. And this wasn't making me happy; it was tearing me into two, leaving me to fight for myself, which so far, wasn't working in my favor.

"It is a misunderstanding on all accounts. There isn't a right or wrong," I whispered, hoping she could soften her heart enough to understand. If anyone would, it would be Risa.

"That's a foolish statement, Allene. You can't be on both sides!" Damien shouted. My eyes squinted in the blackness, overtaking all color.

"Why can't I be on both sides Damien?" I yelled back.

"You have a responsibility to your kingdom, to fight for Valteria and stand by it! Your people have been worried about you and yet you're here, betraying every single one of them. What kind of princess does that?" He threw his hands in the air, clenching them into fists, fuming. "Everyone has been searching for you. Hassan blames himself for something that didn't even happen! He has been suffering over the fact that he couldn't protect you, that it was his fault! How can you justify any of this? How can you think that you can be on both sides?" Damien asked, going from shouting to a faint sough.

It was silent for a moment. I couldn't hold back anymore, I broke down into tears. No one reached out to comfort me or tell me it would be okay. I was left to my own devices of absorbing everything that Damien had just said. I was beyond foolish to think my actions wouldn't affect those at home. Poor Hassan. I had hurt everyone I loved in order to spare myself. I felt completely lost.

Risa broke the silence quietly, saving me from my thoughts.

"Allene, I get it. You're trying to be like Father, to bring peace, but getting in the middle of it isn't the way to do it. Father had to choose a side in the end and now it's your turn. It's not too late to do what's right." Risa's words of grace made my head spin.

I thought about what she said. She opened my eyes to a new point of view. I hadn't realized that I was reliving my father's life. He didn't get to finish it. He could've brought peace between Valteria and Praseria, he almost had. Now I felt like it was my duty to finish his goal and bring peace between our kingdoms.

"Risa, I won't choose a side," I spoke bravely, but my insides held no courage.

She sighed with dissatisfaction. "Then I suppose we will

choose for you. Damien is here now, you can go," Risa said sadly, dismissing me entirely.

Damien shoved me out of the way like I was nothing. He shuffled through his pocket, searching for something. He displayed a key in his hand and unlocked the door with little effort. He had obviously thought through his plan.

He politely offered his hand to Risa as she stepped out of the cell frowning; the first time I had ever seen her dissatisfied toward me, and it hurt beyond words.

"We'll go and leave you to your new life here in Praseria," Damien blurted the words like daggers to my sides. "We need to hurry Risa, the others are waiting." They walked over to the door together, hand in hand as Damien knocked twice and stomped on the ground. I wanted to run to Risa, to hold her back until she could see my point of view, but I was frozen. I was completely lost on how to handle the situation. Everything I said up to this point was just making it worse and I was terrified to continue blundering.

The door slowly opened. Damien was the first to step out, not looking back. Risa turned and spoke words that cut through me, the wounds growing and the pain not diminishing.

"Goodbye, Allene." And that was the last I heard in that silent room, besides my knees falling to the floor, and soon enough, my weeping.

———

· · ·

I sprinted to the castle. My tears were dry. I didn't want to waste moments with sorrow. I didn't want to think about the bad things. I was only thinking of what would come next.

These were the times where I would run to my father, imploring for help, taking his advice, and having the problem resolved sooner than I could've done on my own.

I stopped running when I came to a tree. I slithered to the ground and forced myself to stop thinking. I lay back on the grass, not caring about my dress, not caring who saw me, but looked at the dark gloomy sky and took in the frozen air that burned my lungs.

I heard the trees sway and crickets sing in harmony. I was mesmerized at the glittering stars above, almost telling me to relax. I felt the cold grass press against my sore back. I smelled green earth and felt its life seep through into my skin as it began to itch. I looked at the dark placid sky and its eerie beauty.

I wanted to form myself a wall that no one could pass. I wanted to be left alone. I wanted to become the sky. I wanted to be anything else, as long as I wasn't faced with this situation.

I let my body sink into the ground and felt no more tension in my bones. I needed to clear my mind. Let the air sweep away everything I had ever thought of and start on a blank slate. I enjoyed all these things for many moments, trying not to think of anything. It didn't last long.

I sat up and brought my gaze away from the night sky and the gleaming moon. I had quickly faced reality. What was I to do? With my family not on my side, who was? I needed someone's help, someone's advice, but that someone would have to be trustworthy. I had only been at the castle for a short time and I didn't know anyone well enough to trust them. There had to be *someone*.

After many minutes I relinquished. I couldn't think of anyone. My next thought was to run. Run away and go home. I could catch up with Damien and Risa, apologize for everything, and ignore how displeased they were with me. But I stopped. I remembered why I was doing all of this – why I was staying in Praseria. I went through every reason in my mind, making a list in my head.

First, I wanted to finish what my father had begun. I knew the attacks seemed true. Maybe Valteria was the enemy. Everything I had ever known about Praseria seemed wrong now. If there was a chance I could fix this, I had to take it. Second, Praseria was beginning to feel like home. Everyone accepted me here, more than I ever had been in Valteria. And Aleron . . . he was the hardest part to accept. After tonight, I couldn't deny it. I had finally come to see that I was falling in love with him, and I didn't want to leave him.

Risa was right. I had a choice to make, but I couldn't make it myself. I thought through the whole thing over and over again. I finally got up, dewy droplets from the cold air falling onto my face and brushing my cheekbones as I ran to the castle. I had made sure no one was in sight to see me make my way through a side door.

I galloped up the staircases and followed them to my room. I stopped at Ezra's door, realizing what I needed to do. I urgently grasped the door handle and let myself in.

Ezra was sitting on a chair, worry covering his brow as he put down a book he had been reading. I could tell he was perplexed considering the time of night but I didn't care. I choked and gasped for air, tears starting to come. I stretched out my hand for the door frame, holding up my weight.

I looked at the ground, trying to stop crying. *Allene, get a hold of yourself. Would Father be crying in this situation?*

I shook my head around in confusion.

"Ezra I–" I whispered the words but then he put up a hand, stopping me in my tracks.

"I was anticipating this time would come."

I felt another onset of fear at his words, not understanding what he was implying. I stopped in wonder. Before I could process what he had said and make any sense out of it, he was speaking again.

"My son, Faris, came to me twenty five years ago, looking much like you do now."

My tears didn't leak any longer. My mouth clenched, my eyes enlarged and my heart fluttered with great speed.

Ezra patted the seat next to him.

"I managed to help him when he needed me. Let's see if I can help you too, granddaughter."

CHAPTER 14

I was frozen in the doorway. "I beg your pardon?" I was bewildered.

"A grandfather never forgets the face of his grandchildren, no matter how long it's been. The resemblance between you and your father, however, is very helpful." Ezra slightly chuckled.

"You're my . . . grandfather?" I was still lost. This was impossible.

He nodded. "I am your grandfather," he said, not seeming fazed by the confession.

At first I thought he was lying. He couldn't be trusted; it was a trap, trying to prove my identity. I had no proof that what he was saying was true. My mind had been so conflicted the last few hours of who I could and couldn't trust that I was convinced I couldn't discern between it anymore. But then I looked into his eyes.

They were my father's eyes. They were my eyes. His face

mirrored my fathers. How had it taken me so long to see it? *That's why I have such a unique bond with Ezra.* I felt relief, understanding that I had someone here that I could talk to. I smiled.

"I believe you," I admitted, trying to overcome the tinge of doubt that was trying to overshadow this new realization.

He came over and cupped his hand around my face. I couldn't resist the urge, it felt like my father was cradling me; I stretched my arms out, embraced him and wept. I wanted to release all my emotional weight and Ezra took it with grace.

He rubbed my back, whispering comforting words every now and again. I didn't let go and neither did he. We didn't say a word. The only sound was my sobs.

He gave me one tight squeeze and let go. He was trying to hold a straight face, but there was joy in his eyes.

"How long have you known?" I asked, wondering if something happened that gave me away.

"I knew the moment I saw them bring you into the castle. I made sure I would be the one taking care of you," Ezra said kindly.

"But why now? Why didn't you tell me this from the start?" I grew somewhat irked at the thought. I could've talked to him about everything weeks ago and not felt so alone in my thoughts.

"I wasn't sure you would believe me. I didn't want to appear like I was trying to build false trust or scare you away. That is why I was so harsh to you in the beginning, I apologize," he said sincerely. It was all making sense. Ezra continued to explain, not giving me time to process. The corner of his eyes wrinkled as he smiled.

"There is so much I want to know. About Faris, about you. I was terrified of ruining my chance unless you came to me first, so I did my best to play the part of Ezra the servant." I was trying to stay calm. So much had already happened tonight. Finding out that Ezra was my grandfather was not something I expected to add to my list of surprises. However, I was grateful that this surprise was good news.

"I can understand playing a part. It's not like I've been honest with you about who I am either." I laughed, trying to make the conversation a bit more light hearted.

"But now there is no need for secrets between us," he proclaimed, obviously relieved.

"No more secrets. That sounds really nice right now," I admitted.

"Well, now that you know the truth, I feel we should address what you came here for in the first place. Why did you come to see me, Allene?" Ezra asked, concern returning to his voice.

I was overjoyed when I heard him say my real name. Realizing that someone in the castle knew who I was brought more comfort than I could have imagined.

I had no recollection of my grandfather. We hadn't visited him since the truce between our two kingdoms only lasted a short time. I was around the age of five when that occurred. I knew that my grandfather had been dethroned because my father left his people and had no siblings to take his place. I had no idea that Ezra would still be here in the castle, or alive for that matter. I yearned to know more about my father and what had become of him.

"Ezra, I fear I am following in my father's footsteps," I said truthfully.

"Why do you fear that?" he politely asked, genuinely wanting to understand what was going on. I focused on my hands, clenching them together as I nervously told Ezra the events that had just unfolded.

"During the ball, I discovered Risa was being imprisoned. I searched for her and when I found her she thought I had come from Valteria."

Ezra interrupted, worry coming over his face. "Allene, I had no idea they were keeping Risa. I would've taken immediate action if I had known," he quickly said.

"I believe you," I assured him, continuing my story without skipping a breath. "Damien, my friend, saw me with Aleron and persuaded Risa to believe I was a traitor. I told the truth, knowing I would be condemned either way. They've left, but they demand that I choose a side, which I cannot do. Now I am despised and detached, my whole kingdom will loathe me for not returning in their company. Even my sister, the one person I never imagined could be angry with me, was obviously hurt by my choice," I restated the entire story in summary, the emotions apacely returning.

Ezra paused for a moment, taking the time to think about his reply. "I am glad to hear Risa is safe. I want to propose a question, but I do not want you to take it the wrong way." He appeared cautious, waiting for an invitation to continue.

"What's your question?" I asked. Ezra seemed confused, trying to understand the surreal scenario I had presented.

"If it was that difficult for you to stay here when you had the opportunity to leave, why stay?"

I hesitated to answer. I didn't want him having knowledge of the real reason, I felt embarrassed, but I couldn't lie. I learned my lesson when it comes to lying to those I love.

"I have feelings for a Praserian," I whispered quietly, hoping he wouldn't hear.

"Aleron, I assume?"

I stopped to retort, but proceeded with regret. "Yes, Aleron," I sighed. Ezra and I were quiet for a moment, uncertain what to say.

"Risa and Damien don't hold the same opinion of him that I do," I explained, Risa's words echoing in my head, saying he was a monster.

"I have met a lot of royals in my lifetime. I can say with confidence he is a good man, Allene, with a good heart," Ezra assured me. I nodded in agreement.

"I wish they believed me. I don't know what I should do. I have never felt this conflicted before." I placed my head in my hands, the anxiety of the situation causing my head to hurt.

"I will advise you the same way I advised your father. Follow your heart."

"My father abdicated his throne, he was your only heir. What prompted you to give him such advice? His decision put an end to the Amena dynasty," I pointed out.

Ezra shrugged and made his way to sit down on a chair in the corner of the room, taking a moment to pause as he thought about my question. "I suppose I've always been a fond supporter of being led by the heart."

"That is not common advice from the royalty I've been acquainted with," I took a seat next to him on the floor and let my weight sink into the firm floral rug beneath me.

"Then it seems even more fitting that I'm not royalty anymore," Ezra flashed a small grin and let out a light laugh from his comment. I couldn't help but wonder if he regretted supporting my father considering all that he lost as a result of my fathers decision.

"You could have forced my father to stay."

"Yes, and I would have retained our throne but I would have lost the respect of my son. That was far more important to me than being royalty."

"I can't imagine how difficult all of that must have been, even when you felt you were doing the right thing by self-lessly letting my father determine his own destiny – it still would have been hard."

"It was. But supporting family is the greatest act of love we can show to one another. Others don't feel what you feel and they will look up to you one day for *your* hard choice," he encouraged me, trying to give me support.

"I wish Risa and Damien could see things the way you do."

"In time, they will," he assured me.

"Ezra, you didn't see their faces. I don't think they will ever understand my decision," I admitted my fear, Risa and Damien's disappointed faces flooding my memory.

"You lack faith, granddaughter. I know it's confusing, complicated and not the easiest way to do things, but it's the right way. They will learn to follow their own heart at some point in their life and I promise you, they will understand eventually. People don't know your reasons for doing certain things. I am sincerely proud of you," Ezra beamed.

"Thank you, Ezra," I whispered, letting his advice replay in my head.

"Thank you for trusting me. Your secret will not be told; I promise this is between you and I." He was clasping my shoulders and used a tender voice. Ezra's words were exactly what I needed in this painful moment. He reminded me so much of my father, it made me not feel so lonely after all.

"I appreciate that more than you can comprehend. You always know what to say, Ezra. You're exactly like my father in that way." I still smiled at the resemblance but the mention of him made me hurt on the inside.

"Speaking of Faris, he must be worried sick about you. Tell me, how has he been?" He was eager to know. I was trying to give a cheerful response, but how could you make a positive response to such a depressing, unexpected circumstance. I was lost on what else to say and I didn't want to lie.

"He's actually somewhere else now." I looked at the ground, hoping it would give me the correct words to speak.

"My Faris abandoned you?" Ezra's voice was astonished. I had to tell him the truth, but I would regret telling him the real reason for my father's absence.

"You misunderstand; he only abandoned us because he had no other choice. He was in pain. He fought to stay but it was out of his control." I stopped. I was pushing back tears, restraining my cries.

"He's gone." I finally got the words out.

"You do not know exactly why he left?" Ezra was still oblivious to my hints. It was obvious he needed to hear the actual words.

I stood up and started to walk away, wanting to keep this painful thing from his heart.

"We should discuss this later. I should go, it's almost dawn and I haven't gotten any rest." I ran to the door but he caught my arm at the frame. He was quicker than I expected. This time his voice was fierce.

"Tell me," he repeated, pleading. I squinted my eyes and looked at Ezra. I rolled my shoulder so his arm would fall off of mine. Once he did, I couldn't help but stand there and try to think of an excuse.

"I'm not sure you want to know," I told him, looking down.

"I need to know. I haven't heard from my son in years. I have no connections to any family. Please, Allene, why did he leave?" He said each word slowly, demanding.

I looked at Ezra with concern. He was getting irritated. I was tired of avoiding the situation.

"He was ill. He was too ill, his body . . . he couldn't take it any longer. He's gone, Ezra," I breathed the words as fierce and painful as fire, my heart aching as I said each one.

Ezra's eyes welled with tears as he tried to remain composed. His face turned slightly red as he held his breath. His brow furrowed, reality sinking in. Ultimately, the pain became too much. The sobs made his body shake as he turned his face away to hide his sorrow. Seeing Ezra react, it made me feel like I was reliving the loss of my father. I choked back my own cries, attempting to remain strong in front of Ezra.

Ezra clearly loved him. It was indescribable, the loss of my father, but I couldn't begin to comprehend the loss of a son. And for the first time that I was here, it wasn't Ezra doing the comforting. I reached out, pulling him in closely and held him as he cried.

~

*M*y choice was made. After many discussions with Ezra, I decided I would stay until I was obliged to leave. I needed time to decide what my next move would be. We were confident I wouldn't be caught for who I really was. Each day without conflict of any kind made me more certain of it.

In fact, each day seemed to get better than the last. When I wasn't agonizing over what I left at home, I was enjoying what I had discovered here. When I wasn't enjoying the company of my new friends, I was completely enveloped in thoughts of Aleron.

I spotted him one day outside my window. He was practicing with a large group of soldiers by the beach, training them as he displayed his flawless combat skills. I watched on and off for hours, wondering if he could feel me staring. My heart would race as he would turn toward my window, the sun catching his hair. I kept hoping he would see me. I would wave but never received any recognition back.

The way Aleron held himself was so robust that I could see how he would be intimidating to an enemy. Yet his demeanor, being so good-natured, made him relatable to anyone he interacted with. I admired him more and more, realizing that I hadn't found any fault in him. At that moment, I knew he would be an altruistic type of trouble. The other trouble was finding a way to tell Aleron the truth about me – which I selfishly wanted to avoid as long as possible.

As I was preparing for the day, a hushed knock came to the door. I laid down my comb that I was using to detangle my thick hair and strode to the door completely at ease, expecting to see Noni or Ezra. When I opened the door, my calm was immediately replaced with nervous exhilaration.

Aleron stood in front of me. His left hand gripped the other tightly, his thumb slightly tapping. His head was level with my own, his knees bent as he tried to be at my height for the sake of looking into my eyes.

My insides jumped with excitement, remembering our last encounter. I couldn't help but smile.

My first normal reaction would be to turn away while blushing, but this time I stared back, trying to stay calm. Without another thought, I spoke.

"This is a surprise." My steady voice was accomplished. Aleron seemed to lose his train of thought and tried to quickly gather it before I could notice.

"I told you I'd come to see you," he reminded me, his blue eyes catching my attention.

"I'm glad to see you're a man of your word," I laughed, giving him a slight smile.

"I was hoping you'd accompany me on a walk; if you have the time." His words tumbled out smoothly, like a serene river.

I hadn't expected to see Aleron again so soon. The ball had only been a few days ago. It was a good feeling, my feelings for him. The pleading voice inside of me was enough to convince me to go with him.

"I'd be delighted. Can you wait just a few moments?" I asked for permission, hoping he couldn't see my knotted hair that I had hid behind the door.

"Of course," he replied, turning away to give me privacy.

I skidded inside, softly closing the door just enough to obscure his view.

Grabbing the brush once again and gripping it until my knuckles were white, I combed my hair one last time, forcing it completely straight. I looked in the mirror to see my lavender dress sweep the floor, the sleeves clinging to my skin. I sighed, smiled and walked toward the door with pleasure.

When I opened it, Aleron was looking directly at me, completely composed. He was wearing a blue shirt that battled with his eyes for my attention. His hair seemed longer than when I saw him last, his curls falling into his eyes more than usual. I was so taken by him, I couldn't think about anything else. Then he spoke in a soft, loving tone.

"You look beautiful. Any sane gentleman would say you're radiant, and I would agree without one bit of vacillation." His words were very proper and precise, always sounding educated and thoughtful.

I nodded in his direction and looked to the side. "What a beneficent comment. You look very dashing yourself." My shy voice announced, throwing in my educated vocabulary to compete with his.

Aleron looked pleased, yet stunned to hear such an opinion from me. He cleared his throat and bowed. He came up and offered his arm. I wrapped around his arm with pleasure and walked down the hall where the servants waited to watch us pass by. The gossip was following behind.

"You don't need to bow to me every time you see me. I feel guilty if I don't do the same in return," I said to start the conversation.

Aleron laughed. "If it makes you more comfortable, I will not bow to you."

"That was simpler than I thought it would be," I admitted, expecting more of a push back.

"You didn't let me finish. I will not bow to you *every* time. Perhaps every other." He winked at me, pretending to be professional again as we walked by a maid.

I kept my eyes to the side, for his eyes didn't seem to move from my abashed face.

Our conversation had come to a halt as we seemed to pass servants at every corner. My thoughts were drifting mindlessly to fill the silence. After many moments of quiet, I looked up to study Aleron's handsome face. I noticed his eyes were scrunched up on the sides, realizing something was wrong.

"Is there something bothering you?" I asked openly. His eyes became wide with embarrassment at my comment.

"It's nothing of concern, just a minor issue in the prison. It's been taking up a lot of my time. It's what kept me from seeing you sooner." Aleron placed his hand on my arm, squeezing it softly. I kept my eyes forward, not wanting him to catch my surprise with him mentioning the prison.

"What happened?" I dared to ask, seeing if there was any additional news that I wasn't aware of.

"There was an escape," he answered in hushed tones, making sure no one heard.

"Escape?" I retorted, pretending to be troubled by his response.

"Yes, it was the princess I told you about," he said solemnly.

I tried to act surprised at the news, instead of how I wanted to feel as I reflected back on the fight I had with Risa and Damien. I truly hoped they were safe and that I would see them again soon, that I would restore my relationship with them both. Aleron sensed my concern, not knowing what it was linked to.

"Don't worry, all is well; we were going to set her free soon. It just took me off guard. I am not used to the castle being infiltrated without being made aware. It's unsettling. It caused quite a stir among the men. We trained yesterday as a precaution and I have made sure to double our security measures," he concluded.

I tried to breathe evenly. I pushed the thoughts of Risa's escape out of my mind for the moment, noting Aleron's still concerned facial expression.

"Is that all?" I asked.

Aleron stopped, pulling us around a corner, out of sight of any servants.

"I have been delaying telling you this but I feel it's only right for you to know." He paused, making my anxiety rise, as usual.

"We still haven't had any luck locating your family. We are doing everything we can but it seems no one has come forward regarding the matter. I promise you we will keep searching. I can't imagine how you must be feeling, not remembering your family or life before the attack. I feel partially responsible."

I had nearly forgotten that I was supposed to be a missing Praserian, and at this rate, it would appear to them that I was an orphan. I hated seeing Aleron feel guilty for something that wasn't real. It was becoming harder and harder to lie to him.

Inside, I wanted to tell him the truth. So much of my life, so much of me, involves my past, and it was a part of me that was entirely off limits to share with him at the moment. I could only hope with time that that would change. It was something I planned to discuss with Ezra as soon as I could. At some point my "memories" would need to come back.

"Please, don't waste another moment feeling guilty. It is not your fault. I am just as content with the memories and moments I am having with you right now. If I have to rebuild a new life, I must say this is an excellent start." I placed my arms around his neck, my arm finally well enough to be out of its sling, giving me the freedom to move as I choose.

He smiled at my effort to comfort him. "Can I be honest with you about a silly fear I have been having?" he asked. I nodded, not knowing what he could possibly fear.

"If you don't have memories of your past, what if there is someone else in your life? I noticed your ruby ring the other night. Perhaps it's from another man?" he posed the question. His fear would have been completely valid in this situation. I looked at the ring my father had given me. *I wish so badly I could tell you the truth.*

"Even without my memories, I can promise you, there is no one like that in my life." I locked my eyes on him, trying not to be distracted by his long eyelashes that were resting on his tan skin.

"I have a hard time believing that. The thought of no one having feelings for you, feelings like I do, seems too good to be true," he rebutted. I found myself thinking of Hassan and the few moments we shared, but it was simple, different, and it wasn't the same. I pushed the thoughts of Hassan aside, letting myself enjoy my surroundings with Aleron.

"If there was someone, I hope they wouldn't have let me go in the first place," I said quietly.

"That's a fair point. And if they did, then it seems only right that they lost someone as valuable as you from their carelessness. I won't make that mistake." He trailed his hands up my arms to finally clasp his hands with my own as he kissed them softly, pulling me out of the corner as he continued walking.

"Where are you taking me?" I asked.

He smirked. "Somewhere very special to me."

~

*A*leron led me outside, to a place I hadn't been before. A large stone wall circled around the area, protected, but not watched. We stepped through an alcove and were met by an unexpected site. Flowers. More flowers than I could count.

The ground was painted in a rainbow of colors. Maroon, lavender, peach, yellow, and cream, all dancing proudly under the sun's radiant beams. Vines crawled up the sides of the walls, attempting to break free from its confines. The smell was luscious. I hadn't seen arrangements of flowers so neatly made. Each set of flowers was distinctly sectioned, all color coordinated, row by row. It was breathtaking.

I sighed, letting the flowers' happiness flood into my skin

and let my heart sing with every beat. *Why hadn't Ezra shown me this yet? It's marvelous.*

Aleron had come up behind me, wrapping his arms around my waist while I took in the new sight. I trailed my fingers along a nearby rose, the delicate flower standing up to my touch.

"Do you like it?" he asked, eager for my answer.

"I love it. I have never seen a garden this beautiful before," I said as the sound of a bumble bee whizzed past our ears.

"This is my mother's garden. You're the first person to see it that isn't family," Aleron said proudly.

I stopped dead in my tracks, remembering back to what Ezra had told me of the queen's garden. It was meant to be seen by others only on Aleron's wedding day.

"Your mother's garden? I shouldn't be here; it's personal to your family." I faltered in my walk and Aleron turned to me, wrapping an arm around my waist.

His scent overwhelmed my senses, overcoming the powerful smell of the flowers. All I could concentrate on was the warmth he radiated, making me want to be closer than I was. He leaned in, practically reading my mind.

"I asked for permission. Besides, my mother wanted to know someone's opinion and I thought yours would be valuable. Ezra told me you loved the flowers on your outings, so I hoped you'd enjoy this." I was charmed with his effort to make this special to me.

"You did some homework," I pointed out.

"First to know things around here, remember?" He reminded me again of his constant ear.

"Well, you can tell your mother it is an amazing garden," I

said, still soaking in the closeness between us. He sighed, his head inclining toward mine.

"I would be delighted if you had the chance to tell her yourself." His lips curled into his crooked smile.

"Are you implying that I am going to meet the queen?" I asked in astonishment.

"Only if you say yes to dinner with me and my parents," he declared.

I became flustered. I couldn't believe how close he was. It was all happening so suddenly. I barely knew him, hardly spent any time with him, yet I wanted to be tied to him in every way.

For being the enemy, he was intriguingly hard to resist. I pulled away and decided to avoid the proposal. I was afraid to think what might happen if his parents recognized me for any reason; it was too much of a risk. I couldn't think of a polite way to decline his offer so I decided to steer the conversation in a new direction.

"Spring is my favorite season. All the flowers in bloom, it's the most beautiful time of the year," I spoke sweetly, hoping he would accept the topic.

Aleron became serious, his eyes holding mine.

"I can say I am becoming very fond of spring as well." He leaned in even closer, his hands moving from my waist to my rib cage, forcing our noses to touch. "I've met someone this spring. Every moment when I can't see her I'm thinking of her. She is my every moment. She is extraordinary, elegant, kind-hearted, compassionate, amusing, independent, positive, and she tends to fall to the floor at the sight of me, which I find very flattering. There is some strong and immovable attraction to her that I am drawn to and it is undeniable." He grinned at his remarks.

I laughed at his ability to flirt with whatever conversation I threw his way. He grabbed my hands and held them to his chest. I squeezed them softly, feeling the warmth crawl onto my tender hands, noticing our heartbeats speed up with every breath.

"I wonder who that may be. Coincidentally, I've met someone as well. Similar admirable qualities, aside from the falling to the floor part," I said. He laughed at my humor and joy danced around his face.

I continued, "Although I must confess, there is one thing that leaves me perplexed by this gentleman."

His eyebrows rose and his head came to the side, his lips awfully close to mine.

"What might that be?" He seemed offended but taunting me at the same time. I touched his shoulder to reassure him it wasn't anything to be offended about.

"He acts differently sometimes. I'm unsure of the real him," I said aloud, ashamed realizing I was accusing him of not being real when my identity was being completely concealed from his knowledge.

"Exactly what does he act like?" he asked.

"There's one side to him when he is precise with language, brave, slightly conceited and very much like a prince, a side of him I saw at the ball. There's the other where he tends to act more freely, more courageous and wild, not caring what others think or hear, intrigued with amusement. The first is when he is in public and the second is around me. Why is that?" My desire to know grew.

He cocked his head mockingly. "What is he now?" he inquired to know.

"A little of both. Aleron, you confuse me. I can't decipher who you really are," I declared, clearly defeated.

Aleron pressed his forehead to mine, speaking in a tone so sweet and tender I almost embraced him by the sound of it. "By your observation I cannot give you a decent answer. I would say I am both. I am a combination of what you see. I was born as a prince. It is in my nature to act as one. When I'm alone, or when I am with you, I forget the proper norms, let freedom come into my hands and be what I want to be at that moment. You make me feel new, Amelia. I feel like I discover bits and pieces of who I am when we are together. Does that answer help you?" He honestly wanted to see that I had been put at ease. His answer was well spoken; not that I expected anything less.

I nodded. "Yes, that is precisely what I needed to hear. You are very good at that by the way." I laughed, but to my surprise his eyes became smaller, concerned.

"Is there one side that you like better than the other?" He had displayed nervousness for the first time. My heart sank for making him feel concerned. I shook my head, ready to answer.

"Of course not! There is not one I favor more. They are equal," I laughed. He smiled and leaned in closer.

"You promised me something at the ball which you haven't yet fulfilled. Might this be a proper time to do so?" he asked.

"I do not recall promising anything. Possibly if you remind me, it may come back to memory." I breathed in deeply and shakily let out another.

"I said I would ask you in the future if you would teach me how to dance," he kindly reminded me.

"You never asked me that." I stood my ground, certain the conversation hadn't come up.

"Can we pretend I did?" He smirked, knowing he was caught.

"I don't need to teach you. You were dancing at the ball without any help from me," I concluded. His eyebrows went up.

"That is simply not true! I was hopeless without you!" He jokingly winked at me. "Amelia, I won't lie – I know how to dance. But you are preventing me from making a valid excuse to dance with you right now," he proceeded.

"Aleron, you do not need a reason to dance with me. All you need is a little bit of music,"

With that, I sing a lullaby for us to dance to. Aleron's facial expressions made me aware that he was listening intently, his eyebrows knit closely together in concentration and surprise. I couldn't tell if he was acting with infatuation or confusion, but either way I felt completely admired. It was such a refreshing feeling to feel the same way about him and know it was mutual.

The lullaby brought back a flood of memories. It was one my mother used to sing to Risa and I. In some ways I missed my mother and the longing to go back to Valteria hit me. But Aleron was staring at me intently before I could think about it any longer.

I moved forward while he stepped toward me, pushing me into his chest. I wobbled back into place. Regret came over his face, but I smiled with reassurance.

"I forgot you were leading. That was my fault," I said, comforting him.

I started humming again and he hesitated to take a step backward. He moved to the side, eyes closed tight, concentrating. He came forward and opened his eyes, realizing we had gotten back our rhythm.

"I'm glad your fear of singing in front of me has seemed to disappear," he said, pure joy displayed on his face as he listened to me.

"I'm not singing. I'm humming. There's a difference," I pointed out. He laughed at my reply.

"You are a stubborn girl, Lia. And I admire every bit of it."

Placing one arm behind my back, he turned me in circles around the flower beds. I continued to hum, no matter how much I wanted to laugh with pleasure. He took his hand from my back and spun me away from him and quickly spun me back into his eager grasp. We continued to repeat this cycle until we got lost in the dancing.

Before I knew it, he was humming too, a new song every minute, unable to commit to one. I laughed as he twirled me to the front, then brought me back facing the opposite of him and hugged me tight, ending the song.

I stretched my head up to look at him. "As I said, you are not a poor dancer, evidence has been shown," I announced. He quickly spun me around to face him.

"Flattery I see. Well, evidence also shows that I am going to kiss you." He smiled, leaning in closer.

My face went bright red. My stomach dropped to the point where I felt nervous butterflies. Aleron had created the perfect moment that every girl wished for. *Don't ruin it, Allene.*

I tried to remain calm, answering playfully back. "I don't see any evidence." I mocked every word slowly, pushing my lips into a large smile.

"There will be," he promised, his face being serious. His eyes locked hold onto mine, complete sincerity flooding them. All the flirting and joking fell away as it was replaced with an intimate moment of silence.

I caught my breath as he slowly leaned into me. I shut my eyes and felt nothing in-between us, not even air, just us.

I tried to take it all in and not miss a moment. I felt something warm and smooth touch my lips ever so slightly, and lightly pull away. Before I could say anything his lips touched mine again, fiercer now.

He gripped my waist with one hand and pressed the other against my cheek. I brought my hands around his neck, trying to bring him closer. I had never been kissed before, but the feeling inside of me exploded and at that moment it was all I wanted.

I let him kiss me without keeping track of how long we had been in our own world. I felt the passion build between us, my mind racing. My hands had weaved themselves into Aleron's hair, pulling him closer to me. Aleron let out a small sound at the notion, pausing at my sudden zeal. *Don't get carried away, Allene.* I released my grip, trying to remove myself from the escalation of intensity. Aleron slowed down, sensing it too, ending our moment with a delicate kiss. His hand stayed on my cheek, his arm still wrapped around me.

I opened my eyes to see him smiling at me, his full grin exposing his dimple.

"Is there evidence now?" he questioned.

I smirked. "Too much." I winked at him, trying to hide my slight amount of seriousness.

He thought over the words carefully and took his time to respond.

"I would rather there be too much than not enough," he announced. I embraced him, my arms circling his neck.

"As would I," I said shyly, whispering in his ear.

"Are you absolutely sure of that?" he inquired, his hair falling onto my cheek as his eyebrows knitted together.

"I've never been more certain of anything."

And at that moment, I didn't need anymore evidence to know with certainty that I was falling in love with Aleron.

CHAPTER 15

*E*zra sat at the foot of my bed, looking up at me, smiling proudly. I had just arrived back from my outing with the Aleron and Ezra was all ears for the details.

"Allene, I have never been so overjoyed for anyone before, besides your father. It makes me ecstatic to see you like this. It makes me think of your sweet grandmother and I," Ezra trailed off, reminiscing of his past.

"My father spoke very highly of grandmother. He truly admired her. He often noted her as inspirational. I don't remember her but I have seen her influence in my life, even being gone," I reassured him, hoping he knew that he wasn't the only one who thought about her.

"Thank you. I am happy to hear that it all went well today. I wish you nothing but the best. Please, come find me if you need anything." He uncrossed his legs and stood.

"Actually, Ezra, I do have one favor to ask."

"Anything," he offered without hesitation.

"Aleron mentioned the search for my family today. I don't think I can keep claiming I have memory loss, I don't want to raise suspicion and more questions."

Ezra nodded. "I will find a solution," he assured me and walked out of the room.

~

*T*he days had passed quickly. Aleron had made a notable effort to see me with any free time he had. He was very good at stopping by in the mornings to check in on me before he left for his meetings for the day. It made me grow anxious as I would wait for him, trying to make every moment we shared a memorable one. Today was different; today he had an extra spring in his step.

Aleron had found me reading at my desk. I spotted him out of the corner of my mirror that was reflecting back at him. I caught him staring at me with a crinkle at the corner of his eyes from smiling. I instantly smiled back at him, admiring his lovely blue coat that made his eyes sparkle. *Was this real life?*

"My lovely Lia, I am free until this afternoon. I was wondering if you would be interested in accompanying me to the parlor. I would like to show you something I have been working on." His eyes held deep excitement as he awaited my answer. I tried to pretend like I had a schedule to go over in my mind, act like I wasn't overly thrilled to spend the entire morning in his presence. "That would be delightful."

"This way." He beamed as he took my hand. He swiftly dragged me behind him as he eagerly made his way to the parlor. I wasn't even aware that such a room existed and for good reason. It was on the second floor, which was near where the royal families' quarters were located. It was off limits to anyone who wasn't personally escorted or called on by a member of the royal family.

We entered a room that was decorated magnificently in marble. The pillars and tiles were all constructed from marble and the walls held pictures of the royal family from generation to generation. It was an astonishing sight. My eyes fell on a particular painting. Ezra, my grandmother Irene, and my father.

The painting was placed directly next to Aleron's family. It was hard not to take a moment to appreciate what I was seeing. Realizing that my family, my blood, had such a rich history here.

Ezra looked bold in his king's uniform, his face having only a few resemblances to my fathers. They had the same eyebrows and bushy sideburns. In the portrait, Ezra stood tall, his shoulders broad, exuding the disposition of a king. He stood with a soft hand on my grandmother's shoulder. Her ruby red dress matched her lipstick perfectly, her black hair braided to the side and her hands placed gently in her lap as she sat in an elegant manner. She had light blue eyes and a sweet smile. She was beautiful. My father had her eyes and nose, which I happened to get from my father. It was riveting to see where I inherited parts of my appearance. My father, a teenager in the portrait painting, had more hair on his head than his face. He was tall and skinny standing on the other side of my grandmother, pursed lip smile showing his attempt to be serious. Seeing the portrait made me miss him even more.

So much has changed, both you and grandmother are gone. I got the courage to tear my eyes away from the portrait but Aleron had caught me staring.

"Ezra, not much has changed about him over the years. He looks almost exactly the same," Aleron stated. He was right, the only main difference I could see in Ezra was the change of his once blackish-gray hair now being snow white. He now had a little more of a hunch but he still stood taller than most men.

I nodded. "He briefly told me about his past. He didn't venture into many details though regarding how he ended up being a servant after he had been a king," I said softly, curious to hear the reasoning for it. It was a question I had been meaning to ask and now the opportunity seemed well enough to broach the topic.

"That was his choice. When my father took over the throne, he offered Ezra second in command, to be his Chancellor. He politely refused. He said his wife grew up in a poor family of servants and maids and that they were the most humble people he knew. He wanted to serve his kingdom in an honorable way and medicine had always intrigued him. He wasn't permitted the opportunity to learn it before in his position as king. So he resides here at the castle, tending to those that need his help. He is better than the actual doctor we have now, in my opinion." He smiled with pride. The story didn't surprise me. Ezra did appear to be as selfless as they come, a trait my father must've learned from him.

"It allowed him to help his wife toward the end of her life.

He never left her side. They had a beautiful relationship. One I aspire to replicate." He reached for my hand, holding it tight as we looked at the portrait together.

"That is very sweet. I'm happy he got what he wanted in the end," I said.

"As am I. I truly think he is happier now than he was as king. I can relate. There are days I wish I could give it all up to be something different too." Aleron spoke in hushed tones. "Come now, I want to show you why I brought you here, and I want to avoid you seeing my family portrait. Not my best hair day," he chuckled.

Aleron pulled me in his direction. At the end of the room was a wall made up completely of windows, the light shining through as we faced the east. You could see the hills continually rolling, nothing obscuring the view. I noticed two easels were set up near the windows, the back of the canvas being all we could see.

"Are you an artist?" I asked, slightly shocked but not completely in disbelief that it was another hidden skill of his.

"I dabble. I like using oil paints. The way they translate on the canvas . . . it makes such a stationary, inanimate object, come to life. It inspires me." He smiled, obviously taking pleasure in his hobby. It made me smile seeing how genuine and simple his response was.

"I want you to close your eyes," he said, stopping in front of the easel. I hesitated, not being very fond of surprises.

"Trust me," he commanded softly and I quickly retreated, shutting my eyes. I heard him rustle around a few things and soon enough he said the magic words. "You can open your eyes now."

My jaw dropped. I was staring at a winsome young lady with pure curiosity and innocence reflecting in her eyes. Her smile was tender and her presence was fierce. She was undeniably strong and very aware of herself as the painting portrayed her sitting on the same gazebo that Aleron and I had been in the night of the ball. It took me a few moments to realize that the astounding image was me.

I could feel my heart in my chest as it swelled with gratitude. The fact that Aleron depicted me as this woman brought me to tears. I studied the painting so intently, taking in every detail he managed to convey. A small mole lay at the corner of my right eye, something I thought he wouldn't even notice. He managed to display the green ring that was contained in the blue of my eyes, showing just how much he paid attention.

"Do you like it?" he asked with sincere implication, putting his arms around my shoulders. I found myself beginning to hold back tears of gratitude. Before I could respond he continued.

"I am so sorry, I have offended you. I know I'm not an exceptional artist but I wanted to translate my opinion of you. I obviously didn't give you the justice I was hoping for."

I turned in his arms, sternly staring him down as I watched him stay steadfast under my gaze. "Aleron, don't you dare say another harsh word toward yourself. I adore it. I will cherish this for as long as I live. Words cannot tell you how much this means to me. It is wondrous. I have never seen a painting more beautiful. You have gratified me beyond what I could ever hope for," I said with conviction, assuring him to make no further mistake of exactly how I felt about his gesture.

He sighed and gently kissed my cheek. "I am pleased to hear you say that," he said, smiling from ear to ear.

I turned in his arms again, still admiring his artistic talent. It was realistic and incredibly spot on. "When did you learn to paint like this? I never would have thought of you as an artist," I confessed. I felt him shrug from behind me.

"I began painting and drawing when I was young. My mother has quite the artistic eye. I would sit and watch her draw objects that were near her. I soon became fascinated with the activity and would join her every day, trying to develop the skill. It took me a lot of time to realize I wasn't very good at drawing objects, but one day I tried drawing my father as he worked on a puzzle. My mother was quite impressed with how talented I was at drawing people. Ever since then, I have found joy in painting others. This project however, it was definitely the longest I have ever spent painting someone and obviously, it's my favorite." He inter-twined our fingers and led me to a small bench pushed against the wall, sitting us side by side.

"With all intents of it being a gift to you Amelia, I was hoping that you would approve of me keeping it." I could see he was slightly embarrassed at the statement but I gleaned at his request.

"Please, I wouldn't have it any other way. It makes me happy thinking you have something of me when I'm not there. I would, for the record, not be opposed to painting a picture of you to keep as well." I winked and he laughed.

"Are you an artist then?" he asked sincerely.

"Heavens no. I tried painting once and it only frustrated me. You had a great example to learn from though. My father was more interested in poetry and music. I will have to share some with you sometime," I said, unsure if I was confident enough to display a talent that my father claimed I had but one that I had always doubted. I was convinced he told me I was good because I made such an effort. I guess a second opinion wouldn't be a bad idea, to finally confirm if he was being honest.

"It is reassuring to hear you speak of your family, to know that your memories are back," Aleron said sweetly. I nodded, realizing this was the first time in conversation I had mentioned them. It felt good not having to be as careful around him now that Ezra had fixed the memory loss situation as he promised.

"Speaking of, you can officially confirm that there is no other man I need to worry about barging through those doors to take you away from me, correct?" he said lightheartedly. I nudged his shoulder with mine.

"Correct."

He smiled, his mood shifting. "That's a relief. If you don't mind me asking, what was your family like? Ezra mentioned that they all passed away, that you are alone. I understand if you don't want to discuss it, but I do feel it would tell me a great deal about you," he said solemnly, nervous to see my reaction.

Ezra had mentioned that he had told the royal family that I didn't want to speak of my past because of the tragic loss of my family. He told them I recently had my memories come back and that it wasn't something I wanted to talk about. This helped keep suspicions at bay as to why I hadn't contacted them after my injuries or as to why no one had come forward to report my disappearance. However, we hadn't discussed our story as to what "happened" to them and I had to draw one up on the spot, trying to use as much of my real life as possible.

"Don't be ashamed to ask, I am happy to share with you. My family was small. My only strong bond was with my father. I miss him dearly. He passed away only recently actually." I got choked up talking so truthfully about my father, the emotions still raw and overcoming my barriers. I felt tears come to the corners of my eyes as Aleron swiftly swept them away with his thumb, waiting patiently for me to continue. I swallowed hard, only letting a little bit of the ache I felt in my heart reflect in my hoarse voice.

"He was ill. He was all I had left. I didn't have a very strong relationship with my mother; she was always treating me like I was a mistake in her life that was haunting her every day. I felt regret when she looked at me, although I could never figure out what I'd done wrong. My younger sister, she had a much different relationship with my mother. My sister and I got along quite well but we definitely responded differently around our parents. My sister was always so kind, extremely positive. As a family unit, I felt like I was left behind in many ways. Don't misunderstand, I miss them, I really do. I loved them all. It was just my father and I for a time, until he passed as well."

I tried to enlace the dishonesty with as much truth as I could. I hated lying to Aleron, but I also refused to give up this blessing that had come my way. I had never been as happy as I was now and I selfishly refused to let it go. Even if it meant crossing the line of not knowing anymore if I was actually Allene or Amelia, not able to discern which one was truly me. Aleron held both my hands, his sorrow overtaking him. I could feel him trying to relate to my grief.

"Amelia, you have been dealt an unfair burden. My only wish is that somehow, being here, being with me, it can lighten the suffering you have felt." Aleron was heartfelt as always, making me sink deeper into his consoling grasp.

"You can't begin to comprehend the way you have lifted my spirits and my heart. You have filled a vacancy that has been there for too long. You have given me purpose, Aleron. You have done more than you needed to and I sincerely thank you for it."

I could see the proclamation made him feel at ease.

"I hope you know that it is my every intention to not be the only person you can rely on." His statement was peculiar. I could see he was testing to see if I would pressure him for further explanation and I happily did.

"How do you mean?" I asked.

His eyes became acutely serious, focusing on mine entirely. "It is my wish that one day not only will I be filling that vacancy in your heart, but that you could eventually look to my family as another source of comfort; to be able to rely on them as much as you have come to rely on me. I hope you know I have every intention to give you a family again, Amelia." Aleron spoke with a deep purpose, evidently displaying that he had given the idea much thought.

I steadily studied every word, letting my mind process it. I knew his proposal could never be, that his family would never approve of him marrying a commoner. Even if he knew the truth about my title as princess, they wouldn't approve of that either ,considering the kingdom I would rule was Valteria. I think they would prefer the news of me being a commoner more than they would of me being the Valterian princess.

We would have to face these realities eventually, but not now – I wasn't ready to take on the complicated path we had ahead. I wanted to immerse myself in this moment.

I could no longer feel Aleron's touch. The burning sensation that I normally felt when I was with him was gone. A new feeling had taken its place and the feeling was exuberant. I was overcome with emotion as I couldn't hold back that distinct feeling of belonging – of being home.

I placed my hand on his cheek as I kissed him lightly, trying to communicate without using words. I couldn't muster a response that sufficed for his statement but I knew that sometimes words weren't enough.

I felt Aleron's lips smile at my response, taking it as an invitation. I felt his hand make its way behind my neck, holding me closer to him. The moment was full of earnest anticipation, exhilaration, and infatuation. I felt myself completely let go and be absorbed by Aleron's touch, his lips consuming mine in a gentle yet fierce manner. That fire I felt disappear earlier had instantly returned but with even more heat pulsing through my veins. I could feel myself becoming dizzy as his presence became more vivid, overtaking my senses. We were so consumed that we hadn't even noticed the footsteps that had boorishly entered the vacant room.

Aleron immediately stopped but stayed only inches from my face, his mischievous smile appearing. "Father, mother, good morning," he stated, without taking his eyes off me. I could see he was waiting for my reaction. He was amused as he saw the blood drain from my face and leave me pale as the floor. He laughed and stood up, helping me to my feet.

I kept my eyes down, completely mortified with humiliation and fright, as I curtsied. I was terrified to make eye contact but knew I had no choice.

The king held a blank stare as he looked at Aleron, completely displeased. The queen was attached to his arm. She was stunning. Her thick curly hair was pulled back in a low bun and her violet dress left me in awe as it matched her plump lips perfectly and contrasted her olive skin. Her small diamond crown sparkled as much as her white teeth and she had a delicate nose to match her soft blue eyes. I could see where Aleron got his looks.

The king held a distasteful expression but he still looked handsome. His hair was slightly long, buoyant from volume and combed over to the left side to display a clear part. He had hard gray eyes that wrinkled at the corners from his pertinent squinting scowl. He was a bulky man, his uniform fitted and almost bursting the buttons at his chest. He hid his lips in a stern line, his uptight character shining through. How could Aleron ever think this man would approve of me?

Aleron's mother was content at the sight of us, looking me over from head to toe with a warm smile.

"So this is the young lady I have heard so much about." Her smile didn't fade, but only grew as she spoke. She had the same crooked smile as Aleron but hers had an added dimple on her left cheek. She was intimidatingly beautiful.

"Indeed it is. Amelia, this is my mother, Queen Eveline."

The queen reached out a hand to shake mine, I accepted the hand shake and slightly nodded in my direction.

"And this is my father, King Vincent." The king did not offer his hand but only a curt nod. I curtsied again, realizing I was too intimidated to do anything else.

I couldn't figure out why I was so overawed by their presence. I was royalty myself. This was something I was used to everyday. I quickly realized I wasn't unnerved by their status, I was daunted because of how much their son meant to me and I realized how vital their approval would be if this was really going to grow into what Aleron claimed it would be.

"Amelia, please, no more curtsying, my dear. I feel like we are already so close. It is a pleasure to finally make your acquaintance," Eveline said softly, her voice ever so gentle.

"It is an honor to meet you as well. I want to thank you for letting me stay in your home and for all the care you have given me. I am in your debt," I said, trying to read Vincent's face as I could feel his stare.

This was the moment I was hoping wouldn't come. It was the entire reason I tried to avoid Aleron's offer to have dinner with his parents. I was afraid of being caught and I felt like somehow the king could sense something was off.

"Don't be silly, I have seen the effect you have on my son and I am grateful that you have come. I have not seen him in such good spirits in a long time. You are welcome to stay as long as you wish," Eveline answered again. She was very gracious. I could see why Aleron looked up to her, she was amazing.

"We did not mean to interrupt you; we will be on our way. Amelia, hopefully in the near future, you and I can sit down and get to know one another better. Eveline and I have business to attend to. Good day," Vincent said, forcing his wife to turn awkwardly away from the conversation, her head lingering behind.

Aleron nodded to his mother and let out a long sigh as he watched them walk away. As soon as they were out of sight, Aleron grabbed my hand and sat back down, searching my face to understand what I was thinking.

"Aleron, that was . . ."

"Awkward, yet completely right. They witnessed exactly how we feel for each other and I find no shame in that." He spoke with such confidence that I almost believed what he said.

I shook my head. "A little too much of what we feel. I think a little less would have gotten the point across. Did you know they were there?" I asked, eyeing him suspiciously.

He laughed. "No! I could tell how ashamed you were. I would never intentionally make you go through that. I apologize. It won't happen again if that's what you want . . ." He bit his lip, mocking me and testing to see how far I would take it. I lightly shoved his arm.

"That is not at all what I meant," I laughed to myself, trying to let the flirty mood replace the awkward one. I was full of relief that the moment of meeting his parents for the first time had finally come and gone.

"Good, I don't think I could've survived otherwise," he teased and gave me a quick kiss. I made an effort to smile but soon realized I couldn't let the moment go.

"Aleron, your father, I couldn't help but notice that he

seemed irritated by my presence," I admitted, wanting to understand.

Aleron held a grim expression, realizing we couldn't move on until we had talked about it. "Ignore him, please. My father doesn't fully understand why I did what I did. He doesn't understand how it is possible that we have the relationship we do. It was probably my mistake anyway, I confided in my mother about my feelings for you. She is a very good listener but she is also a dedicated gossip. She told my father how serious I am about you, to the extent of seeing a future together, and I knew my father wasn't ready to hear that. I can promise you he will come around. My mother fully supports us, Amelia. She only wants to see me be happy. My father on the other hand . . . he likes his own agenda to be dealt with first. Just give him time," Aleron said with such assurance that I wanted to hang on to every word of it. I wanted to believe it all, but I knew the support of his father was highly unlikely.

"You heard all about my family. What is the relationship like with yours?" I inquired, trying to understand his family dynamic.

Aleron took a moment to really consider his answer. He finally sighed.

"My family is more complicated than it appears on the surface. Are you sure you want to hear about it?" he asked with uncertainty. I couldn't help but laugh. If he considered his family complicated than what was mine? *If only he knew.*

I nodded my head, urging him to press on.

"Suit yourself." Aleron leaned back, extending his legs out in front of him, placing his hands behind his head. He was acting like we would be there a while, if it was really what I wanted to discuss. I ignored his dramatic attempt to avoid the question. Aleron gazed my way, seeing that I was listening.

"I had a wonderful childhood. I loved growing up in the castle. My mother and I are extremely close. My father is a great leader and he is skilled in battle. From a young age, being a prince, I had to train to fight. I had a partner who was always slightly better than I was. I constantly fell in his shadow. It was infuriating for me for a long time. I was jealous that when it came to training he was my greatest competition, and when it came to anything else, he was my greatest friend. We would do everything together, nothing could separate us." Aleron had transitioned into a day dreaming state, reliving the fond memories.

"What was his name?" I asked, not wanting him to stop the story. I was intrigued to learn more about him.

"Killian – he is my brother." He had hardly even whispered the words loud enough for me to hear, but I was certain I wasn't mistaken. I was caught by surprise, my jaw gaping slightly. Then I remembered what Ezra had said the first day I arrived in Praseria. He said Aleron was the only *present* heir to the throne. I found it peculiar when he mentioned it. I had almost completely forgotten about it until now.

"You have a brother?" I couldn't begin to comprehend the thought of another version of Aleron.

"Yes, he is a year older than me. He was the pride of the family. He was a great many things."

I could see the hurt on Aleron's face and I couldn't help but still be confused by the news. "I don't want to push you to discuss anything you aren't comfortable telling me, Aleron."

He squeezed my hand tightly, the memories erased from his eyes and his focus clearly being on me. "Amelia, I am comfortable telling you anything. I just haven't told anyone about this before. It's a good feeling, having someone to share your past with."

I nodded in understanding, appreciating his honesty with me and feeling guilty for the shadiness of my stories as he was being so open with me.

"He left two years ago. As much as my father adored him, he didn't return the same appreciation. My father pushed him too hard, to the point that I knew he was driving Killian away. I distinctly remember the night that Killian had pulled me aside to ask me to flee with him. We were inseparable and I knew my father had pushed him to do things that he wasn't fond of. Killian grew tired of my father's manners and wishes that he had for my brother. Killian realized the only way to escape it was to leave. I was prepared to go with him. He had friends spread out over many of the kingdoms that he planned to stay with and to start a new life. He was never happy that he grew up in royalty, having the responsibility of so much without it being voluntary. I almost went with him, but I couldn't bear to leave my mother. If Killian left, my mother would have no one. She would have no one to inherit the throne or to look after her, to carry on the second genera-tion of our royal line. I stayed behind and Killian left.

"When it first occurred I thought he was courageous for not letting our family determine his future. As I have grown and understood through my father's eyes the responsibility we hold as the royal family, I realized that Killian was a coward. I know my father doesn't see me the same as my brother but I do know he is proud of me for heeding the responsibility I have as prince of Praseria," Aleron spoke so softly, afraid someone would hear him.

I hadn't realized that Aleron had been through as much as he had. I wish I could explain that I could understand how he felt about being less than his sibling but yet still being so close. That was my relationship with Risa almost exactly. I wanted to relate to his pressures of royalty but knew I had to stay quiet. I could feel the weight that Aleron had placed on his shoulders, being all his family had left. I was proud of him too – proud that he was honorable beyond measure.

"Aleron, I am deeply sorry to hear that your brother left. He was a fool for leaving you behind. Praseria is proud to call you their prince and, shortcomings of your brother aside, I know he would be proud of the man you have become." Despite the betrayal I could see in Aleron's eyes, I could sense he still yearned for the respect of his brother and he took comfort in my words.

"Thank you. I know your family would be immensely proud of you too, Lia." He kissed my lips one more time, trying to make me believe I had something to feel accomplished for. I was washed in shame realizing the mess I made, the façade I had convinced him to believe was me. As much as I was being *myself*, it wasn't actually who I *was*. I didn't deserve his comfort or his understanding. What if he knew the truth? Would it change his admiration toward me? Would it change us? *If only he knew . . .*

CHAPTER 16

My mind was starting to get the best of me. I was becoming my own worst enemy. It was ironic considering the situation I was in. I had filled myself with doubt of everything that had been happening. The idea that Aleron discovering the truth could shatter everything we had built made me question how deep our love really was and it was slowly consuming me. I kept wishing I had said more and had been honest with him. I kept wishing I would have responded differently to his roundabout way of saying he wanted to marry me one day. I wanted it all to be slightly different but still as perfect as can be. I was wishing for a fantasy.

No matter how hard I tried to stop it, my thoughts always drifted back to Aleron. I planned to see him in two days. He promised he had another special surprise for me. I hoped I would encounter him at least once before then. It was getting harder to imagine going a day without seeing at least a glimpse of him.

I concluded I would go speak with Noni, ask where she was the night of the ball. *I can't believe it's been that long since I had spoken to her.* I had subconsciously avoided her. I knew I would have to give back the lovely dress and shoes that I had successfully dirtied to a point beyond repair. The grass stains from my sneaking around had painted the dress from white to a light shade of green. I was nervous to see her reaction to the damage I had done. It also would be a wise idea to get a new dress for my date with Aleron, if Noni trusted me with another one that is.

I walked into Noni's room, keeping the dress and shoes behind my back as much as possible to avoid the conversation right away. Noni jumped up at the sight of me, her face happier than ever. She was sewing a white dress, more beautiful than the one she had made for me. It had rows of beads, pearls, crystals, flower lace and ruffles. It was no question that it was for something special.

"What is that?" I questioned.

Noni bit her lip, about ready to shriek. "My wedding dress!" she cried out.

My jaw hung low, my mind was racing with questions. "Noni, that is wonderful! When did this happen? Why didn't you tell me sooner? Who are you engaged to marry?" All my questions came out hurriedly.

Noni set down her dress and came to my side. She looked around and moved some fabric off a chair. She shoved me down into it and sat happily on the floor, getting a peak at the green dress behind my back. She pointed at it, giving me a glare.

"Is that what I think it is?" she accused. I gave a sheepish smile.

She waved her hand in the air. "Oh I don't even care, I can be mad at you later," she giggled and I let the dress be placed by my side as I listened.

"It happened so fast! At the ball, Simon asked me to go on a walk with him. He took me down by the ocean, just before the sunset. It was beautiful and at the end, he proposed! I wasn't expecting it at all. I must say, I didn't think Simon and I would ever be together. I mean, I was always fond of him but I never thought I was *in love*. Now I can't stop thinking about him. I am blissfully consumed! In the moment it felt right. I couldn't stop myself from saying yes," she explained.

I smiled; I was so happy that Noni had found someone to share her life with; I was starting to wonder why a girl with such high and cheery spirits wasn't yet married.

"Simon, the guard?" I assumed.

She nodded. I thought of gleeful Noni next to serious, determined Simon. It made me chuckle. They would balance out each other nicely.

"When will the wedding take place?" I asked.

"As soon as I can get this dress done, so surely soon. You know I work fast. We plan on having it in the church in town," she chirped.

"Noni, I don't know what to say other than congratulations!"

"That's all you need to say. Oh, please tell me you will attend it, won't you?"

I thought of the wedding. I hadn't attended very many. I had a distant cousin get married once, but because of our status as royals they insisted on having a dinner party to not attract a large gathering of people that would possibly focus on my father, mother, sister and myself, instead of the bride and the groom. A commoners wedding would be a new experience.

"I would be honored to attend," I said honestly, excited that I had been invited as a guest.

"Delightful! Simon will be very happy too! Now obviously that isn't all you came for. What may I help you with dear?" she inquired, getting back to the point.

"I was hoping you could make me a dress. But I do not want to distract you from your progress with your wedding dress. I have plenty of other dress choices I can choose from your collection," I assured her.

"Nonsense. Of course I can make one for you! What is the occasion if you don't mind me asking? I pray it doesn't involve . . . whatever it was that destroyed my masterpiece," she said dissatisfied as she eyed the fabric beside me.

"Just an outing. Nothing that will harm another dress," I concluded, trying not to allude to anything more.

"With?" Her eyebrows went up.

I gave in. "Aleron." I grinned.

The needle went slack in her hand. She jumped off the floor, dropping her dress and squealed. She grabbed my hands and hurled me off my seat and into the air, hopping around with joy.

"I knew he fancied you! How romantic! Ah!" She clapped her hands together and jittered her feet.

I chuckled. "I was shocked. It seems we both had every-thing fall into place at the ball," I pointed out.

"Are you happy?" she asked, as if it was even a question.

"Overwhelmingly so," I replied.

"Wouldn't any girl be? You are *so* lucky! I'll have it ready the morning after tomorrow, I can make something breath-taking and simple. Will that do?"

I nodded. "Yes, the outing is in two days. You are so kind, Noni, to take the time to make me a dress," I said.

"That is what friends are for, Lia. Besides, I would love to have the prince as a guest at my wedding! Attending with you, of course. I will be sure to make the perfect dress for another perfect night. If I am going to get it made in time I must start now." She turned, shooing me away.

I chuckled at her reply. "Of course, I'll leave. Thank you."

～

I skipped through the halls, thinking only of Aleron. I came to my room and gave a small jump in the air before I opened the door. I shut it, hoping for a knock to startle me and fall to the floor. Surprisingly, my wishes partially came true.

A knock came to the door. The anticipation for the face I hoped to see quickly faded. It was Lottie. I frowned. She didn't wait for me to answer the door and let herself in. She skittered to my side, holding a piece of paper.

"For you." She extended her hand and placed the letter in mine.

I nodded. "Thank you."

She curtsied and left the room. I hadn't received any letters while I was here. I was highly suspicious as to who would be writing to me. Maybe it was from Aleron.

I brushed my finger tip under the envelope, opening it without effort. Neat handwriting covered the page as I read.

My dearest sister,
You are probably not expecting a letter from me, but I feel respon-
sible to inform you about what has been going on at home. Everyone
is worried about you and it has gotten much worse since my return.
Damien has told mother of your whereabouts and she is coming for
you at once. She knows you are with Aleron and she knows what
happened to me. She believes that he has you kept captive as well,
despite me insisting you are there willingly. When she arrives, I
fear for the repercussions that will follow.
This is all to warn you, to hopefully give you enough time to sort out
what you can. When you get this, I assume she should arrive in
three days time. I hope this has gotten to you soon enough to prepare
for her arrival.
Allene, I would like to apologize to you for everything I said. I
understand why you did what you did. As sisters, I hope we can still
trust in one another. I know that you will do what your heart tells
you and if you believe you should stay, then stay. I hope you know I
am always on your side. I wish you good health, love and luck.
Your loving sister,
Risa Clarisse Amena

My heart jumped into panic. My fingers went stiff as I read the letter four more times, absorbing all the words. I was grateful that my sister had informed me of what was happening, but what was happening was my worst nightmare. It was not something I had thought would ever occur.

I knew Ezra could help but I didn't want to tell him what was happening. I didn't want to hurt anyone else by involving them with my complicated situation. I needed to resolve this myself; this was my problem, not his.

If Laerina was going to be here in three days, I would still have my outing with Aleron. Then I could run away; no matter how much I wanted to stay. I could tell Aleron the truth after our outing, see his response and hope for the best. *True love would conquer this, right?* My father and mother did.

I had a decision to make and it wouldn't be easy. There was only one option that seemed right and that was the one I had to choose.

~

I ran to the stables, trying to get the unfortunate news out of my thoughts. I hadn't visited the pasture in weeks, and the offer from Kendra to ride when I was better pushed me to run harder at the thought of the amazing horse.

I came to the field where the horses ran wildly. I stepped back at the sight. How was I going to get through without Ezra?

I took in a deep breath of air, feeling it warm my body. I had done it once, I could do it again.

Without giving it much consideration, I took a step forward, scampering through the pasture, avoiding every steed I could. Many times I wanted to shut my eyes, but I knew that would make my chances of getting past unharmed even more unlikely. I was getting closer to the barn when a horse brushed my leg.

The beast continued its scurry, but left me toppling forward onto the ground and leaving me on my back. I heard another coming my way, full speed in my direction.

I wanted to move but some unseen force wouldn't let me. I felt no pain, but my body was rigid. The hooves were drawing nearer and I cringed, my arms now covering my face. The hooves brushed close to my side, but I was not trampled. Instead something caught me in a stronghold, a grunting noise sounding in my ears. I was thrown in the air and placed swiftly on the back of a horse. Vibrations came into my body, making me shake and tremble. Did I dare open my eyes?

I forced my gaze open to see a young man, probably in his twenties, carrying me to the barn on a pale arabian. He didn't look at me, so all I saw was chocolate hair that barely came to his ears. It was messy and his clothes were filthy but his struc- ture was something any girl would drool over. His arms bulged large, his chest heaving with every bounce the horse made.

He came to a slow stop, jumping off and facing me, eyes exhausted. He looked up at me, a smirk on his face. His face was as attractive as his structure. Freckles covered his nose. He had sea blue eyes, full lips, and pink cheeks. Any girl would find him handsome, aside from his wardrobe of course.

I shyly looked at the ground, rocking on my heels. "Thank you," I said with gratitude.

He smiled. "What were you doing? I would strongly advise

against braving the pasture without assistance." He sounded like he had been lounging for hours, not using his voice unless needed. It was a deep tone that left tingles in your stomach.

"I came to visit a horse that I missed an opportunity to ride. I thought I could cross on my own. I promise I won't be making that mistake twice," I apologized.

He shook his head laughing. "It wasn't a problem. I was just wondering why you put yourself in that death trap without any protection." He leaned across the horse, extending his hand.

"Trae, Trae Kipson."

I placed my hand in his and he kissed it gently, letting go of it shyly. I let my hand come back to my side and said my name in reply.

"Amelia."

He smiled. "Amelia? I haven't seen you before, but I've heard your name," he paused, trying to put his finger on it. "The prince saved you didn't he? Now that explains why you put yourself in harm's way. You better not make that a habit; handsome men like us won't always be around to save you." He chuckled at his own joke, waiting to see if I was amused.

I cracked a smile, acknowledging it was a clever and egotistic comment.

"I was shocked by what I saw that day, he has never been that reckless," he concluded.

"So I've been hearing. Wait, you were there?" I inquired, dismounting the horse and landing safely on the ground next to him.

"Absolutely, I never turn away from a fight. I support

Aleron and his decisions entirely. I've been in every battle he has ever fought."

"That is very commendable of you; I imagine Aleron is grateful to have you by his side," I said.

"I hope so! Could I help you find the horse you came for?" he asked.

"Actually, I came to see Kendra. Is she here?"

He shook his head. "She left to visit her ma. She will be gone for a couple days and asked me to watch over the horses. It's different working in the stables. Being a warrior takes hard work, but this . . . this is dirty, disgusting work. I don't know how she handles it!" He pointed to his clothes as an example.

I chuckled. *Now he made sense.* "Maybe I'll come back later then." I started to turn away when Trae stopped me.

"Sure I can't help with anything?" he offered. "I am done with all the chores."

I thought about it. I shouldn't take Aleron's horse without his permission. Besides, Trae wouldn't know how to handle a horse like that if he was just tending to them for a little while. I nodded at his offer.

"You could help me get across the pasture and back to the castle gates. I can manage from there."

He laughed and mounted onto his horse, offering his arm. I laughed too, grabbing it but not having to pull myself up. He did it without effort, like I weighed nothing.

"Hang on; this could be a bumpy ride."

I grasped his shoulders and opened my eyes, watching the stallions and mares zip past as we sprinted to the gates without conflict. He handled the horse like it was the easiest thing. I suppose he was a knight and had some experience riding horses, but it still took me by surprise.

The ride was smoother than he said it would be, hitting an occasionally high bump, but never throwing us off.

He forced the reins back, the horse protesting but finally giving in and letting me topple off with the help of Trae. I straightened out my clothes, making sure nothing had gotten on them to show I went outside.

"Thank you again. I am in your debt," I told him, after seeing everything was spotless. *I've been having to say that a lot since coming here.* He shook his head unpleased.

"No young lady is ever in debt to me. As a knight, helping is what I do best. Besides, we're friends aren't we? It's the least I could do. If anything, I am in debt to you."

I blinked and pondered what he said, scrunching my face.

"Why would you be in debt to me? I didn't do anything but cause chaos for you."

He laughed with enjoyment. "That's where you're wrong. You made my dreary day entertaining by providing action that any man is looking for."

I was stunned at how gentleman-like he was, but did not argue any longer on the subject.

"It was an honor," I chuckled. He slightly leaned down, to indicate a bow. I curtsied slightly.

He held the reins in his hands and threw them up, making the arabian come up on its back heels.

"I hope to see you again, Amelia! Farwell!" he yelled his goodbyes, and took off in the other direction, leaving me alone, laughing with cheer, and finally receiving the merriment I had gone searching for.

CHAPTER 17

One day had passed. Tomorrow my mother would arrive. I had no idea what to do with myself today while I waited for my evening with Aleron. I was fresh out of ideas. My injuries were finally healed and Ezra had been tending to other ill patients among the castle, leaving me alone and restless.

I had gotten dressed and ready for the day, taking more time than I usually do. Without anything else to occupy my time, trying to look perfect was a good way to make up for all the hours left in the day.

After getting myself ready, I decided to go visit Noni. She was always an entertaining person to be around and right now I could use the entertainment.

As I stepped outside into the bright hallway, I couldn't see anyone in sight. The halls were empty. I pushed myself up to the right side of the hallway, my hand trailing its way down the stone, feeling the cold rush through my fingers. I slowly walked down the hall, not in a rush, taking it easy. At least I *was* taking it easy until I heard a familiar voice. The hairs on my arms stood up, my stomach forming into knots. *Aleron.*

I could barely contain my excitement. I knew he was close. He was whispering to someone. I turned around to see if he was behind me, but he was nowhere in sight. I stopped walking, and concentrated on where his voice was located.

". . . you know it's not what you should . . ." I could barely make out what he was saying but I was positive it was ahead of me.

I started walking again, this time I took tiny steps, making sure I made no sound. Aleron's voice sounded concerned and I didn't want to upset him by startling him in any way.

As I got closer, the conversation was easier to understand. I could see a light from the kitchen and two shadows in the room. Two male figures. One was definitely Aleron. The other figure was unfamiliar, I wasn't sure who it was.

I sped up my walk, stopping a couple feet away from the opening. I checked the halls to make sure no one was in sight or watching me. As far as I could see, I was alone.

I sat very still, dead silent and listened.

"Father, it's wrong. It's *all* wrong. I want to change what happened," Aleron whispered.

"You've grown weak, my son. I thought higher of you. I can't believe what you are saying," rebuked a rough voice. *Vincent.*

I crept closer, daring myself to peek through the hinge. I held my breath as I let one eye come close to the wood, my sight hardly being obscured.

Aleron was far away from his father. His father was

looking at Aleron with complete disgust and Aleron stared at the table, not looking up.

Vincent and Aleron looked so much alike, aside from their age. They had the same facial features, except the king had strands of silver peppering his hair and a few wrinkles around the corners of his cold eyes. I knew I shouldn't eavesdrop on royalty or private conversations, I know I wouldn't appreciate such a thing. But my curiosity got the better of me. I continued to listen.

"You don't know her," Aleron murmured.

"And you do? Son, you haven't even had time with her, aside from the ball and your few outings. You cannot tell me you are attached," he hissed.

"But I am. She's different – it's all so different. I didn't expect this to happen," he said back.

The king moved closer to Aleron, gripping his shoulders. His father stared at him, waiting for Aleron to meet his gaze. He slowly lifted his head up, eyes in slits.

"If you grow weak, weaker than you are now, I will take care of it myself. You have lost vision of the true treasure. She is not worth the risk of losing it all," he spat at his son.

"You act like you know what's best for me; you act like what you are doing is for good. You are a conceited, hypocritical, selfish man. You disgust me." Aleron's words were sharp and short. With that, Aleron shoved his father away and started walking to the door.

I didn't have time to react. I began walking backwards, slowly, hoping I could get enough distance to make it appear as if I was just walking the halls.

"Aleron!" Vincent yelled to him. It made me jump and I

stumbled backwards, tripping on the corner of a rug. A loud thud came from my landing. *No!*

Aleron ran out of the kitchen, searching for what made the sound. His eyes found mine and he rushed over to me.

"Amelia, are you all right?" His eyes held deep concern. He reached down and helped me up.

I brushed off my dress and regained my composure, my cheeks going their usual shade of red from embarrassment. "I'm all right. I will eventually stop doing that every time we meet." I tried to humor him and he gave a weak smile. I could tell he was upset.

"I heard someone yell your name and it startled me." I gave a brief smile and turned my head away from him, trying to compose a lie. I had the hardest time lying to Aleron.

He gripped my shoulder, forcing me to look at him. "Did you hear anything besides that?" he asked.

I could see the hurt in his eyes. The answer was yes, but I bit my lip. "No. I was just walking through the halls and heard your name," I lied through my teeth, trying not to crack.

Aleron let out a deep breath, a sigh of relief. "Well, I won't complain about seeing you a few hours earlier than planned. I am looking forward to tonight." He wrapped his arms around me, embracing me. I embraced him back, looking over his shoulder.

The king stepped out of the kitchen and without looking back at us, started walking away, but before he turned the corner, I saw him mutter something under his breath. He took one glance at me and was gone.

~

*T*he day went by too fast after that. Before I knew it, a steady knock came to the door, the one I had been waiting to hear for two days.

The dress that Noni said she would make was securely fitted on my body, the crimson color making my skin flash with every step. I was amazed at the impeccable fit she achieved in such a short amount of time. It didn't have many embellishments, but the silk fabric spoke volumes all on its own. The pearls she lent to me to wear around my neck gleamed when turned toward any light, and my hair lightly tapped my shoulders with every smooth glide I took. I stretched my hand for the door, but found it opening on its own.

Aleron stepped in, matching me with his maroon tunic and fancy leather boots. I learned that each of our outings Noni intentionally would make sure our outfits were coordinated. Her efforts made me smile.

Aleron had a much lighter spirit about him than when we encountered each other earlier. He was a breath of fresh air. His hair was perfectly swept behind his ears, his eyes glowing. I stared in awe at his perfection.

Before I could even greet him, he caught me in a welcoming embrace and lifted my feet off the ground, twirling me round in circles like a child. My head started to spin and my laughs made me shake. He set me properly on the ground but still held my waist so I wouldn't fall over from the dizziness.

"Enter?" I said mockingly, seeing his reaction to his wonderful introduction.

"I couldn't wait for you to open the door. Even a few hours without seeing you was a few hours too long. I needed to see that you were well . . . and still as beautiful as I last saw you," he added. I blushed underneath the hand that he held to my cheek.

Memories of the last time he saw me came back. The conversation he had with his father. It had been weighing heavily on me, lying to Aleron about not overhearing them. I wanted to know what it all meant. I had decided we had a lot of important matters to discuss tonight, when the time was right.

"Are you still worried?" I asked.

He scanned around the room and started to hum and then he opened his mouth, paused and spoke in a hushed tone.

"Not at all. You seem well. Am I correct?" he asked.

I thought about my week. Any falls, any injuries, any problems. The only one that came to mind was my mothers soon-to-be arrival. I cringed. Thinking of his reaction made me want to burst out and cry. If I had any luck left, maybe it would turn out the opposite of what I was expecting, but the odds were unlikely.

I sighed. *Just enjoy every second you are given with him, let whatever happens, happen.* Aleron had noticed me cringe.

"What is it?" he asked, concerned.

"Earlier I embarrassed myself from falling in front of you for the third time. This is the first time I have successfully stood on my feet in your presence." I gave him a playful wink. I could see his worry melt away.

"So yes, you are correct. I am well. More well than I should be," was my honest answer. Aleron bit his lip, staring at me intently. I grew uneasy from his stare, frozen in place.

"Aleron, you're staring," I accused him, shyly turning away.

Aleron caught my arm, pulling me close. "I can't help it if you're stunning, Amelia. I don't know how to focus on anything else," he said in a delighted voice, kissing my cheek.

I looked at him, letting my eyebrows push their way up with hope.

"You could show me the surprise I've been waiting for. Is that distracting enough?" I let my idea be a tempting offer, hoping that it would lead us out the door. My wish came true.

"That is something to consider. Now that you mention it, yes, we should be leaving."

He didn't offer his arm this time, he offered his hand. I took it, smiling. I wanted to pinch myself to make sure that this wasn't my imagination. Since I couldn't pinch myself, I squeezed Aleron's hand tightly and released the pressure it gave. Without a word, he squeezed it back, but he didn't release the pressure, instead he kept no space between us. Letting him lead, hip to hip, arm to arm, we walked down the hallway.

We strode down the halls at a very steady pace and I didn't argue with it. Usually I was wanting to rush, but this time I wanted to go slow and take it all in, hoping it would make time pause for us. I never wanted this happiness to end. I was faced with the agonizing realization that after tonight, it very well could.

I knew people were staring at us, but it didn't bother me and it didn't seem to bother Aleron either. I didn't pay attention to where we were going, I was too distracted by my thoughts, feelings, and walking at the right pace.

Aleron stopped walking but my legs wanted to go on. I came to a sudden halt and studied the room I had entered.

It was dimmer than I thought it would be, but there was still a soft glow in the room. Candles were lined up on tables and shelves, masking the room in a faint light that glimmered. There was a crackling, roaring fireplace a long way in front of me and cushions were set beside it. A short table was at my right side and the smell of soup filled the warm air. The room was quite small for a castle and it seemed like it hadn't been paid very much attention too. But it had a cozy feeling that made it happier than any place in the castle I had seen yet.

I smiled and turned to Aleron, still hand in hand. "This is a wonderful surprise. The most wonderful surprise I've ever had," I declared truthfully. He looked at me with serious eyes.

"Really? The *most* wonderful?" He didn't sound sure of my words.

I sighed with glee. "Why wouldn't it be?" I questioned.

He shrugged, lifting my arms with his, placing them over his shoulders.

"I wanted tonight to be just us, away from watchful eyes. I thought dinner would be nice, since we hadn't done that yet and I assumed the setting would make it that much more private and extravagant," he answered.

"It's lovely. You continue to amaze me with how thoughtful you are, Aleron." I stepped away, taking only his hand, pulling him toward the table. I gathered my dress under my legs making sure the fabric wouldn't wrinkle and gladly looked over the supper.

Lamb was the largest dish, proudly displayed in the middle of the table. There were potatoes, purple carrots, pears in a bowl, manchet in the middle, vegetable soup to my left, and corn on my right. It was a feast fit for more than two people, and knowing Aleron there would be dessert too.

"You didn't have to do all this," I pointed out.

"Of course I didn't, but there are always exceptions, aren't there?" He took a seat, looking at his plate.

I nodded. "I am more than happy to be your exception. However, you are going to make it very difficult for me to ever compete with your thoughtful date ideas."

He smiled. "I am relieved to hear that you want to have more," he said, laughing.

"Now, I don't know about you, but I can't resist the temptation of this food. Shall we eat?" he asked for my permission, his stomach making a quiet rumble.

"Yes, please. Letting this beautiful food get cold and seeing you dying of hunger . . . it's unbearable." I glanced at his stomach as he grasped it with his hand, Aleron blushing for the first time since we had met.

We ate in silence, not wanting to disturb one another's joy in eating such delicious food. I picked up a thick slice of bread as he sipped his blocky soup. I laid the bread on my palm, warming my hand while I quickly broke off a piece and popped it into my mouth, heating my tongue. The bread was soft when I bit into it, something I hadn't expected. In Valteria usually the bread was harder, slightly charred, and I enjoyed the gentleness more than I thought I would, taking another slice without hesitation.

I then ate my soup. The soup was thick and rolled down

my throat with protest, but the feeling didn't stop the fascinating taste. As I swallowed, a hot spice was welcomed on my tongue. Cayenne maybe? I shot my hand forward for the water pitcher, letting the liquid pour only half way into the cup before I started to swig it down in many gulps. The spice became dim but still wandered in my mouth no matter how much I drank.

I dropped the pitcher and looked at Aleron. He stopped eating and stared at me in a mocking smile. I urgently grabbed the cloth on my lap and wiped away the remainder of water droplets on my lips, ignoring his smirk.

I timidly looked away and started eating again; blowing on the soup this time like nothing had happened. I swallowed slowly and the fiery taste came back as fast as it went, making me want to gag, but I held in the pain and resisted grabbing the water, acting like I was just having a moment.

But no matter how long I tried acting normal, Aleron would not remove his eyes or his large growing smirk. I repeated the cycle again, this time having better composure. Aleron's locking gaze didn't flicker as he continued to stare in my direction.

I dropped my spoon and gazed back, hoping that if he saw that I was looking he would stop, but of course he carried on. I finally broke.

"What are you smiling about? I haven't done anything but eat. I see nothing amusing about it," I admitted my thoughts to him without regretting one word.

Aleron kept smiling and after a long moment of the fire crackling he spoke very softly. "I don't know why I'm smiling.

Haven't you noticed that whenever I look at you I *always* smile?" he confessed.

"So you aren't laughing at my struggling attempt to mask how spicy this soup is?" I said, doubting his excuse.

"You think the soup is spicy? I just thought it was my longing stares that were making you look so uncomfortable," Aleron mocked, holding back another laugh.

"You're impossible," I chuckled, pushing the soup to the side.

"Impossibly smitten." He winked, turning back to his soup without hesitation. The spice obviously didn't bother him.

I took the moment to ask a question, one I needed to know before I told him the truth, just for reassurance.

"Aleron, you make me incredibly happy. Happier than I have ever been," I stated, reaching for his hand across the table. He swiftly took it and kissed my wrist.

"I promise that I will continue to make you feel that way," he promised, his eyes full of sincerity. *Here is my chance.*

"Aleron . . . if I was taken away, for any reason at all, would you come after me?" I asked the question with regret, feeling like an imbecile.

The question took him off guard as he pushed his eyebrows together and responded. "I believe you already know the answer." He smiled but saw I was expecting more. I needed a definite answer. After many moments he said what I was waiting for.

"Yes, I would no matter what," he reassured me.

I briefly grinned and intertwined our fingers. I turned back to my plate to focus on eating, not knowing what to say back. I was grateful he didn't push to understand my odd question. He began eating too and his smile never disappeared.

Dessert came sooner than I thought and was hard to consume given the amount of food I had already eaten. Éclairs. The pastry was dripping down my chin, the pudding not making it quite into my mouth. Luckily it was the same for Aleron, pudding spilling from the sides, chocolate smeared across his cheekbone. We finished our Éclairs and finally stood up, wiping away the remains of the delectable mess.

"That was the most exquisite meal I have ever had," I concluded.

He brushed leftover crumbs off his tunic and smiled widely. "I have to agree. We can both thank the chef and pastry boy later if you'd like," he suggested.

"Once again, being quietly thoughtful. It is an amazing quality, Aleron. I can see why you are an example to so many of your people," I said admiringly.

Aleron didn't lose his smile, but his eyes briefly flickered away from mine, almost in shame.

Silence followed my remark but my footsteps broke it. I lingered toward the fireplace, sitting on the cushions. Aleron followed and sat next to me.

I stared at the fire, waiting for time to stop. We had a delightful conversation for what seemed to be hours, holding each other closely as we embraced the fire's warmth. Time showed no hint of retreating and it was a brutal reminder that I was approaching a hard conversation.

I sighed, knowing I had to tell Aleron the truth before it was too late, but my lips would not move. My mind would not work. My heart practically stopped beating. I took in a deep breath and thought about what I was going to say, *again*. I went through it over and over, changing something each time from the original way I had rehearsed it.

Our conversation had finally died down into silence and I knew I could break it. But I waited to see if Aleron had anything to say before I spoke, not wanting to ruin the precious moment.

What will he say once he knows? What will he do? Will I regret this? Should I wait for my mother to come and just play along? Maybe I shouldn't tell him, maybe I'll run. It might be easier that way.

Last minute questions and worries filtered into my mind and hesitation became something natural. I had lost the courage to tell him the truth. But I *had* to, no matter how much I didn't want to.

I felt his fingers tickling my wrist, his breath in my hair. It was perfect. I wanted this every day for the rest of my life. I knew that the reality of getting there had to start by facing the truth before we could move forward.

With that in mind, I finally gained the resolution I needed to begin the difficult conversation. I started out with a question that didn't have anything to do with confessing the truth.

"Why did you pick this room? I haven't seen it before."

He smiled with relief in his face at the sound of my voice.

"This room is hidden. It's far away from everyone and everything. Many people know of its existence but they never disturb me here. This is usually where I spend my time if I'm not at the beach. I found it helps me think. Just as it did for the previous prince. He had many great ideas in this room."

My eyes brightened and my heart lifted. If this was where my father had great ideas maybe some of his luck would rub off on me and make my situation go away.

"Which prince?" I queried.

"Faris Amena," he whispered.

"Tell me about him?" I continued, realizing his unintentional conversation was leading perfectly into what we needed to discuss.

Aleron nodded. "I only know stories. I was born right after he left for Valteria. Ezra is really the only Amena I have gotten to know. Based on stories my mother and Ezra told me, he would have been a great king. My father, as harsh as it may sound, is nothing compared to him. I can't help but wonder if Faris would be disappointed in the way my father rules. How I rule . . ." he announced, a slight sadness in his voice.

I took his hand and stroked it with solace. "That is simply not true. You are more like Faris then you think. I know he would be incredibly proud of a successor such as you for Praseria." I silently let him soak in my truthfulness, waiting for him to ask me more about it.

Aleron squinted. "You knew him?" he wondered, seeming bewildered by the connection. *Here it goes.*

"I knew him better than anyone did." I flinched at the pain of the memory of his funeral, of him being gone.

"You act like he's dead," Aleron said with humor.

I looked up at him with sorrow, trying not to be offended by his innocent humor.

"He is," I silently said, barely even a whisper.

Aleron looked shocked, not making a sound. He didn't speak or move for many moments. My heart was racing rapidly in my chest, my eyes trying to hide the panic I felt surging through my body.

"But how did you know him? You are younger than I am, it's simply impossible that you have met him here in Praseria. How do you know he has passed away?" he inquired to know.

I took in many deep breaths to respond truthfully despite how much my mind was telling me otherwise. "Aleron, can't you see it? I am . . . I am his da–" before I could finish the words someone burst through the door in panic. It was Lottie, her chest heaving. We both sat up straight in surprise and Aleron squinted in her direction.

"Your majesty, I apologize for the disruption but the king and queen are away tending to some business in Lokali. They have an unexpected guest, one that is not willing to wait for their return," she gasped. Aleron didn't look worried but held complete ease.

"Who is at the gate?" he wondered.

Lottie was gasping rapidly now but sputtered out the words. "Laerina Amena, Queen of Valteria," she croaked.

My heart stopped and I looked down, my eyes closing shut, my face turning red. My breathing came to a halt. What was I to do? I wasn't ready! She was a day earlier than expected.

Aleron looked at me, shock surrounding his beautiful eyes. I let his arms grasp mine; I wanted to collapse into them, but resisted with all my strength.

"Thank you; please assure the queen I shall be with her in a moment."

Lottie rushed out of the room, feet pounding behind her.

I wanted to cry, I wanted to take Aleron away with me.

What was she doing here so early? I hadn't told Aleron the truth yet.

"What is the matter? Everything is going to be fine, I promise." He tried to reassure me, observing me hold back a sob.

I shook my head back and forth. "No, it's not. It's all going to be ruined. You and I . . ." I cried. Why didn't I just go home when I had the chance? Why did I make myself miserable?

Aleron took me in his arms, letting my head lay against his chest. After a few moments, he shifted me away from his body, my crying not stopping.

"Lia, I don't understand what you mean and I want you to explain everything, but we need to hurry before the queen gets angry. You can come with me. I promise we will continue our conversation right where we left off," he said.

He stood up and pulled me to my feet. I reached for the fireplace for support, not sure what to do. Aleron wrapped his arms around me, holding me close.

"It's all right, Lia. Don't cry." He lightly kissed me on the cheek, trying to soothe me.

Aleron took my waist and helped me over to the other end of the room, holding the door open while soothing my worries. We were half way down the hall and my crying slowed. I had to admit the truth before it became a wreck, before I lost the chance to have him hear my side of the story.

"Aleron, please wait! I have to tell you what I was going to say," I insisted, trying to pull him back.

"There isn't time. After. I can't keep her waiting," he told me. He spoke like we had all the time in the world, when truly we had a slim chance of seeing each other ever again.

I couldn't stop him; I considered blurting it out before we got there but the hallways were filled with servants and maids, the privacy factor to discuss the matter, gone. I held it in, discouraged and full of fear. I cowardly hoped he was right, that it would all be okay and that we would have time to talk afterwards. It seemed all I could do was pray and I didn't stop praying until I had to.

We came to the entrance of the room, Aleron holding my waist tightly, my arm wrapped around his back. Since all seemed doomed I might as well enjoy my last moments with him.

I stopped at the entrance and turned to him. "Aleron, I have to say something important." I choked back a tear, holding my ground.

"What is it?" He brushed his hand over my cheek, the tingling sensation he emits being left behind.

"I've fallen in love with you." I looked down, holding my breath for his response to my confession.

He tilted my chin up, his eyes keeping hold on mine. The blue reflection in his eyes danced as he showed incalculable joy at my words. He smiled his charming crooked smile.

"I feel slightly robbed that I didn't get to say it first," he mocked.

I laughed at his comment, not expecting it to happen that way either.

"But your courage, it's just one of the things I love about you. *I love you*, Amelia," he whispered the simple words that were left ringing in my ears. *He always knows exactly what to say.* He couldn't have created a more perfect moment for me to hold onto after all of this was over, before entering the trap that I was about to proceed into. All he wanted was to make me feel safe and secure, and that is exactly what he accomplished.

He proceeded to gift me with a gentle kiss, leaving a warm feeling in my heart, one I would treasure always.

Finally, the moment wouldn't be delayed a second more. Securing his hand in mine, we entered into the silent room, where everyone waited for my long return.

CHAPTER 18

*M*ore people were in the room than I had expected. Dozens of maids and servants lined the walls. I was surprised to see townsfolk as well among the group. They must have seen my mother approaching and came to watch the unexpected meeting.

I started to spot familiar faces of my friends. I first noticed Noni who stood with Simon by the doors as they held no expressions toward us. Trae looked addled and had his hand readily placed on his sword. Terris was nibbling at his thumbs. I saw Lottie, standing to the side of Laerina and my body went ice cold and rigid as I could feel her stare burning into my skin. I tried to move my focus elsewhere, hoping to not give away our familiarity.

Faces of interest kept moving to the enemy and back to Aleron. Some eyes scowled at the queen, others looked to their prince in panic. Only a few faces looked at me – Noni looking worried, Lottie looking confused and out of breath.

Trae didn't move his eyes away from me, no smile, almost like he knew what they came for.

But one stood out from all of them. Ezra. Tucked away in the back of the room, keeping out of the sight of my mother. I locked my attention on him, finding comfort that he was there. He knew what was happening and continued to watch me. I tried to understand his expression but I couldn't tell what his eyes were communicating. Run? Speak? It seemed he couldn't move but his eyes had become narrow while looking at me, depression crossing his face. Yet I still felt I could trust he would be my friend afterwards and I could sense he would want me to come and visit. *If they would let me come visit.*

Laerina stood in the middle of the floor, eyes infuriated, mouth quivering. Damien stood beside her, lividity still in his eyes. Dirt was smudged on his aging face that suddenly looked like a man and no longer a boy. Ajax stood by my mother's side, sword in hand, eyes narrowed toward me. The one thing I did not expect I would see was right in front of me. Hassan.

He was as brave and courageous as the first night we met, not bearing any smudge of dirt or sign of exhaustion from their journey. He was holding tightly to his sword as well, his eyes fixed on Aleron holding me smugly as we glided closer to them.

I had successfully pushed thoughts of Hassan away over the last few weeks. I felt horrible not thinking of how this would affect him and our friendship. What about Freira? Would she be angry with me too?

I looked at Hassan who briefly flickered his sweet gaze in my direction. I saw that he was not enraged like everyone else was. He held an expression that made me feel even guiltier: dismayed, appalled and slightly offended. His eyes slightly squinted as he looked at me and I couldn't help but give him an apologetic stare back. What was I going to say to him? He sighed and looked at Aleron now, in a prepared stance for whatever was going to come.

Aleron came to a halt several feet away from the queen, nudging me slightly behind him, using himself as a shield. He bowed slightly, his face composed, the prince in him shining through. Laerina scoffed and jabbed her finger toward him, completely losing all self-control and manners.

"I have come for your full admission of guilt," she bellowed loudly for the whole group of people to hear. Her yell echoed through the room, vibrating the walls. Everyone in the room stepped back, terrorized at her surprising approach toward the prince. No cordial exchanges, straight to business.

Aleron looked at Laerina, cocked his head to the side and tried to act perplexed. He didn't let her anger fuel any emotions in him; he was trying to take control of the situation by not appearing to be fazed.

"Queen Laerina, it is a pleasure to meet you. I am Aleron Hadway, Prince of Praseria. I suggest we move this discussion to a less public format," Aleron encouraged kindly, ignoring her comment. His calm demeanor only fueled her anger more. Laerina growled at him, stepping forward.

"You've crossed a line. It wasn't enough for you to attack my kingdom, *my people*, but you kidnapped my daughters too. Do you deny what you have done? Or shall I say more? I assure you, *Prince Aleron*, I have much more to say and I do not have any intention on withholding it from the public eye," she exclaimed.

Ajax stepped forward, pressuring Aleron to quickly respond. Aleron didn't let himself become flustered as he still attempted to take control of the situation.

"It's true. I was trying to make a point without harming your people, out of courtesy. A characteristic you didn't spare for mine. If you are here for admissions, how about your own. Do you confess to burning our land, leaving my people almost nothing to eat?" Aleron said his words calmly, showing no sign of panic, leaving everyone in the room comforted by his honesty. Even I was surprised by his blunt response, it was refreshing to see he wasn't trying to play any games.

Laerina faltered before proceeding to speak. She shook her head in retort. "I do not recall such a thing," she insisted.

I gasped and she looked at me directly, surpassing Aleron as my shield, her glare penetrating right through him. I wanted to say that I saw it, I wanted to say that she was a liar, but this was for Aleron to handle, not me.

"My people suffered greatly by your hand. You left Praseria and other kingdoms with no choice but to retaliate. If it is truly necessary to remind you of your actions, I would be happy to show you proof," Aleron stated collectively and kindly.

Laerina laughed. "Proof? Nothing was done! The accusation of burning your land will be a conversation I will have with the king and queen, not their substitute," she insulted, trying to make him lose his temper.

"Understood. You are welcome to wait for their return. If there is nothing else I can help you with then, I will dismiss myself," Aleron said, clenching his jaw as he tried to not seem irritated by her comment.

"We aren't finished. I am not leaving until I get what I came here for," she replied, stopping him from turning away.

He sighed, obviously becoming irritated. "What did you come here for?" he asked.

"My daughter. Once you return her to me, I will leave in peace," she concluded loudly.

Aleron looked confused, as he should. I felt his hold tighten as he grasped my hand. "I apologize but you have wasted your time coming here. Your daughter escaped days ago. No one has seen her since," he said.

"Yes, one of my daughters escaped. Must I remind you of the other?" Laerina mocked his facial expression, trying to make him the fool.

I noticed Ezra's face sweating, sorrow feeling his eyes.

Aleron gaped widely. "Do not mock me any further. I held captive only *one* of your daughters. I will kindly ask again, is there something else you want?" He scrunched up his eyes in suspicion.

Laerina was becoming impatient, her foot tapping the solid ground. The anticipation was building for everyone. I noticed Hassan staring at the rug. Damien tried locking eyes with Aleron and I buried my face into his back, trying to be invisible.

"Stop trying to play witless larks on me, boy. Hand over my daughter; it would be very unfortunate for your parents to be welcomed home to an incident." She cocked her head to the side, challenging him.

I started to feel heat burning inside me. I wish they

wouldn't have let her in, I wish they could've kept her out of the castle. I shot a pleading stare at Damien but he didn't even glance in my direction. *Allene, you speechless coward, say something! Anything!*

"I am not intimidated by your threats Lareina, and I am not playing *witless larks* on you. I will not tolerate this conversation any longer." His voice for the first time sounded annoyed. I could feel his arms slightly shaking. Aleron was angry. I had never seen Aleron angry.

Laerina exploded, "Do you think I'm blind? Do you believe I have forgotten who my own daughter is?"

Aleron was not offended but more provoked every second she spoke, his patience running thin. "Dear queen, I question if you are in the right state of mind! Enlighten me, who *do you* believe your daughter is so we can straighten out your confusion," he spat back each word, his hands now in fists.

Laerina rolled her eyes, her temper somehow being contained as she realized she had broken him. "The young lady you are embracing with such nauseating affection. Allene Amena, princess of Valteria," she said each word with an unpleasant tone and didn't hold back her disgust at the sight.

Aleron's gape became larger in seconds. He turned to look at me, letting his guard down as he was searching my eyes for answers. He grasped my arm and brought me parallel to his side, his protection of me diminished

"You think Amelia is your daughter? Do you really think I am that much of a fool? She is a Praserian. She bears no resemblance to *you*, in any form for that matter," he spoke with conviction, insulting her character.

He obviously pushed Laerina over the edge as she boldly spoke directly to Aleron.

"Amelia?" she scoffed. "Very creative, Allene. It seems my daughter knows how to survive in the enemy's home. You believed a complete falsehood. We may look nothing alike but she is my daughter. Her father is Faris Amena. Your old prince," Laerina declared.

Aleron's eyebrows went up, his head shaking back and forth with disbelief. I could see the hurt flood his eyes and my heart drowned at the sight.

Aleron lightened his grasp, stepping away from me. The way he looked at me now made it obvious; he could finally see it. He was trembling. I wondered if he knew I was going to tell him. I wondered what he felt. I wondered if this was the last time I would see him.

He tightened his eyes together, his lips slightly parted. His hands clenched into fists, his eyes finally opening slightly to infuriatingly stare me down. But even with fury shading his eyes, you could see a hint of marvel. I knew he didn't know how to feel, but I could also tell he was thinking of his promise as his rage slightly subsided. He was confused, he was hurt, and I hated that I was the cause. I looked directly at Ezra, trying to find some spare hope.

He had turned away, not wanting to witness what would happen. I saw Hassan also wearing the same look, almost smiling at what he just saw. No one had anything to say and an uncomfortable silence fell over the room. I meekly said the first word that would break the impenetrable silence.

"Aleron, I tried to tell you," I barely whispered, stepping toward him, trying to block out everyone else in the room.

Aleron was not interested in looking at me, obviously feeling betrayed by the news of my identity.

I turned to look at Damien, worry crossing his face. Should I tell them what happened? How I wouldn't have been in this situation if my best friend hadn't insisted I sneak out? Or should I be the bigger person, letting this one slip to attempt to restore our friendship? I wouldn't fair-weather my friend, even if it did provide me some temporary mercy.

I bounced my eyes off everyone. I felt so alone in a room full of people that all loved me . . . at one point at least. I cowardly looked down, not knowing what to do.

Laerina finally whispered something to Ajax and started to turn toward the door. "We are done here," she bellowed, not turning back.

Hassan followed after Laerina. Ajax and Damien were coming my way, preparing to take hold of me. I wanted to run but knew it wasn't worth it. I knew now that I was, without a doubt, never welcome here again. I saw Noni crying and Simon helping to calm her down. Trae was shaking his head and Terris's mouth was wide open.

Ajax seized my right arm, grasping it tightly, still holding the sword in the other hand. Damien took my other arm, but lightly braced it, his eyes soft. Almost like a thank you for not giving away what he had done and sorry for doing it in the first place.

Ajax started out of the room, pulling me along without concern that he might be hurting me. We came to the door and I twisted my head back in the direction of Aleron. He didn't hesitate or tell them to stop, he didn't move a muscle. I know he wanted to protect his people, or maybe he was absolutely disgusted with me. I let the promise he made to me, about never letting me be taken away, that he would come after me, that he loved me, echo in my mind. It was all I had to hold on to, the foolish hope that he would keep his word.

His fist was still clenched but he locked eyes with me for one second, seeing us both shed one last tear before everything we had was gone.

CHAPTER 19

The smell of fire was unwelcoming in the blend of scorching air, yet it still swarmed around the tightly enclosed tent, releasing intense heat and foul smells.

I replayed the last few hours in my head. My mother had heard my whole story and how the mishap all began but she refused to believe that what I said was the truth. Only two people believed me – Damien and Risa – who actually witnessed what had happened.

I was surprised to find Risa waiting on horseback outside the gates. She didn't want to enter inside the castle, afraid to be held captive again or make the situation worse. She and some guards hid in the trees, waiting for our return. Her concerned eyes held deep pity as she saw me coming toward her direction.

Ajax and Damien did not release me until we arrived at the camp. Ajax had told Damien he could handle me without extra assistance but Damien hesitated to move. I was grateful he did. Ajax would have thrown me into the tent aggressively, knocking me out on the hard floor if Damien weren't there to stop him.

I was not permitted to leave the tent, and constant watch was being kept over me to make sure I didn't attempt to. We would camp for a couple days as everyone regrouped and Laerina plotted her next choice of action.

My mother hadn't talked to me otherwise. After hearing my story, she treated me like a prisoner. She refused to be sympathetic about the situation. I was doing the same thing she had done with my father; pursuing a "forbidden" love. It was beyond hypocritical but she wouldn't admit it for even a moment.

I was glad to see she let Risa and Damien visit as they pleased. They were the only company willing to approach my tent and actually be kind to me. Damien had apologized for his horrible behavior and I gladly accepted it, immensely happy our friendship still existed. I tried to explain to him everything that happened and both Risa and Damien seemed to believe me. It was comforting knowing I could justify my actions, even just a little.

I laid down on the blanket that was placed in my tent, giving off an even harder feeling than the ground. I turned over to my stomach, my back aching. I couldn't help but think of Aleron's face whenever I was sitting in silence.

Flashbacks came into my mind and quickly faded away, being replaced by another wonderful memory. I remembered our first dance; our encounter at the beach, all of our conversations. I thought of the dinner, tasting the soup in my mouth at the thought of it, his smile making my heart jolt. I remembered the first time I saw him. I thought of when he confided in me about his family dynamic, his sweet concern for his people. I remember him saying "I love you." His words rang in my head. I repeated them, trying to realize that they still might be true, however, I doubted more than I believed.

One memory I swore to never think about passed through my mind and no matter how much I tried to push it out, it refused to budge. Our last time seeing each other. The last second we locked eyes. The shock he held. The memory kept playing back and every time new tears came with it.

~

I heard the guards gossiping about me in the evenings. Discussion of my alleged betrayal, how disappointed they were, and how they despised me more than ever. They intentionally would say it loud enough for me to hear. Every time a cruel saying came out of their mouth, it made me weep, knowing that I could have stopped this from occurring. I was a terrible princess for Valteria and everyone believed it. Even *I* believed it.

Ajax was commenting on my behavior, tears splattered over my face when I heard him pause for a brief moment. He stopped gossiping about me as someone approached him, speaking softly.

"Proceed." Then his conversation began again, this time farther away, barely in ear shot.

My tent entrance slightly moved, showing a tall shadow, bulky arms, and a beautiful structure. I cleared away tears with my hand, trying to catch my breath and compose my face. I was grateful for the lack of light in my tent at that moment.

I propped up my elbow, helping me get into a sitting position. My eyes were closed and when I opened them, I was astounded to see him.

Hassan sat next to me, eyes in pain, distress displayed on his attractive face.

I fidgeted with my hands and tried to stay calm. One tear leaked through my eyes, but I didn't care. I let it proceed slowly down, reaching my chin and pouring off into Hassan's outstretched hand. He closed his hand softly and brought it away from my face, more tension coming over him.

I heard Hassan take in a breath of air and meet me on the ground, now facing each other. Then I listened to his low level whispers, trying to keep his voice out of earshot of the guards. "I hate seeing you like this. It's not right," Hassan muttered, leaning in a little closer so I could discern his words.

I crossed my legs and brought them to my chest, letting my arms wrap around them in a comfort that didn't cease my crying. I didn't respond to him. What was I to say? I am so sorry I completely forgot you even existed and made a horrible mistake, how can you forgive me? He understood that I was speechless so he took the liberty of filling in the silence.

"Can I help in any way? What will make you happy again?" He wiped another tear from my eye. I took in many breaths, finally my sobs coming to an end. Hassan waited patiently for my response as I pulled myself together, another admirable quality he bestowed.

"Can you get me out of here for even just a few moments? I loathe being confined to a stuffy tent," I confirmed.

Hassan looked through a slit in the tent toward Ajax and back to me. "That might not be possible at the moment," Hassan said with a pitiful stare.

I sighed. "I assumed as much," I huffed wistfully.

He let out a long breath, really thinking about what to say. "Allene, I'm sorry about everything that happened. I know I could've prevented it if I would've just trie-," I stopped him, letting one hand go, letting it cover his mouth gently.

"No, I apologize. Hassan, I don't know what else to say but that." I looked down.

Hassan tilted my head up, smiling warmly. "You don't have to say anymore. But I want you to be happy; I want to see your gorgeous smile. How can I make that happen?" Hassan teased, his flirting tying my stomach into knots, reminding me of the fondness I felt towards him. *I can't believe I had forgotten about him.*

I sighed. I was mulling over how Hassan could help, thinking of what I missed that could make me happy. Then I remembered why I had forgotten so much in the first place.

Aleron. I missed Aleron the most. I missed Noni's outbursts and amusement. I missed feeling like I was wanted. I needed Ezra's advice. I needed to smell the flowers again. I wanted to hear Terris talk in terms about baking and cooking that I didn't understand; I needed to gag on the chef's soup. I wanted to dance and let everything that I worried about be swept away. I needed friendship. I needed them. Without much consideration, I vented all my burdens of longing to Hassan.

"I *need* them. I need their comfort; I need their friendship and acceptance, their respect. That's all I need," I whispered the truth.

Hassan looked displeased. His jaw went slack and we sat for many moments staring at one another. Finally, Hassan spoke, but in a tone and answer I didn't expect coming.

"We barely know each other but I can say that I have seen how your sister and Damien treat you. What have they been doing then in your eyes? They haven't given you comfort, they haven't given you acceptance or friendship, they haven't given you any of that, ever?" he asked, astonished and wounded by my harsh words.

I shook my head. It came off wrong. I tried to fix what I had said, realizing my error. "No, it's just . . . I don't know how to explain it. It's different. Hassan, you don't know how it feels being rejected by those around you your entire life. Being called an enemy and then finally finding some place that you're accepted. I felt connected there. Imagine being taken away from that new reality and ending up in a smelly tent with even more rejection than before, feeling like an imbecile." I admitted my feelings and thoughts with no happiness lingering in my voice.

He shook his head, biting his lip, not knowing what to say next. "Allene, you left Damien, Risa and me feeling utterly hopeless. We don't know what else to do to make *you* happy. More importantly, we can't comprehend what was so awful that made you feel compelled to leave Valteria in the first place."

"I didn't leave, I was mistakenly taken," I said in defense.

"Exactly. You were taken by accident. Risa was kidnapped

intentionally. I don't understand how you can claim these glorious feelings toward these people, toward Aleron, when their intentions were malicious at heart. We, on the other hand, haven't stopped worrying about your well-being ever since you went missing."

His words made me go silent. I was still in awe at my complete selfishness that somehow I still hadn't learned from. He was right and I knew it. I felt horrible. *What had I done?*

I clenched my teeth, my heart drooping, feeling like it was taken and leaving my insides vacant, without any feeling at all.

"Hassan, I cannot describe how awful I feel for the way I have treated all of you. You deserve so much more. I hadn't even thought, I was just . . ." I shook my head and finally released it, letting it hang low. He brought it up, scooting closer, letting me fall into his chest while he stroked my arm.

No sobs broke through, only whimpers and regret. Hassan tried to hush me, but nothing could stop the guilt I felt.

I was sore from holding back sobs, a burning sensation building in my throat. I gave up in a desolate relinquish. Hassan's voice was nice to hear rather than my galling, aching cries that didn't help anyone. He tried to steer the conversation in a new direction.

"We haven't talked since our parting at the Gala. I want you to know that I liked your façade of being Amelia." I heard him hold back a snicker. I could feel a smile emerge from my lips from the reminder of that night. I had grown so used to the idea of being Amelia that I had almost forgotten that the Gala, my time with Hassan, was where it all began.

"Damien came up with it. I can't take any of the responsibility."

"He was always condoning mischievous scenarios. Can I tell you a secret?" Hassan asked with slight hesitation in his voice.

I nodded my head against his muscular chest as I tried to hide how much I enjoyed my given situation at the moment.

"I knew your identity when we were at the Gala."

Hassan's words took me by surprise, a million questions coming to the surface.

"You did? How?" I asked in astonishment.

"Not that your disguise wasn't convincing, but you were the only person with blue eyes at that Gala. Aside from that, Damien had told me all about you. I'm ashamed to admit I know more about you than you probably realize. I feel like I know you."

I processed this new piece of secrecy that explained more of what had gone on that night. It explained the sudden urgency from Damien for me to attend the Gala. It didn't explain however why Hassan agreed to Damien's shenanigans.

"Wait, you knew I would be there that night?" I asked, pulling away slightly to observe his response.

"I didn't know Amelia would be, but I knew Allene would," he said timidly. He continued, "Damien had written me letters about his best friend for years. He didn't tell Freira much. He was afraid she would get the wrong idea. I hope it doesn't bother you that my intentions of attending the Gala, partly resulted from my interest in you."

I let Hassan's confession sink in. He was honest, and it was a quality that I appreciated more than ever at the moment. I could trust him and I took reassurance that I had someone I could rely on. What made it even better, is that person being Hassan. I could feel the repetition of butterflies that I experienced at the Gala. He was an unexpected safe haven.

"It doesn't bother me at all. In fact, I am extremely flattered. I wish I could convey how much that means to me that you would do that for me. I feel silly that I lied to you about who I was when we first met. It seems I've had a record of that as of late." The constant pressure to lie the last few weeks, in Valteria and Praseria, to everyone I met, had become exhausting. My thoughts immediately veered back to Aleron, along with the pain associated with it.

Hassan could see the burden return, his efforts for light conversation sent to a halt. He wrapped an arm around me, squeezing me close as if to take away the weight I could feel inside.

"Allene, I am relieved that you are safe and out of that man's vicious hold. I am so sorry that you were put through that," he declared.

"It didn't feel vicious . . . it *wasn't*. It's all confusing when I look back on it."

"I don't mean to overstep or voice my opinion, but from an outsider's perspective, it seems a lot like lust. I can imagine that could cause some unresolved feelings and tension," Hassan whispered softly, as if he spoke above a certain level that I would be offended by his bluntness.

As refreshing as it was to be speaking so candidly, I became defensive. My feelings for Aleron were still there, despite all the conflict. It was too soon to let go and give up on something that felt so right. "For some it may seem that way," was all I could say in response to his choice words.

Hassan had pulled me to the side, gazing directly at me as he approached the sensitive topic once again. "Do you think you love him?" he asked, a slight sound of disappointment taking over his voice.

I didn't want to say the words out loud, seeing that Hassan did not approve of my feelings. I briefly nodded in response. Hassan sighed slightly, his posture growing taller as he continued with his lecture.

"Allene, everyone has a first love. First love isn't always everlasting love. I speak from experience," Hassan said surely.

"But not every love story is the same," I protested against his point.

"You're right, they're not. But this love story that you have with Aleron was built on a foundation of deception and lies, with intents other than progressing in your relationship. From what I could see, he wasn't seeking love, he was seeking power. Do you think that is what everlasting love consists of?"

Hassan's voice didn't pose the question to make me feel foolish, but seeing things from his perspective made my brain catch up to my heart and that brought a rude awakening.

"Aleron, isn't power hungry. He loves me. He promised he would come for me." I tried to convince myself more than Hassan. He wasn't going to indulge in my fantasy.

"It seems a little too good to be true. Doesn't it seem to have happened quite fast? How many moments have you had with him? You were in Praseria for a mere few weeks. I don't say this to hurt you more, but to ensure that you won't be hurting worse in the long run." His voice wasn't raised but his tone cut through the hot air, piercing my heart.

Hassan had gently reached for my hand, holding it gently as he noticed the shock that flooded my face. I tried to prepare to answer rationally and logically. My head dropped to my chest, not wanting to believe anything he said. Once again, he filled in the dry silence.

"Allene, there is more out there for you. There is more than Aleron, more than Praseria. You can find what you are looking for but you need to allow yourself time to experience other opportunities. I hope that one day you could possibly consider me as one." Hassan's gaze was one with mine, taking away my flurry of emotions for a brief moment to only feel happiness.

How could this be real? Hassan was collected, he was observant, he felt wise. I wanted to listen to him, to let go. Logically, he was right, and for the first time since I left Praseria I felt a sense of hope that the future held more for me than I was allowing myself to see.

"Think about what I said, Allene. You can depend on me, for whatever you need."

I didn't know what to say. I noticed a smile returning to my face, not being able to discern the feelings that were coming alive. He had left me speechless and I could see that he knew I needed assistance in knowing the direction to go from here.

"Sleep well," he whispered, loosening his grip as he hesitantly started backing away. He bowed low to the ground and started to turn to go.

"Hassan, wait." I stood up and approached him timidly.

He was slightly perplexed by my resistance to him leaving. I let my feelings take control of the moment as I kissed his cheek lightly, feeling his face turn warm underneath my lips.

"Thank you, for everything. You are always welcome to come back. In fact, I would be delighted if you did. Good-night," I whispered, hugging him close.

Hassan grinned shyly but proudly, exiting with a smile. Finally, in quite some time, I had done something right.

⁓

The early morning sun was blocked from my view, the tent defending any sign of light. The discussion Hassan and I had kept me up almost half the night, thinking of what he said.

Was he right about Aleron? After all that has happened, could I find it in myself to really love someone other than Aleron? I still felt bound to him, part of him, like nothing could tear me away. The feelings I felt for Hassan last night seemed different, but they were undoubtedly real. Was the potential for new opportunities truly there, possibly with Hassan?

I was mesmerized in my thoughts as I watched a small black ant make its way into my tent and successfully find a crumb of leftover bread that I had no appetite for from the night before. I was fascinated with how quickly the little ant had packed the meal on its back and scurried to the door. I was always amazed at the examples ants made. Being able to carry double their weight and being one of the smallest insects in such a large world, I was always in shock how they survived.

At that moment I drew a new sense of inspiration from the humble ant. I needed to handle a load that felt like double my weight and endure the world around me. If a tiny insect could do it, then I surely could.

A rustle came into my heated tent, making me jolt up right at the shock of fresh air, my heart pounding. Sunlight seeped through the tent flap, revealing Ajax standing in front of me, his face more than serious.

"The queen has asked for you. She wants to speak with you right away. I shall escort you." He offered a hand to help me up. I scratched my eyes at the sudden light and soon took his hand, stumbling backwards from the tingling in my legs. Ajax put a hand behind my back and pushed me up. Rudely, he took his hand away, placing it behind his back.

"I am supposed to escort you safely. Watch your step," he barked, not waiting for my comment, but tugging me out of the tent, my feet straining to keep up.

Trees surrounded the camp, but not many. Few leaves were left on the bare branches, insects having no interest in the surroundings. The ground contained very little green. It had more rocks, dirt, branches and bark than lush grass. Tents formed a large square where logs were rolled into place for seating. A campfire was in the middle, pots and pans on the side from a recently cooked breakfast, leaving a mixture of spices and foods to smell in the warm air, unable to determine the specific dishes from the amalgamation of scents.

The sun peered over the mountains, the sky dull without

clouds. The air was somewhat colder outside, but the sun was pushing it aside with persistence.

Risa was seated on the nearest log, Damien sitting next to her. Hassan sat on a tree stump to the right of them, eating eggs, cheese, dried fruit, and buttered biscuits. Risa and Damien were just finishing up.

Risa craned her neck toward me smiling widely, something anyone could expect, but her smile helped a grin emerge from me as well. Hassan briefly smiled, straightening his back and unfolding his legs, sitting properly at my entrance. Damien stood up and hopped over to me, plate in hand.

"Allene! Nice to see you out of your tent for a moment. Breakfast is delicious, I cooked it myself. Well, most of it anyway. The biscuits were leftovers and the dried fruit . . . and the cheese, but the eggs were all me. There's a plate ready for you next to Hassan and extras in the pan. Help yourself, there's plenty. I don't know what you ate in Praseria but you look like you could use seconds." Damien patted my shoulder and headed off in the other direction to clean his plate.

I laughed at his comment, happily realizing our old friendship was certainly back and that the boyish version of Damien was still held within him. It made our previous two encounters in Praseria practically disappear, reminding me that true friendship always wins out in the end. I hoped we wouldn't have to go through those feelings of anger toward one another ever again. Damien meant too much to me to jeopardize that.

Ajax tightened his hold on my arm, faltering and considering whether or not to let me go. Hassan had his eyes in slits, flashing them to my arm, turning red.

"Ajax, stop hurting her. You've already accomplished enough with your shameful and imbecile comments. Let your princess eat her meal." Hassan sounded smug sitting on his stump, not worried what might come next from the knight.

I sighed when Ajax let go of my arm, my pale color returning slowly, the pain withering away. Ajax eyed Hassan for a brief moment, Hassan returning the stare without any sign of worry. Ajax huffed and stepped back from me, finally turning away, infuriated at Hassan's unexpected outburst.

I took long strides toward Hassan, taking a seat where my plate lay. The temptation of food was strong as my stomach grumbled. The smell was too sweet to ignore. As punishment, the last few days I have been graced with having vegetables, oatmeal, and cheese. Compared to all that, this was a delight.

"Thank you for that." I returned his wonderful outburst with gratitude.

I grabbed my plate, retrieving the fork and stuffing the eggs in my mouth, it was one of the best meals I had had in days. Damien was right, they were delicious. Better than I thought they would be, as I was quite surprised to see that he could cook.

"My pleasure. Anything I can do to help," was his happy response as he watched me closely.

"These eggs are amazing," I told them of my thoughts, taking another heap full.

"I guess men have some talents that we didn't know of," Risa grinned brightly, mocking them.

Hassan chortled. "We have many more Miss Risa, so many you couldn't imagine all of them. Keep that in mind."

Risa raised her eyebrows. "I have no doubts whatsoever."

Hassan smiled at her retort. I viewed the area, seeing no sight of Laerina, who summoned me from my gruesome tent prison.

"Where's mother?" I asked Risa, looking around again, making sure I wasn't blind and missed her presence.

Risa laughed, finishing the last of her eggs, setting it to the side. "In her tent. She hasn't come out since yesterday morning. I was surprised when I heard she wanted to see you."

"Is something wrong?" I questioned my sister, eating my biscuit.

Hassan answered for Risa. "No one knows. Sometimes we can hear her whisper to herself, other times she cries. I personally suspect she is suffering from anxiety and panic attacks," he explained.

I nodded, shoving the last of the biscuit into my mouth, having trouble gulping it down. The biscuit had me gagging in protest, asking me not to proceed any further.

"Water?" Hassan offered a cup of water and I took it, not seeing if someone had already taken a sip out of it. The water helped the sticky biscuit make its way down my throat, leaving me unharmed but gasping.

I looked up at Hassan, trying to catch some air to heal my sputtering. "Thank you," I said the words more clearly after every breath of air took in.

"Nonsense, I don't want you choking on my watch." He smiled.

I looked to Risa, trying not to think of the conversation we had the night before as I saw her inquiring about our exchange. I stood up, the blood rushing through my body, swaying me. Before I had the chance to catch my balance, Hassan had made his way to me, offering his arm.

I frowned. I had become a damsel in distress in his eyes, and it seemed to only happen in front of him and Aleron.

The realization made my head spin more. Is that what love does, make you lose all sense of self? It couldn't be. Besides, I couldn't have feelings for them both, could I?

I sighed and looked at my mother's tent. Anxiety attacks were something she had always suffered from throughout her life. Part of me felt guilty knowing I was probably the cause of the most recent ones. It would explain why we have stayed camped here for so long. When she was in this state, being alone is what she preferred.

"I probably shouldn't keep her waiting much longer."

They both nodded their heads in agreement. Hassan took my arm again smiling.

"Maybe I should escort you there, for safety reasons."

I nodded and walked to the tent. I had managed to avoid a couple large rocks, some branches, and my feet. Just to be safe I kept my feet far away from Hassan's, afraid I would trip over them and make us both fall over.

He released my arm when we reached the tent, no injuries, no falls, no pain. Hassan laughed. "First time without a stumble. We'll keep working on it later." I smiled as he became more serious. "I'll be nearby if you need anything." He bowed and I curtsied before he jogged away to join Risa. As I turned to the tent, I didn't realize that I was plummeting into something completely unexpected.

CHAPTER 20

The tent was brighter than what I thought it would be. Flaps were pulled up to let the sun shine through and the air smelled of fresh earth, much more welcoming than the stench in my polluted tent.

Laerina sat at a table with one empty seat across from her. Two guards were at the sides of the entrance, not letting me proceed until told.

Laerina had been staring down at the ground, not realizing my presence. I hadn't recognized the guards, but apparently they recognized me. One huffed at the sight of me and the other cringed.

Laerina waved her hand in the air, eyes still searching the ground. "Let her in. Stand guard outside," she whispered her silent demands, her eyes searching for something invisible. The guards obeyed and retreated outside, leaving us to be alone. Laerina didn't speak, eyes still intending to stare and not look up at me.

I examined the tent. A cot lay in the corner; maps were kept in the other. A small food stash that hadn't been touched was on the table and a blanket was laid neatly over her chair.

The silence stretched on, forcing me to bear it. It overwhelmed me when nothing was happening, when I couldn't hear anything. It seemed like all of my other emotions were absent. My head left spinning, trying to move, trying to use my voice, trying to hear something instead of the quiet air, trying to smell or taste life in the room. I had to escape the drowning silence.

"You wanted to speak with me?" I declared loudly, feeling everything in the air loosen at the thunderous sound. No tension was left, no headache or silence, only Laerina, finding simple words to respond.

She looked up, not at me but at the seat in front of her. She responded like she was speaking to it. "Yes, I did. Come take a seat, I don't know how long this conversation may last," she spoke honestly.

I approached the seat, tucking my dirty dress underneath me before fully lounging in the wooden chair.

Laerina was finally looking at me, no smile or life on her face. She fidgeted with her hands, placing them calmly in her lap, one overlapping the other. It was a rare occasion to see my mother appear uncertain or vulnerable. The situation made me uncomfortable, not knowing how to react. I crossed my legs at the movement of her rubbing her thumb and set my eyes back on hers. This time she spoke first.

"I don't know where to begin," she quietly told me.

My forehead creased, face twisted. "What do you want to

talk about? Why did you ask for me?" I threw out some conversation topics, but she didn't bother taking them.

"Allene, I am not very fond of telling stories, but today there is an exception. I was going over your story in my mind and realized you left out how you got your name. I figured you did not make it up yourself, but probably had help from another individual." I felt my nerves churning in my stomach. I had avoided disclosing that tidbit of information about Damein's part in it all. I did not want to lie *or* tell the truth. Gratefully, Laerina made my torment short lived.

"No matter, I do not wish to discuss that.In fact, I don't want to bring it up again. I shall proceed to tell you a story. *My* story. Your father shared his version of how we met, correct? I wish to share my part of the story and how it affected me as a queen."

My ears perked up at the tantalizing offer to hear my mother share something personal about her life. She was never one to tell me stories, that was my father's department. She proceeded on.

"Allene, it's not easy being royal. When I was young I was raised to believe royalty was the only joy in life, that my family was incredibly blessed. I had always dreamed of certain dresses for my crowning. I had made lists of food for banquets for special holidays or occasions. I thought of balls and seeing all the young ladies ravishing dresses sparkle in a grand ballroom, but mine standing out among them all. Everyone bowing to me and giving me gifts . . . it brought me sincere joy and love for being of royal descent. That is what I grew up to think life was and what my life would be.

"I never had thought of love. I understood being loved,

being admired, because as royalty it was a commonality and it was something I was trained to enjoy. I had never dreamed of me being *in love* with someone. I thought everything about it was false. I was convinced that love was only a way to get your heart broken. A consequence that I feared, the result being vulnerability, true love didn't seem fit to consider given my position.

"Or maybe it was a way to defend myself from the thought of an arranged marriage. It is so common for royalty, I didn't want to give myself hope for something that wasn't just political. Marriage, love, when done right, I had never paid much attention to how it brought joy to other people's lives. I focused on only how it hurt their lives to convince myself I wouldn't be missing out. I had no intentions of finding love, or for it to find me. I thought I would neglect it when it first came into sight. But I was very wrong and let me share why.

"My grandmother had held a party to celebrate her birthday and everyone in Valteria was invited. A mysterious man had attended; no one had ever seen or heard of him. A friend of mine had told me he was rich. Another had said he was handsome. I became fully curious about the man and intended to learn his name. I had asked many people in attendance that night, but they had told me he wouldn't share his name with anyone, *"until he found what he was looking for"*. He definitely was a mystery and people lost interest in him quickly, assuming he was an odd commoner. Except for me.

"I grew anxious at the party not being able to approach and make a conversation. I swallowed my fear and I asked the mysterious man for the next dance. He gladly accepted the invitation, just as I hoped he would." She paused, smiling from reminiscing of that night. I moved into my seat, getting comfortable, imagining her memories with her, already knowing what would be coming next. And soon enough she proceeded to tell the heartwarming story.

"The next dance he found me, took my hand, dancing without a word. The first thing I asked was where he was from and his answer made me irritated. He told me it was private. I disliked feeling indignant and I was not going to let that be his answer. I pushed the feeling aside, smiling and laughing at random moments, trying to gain his trust. It seemed to help. I felt comfortable enough to ask his name. He told me his name was Faris and I felt special when he confided in me. After that, every dance going forward he wouldn't hesitate to ask me and I would be delighted to dance again.

"After that night, we started seeing each other everyday, going on walks and outings, sitting in the creek and taking turns pushing each other in. We fell in love and soon we were engaged." Laerina stopped, hurt flooding her expression. The next part of the story seemed to invoke some bleak memories.

"My fear had come true. I was heartbroken. I was forced to throw him out when war came our way. He had confided in me about his true identity, leaving me no choice. It was very confusing at the time, not knowing what was real and what wasn't," she whispered in regret, like some memory had torn her in two. She stopped talking and began to weep, her chest elevating and her hands covering her face while the tears dribbled out from the sides.

I leaned across the table, rubbing her arm and back, talking in hushed tones trying to assure her. "Mother, it's all right." I was taken off guard seeing my mother behave so openly and emotionally. It was a sight that I hadn't seen before and it left me uncertain how to handle what had unfolded.

Laerina kept her cries low and murmured when she tried to speak. "Your father was my greatest love. I was his greatest heartache. I don't want the same suffering for you." She mouthed the last word as she started blubbering again.

What was troubling her about the memory? Everything had gone right in the end, hadn't it? They were married, they ruled over Valteria, everything she had hoped for and yet she was crying like it all was a horrible mistake.

"Mother, father adored you. You did not bring him heartache."

"You're wrong. I thought our love would be enough. But deep down, I knew his decision pained him in a way he would never admit. By choosing me, by choosing love, he forsook his family. The things he held so dear in his life, the people he was closest to, gone. He knew he was making a sacrifice but it is one he never fully accepted. The damage of choosing me severed all the relationships he built in Praseria. They lost their prince, their future king, and their son. Seeing your relationship with Aleron unfold, it is uncanny in its similarity to your father and I."

"That is why I was confident it could work in the first place. Seeing your story, your happy ending, it gives me hope that I can have mine," I proposed.

Laerina shook her head, upset by my reply. "Allene, our story did not have a happy ending. In this case, you are playing the role of your father. And as your mother, it deeply hurts me to think about the possibility of your love story being patterned after ours. Risa and I, we have already lost your father. I fear that by you choosing Aleron, we will lose you too. You could lose us. And that is a sacrifice and impact you need to heavily consider."

She coughed and bit her lip, trying to hold back another sob. She took in large breaths, her lip still between her teeth, holding back a wail. She grasped the table and stared at me, barely being able to speak. "I cannot talk about this any longer. I trust you will take my words to heart and really think about your future."

Her words left me feeling burdensome. Did she really mean all of that? Did she sincerely think she caused my father heartache? I sympathized with the notion, digging deeper with better understanding of my mother.

"Leave me please." She ordered and bit her finger now instead, letting her head fall into her hands, her knees coming to her chest as she wrapped her arms around them. She seemed so innocent, in peril, my scrutiny towards her was beginning to melt away.

I did as I was told, silently leaving my mother in her tent to mourn over her memories and fears alone.

~

*A*jax waited for me outside the tent, Hassan coming up behind. Ajax walked faster to my dwelling where he threw me in without a word, securing the flap close.

I heard them arguing, Ajax not letting Hassan in and Hassan apologizing for his outburst earlier that morning. I listened because they were the only things to listen to, everything else was dead silent. I heard Damien come into the argument demanding them to stop, saying how they were behaving like toddlers and they instantly went quiet.

I saw Damien's shadow walk around my tent and out of sight and then Hassan's shadow came into view. He stopped at the back of my tent as I scooted toward him, letting my ear rest on the fabric.

"I'll be back, I promise," he muttered under his breath. I didn't dare speak so I nodded, hoping he could see my silhouette.

He held up a hand to my tent, but quickly ran away before he could be seen by Ajax, knowing somehow he would fulfill his promise.

Ajax went out of view, probably sitting some yards away in case Hassan tried to make his move.

I sat up, listening to the crickets tune and the fireflies buzzing around with glee as night approached. The moon had cast a shadow over my tent, making it colder inside than I wanted it to be, almost making me prefer when it was hot.

I reached for my blanket, wrapping it around me, shuddering whenever the shadow of the moon grew. I could see a small glimmer of light through a hole in my tent. The guards had made a fire, telling stories of when they went to war or the injuries they had received as they trained to be knights when they were young. The stories distracted me from my obsessing thoughts involving the story my mother had cut short. I was grateful to try and focus on something else.

One story had me giggling quietly when a man spoke of how he saved a lady from a wild pig. He had suffered a large cut in his leg and swipe on his thigh, but nonetheless he saved the girl by putting her on his back and climbing up a tree to escape the wild hog. I laughed at the image of a cute pig getting the better of a grown man clinging to a tree for safety.

I decided to lay my head down on the hard ground, listening to things from afar as it traveled secretly through the earth. I could hear the vibrations of footsteps and the conversation being carried through the dirt and into my ear. The words were slurred yet calming, like a boat rocking, making my eyes droop.

I tried to stay awake, to listen to their ridiculous stories, but before I had time to stop myself, my eyes fell and left me in an abysmal sleep.

CHAPTER 21

A shriek broke away from my throat, disturbing the silence that enveloped the piercing night. A soft, urgent hand shielded my mouth as it earnestly pulled me into a resilient grasp. My head had found itself firmly against a man's chest.

My mind was completely jumbled with fear. Alert and mentally ready for anything, I tried to breathe in. I couldn't help but panic, the gruesome feeling and realization that I had no control over what may happen took my breathing to an entirely new level of hyperventilation. I tried to define the man by mere evaluation of possibilities but I kept losing focus.

I couldn't hear the guards move at the sudden sound I had made, only deep breathing could be perceived. What was I going to do? I had to try something. I attempted to twist out of the mighty hold that was now cutting off air to my lungs.

The arms locked, getting tighter and tighter the harder I attempted to fight back.

The man trapped my legs and curled me into a ball against his chest, pressing me nearer, insistent to hush me. The lack of air was beginning to make me feeble. I surrendered for a moment, bringing me back to the night's penetrating silence.

I tried breathing in and out but the hand prevented me from doing so. We both listened to the guards, but no one stirred at my silent fighting. I wanted to scream out to them. The entire point of them being there was to keep watch, not sleep through a kidnapping.

The man released his grip on my mouth but still snuggled me to his chest. I tried to move away from his arms, inclining my head to bite his hands, but he moved them before I could. I dropped to the floor, throwing my hands up to slap him. He quickly caught my hands and held them in his.

"Allene, stop! It's me. Stop!" he implored below a whisper.

I froze, my hands rigid. That voice. I had only heard it in my mind everyday and in my dreams every night. Was I still dreaming? Was I really awake?

I fell to my knees, trying to see through the darkness and gather the outline of his figure. He brought my hands to his smooth, warm face. I cautiously traced his every feature with my cold fingers and I gasped realizing it was real. It was him.

"Aleron?" I queried. I felt the face move up and down in a brief nod. I couldn't believe it. My heart dropped into my stomach. What was he doing here? After everything *I* did, why would he come back?

"Allene, thank goodness you're all right. You are well, aren't you?" He breathed warm air into my face and my head urged forward for more. I threw my arms up and around his neck, begging for an embrace in return as I inhaled the clove scent that bounced off his skin. He hugged me tightly and soon let me go, just holding my hands and waiting for me to respond.

I did this without thought. "I am better now. How did you get past the guards?" I asked in astonishment.

He shrugged, staring at me in the darkness. "It wasn't difficult. I waited until they were asleep. They have a slight drinking problem, probably something you should address with their supervisor. Not the best men for your protection," he mocked halfheartedly.

I nodded, realizing their idotic comments and stories were a result of alcohol. How sad our situation looked trusting our safety to drunken fools, their supervisor Aleron mentioned being one of them.

"How did you find me?" I asked.

"I followed you here, waiting for the right moment," he explained in his deep, enchanting voice.

"You shouldn't be here, if you get caught I–"

Aleron hushed me. "I'm not alone. Trae is keeping watch for me nearby," Aleron assured me, seemingly calm.

My eyes widened, more questions popping into my head. "I'm surprised he came with you," I said candidly.

"Why are you surprised?" Aleron asked.

The amount of shame that washed over me at that simple question made me utterly embarrassed. "I saw the look on his face when he found out who I was. I saw the look on every-one's face. They all must hate me." I had to be honest with myself, I knew the damage I had caused and how I must seem in their eyes.

"They don't hate you, Allene. They are worried about you. *I've* been worried about you," Aleron spoke softly.

"You don't have to lie to me, Aleron," I protested, trying to display courage. I was used to being disliked by people, it was something that didn't faze me much anymore, it was just reality. I knew I was an outsider, a trait I carried wherever I went.

"Don't do that to yourself, you are still the same person, we all realize that. Nothing has changed," Aleron persisted.

"We?" I wondered who he had spoken to.

"Ezra and Noni," he answered my question quickly. Hearing their names made my heart ache, I missed them both already.

"They spoke with you?" I asked, surprised they would confront Aleron about me.

He nodded. "Yes. Noni gave me a stern warning that if I didn't get you back in time for her wedding, I would deeply regret it." Aleron laughed at the thought. It sounded like Noni, willing to challenge a prince for the sake of her big day. I smiled, relieved she still wanted me to be a part of something so important.

"And Ezra?" I asked. I had been waiting for the right moment to tell Risa about meeting our grandfather. It was weighing heavily on my mind, the look of sadness on Ezra's face when my mother arrived.

"He told me to tell you that you are stronger than your father and him combined. That he's certain you can handle what's to come," Aleron whispered, trying to imitate Ezra's comforting voice. I could practically hear it.

"I didn't get a chance to say goodbye to him," I thought outloud, regretting my departure. Aleron looked puzzled.

"What is it?" I questioned.

Aleron shook his head. "It's still difficult to comprehend that Ezra is your grandfather. That you are a princess . . ." his voice trailed off, losing his words as he stared into space.

Aleron had every reason to be shocked. As nerve racking as it was to have him know the truth, it was like a weight had been lifted knowing I no longer had to lie to him. Even if knowing the truth meant we might lose what we have.

"Are you angry?" I couldn't help but ask. I tried to brace myself for his response, expecting the worst. A small chuckle escaped his lips and he exhaled with a silent laugh.

"No, I'm not angry. Surprised, but not angry. I realized as soon as you left that I made a dreadful mistake by letting you go." Aleron seemed disheartened by the memory.

"I made a promise to you Allene; I swore that if anyone took you away that I would come for you, remember? You would be amazed at what I can accomplish once I have made a promise." His words were practically music to my ears, numbing my body as I absorbed everything he was saying.

I let my knees sink deeper into the floor, catching my breath. He promised me and he fulfilled his promise. *Maybe he really did love me. Maybe we still had a chance.*

I muttered my response, practically breathless. "Remember? I haven't been able to stop remembering every moment I have had with you. I thought after my mother came you would never see me the same way. I lied to you Aleron, and you have no way of understanding how horrible I feel." I let my head fall in shame, but he caught it in his hands, lifting it up to view his. Even in the dark I could see his teal eyes, glowing brighter than the moon, sparking a light inside me. I saw a faint smile on his face.

"My beautiful Allene, if it wasn't for what you did, I may have never gotten the opportunity to meet you. And what a shame that would have been." Aleron caressed my cheek, making my head fall into his hands. "I still have great plans for our future, no matter how grim the circumstances may seem," he assured me.

I couldn't help but laugh as tears of relief were about to pour out of me. I held them back by looking into his eyes and realizing that everything was going to be okay. He still loved me and that was enough.

I sighed and stared at my hands, watching Aleron pick me up and fold me into his chest, cradling me in his arms. He spoke against my hair, not bothering to move.

"I love you," the whisper of Aleron's reassuring words made my mind soar.

Silence came over us for many minutes. We listened to what was going on around us, hearing crickets chirp and the snores of the guards. It was relaxing and being in Aleron's arms again was a dream come true. I was afraid to talk, the looming possibility I'd wake up from this amazing dream was too much of a risk. We embraced each other in silence, no words needing to be spoken.

After a while the silence took a turn from comfort and insecurity arose. Aleron hadn't moved or said anything at all. I could barely feel him breathing.

I turned in his arms, searching for those blue eyes that lit up his face. His eyebrows were furrowed in concentration, biting his lip, and his grasp around me tightened. He saw me looking up at him and stopped. Something was on his mind and he knew I could tell. He sighed with remorse.

"What's on your mind?" I asked.

Without even a glance toward me, he stared into the corner of the tent, his words barely able to be heard as his lips brushed against my hair. "Your name. I'm having a hard time calling you Allene. I think I prefer calling you Amelia," he cautiously said, waiting to judge my reaction.

I smiled. I liked the name too and I was more than all right with being called Amelia. It made me feel like I was in Praseria again, bringing me back to my favorite moments. Noni chatting away, Ezra's stories and conversations, Terris and his pastries, Trae's quick save and Kendra's love for horses. I wanted all of it again and smiled at the memories that came back and filled my thoughts.

I looked up at Aleron with a kind face, a chuckle escaping my lips. "You can call me whatever you like. I'm yours."

He laid a gentle hand on my cheek, a smile growing on his face. "And I am yours," he said back. The words rang in my head, making my head spin in circles and sent my heart fluttering at full speed.

Aleron stopped the ringing in my head with a disappointed sigh. His eyes flooded with worry, leaving a frown on his face, mirroring mine.

"What is it?" I asked.

Aleron shook his head, another huff filling the room with hot air. Maybe it was his father. I was meaning to ask him about the fight they had and if his parents knew what had happened yet. It was a conversation I was trying to avoid, I wanted to preserve this moment as long as possible.

"I had a feeling they wouldn't tell you." His head fell.

My brows hung low, my eyes searching Aleron's dark face. "What have they not told me?" My voice was shaky, my body quaking, afraid to hear what he had to say.

He shook his head. "Your mother has declared war on Praseria. We tried negotiating but she refused. We can't have more land burned or our people's lives put at risk. We are preparing as many men as we can for the battle."

My mouth hung open. *What is she doing? Why is she declaring war? What has she done?*

"Aleron, there is no reason for her to want war and there is no reason for you to either," I pleaded, wanting to end my misery for the feud that was held between the two sides that I loved.

"Lia, what other choice do I have? Let my people perish? Your mother has all the reasons she needs. She believes we kidnapped both her daughters. I have to do something and sitting around waiting for the worst is not an option," he explained.

I nodded. He was right; he had a responsibility to his people that he couldn't abandon. But then I realized something horrible. My voice shook, my body trembling, leaving him vibrating too while I spoke.

"You . . . you're not going to be fighting in the war, are you?" I gulped waiting for his response. I knew the answer to the question but I was hoping for another miracle tonight, a prayer pleaded in my heart. I guess one miracle in one night is as much as I can ask for.

Aleron looked away when he answered, his hands sweating. "I have to. I'm the prince, the leader of the army. I have to lead them into battle to fight alongside them," he whispered the dreadful words, leaving me feeling alone in the darkness, his touch dim and my face cold.

Aleron looked at my terrorized face, cupping it in his hand, trying to give me comfort. "I will be fine, I promise. Nothing is going to hurt me; I am very good with a sword. I have prepared for situations like this ever since I was young," he whispered the chilling words.

That didn't make me feel better, that just meant more of my people would die at his hands. I didn't know which one to pray for, Aleron alive or my people safe.

I sighed in defeat. What could I do? I was a powerless princess, completely shut out from all of society or having any ability to change the direction of either side.

"Maybe I could talk with my mother. There has to be some way to change her mind. I don't want to see either of our kingdoms have casualties," I quickly said my conclusion.

Aleron shook his head sadly. "Your sister has already tried to reason with your mother, my negotiators told me so. We even offered land, but she said it wasn't enough to undo the bad blood we've caused. The words she told my negotiators exactly was she wouldn't stop until I am in a grave, that it's the only way to put me out of reach of her family."

I stopped breathing at his painful words. She couldn't kill Aleron, she couldn't take away my new reason for living.

"As long as I am alive that will never happen," I assured him, trying to control the uncontrollable.

He took my hands, covering them with his and placing

them in his lap. "I just want to see you safe. It would hurt me far worse to lose you. Please promise me you won't interfere in any way. Promise me you won't and everything will be okay." His hands tightened around mine as I looked into his pleading eyes. How could I say no? How could I say yes?

"I can't promise you anything. I can only promise you that I will do everything in my power to make this right," was my answer.

He sighed and spoke with slight irritation in his voice. "You *have* too. Please, just this *one* time, don't be stubborn. This is the only thing I have ever asked of you. Please," he mouthed.

I looked away from his imploring eyes. It felt wrong to dismiss his one request, considering all I had put him through and all he had done for me and forgiven. I didn't want to be selfish, but it was hard not to.

"It affects me too, Aleron. I have a reason to get involved, don't I?"

"Yes, you have every right. But you also have every reason to stay safe," he explained, pressuring me still.

"Aleron . . . you're putting your life in danger, my people, and yours. People that are innocent. I can't watch us try and kill each other. All I want to do is talk to her, if I -,"

"Allene, please." His eyes caught mine, exactly what I was trying to avoid. I knew I would falter, my courage diminishing as I looked at him.

"Please," he repeated, this time coming only an inch from my face, knowing I'd give in soon. He put his hand on my cheek and tried a new tactic. He kissed me, not letting me interrupt again.

Part of me wanted to protest but another part of me knew I wanted to give in. Aleron's lips were soft against mine, silently pleading with me each time he broke away. He had a renewed sense of urgency as each kiss grew more intense, a hunger being sensed by both of us.

Aleron's hand had slowly made its way from my cheek to my thigh, gripping me tightly. His hand felt strong as he pulled me onto his lap, insisting on being closer.

The emotions that were erupting between us were making me dizzy, losing my train of thought. He was successfully making me forget what we had been talking about.

The strong headed side of me shined through, slowing down his unfair attempt to distract me. I pulled myself away, trying to gain back his attention on the matter. His breath was warm against my face and that was all it took. I sighed in defeat. I couldn't see him suffer any longer.

"I promise," the faint words tumbled out of my mouth. *Curse you Allene, for instantly letting him get what he wanted, promising him without even thinking what you should say.* I had courage but Aleron had a way of letting my guard down.

"Thank you. You just made me feel entirely better," he admitted.

He released my hands that had found themselves inter-twined and laid them flat on top of his. His fingers were an inch longer than mine. The observation of the difference made him chortle, and in result, made me do the same.

I closed my eyes thinking of any other questions I might have for Aleron. This was all happening so fast. Another war to handle, more lives in jeopardy, and I had to stay on the sidelines.

"When will the war begin?" I asked. I was not sure I wanted to know the answer, but it would be better to know what to expect.

"In three days," he said solemnly.

My eyes flew open. "That quickly? How long has this been planned?"

He pondered my question and had no trouble responding. "Four days."

I sighed. A week to deliberate and prepare, that quickly? How could this be happening? I wanted to scream and run to my mother, pound on her tent and plead for her to end this nonsense. I knew it wouldn't do any good. I would probably give Aleron away, making the war situation even worse or the guards would hear me and take him away.

His hands wrapped around my waist, letting my head lay on his shoulder. Since the conversation had taken a solemn turn, I decided now was a good time to approach the subject of Aleron's father.

"What does your father have to say about all of this?" I whispered the words, wishing I didn't have to ask the question in the first place.

Aleron squeezed me tightly, feeling rigid from my question. "It doesn't matter what he has to say," Aleron said shortly, clearly not wanting to discuss it either.

I paused, taking the time to thoughtfully consider what to say next.

"He's the king, Aleron. As much as you may wish that it doesn't matter, it does," I whispered faintly.

"He lacks impartial and honorable judgement. His opinions hold no merit in my eyes," Aleron said stringently, clenching his jaw.

"But that doesn't mean his opinions aren't valued by others. Between my mother claiming she wants to see you dead, and your father obviously not supporting us, even *before* he knew my identity . . . it feels like the odds are completely against you and I."

Aleron pulled back, looking into my eyes with deep concern. "Don't give up hope. We don't know where my father stands," Aleron claimed.

"I overheard you two fighting in the kitchen. He made his stand very clear," I confessed to eavesdropping, not feeling ashamed since Aleron tried to conceal it. Aleron let the realization sink in, giving a moment of silence as he thought over my words.

"Right now, there are more important things to handle than our parents' opinions. I know it's a lot to take in, Lia. For the moment, you need to stop worrying. In time, all of this will be past us and everything will be the way it should be," he spoke with hope and confidence, the opposite of what I was feeling. All hope, courage, confidence, true pleasure, was gone, washed away as quickly as a river current. With only a few words, that's all it took to rob every feeling of happiness from me.

"I hope you are right. I really do," I whispered, holding him closer.

"When have I not been right?" his eyebrows went up in wonder, forcing a small grin.

"Ah, yes. How could you ever be wrong?" I tried to joke but no sound of enthusiasm came out of my voice. Aleron still chuckled softly, trying to show that my effort was worth it.

"I want you to relax the next few days. I'll come for you after the war. We will talk to your mother and my father and work this out. It'll all be all right," he said, trying to comfort me and give me something to look forward to.

I shuddered at the word. *War*. Who invented such a thing? It was cruel and now the love of my life was going to be in the middle of it, leaving me worrying if he was going to survive and wondering if I was ever going to hear his laugh again or see his smile. I was grateful for memories but I would be more grateful for persuasive power to end all of this hideous nonsense.

Aleron was rubbing my back, not rushing me to answer. The cold air was creeping all over the room, making me yearn for his warm touch to stay.

"I will hold you to your word," I whispered, releasing the heat of his hand at my reply and feeling the cold take over me.

Aleron grabbed my blanket and bundled me tight. He laid my head on the floor; the air was caught in my chest when I realized how hard it was. Aleron hunched down to my level, carrying a hard smile on his face. He looked sad and distressed, but tried to hide every bit of it.

"You need to rest. Sleep well, Lia. Remember your promise and I'll remember mine. Have faith." He paused just long enough to look into my eyes. He gave me a lingering look that I had never seen him give before, almost a signal of some sort. An exchange of secret words I had to try to discern for myself.

Before I had the chance to ask what it might be, he gently

swept his lips over mine and left the tent as silently as he came in. That was it, he was gone.

I stared in the direction he had left, hoping he would come back, sweep me in his arms and take us far away from everything. I stared for a long while, my eyes barely staying open when I realized he wasn't coming through the door again.

The conversation with my mother was creeping in, trying to give me doubts. Was she right? Did my father have regrets? Could I lose everything? I was left alone in the cold dark night to be consumed by the horrible news of what was to come and the debilitating decisions that it required of me.

CHAPTER 22

*I*n the morning they let me leave my tent for breakfast. I liked having breakfast, it was the time of day where I could see a couple blossoming flowers and my friends gleaming faces after they had just woken up.

Damien's hair was a huge mess, sticking off the top of his head like he was struck by lightning. His pants were rolled up and he wore a short sleeved shirt, despite the cold morning air.

Risa's hair was in a long braid, eating in her stunning blue gown. She looked like she hadn't been sleeping for hours but rather had been wide awake preparing for a ball. She wore her same glittering smile, signaling to me that there was an open seat next to her. Hassan was nowhere to be found, probably still asleep in his tent, waiting for the birds to wake him.

I tucked my gown to the side, searching for a plate when Damien yawned and shoved one onto my lap. Bread and honey hugged one side of the plate, a mashed potato on the other side, while watery porridge mixed with sugar bled into the rest of the meal. I had never had a potato for breakfast. I didn't need to ask if Damien prepared the food, the sloppy preparation was enough of an indication that he had.

"Did you sleep well, Allene?" Risa asked, stabbing at her potato without much interest. I took a spoon, stirring my porridge, nodding with delight. I didn't mention Aleron, but I did eventually sleep after his visit, leaving me breathless as I dreamed of him all night.

"One of my better nights rest, actually."

Risa's eyebrows inched up on her head. "Oh? Why so, if you don't mind me asking."

I stared at her with a smile. "No reason at all," I lied.

Risa rolled her eyes and turned to look at Damien. He was munching on his bread and didn't even realize that she was staring. He looked up at the sudden quietness, meeting Risa's gaze. He understood quickly, shaking his head.

"Oh, I get it. This conversation is for women only, isn't it? Nope, I am sorry, I am not moving from this spot until I am done eating. If Allene has something to tell you she can tell me too. I'm more sensitive than I look," he huffed in a sleepy tone, yawning.

Risa giggled and I could see a slight smile on Damien's face, almost like it overjoyed him to make her laugh.

"It's all right Damien, you can stay," she assured him, still smiling.

"You're quite grouchy when you're tired Damien," I laughed.

He grinned without amusement, chewing again, leaving

Risa and I chuckling. That was how the rest of breakfast was, laughing at anything Damien did.

Once we were finished, my belly was sore from laughter and the sudden stop of Damien's jokes was a relief to my bones. After the giggles were gone, my mind was forced to wander, remembering last night. My heart stopped at the image of Aleron's worried face, but soon it sped up like a hummingbird's wings, beating fast at the thought of his news. *The war.*

I had to find a way to stop the war from becoming a bloody mess. I couldn't bear risking Aleron's life or my people's. Besides, they didn't deserve war. It was my mother's mistake burning their land, causing this rift between our two kingdoms, not theirs. They were fighting for her when she should be fighting alone.

I struggled against the temptation to ask about the war. I had to find out everything I could, see if Risa and Damien were aware of it and if there was some incredible way to stop it.

I fidgeted with my skirt, looking around at the pale sky and landing my gaze on a rustling tent. Hassan stepped out, his hair flat and red marks on his left cheek from sleeping all night. He stretched his hands toward the sky, letting out a loud groan. He began slowly walking, still half asleep as he took a seat next to Damien.

He yawned a couple of times before realizing I was there. His hands ran through his hair, making it stand straight up and then right back to being flat, the thickness of his hair weighing it down. He sheepishly grinned.

"Good morning, Allene. Sleep well? No injuries?" His grin

grew. He moved his eyes away from me, sniffing out breakfast and loading everything onto his plate.

I smiled but quickly retorted. "I did sleep well and as far as I could tell I am doing much better with my balance."

He started shoving food down his throat and gulped it down to respond. "That's a relief to hear." He gave a playful wink and immediately returned back to devouring his food.

We sat in silence as I was trying to build the nerve to ask about the war, but every time I thought I could, it would slip right from under me. I sighed and forced my lips to move, the sound barely coming out.

"Has anything happened lately that you guys haven't told me?" I looked at my feet, studying every part of them. I wiggled my toes, the silence stretching on longer than I anticipated. I couldn't see their faces but I knew they were probably looking at me with confusion and concern.

"Why would you ask that? What would happen that we wouldn't tell you about?" Damien asked.

I shrugged, still looking down. "Being confined, left alone, makes me feel . . . lost, uninformed, like a big secret is being kept from me. I heard whispers from the guards and I thought I heard something peculiar the other night. I was just making sure nothing was going on that I wasn't aware of, that's all," I confessed, trying to place blame on the drunken men whose tongues would accidentally divulge secrets, hoping it would convince them that I knew.

I finally gazed up at them. They all were looking at each other like they wanted to talk but didn't know if they should. Of course, Hassan sighed and relinquished.

"Well, if no one else is willing to jump in on the topic I

guess I will. One thing has happened. We aren't supposed to tell you. But I feel it's unfair to leave our princess in a tent not knowing what's going on." He looked around to see if anyone objected to him telling me their big secret. No one moved and Hassan proceeded.

"The Praserians are forcing us into war. We are going back to Valteria today and in three days the war will begin. Our army is large, we are just hoping it's large enough. With Praseria's past alliances, who knows who they might have fighting along their side. Our men are being trained at this very moment, getting prepared," he reported the news in a light hearted voice, making it sound like it was good to hear. All I heard was, *"we are going to try and kill the man you love for the good of the people."*

My mouth gaped, but not because of the news of the war, but because of the lie. What was going on? I thought my mother had declared war, not the Praserian's. My mind was tired of being bewildered and confused. Nothing seemed to make sense anymore. I found myself asking the question of who was telling the truth far too frequently the last several days. I had no reason to believe that Aleron or Hassan had ever lied to me. The fact of the matter was *someone* was lying to me and my intuition to discern who it was seemed obliterated. *I guess this is the consequence of being on two sides, it's impossible to know who's right.*

I let my head fall into my soft hands, letting them rub my temples. I was tired of being confused and angry, not knowing whose side to take. What was I to do? Tell them what Aleron had said and risk them being angry, or go along with it and clarify later on?

At the moment I was wondering when it would be over, if it was *ever* going to be over. When would all of this chaos end? It seemed to be going on for an eternity.

I sighed, letting the tension in my neck and shoulders fall, the pain of it all being lifted to the heavens for the strong angels to bear for only a moment until I could catch my breath. Once I let my lungs relinquish the nourishment, the pain was dumped faster than I could blink and the loneliness set into my aching heart once again.Everyone was starting to crowd around me, concern on their faces.

"What's wrong, Allene? Are you all right?" Damien asked.

"You're quite pale, you look like you might faint. Do you need some water?" Risa inquired, wanting to help in every way.

I shook my head and met my eyes with hers. "I'm just overwhelmed. War? So soon?"

She nodded. "I know it's a lot to take in, considering every-thing that has happened. Mother had no other choice but to defend us. Negotiations were unable to be made with Praseria and they are still in the dark about father's death, for the moment at least. If we wait much longer, they will think we are even weaker without our king. We will only be made more of a target, by Praseria and others. We are all overwhelmed, you're not alone," she said, trying to relate to my pain.

I had almost forgotten that Praseria was unaware of my father's passing. Well, everyone aside from Ezra. Part of me wished he would have told Aleron the news when they spoke earlier to spare me the dreaded conversation. I realized now it may not be something I have the chance to tell him myself, he may hear it through other sources first. I couldn't decide if I preferred it that way or not. I had likely lost the opportunity to have him hear it from me.

Overall, Risa had a point, the death of a king generally left kingdoms fragile. It was only a matter of time until it would cause Valteria even more disarray.

"Are you sure *they* declared war?" I needed to get as close to the truth as possible.

"As far as we know. Mother announced it four days ago, she received a letter," Risa said, reading the hurt in my eyes.

"A letter? Did you see the letter?"

They all shook their heads, making me sigh with finally getting somewhere. Maybe Laerina was lying. She lied about burning their land so why wouldn't she be lying about this?

"Anything else?" I asked.

Damien exchanged a worried look with Risa. He sighed and spoke to me, staring at Hassan to see the reaction to his words.

"The guards found footprints by your tent earlier this morning. A man's footprints and plenty more in another area not far from here. Nothing was there. Whoever it was left hours ago. You didn't hear anything last night did you?" Damien asked.

I caught my tongue, wanting to explain the situation. I stopped myself, knowing it would ruin everything, maybe even make it worse. Aleron was safe and I needed to do everything in my power to keep it that way. Hassan had stopped eating, the immense effort it took him to remain calm was displayed all over his anxious expression.

I shook my head, knowing if I spoke my voice would crack and they would know I was keeping a secret.

Damien didn't bother to ask anything else, but everyone's face was still frozen, like something awful was going to happen.

"We will be leaving soon. I should go pack," Risa said. She put her hands on her knees and used them to lift herself up. She stared down at me and covered her mouth with her right hand.

"What?" My voice was alert, my body not wanting to move now looking at her terrified face.

"Allene, you are filthy! When was the last time you bathed? Come with me, I am taking care of you first!" She reached down to take my hand and all of my body went limp, realizing there was nothing to be alert about, but something to dread.

She pulled me to my feet and I wanted to pull back until I thought about her question. I hadn't bathed in at least a week. I smelled my hair. It smelled of pinecones, dirt, fire, and biscuits. I hadn't seen myself in days to know how dirty I must've looked. My face went red in embarrassment as I had just been with Aleron. He hadn't mentioned a thing.

Risa pulled me behind her tent where a large bucket of water was laid off to the side. She ordered me to wait and came back with a tattered rag and a bar of soap. I took the bar of soap as she hurled me toward the bucket. Without warning, she grabbed my head and dunked me into the water.

I squealed loudly when she brought my head up for air, the ice cold water running down my back and arms, my teeth clattering. I wanted to yell at her but my mouth was too frozen to move and I was too surprised to speak. Risa didn't take notice but started scrubbing my arms, not realizing I was still in my clothes. She was humming as I shivered and once she was done with my arms she began speaking as she worked down my neck.

"Really, Allene, could you not smell yourself? It's disgusting." I couldn't answer; the cloth was hard on my neck, hurting every time she pushed it down. She dunked my head in the water again, making the burning on my neck become unpleasant as it turned ice cold.

"R-r-risa, a warning would be nice," I muttered through my lips, reaching for the rag without permission.

She backed away, smirking, letting me dry myself off with a towel that had been draped over the tree. I placed the towel over my hair, scrunching it so some of the water could be absorbed. I huffed once, some warmth coming back into my body and my teeth eventually stopped rattling.

"That's better! You are going to be riding next to me so try to hurry and gather your belongings. I want to make it home by nightfall. I am tired of sleeping in tents, and my feather down bed is calling to me. Meet me here when you're done," she instructed. She skipped off in the other direction as I paced back to my tent.

I didn't have much to pack aside from some clothes and blankets. The guards hadn't given me much else and it's not like I had brought anything with me to my unplanned visit to Praseria. Suddenly, I realized I wasn't forced back into my tent by anyone, I had come back by myself. No one had been there to stop Risa from bathing me. Aleron might still be nearby and my desperate hope to see him again caused me to venture outside.

I poked my head out of the tent and found a new man watching me. He was sitting cross-legged on the dirt, eyes searching all around and focusing on me. His hazel eyes were soft, his arms were scrawny and his brown hair was sticking to his head.

"Allene, please stay inside your tent until we depart," the sweet voice asked calmly.

I didn't do as he asked but instead grabbed my blanket and clothes and let my foot peek its way through the tent and onto the ground.

"Risa had instructed me to meet her by her tent so I could ride with her on the way home."

The man came to his feet, almost flying toward me, trying to stop me but realized he couldn't. He tried to compromise.

"Do you mind if I watch from a distance? I am not supposed to let you out of your tent, so if I let you go I would have to at least escort you from afar. Is that all right with you?" he asked kindly.

I wanted to wrap my arms around him and pat him on the back. He was the only guard who let me out of my tent. He was the only guard who had asked permission to escort me. He wasn't grabbing my arm, instead he was letting me walk on my own. His demeanor actually reminded me of someone. *Risa.* Then the wheels started turning.

I smiled. "I would love that. In fact, would you like to ride with us?"

A small smile quickly came to his lips and vanished just as fast. Even though he wasn't actually smiling with his lips any longer, it was overflowing in his eyes.

"If you wish. Is it all right with your sister?" he questioned.

"I know she won't object at all," I said truthfully.

He nodded. I grinned and walked to Risa's tent. He stopped at the doorway and motioned for me to proceed in. I ducked my head under the flap and saw Risa picking up the last of her clothes.

"I'm all ready, what about you?" she asked.

"All packed, I even managed to bring you an extra surprise," I confirmed.

"As you are fully aware, my last surprise didn't end so well . . . besides, what could you possibly surprise me with?" She locked her gaze on my hands and her eyes fell with disappointment to see only my belongings. Poor Risa, I hadn't taken the time to consider how awful she must feel being played as a fool from the Praserian's coup. If I was in her position, I wouldn't much like surprises either.

"It's outside, silly girl. Come with me, no reason to fear this surprise." I took her free hand and led her through the tent and to my new guard.

Risa's smile was mirroring the guards. They locked each other's gaze and didn't seem to move. I tried to stay silent but couldn't take it any longer. I skipped to the guard and cleared my throat.

"Risa this is . . ." I stopped, realizing I didn't know his name. He didn't take notice but finished my sentence.

"Marshal. It's a pleasure to make your acquaintance, princess." He bowed, taking hold of Risa's hand. Her face flushed pink, a giggle escaping her lips.

"Likewise." She forgot to curtsy, staring at him, dumbstruck. *Match made in heaven.*

"Marshal is going to be escorting us home," I told her.

"How generous of you. Shall we be on our way?" she asked.

Marshal nodded. Risa bent over to pick up her bags but Marshal swooped them up into his arms before she had a say.

"Please, allow me. If you lead me to your horse I will get you set up," he offered. Risa didn't glance at me, but quickly ran to her horse in the other direction taking Marshal with her, leaving me alone.

I sighed at the sudden silence; the company I had hoped for was gone but it seemed my attempt to rejuvenate surprises for Risa was accomplished and that was something to be proud of.

I took long strides to the campfire, clutching my belongings to my chest like priceless items. I found Hassan in the middle of a group of soldiers, about to mount onto his horse until he spotted me.

"Allene, will you be riding with me? Damien already left with Ajax and the queen, leaving me with, well . . . no one." He waited patiently for my response, stepping backward then forward to entertain himself.

I smiled. "Seems we were both abandoned by our siblings then. I would love some company," I replied. He grinned widely and offered his hand, lifting me onto the horse without even a huff. He took my belongings and shoved them into a sack and proceeded to throw himself onto the saddle, avoiding making direct contact with me. His additional weight rocked the horse.

He grasped the steed's neck to steady himself, making the horse step backwards, his body pressing into mine. Hassan let go and winced, shifting himself forward to give me space, waiting for the horse to recover. Hassan tapped the horse lightly, making it walk.

I lightly placed my hands at Hassan's waist, afraid to give him the wrong impression. He seemed to ignore it anyway and silently pressed on.

A slight breeze was rustling the trees, no sounds about except the horse's slow, rickety steps that shook us every time his hooves touched the ground. The sun was peeking through the clouds with a ravishing welcome.

I threw my head back, letting the sun soak into my skin, the feeling of light instead of darkness brightening my spirits. I grinned at the change and released my arms to point them toward the sun, letting it tingle down my hands and into my feet.

I sighed and placed my hands back on Hassan's waist and let my head slowly come up, meeting Hassan's soft eyes and a small smile.

We continued the long ride in silence. I popped my head up to view over his shoulder. I saw a couple horses in front of us, far off. I tried to define them. I could see Risa, a few guards ahead of her and a couple behind. I let my head sweep back to see if anyone was following.

I vaguely saw where our camp had been. Everything was packed and gone, but in its place was a whole group of soldiers departing. Soldiers in maroon. *Praserian soldiers.*

They soon all ran into the trees, leaving one man alone on his horse. Recognizing the large, ebony friesian, I turned my gaze to the rider.

Aleron was staring directly at me, face hard as stone, but

when I met his gaze his lips twitched and soon formed a large grin. Only his eyes were squinting with worry.

I waved at him slightly, trying not to draw Hassan's attention. My lips pressed into a line, remembering all the things we had discussed.

His eyes dropped to the ground and back at me, his face unreadable. He kicked his horse and off he went into the trees, becoming just a ghost to my eyes.

CHAPTER 23

*W*e had made it back to the castle without any obstacles. I was shown to my room without any greetings, without any smiles, without a word. Instead of bows and questions, I was given glares. Some turned their heads the other way, others ignored my very presence. Luckily, Hassan refused to let me go alone and accompanied me, letting me know at least one person knew of my existence.

We had made it to my room, Hassan closing the door and sinking into the rug. "That was a long ride." He patted the rug next to him and I let my back lay on the hard rug like it was as soft as cotton.

"Very," I said, propping myself up on my elbow and using the other hand to comb through my hair. It was all tangled and I cringed at the idea of combing through it, knowing I'd probably take out heaps of hair in the process.

Hassan laid down, closed his eyes and acted like he was in a deep sleep, not moving at all. I tried doing the same but found that my endless energy wouldn't let me keep my eyes shut for even five minutes. I gave up on the idea of rest, instead listening to Hassan's small breaths of air.

After at least fifteen minutes of listening to Hassan's breathing, I started to become weary. I opened my mouth, wanting to speak but quickly shut it, realizing that he really might be asleep. I started coming to my knees to exit the room until his eyes jerked open and he came to a sitting position.

"Where are you going?" he inquired to know.

I laughed and let my knees sink back into the floor. "I thought you were asleep so I was going to let you rest. But apparently I don't have to anymore," I told him.

He chuckled and lay back down, eyes still open. "I don't sleep during the day. I don't sleep very much at night either," he admitted.

I stared down into his eyes with an addled expression, but my thoughts wouldn't stay on his sleeping habits for long. They moved to more important things. Which resolved into my least favorite thing: questions.

I was so tired of people asking me questions, just as tired as I was having to ask others for the answers. It seemed like an endless cycle that no matter how hard I tried and no matter how many times I asked; my questions were never *fully* answered.

I took in a deep breath, shaking away the obnoxious thoughts. "Hassan, may I ask you something?" I tried not to sound aggravated by my burning question.

"Anything," he said gently, not noticing my tone.

I hesitated to ask. He would tell me if I needed to know,

wouldn't he? Well they didn't tell me about the war upfront and that was something I needed to know, so maybe he wouldn't. Either way, I proceeded to ask.

"This morning, after you all talked about the footprints by my tent, it seemed there was something else you all were worrying about. Something important. I don't know if it was my imagination or not, but if it wasn't, will you please tell me what it was you were all distressed about?" I began playing with my hands, trying not to look up but my eyes somehow found his face.

Hassan closed his eyes tightly, his lips pressing together. He sat up, letting his hands brush through his hair, eyes still shut.

"Allene, I don't want to answer that," he whispered.

I sighed, letting go of my hands. "You said–"

"I know what I said," he insisted, shaking his head.

I felt my insides go numb, realizing the question must've been irritating him all morning and I just made it worse.

He shook his head. "You need to know, I just don't want to be the one to tell you."

He caught his breath and took my hands for reassurance. He let them drop onto his knees, grasping them tightly. He didn't meet my gaze, he didn't move, the only thing that I heard was a whisper. The whisper came in one quick breath.

"I am fighting in the war and so is Damien."

My heart beat stopped, my eyes became watery within seconds and my voice was sharp. I let one tear leak through as Hassan squeezed my hands and met my gaze with a sad expression.

Hassan was well fit, could ride a horse and use a sword,

but he'd never been in a war and he wasn't a knight. He'd die. Even worse, Damien! He wasn't even of fighting age yet.

"What? That's absurd, you can't! Neither of you can, I won't let you," I sobbed, feeling my chest huffing.

"Allene, we have to," he spoke calmly and with regret.

"No, you don't! I am giving you a way out of it."

He shook his head at my option. "I don't need a way out of it. I already gave my word."

"Hassan, I am ordering you not to. You aren't even prepared, you're not a soldier. You'll die, you both will!" I shuddered at the thought. The war was becoming even more real now. I couldn't lose Damien, he was my best friend, and I already almost lost him once from my own mistakes. Hassan was too much of a saint; I couldn't stand the thought of them losing their lives on a battlefield.

"I won't die." He laughed, finding humor that I even said such a thing. He managed to stop my crying but I almost screamed with frustration.

"How can you keep that promise? You can't, you have no way of knowing what will become of you!" I shouted.

"I was the greatest sword fighter there was in Selvet. I am a natural at jousting. What experience I have, it will do. It will bring me back to you," he spoke with certainty. I sobbed some more, his words not helping.

I eventually stopped crying, but the ache was still lingering in my throat. I swallowed, hoping the pain would disappear and was officially exhausted from my relentless inconsistent crying over the last few days. It was finally getting to be too much, my emotions left me at a complete breaking point.

"What were you thinking agreeing to all of this? Why

would you offer to risk your life?" I asked the main question without yelling, one success of the day.

"I was thinking of Valteria, my family. You. I want you to be safe; I can't let them take you again. I will do everything I can to protect what I care about and if it means fighting in the war, so be it," he concluded softly.

I smiled and placed one hand on his cheek, the warmth of his skin made my hand burn, so I pulled it back but kept the smile that seemed to make him grin too.

Aleron said a similar thing. I felt guilty, both of them saying they were fighting for me, when it wasn't needed. It was an awful position to be in when the people I care about are being put in harm's way by other people I care about. It was all so complicated, but Hassan had already committed and I had to thank him.

"Hassan, thank you. Just promise me–"

"I'll be safe and I'll keep *you* safe. I promise."

~

I clenched my hands into fists as I walked past another maid, her gray eyes mocking, her silver hair flat and her voice intending to be rude.

"Look who it is. I believe Praseria is the other way your majesty. Unless you're looking for the prison, it's down two flights of stairs and to your left," she hissed.

I stopped walking; my fists became blades that lay by my sides. I took one small breath and tried to play back. I cocked my head toward her and smiled, acting like I took the question seriously.

"Thank you, and what direction would lead me the farthest away from you?" My reply was snark, but I was growing tired of swallowing people being impolite. The maid was not amused, her lips went into a line.

"Are you aware of what you have done to Valteria?" She stepped closer, pushing me back. "We are ruined because of you and we are all going to pay for your mistake. When I say all of us, that includes you." Her voice became soft, but the softer it was the sharper it felt.

"Watch your tongue, don't forget your place. You have no right to speak to me that way. I was trying to do what was right for Valteria," I said firm and harsh.

"Doing what was right for Valteria or what was right for *you?*" The maid didn't falter at my rebuttal, she was not even slightly intimidated by my defense.

I couldn't speak. My words were gone but the old maid continued to speak.

"Princess, you are the only one who can make this better. You are the future of Valteria. It is on your shoulders to decide if Valteria is destined for a beautiful fate or a tragic one."

We were silent for many moments, the lady staring directly at me and giving me the shivers. The old maid straightened up and coughed, waving her hand for me to proceed to where I was going to go.

I pushed my legs as hard as I could but was having trouble actually bending them, so I began gliding to Risa's room. I finally bent one knee and the other started to loosen too, until I was sprinting to Risa's room, hearing my thunderous footsteps echoing through the deserted corridors.

When I reached Risa's room, the door was already open. I threw myself through the doorway, not thinking twice, only wanting to escape the stares. I froze as soon as I realized my mistake of not knocking. I tried turning back but it was too late, I was caught.

Risa and Marshal were holding hands, caught leaning into one another, both of them entranced. The sound of my entrance left their faces full of shock, mirroring mine. Risa quickly shook Marshal's hand like they were just saying good-bye.

"Thank you for bringing my handkerchief Marshal, it's very kind of you to return it to me." Risa pushed her eyebrows up at Marshal's perplexed face. He understood and swiftly pulled out a handkerchief, handing it to Risa.

"The pleasure is all mine," he responded.

Marshal let go of her hand and bowed to her. He nodded to me and ran out of the room. I placed my hands on my hips, eyeing her with a smile. Once she realized I was staring at her she jumped back and grinned.

"What?" she asked.

"Absolutely nothing," I lied casually, picking up one of her glass figurines that she displayed at the entry of her room.

Risa furrowed her brow, but wore a slight smile.

"Allene, you cannot smile like that and say 'nothing'. What is it?"

I laughed and threw back my head, my arms reaching for the air.

"Risa, do not attempt to deny it, you know I saw, " I stated the obvious but Risa wouldn't budge.

"I do not know what you are talking about, Allene."

We were silent for many moments until Risa sighed, tapping her foot.

"Tell me what it is you want to say," she blurted.

"Marshal and you? I saw it right before my eyes! How could you have not mentioned it to me?" I asked her.

She sighed but smiled, indicating my outburst was accurate.

"I felt it was not important to say a word about it until I was completely sure of the way he felt. I didn't want to over exaggerate. After all, we literally *just* met yesterday." She chuckled and was looking off into space, almost like I wasn't here.

"Are you sure now?" I interrupted happily.

She sighed again, this time with pleasure.

"Possibly, but this is just our secret. Can you imagine how mother would react to my interest toward a guard? He hasn't even achieved knighthood yet."

"Risa, it could be no worse than her catching you with the enemy prince . . . trust me, it's worth a–"

"No, please, Allene! Do not speak of this, not ever again. I need time." Risa grabbed my hands and dropped to her knees begging.

I crouched down to her level, my lips tight and my heart aching at her reaction. It was such a shame that we feared the reaction of our mother, of her disapproval, robbing ourselves of our own happiness for the sake of hers. I sighed with thoughts of Aleron.

"Time. That's what we all need." I bit my tongue, wishing I wouldn't have said anything.

Risa placed a hand on my forehead with worry. "Allene are you—"

"I'm fine, forget I said a word," I muttered sadly. I turned my head away from her hand and made my legs straighten until I was standing and staring out the sunny window. Fluffy clouds passed through the sky, moving slowly, my eyes barely catching the movement. The sun was casting a blanket of light on the grass, the energy of it all sparkling.

I heard Risa sigh, my gaze returning to her. Risa still held a small grin but her face was filled with deep concern that echoed my own. She looked around the room casually and set her eyes on me.

"I assume you did not come to discuss Marshal and I. What is the reason for your visit?" she queried in a joyful tone, trying to lighten the darkened mood in the room.

I nodded, trying to change my lips into a smile, but my lips returned to a frown realizing why I came in the first place. The room felt less bright every second.

"Risa, I've been thinking about the situation we are facing. I have given it a lot of thought and I would appreciate your support. I am going to leave Valteria."

Risa gaped. "What? Allene, you have officially lost your mind, we just got you back." I could hear the disbelief in her voice.

I let my eyelids drape over my eyes and I could feel my stomach ache uncomfortably. But I somehow proceeded to speak with a faint whisper.

"I'm not meant to rule Valteria, it's obvious I have only caused harm to the kingdom. I've made everyone look like a fool and this whole war is partly because of me. I need to try to make it right and I think the way to make it right is for me to leave entirely."

"Allene, that's not true, you're just right for Valteria. You are the spitting image of father. We need you. Do you remember what father did? How it all began? At first it seemed like he was making everything a mess, but what happened in the end? He saved everyone in Valteria, on more than one occasion I might add. I have no doubt that you will make things right, but you'll make them right by staying here."

I chuckled. "You sound just like Ezra." The words came out before I could even realize they had been said.

Risa paused. "Who is Ezra?" she asked, confused. Now was not the time to dive into this, but I didn't have another choice.

"He's our grandfather," I said timidly. Risa's face lit up at my reply, her excitement difficult to contain as she tried to stay in place.

"As in father's father? An Amena? Praseria's old king? That grandfather?" she asked every question imaginable to be sure it was clear. I nodded, smiling at the thought of how happy I was to finally have a memory that I could hold onto of my grandfather.

"You've been keeping a lot from me about your time in Praseria haven't you? I want to know everything. What is he like?" Risa beamed with curiosity.

"He's a lot like father, gentle, kind, sincere. He took care of me while I was there. He recognized me right away," I recalled.

Risa squealed from excitement. "Allene, that is incredible! I never imagined either of us would have the chance to meet him. What about grandmother? Did you meet her?" Risa asked.

Discussing my time in Praseria was growing more and more difficult. It felt like the joy I experienced there was going to be taken away from me if I talked about it openly. I wanted to keep it to myself, to not hear anyone else's opinions of my time there, whether the comments were good or bad.

"We should talk about this later, Risa. I don't think I can handle another heavy conversation," I admitted. The light in Risa's eyes dimmed, picking up on the mood I was emitting.

"Allene, this just gives another reason for you to stay. You need time to recover from everything that has happened. I don't think it is wise to be making an important decision, such as abandoning your throne, before you have even had time to try and sort things out." Risa's tone became one of contemplation and empathy. She shook her head multiple times and that seemed all she could do for many moments.

"And if that reason still isn't enough then consider this. I need you, *we need you*. You cannot abandon us. The only way I can see you making things worse, is leaving us at the time that we need you most. You've left us once, don't leave us again," Risa pleaded.

"I am only thinking of the good of the people. They have mother and you to rely on. They don't need me too," I mentioned.

Risa grumbled with a small smirk at the thought of just them ruling. I smiled too, the first time in a while.

"I cannot do this without you. Mother is not going to live forever, and when she is gone I need someone else there to help me through everything this world will throw at me. I *need* my sister, I need you, Allene. I hope you will find refuge in needing us too. Please let that be enough to stay." Those were her faint words. Risa was silent for a minute but she realized she couldn't end her speech there. She patted my shoulder and chuckled.

"Besides that, I *want* you here. I want my daft, loving, sweet and gentle sister with me on all my journeys. Can you do that for me?" she implored.

Risa tugged me into a loving embrace. I didn't pull away but hugged her back. She was always providing beneficial advice, laughing when it was silent, and having a warm heart toward everyone. When she ended the embrace her face was glowing, making mine beam in return.

"I also can't bear the thought of you being alone. I can't fathom where you would go and I will not let anything happen to you again. Allene, stay." Her eyes enlarged while mine closed, searching my mind for the true answer. I didn't want to worry about going back on my word, so I gave her no words at all, just the faintest nod. I realized if I told her I'd stay, I could keep my word . . . but only for a little while.

CHAPTER 24

*D*amien and Risa had tried to distract me for the last day, playing games of cards and checkers to pass the time. Or so they said. Part of me felt they were keeping watch over me, ensuring I didn't do anything foolish, hiding behind checkers and cards as their excuse to supervise. Hassan was off helping prepare supplies for battle but I found myself yearning for his upbeat presence too.

No matter the true intentions of our time together, we all knew what would be coming and we couldn't shake the mood of impending doom that seemed to overtake the castle walls. We took advantage of the opportunity to catch up, just like we used to.

"Damien, whatever happened with you and that girl at the Gala festival?" I asked innocently, prying to know more about his secret love life. I had just lost another game of checkers to Risa, growing bored of the repetition. I had never been very good at checkers, but I would at least win every now and again. Risa must have been practicing.

"There are much more interesting topics that we could discuss," Damien replied, trying to shift the conversation in another direction.

"Like?" I took the bait to hear his suggestions.

"Your flirtation with my brother, Risa's new obsession with Marshal, there are literally countless more topics worth gossiping about than my life." Damien raised his eyebrows.

Risa went pale, lightly hitting my arm with disatification. "Allene, you swore not to tell anyone, you gave your word!" she said sternly.

I raised my hands in defense. "I didn't say anything, I swear."

"She didn't. It's that obvious, Risa," Damien confirmed.

Risa huffed, rearranging the checkers board like she didn't believe it for a second.

"You dodged the other topic Allene," Damien mocked.

"I didn't dodge it, there just wasn't anything to say," I replied.

"You're just as subtle as Risa I'm afraid, you are both terrible at hiding things. I really should offer to teach you how to be better at it, but then I would miss out on all the fun of seeing your shocked faces when I know more than you think." He chuckled at the thought. We both rolled our eyes, not letting him pester us any longer.

"There is something I don't know however. What did Laerina discuss with you the other day? It seemed like she wanted you for something serious," Damien said, not worried about overstepping. He really was like a brother to me. Risa's interest peaked as well at the sudden mention of it.

"Yes, what did she say to you?" Risa asked. My mother hadn't been seen by any of us since arriving back at the castle. The conversation between her and I remained unfinished. As awkward as it had been to see my mother that way, I wanted to know the rest of the story, understand why she felt it was important to speak with me in the first place. She hadn't told me much of anything that I didn't already know.

"I wish I knew. She asked me to leave after getting emotional about her and father's story."

"That's what she wanted to talk to you about? Mother never speaks about their love story, or really anything involving her past," Risa said perplexed. I shrugged.

"It was odd, she didn't seem herself. I was partially expecting a lecture about everything that happened in Praseria. It wasn't a conversation I anticipated."

"I'm glad she didn't reprimand you. I want to leave Praseria and everything else in the past, pick up where we left off, like it never happened. I'm tired of all of us thinking about it," Damien said, quietly protesting.

Risa nodded. "I agree with Damien, no reason to drudge up the past. Mother might have had some nostalgia being in Praseria, maybe that's why she brought it up? I have no doubt it made her think of father. But we are home now, we don't have to bring it up again." Risa reached for my hand, squeezing it lightly. *I wish it were that simple to forget.*

A quiet knock came to the door in the drawing room we had been hiding away in. It was mother's personal messenger, Henry. He was an older man, tall and skinny. His blond hair was patchy and wispy. He had a tender demeanor and for being a messenger, he had always been more reserved.

"Your majesties, the queen requests your presence in her chambers." He turned, walking away, expecting us to follow right away. Risa and I exchanged looks.

Damien waved his hand in the air as he slouched deeper into his seat. "I'll be here," he said, closing his eyes, looking like he was ready for a nap. Risa picked up her dress and nodded for me to follow her, leaving the checkerboard behind us.

Henry was quite far ahead of us. Risa and I walked arm in arm as we approached our mother's room. Henry waited patiently in front of my mother's door until we caught up and with a gentle knock, Henry opened the door, escorting us inside.

My mother's room was quite the opposite of the rest of our castle. It had a lot of details to observe. Mother collected rocks, it was an interest of hers ever since I can remember. Different stones and colors surrounded her room, some glittering and shining in the light of the sun that came through her large windows. My favorite was a large chunk of amethyst that sat on her bookshelf. My mother was standing next to it actually, studying the other rocks that were displayed near it.

Henry announced our arrival. "Queen Laerina, Princesses Allene and Risa Amena." His announcement could barely be heard in the large room. He turned around and walked out, shutting the doors behind him. Risa and I waited for our mother to acknowledge us, standing patiently by the door.

Mother was dressed in her nightgown, also something

unusual for us to see her in, especially this late in the day. She turned our way, her hair not in its normally perfect braid, her eyes had dark circles and her face was drained of almost all color. Her eyelids were puffy and red, she did not look well.

Risa didn't wait to be spoken to first, she approached my mother quickly, the sight of her alarming us both.

"Mother, you should have called upon us sooner. Are you unwell?" Risa asked.

Laerina threw a hand up to stop Risa from coming closer, finally looking at us.

"I have some matters to discuss with you both. Sit," she demanded, pointing to the couch in the center of the room. Risa wasn't going to ask the question again, quietly obeying her orders. We sat down on the couch, realizing mother was not in the mood to be spoken to. She wanted to get straight to business.

Laerina passed back and forth, trying to keep her composure as she spoke.

"As you both know, the few times we have been at war, your father would oversee battles to help command the soldiers and lead them. I was hoping we would have a new king before another war occurred to step into this role, but seeing as neither of you are married, it leaves us with few options." She paused, ensuring we understood, then continued.

"It is important that I stay at the castle. The people are very unsettled and we need to show a strong front as a family to give them hope. I have decided you both will participate in overseeing the battle in two days to help command the soldiers in my place."

Risa and I both gaped in shock. Risa was quick to reply. "Mother, I do not support this. Why would we go near the battle? We can show support by being here and having Ajax oversee the commands."

"The people doubt where our family's loyalty lies. By supporting the troops and leading the commands, it will clearly show your allegiance to this kingdom," Laerina said.

Risa objected. "My loyalties have never been questioned, this is absurd."

"It's not yours the people are worried about," she replied, looking directly at me. Risa was now silent, unsure how to proceed. We all knew mother was only talking about me. It was not fair to drag Risa into this mess when I was the problem.

"You're talking about me," I said.

"Indeed I am," she replied. I looked at Risa, who had become silent now that the conversation had shifted in my direction.

"Let me go then, Risa can stay here with you," I suggested. I knew she was only wanting me to go out of spite, forcing me to watch and prove some hidden agenda she has against Aleron.

Laerina shook her head. "Risa is going, I don't trust you to go alone," Laerina replied.

"Why not?"

"I am no fool, Allene, the soldiers are supposed to obey your every command if you go. With your twitterpated heart, heaven only knows what you might do to save your Praserian prince. I know you object to this war and my decisions for this kingdom. I intend to make a public statement by having you go in my place, but don't be mistaken, I don't trust your judgement in the slightest. That is why Risa must go with you."

She meant it when she said it was a public statement. I was no help with battle tactics, and even if I was, I would never offer to help in this situation. She already made it clear she saw right through me. There would be no order from me to retreat and stop the war. My objections had been noted and dismissed. I yearned to help Aleron in some way but all my efforts had so far proven worthless.

"It's all right, Allene, I will go with you. We will be back before we know it," Risa said sweetly, trying to change the mood in the room. I know she didn't want to go, she was very brave for pretending to be okay with it. I was scared too, but it seemed we had no choice.

"It is settled, you will take leave in the morning. You are dismissed," Laerina said, motioning for us to exit the room. Risa and I picked up our dresses as we made our way to the door.

"Allene?" Laerina said.

I turned, my lips in a hard line. "Yes?"

"Do not be slow to remember where your responsibility lies," she said firmly.

I nodded, not wanting to give her a verbal reply. *I wish I knew where my responsibility was, it would make all of this a lot easier.*

As awful as it was thinking about watching and commanding the war, I oddly took comfort in the idea of being close to Aleron during the battle, even if it was under such ghastly circumstances.

~

*T*he time had arrived for the army to depart. We had ridden for hours, no one complaining or mentioning the time. My constant audible sighs of impatience made the soldiers grow irritable. Each time they would wince, thinking it was someone else and I silently chuckled, making it a game.

Ajax was leading the warriors with gallantry, each step his horse made rang in my ears repeatedly. When I wasn't sighing, every silent breath a man took in felt like a sword in my stomach and was as loud as a thunderstorm. It all came too fast. One day I was living my dream, the next I was living my worst nightmare and there was no one to wake me up. The war was going to begin in a matter of hours and I would be forced to watch those I love attempt to kill each other. I shut my eyes and let my horse walk at the end of the group with Risa tagging along by my side.

For the last two days, Risa had been tirelessly trying to get everything off my mind, trying to make me feel better and distract me, but nothing worked. I tried to stop thinking entirely, let everything go and be happy but how could anyone in their right state of mind find any joy in what was about to come?

I let the horses' footsteps vibrate through my whole body, leaving a numb tingle in my feet, but before I could blink the feeling was gone. I opened my eyes to see Risa trembling, her shoulders shook and her eyes were blank. I stretched out my hand and laid it on her shoulder, feeling her begin to stop.

"Risa, what is troubling you?" I queried. Risa grimaced and

looked toward Marshal who was in the distance. He was by a clearing of trees up ahead, his face looked concentrated and determined. Risa turned away quickly and threw her arms up to the darkened sky.

"All of this! Marshal isn't safe and I have to watch him fight for his life with no justifiable cause! Mother's cold blooded heart knows the pain of losing someone and yet she happily will let us share her sorrows. I'm scared for Marshal, I'm frightened for you and I, and . . . well, everyone is in danger and I can't bear to see it." She released her neck and held onto her horse tightly for comfort, but no matter how tight she held, the sobs wouldn't stop.

I had never seen Risa like this. I had no idea how to handle it. Usually she was the one comforting me, not the other way around.

I patted her back repeatedly, tilting me off the steed many times and my hand grabbing the mane before I could fall flat on my bosom. The patting didn't seem to help either of us so I whispered and hummed. Many minutes after she was breathing heavily, the cries were gone and a smile was on her face, doing her best to return her generally happy demeanor.

I snickered. "Risa, everything is going to be alright." We both knew that my words could not be absolutely true, but it was enough to comfort Risa. She sat up straight, her breathing even, as she stared at me for many moments.

I felt uncomfortable knowing that she was looking at me but not saying a word, so I fixed my gaze on her and once I did, Risa spoke in a soft voice.

"Allene, you're a better role model than you realize."

I tried laughing but instead a quick breath came out of smiling lips. "I beg your pardon?" I managed to say.

Risa nodded to my comment and looked fascinated. "You're watching all of your loved ones go to war, you're watching them suffer, yet here you are so serene and. . . well, I wish I could act the same. You don't even seem worried about. . ." Risa stopped speaking. I tilted my head to the side, wishing she would continue, but she did not.

"Worried about. . .?" I began, acknowledging her to proceed.

Risa bit her lip, seeming like she regretted mentioning it in the first place, but continued. "Hassan and Damien, but more importantly, Aleron. I haven't heard you mention him in two days," she pointed out. I was hoping she wouldn't notice.

I looked at my hands, his name making my body throb. There was a reason I hadn't mentioned him, it was too much pain for my heart to handle. I was trying to hide it. I was trying to clear him out of all my memories, but the effort was wasted, it was too late. Aleron would forever be in my thoughts.

A small clear tear leaked through my squinting eyes. "You're wrong, Risa. He's all I'm worried about. I would rather die myself than watch him suffer." My voice was low and slow, my lips pressed into a straight line. My hands rubbed the back of my neck, my mind forming a picture of his perfect face.

"Allene . . . I'm sorry I even–"

"It's fine," I said quickly, not wanting to hear another word on the subject. Risa fell silent, the discussion brought to a standstill.

Rain soon pattered the dirt, resolving into small puddles of mud. Some thunder boomed miles away, faint to my ears, for the wind hushed all sounds. Our country and wildlife seemed to always fit the mood of our people. It was almost like our earth was bonded to our emotions, and right now it was crying with us. Crying for me, my father, and our soon to be broken land.

The rain was a drizzle and the little droplets glistened in my ebony hair. My dress was becoming wet, as well as Risa's. Risa pulled a cloak from the sack on her horse and draped it over herself for protection. I stretched my hand out to find my own cloak, but decided it wasn't worth it now. I was already drenched and it would only get the cloak wet, so I went on letting the rain saturate my pale skin.

Ajax yelled a command, but all I heard was a hum. All the soldiers came to a halt, forcing me to quickly reign back my horse before I could run into them. Marshal looked back to Risa to show a faint grin and then returned his focus to Ajax. I couldn't spot Damien, but toward the front I saw a head swiftly look to me. It was Hassan. His face held no expression. He slowly sighed and looked back to Ajax.

A man, one behind Hassan, nodded and slid off his horse and started running toward Risa and I. The poor soldier was trying not to seem bothered having to run in a complete downpour.

"Please, if you will follow me, I shall escort you to a safer spot, your majesties." He took our horses reins and led us into the trees, leaving everyone else behind.

The man had taken us quite a ways. We were in the middle of a hill, surrounded by bushes and trees. There was a small hole the trees formed that revealed the Praserian's coming from the other end of the battlefield, marching with wicked grins. They had a determination in their eyes that made me shiver.

My face froze at the sight of the man in front. Aleron. His hair stuck to his head, his eyes squinting when water fell on his face. He wore gold battle armor that glistened whenever a droplet of water fell on it. He placed his hand on his sword, preparing to draw it at any minute. He looked at the Valterian soldiers in front of him, gazing all around, like he was searching for something. Three other men were at the front with him, one patted his shoulder and his search ended. I could not tell who they were, so I stopped staring at them and focused on the soldier behind me who was trying to capture my attention.

"They cannot see you up here unless you go through the trees. Do not try to move any closer than you are now. If you have any orders to give during the battle, my messenger will deliver them to Ajax to ensure they are met. If anything happens, if they do spot you, I want you to run up the hill and don't come back down until someone retrieves you." His voice was monotone and it made me tired just to listen, we both nodded so we wouldn't have to hear it again.

The soldier was on full alert, looking all around, sometimes going into the trees if he heard something. All I could do was look at the ground, the anticipation of the battle growing. Soon enough, the battle would be in full swing.

I could feel the tension in the air, the eerie silence that blanketed the area despite thousands of people being present. I didn't want to see what was going to happen, it was all too much, but one sound was all it took to grab my attention.

"For Valteria!" I heard a yell and many shouts following after. I heard feet and hooves traveling toward each other. I dared myself to look up as I repeated prayers in my head. I could only hope Aleron would be able to defend himself and be well enough protected by his men. Damien and Hassan had been positioned toward the back of our group soldiers, so I prayed they would hardly fight. As much as I didn't want Aleron having to lose the battle and surrender, I knew my mother wouldn't budge. I prayed he would surrender for the sake of everyone. It was the only way to avoid people getting hurt.

Men were meeting each other quickly and as soon as they did, a sword struck another man's shield. The swords metal was louder than the thunder and many horses were slipping when trying to run. The battle seemed very even, each side holding their own.

Risa seemed shaken by the commotion, trying to ignore what was in front of us. I wanted to do the same. After what felt like hours and the soldiers becoming a massive pool of metal armor, I tried looking for Hassan and Damien. I took all the courage I had to actually search out my friends, but the hopes of seeing them ok was enough for me to dare myself to look. After minutes of searching, I couldn't spot either of them, which I hoped meant they were still at the back, not having to confront the battle.

"Soldier, is there any word of the possibility of retreat?" I asked the guard nearby, trying to drown out the shouts and cries that were becoming more frequent on the battlefield.

Risa had placed her hands over her ears, closing her eyes trying to escape it all. The soldier shook his head, not fazed by the scene, knowing this is what he trained for.

"Praseria hasn't sent any messengers or raised any flags. Don't fear princess, we won't give in," he said firmly, obviously not wanting to even discuss it. *He must have spoken with my mother, she wasn't kidding about them ignoring me if I mentioned retreat.*

Then I heard a loud cry that I recognized immediately, snapping my attention back to the battle before me. I wiped my head in the direction it had come from. Damien was leaning over a man, the sight of it clearly in my view. Damien's sword had found its way into the man's chest. Damien's eyes looked terrified but a loud cry of joy escaped his lips as he charged for another man without thinking twice. Damien came to a stop when a man much larger than him swung at his feet unexpectedly. Damien jumped back just in time and seemed infuriated by the attempt. I had never seen this side of Damien , it was fascinating and terrifying all at the same time.

He took a few steps back, almost in a teasing manner, screamed and charged at the man. The man prepared to strike but Damien threw his sword like a spear, striking the man in the knee. Without another breath he fell flat onto the ground as Damien finished him off with a smile. I shuddered, turning away from the gruesome sight of my best friend.

I looked at Risa who had opened her eyes again, her face filled with pure horror, like she had just seen a ghost.

"Risa we don't have to–" but she cut me off by pointing in

the direction she was looking. I stared in the direction her finger was guiding my eyes to.

My feet instantly went numb, my senses on such high alert that I couldn't feel a thing. My lungs couldn't form any more air. I searched for it desperately, to save me from the feeling of water collapsing all around me. Finally a small breath was made and I blinked once more to see if it was all real. Hassan reared up his horse and soon enough was charging toward a man shining in gold; Aleron.

Aleron ran out of the way, swinging in mid air, pushing Hassan to retreat. Hassan took his sword and swung back, making the swords compete against one another. Aleron was caught off balance by the motion, but managed to grab his horse's mane and pull himself back up.

Aleron stepped back as Hassan moved forward. I could see their lips moving but couldn't tell what was being said, it was obvious however that Hassan was not happy.

Stop! Stop! Stop! I wanted to run, run to both of them but what was I to do when I got there? It wouldn't be safe, I probably wouldn't be able to even reach them if I tried. Besides, the guard wouldn't let me pass the clearing, and with one sound I could ruin everything. I bit my lip hard, not realizing the pain until moments later as I tasted blood on my tongue.

I watched them fight like it was a bad dream I couldn't wake up from. My heart sank with every wince Hassan made and every grunt that escaped Aleron's lips. I tried to stay still, not move, knowing I would be tempted to run to them if I did. After many minutes of watching Hassan barely being swiped and Aleron falling off his horse multiple times, I gave up. I couldn't just stand here and let two people I cared for try to kill each other.

I gripped my horses reins, ready to sprint in their direction, but a small sound made me stop. I turned to see Risa staring at me as she then flickered her gaze to Aleron and Hassan. She turned back to me with sadness, already knowing what I was about to do.

I sighed. "Risa, I'm sorry," I whispered regretfully.

Risa looked up the hill to the soldier who was looking around a bush. Quickly returning her gaze to me she sighed. "Go," she confirmed in a whisper.

I patted her shoulder in silent gratitude and quickly kicked my horse, sending it through the trees and running down the hill with a loud yell behind me, forcing myself to commit to my plan.

The delayed realization of what I was doing set in. I was entering a battle ground. An untrained princess ready to stop a war with no sword or armor. *I was an absolute genius.*

Could I stop it? Could I have stopped this all along? I felt insane and afraid but I didn't look back. I looked forward to what needed to be handled and I knew I was the only person who could make it stop. Hassan turned his head at the noise, but Aleron didn't notice.

Hassan screamed at me even though I couldn't understand a word he said. Aleron swung back at Hassan who ducked before he could be hit.

"Hassan, Aleron, stop!" I screamed at the top of my lungs, my throat becoming tight. Aleron's sword froze at the sound, my attempt to be a distraction to them both was working.

I propelled my horse, sprinting at its fastest down the hill.

Aleron and Hassan had pushed one another toward the bottom of the hill, almost like they knew where I was and purposely chose that spot to fight in the first place.

Aleron turned his horse in my direction, as well as Hassan, both scampering toward me, neglecting each other's presence.

I kicked my horse again, harder this time, trying to gain speed to meet them, but the mud was too much. The horse's legs tangled as I toppled forward into the mud, landing hard on my back.

My eyes flew open, my vision blurry. I saw my horse taking off without me, leaving me on a battlefield with no weapons and no way of escaping my draw with fate. Nothing hurt but I was perplexed as I lay in the mud, not wanting to move, until I heard a shout that seemed to awaken me from my daze.

"Allene, get up! Run! Hurry!" I looked up to see Hassan speeding ahead of Aleron, trying to get to me before he could, but before he could say anymore, a man came out of view and hit him on the side of the head, plummeting him into the mud, unconscious.

"Hassan!" I yelled. I propped myself up onto my elbow, trying to get sight of what had just happened. The man picked Hassan up and started carrying him in the opposite direction.

Aleron didn't break his glance at the sudden event, but stared at me as he inched closer, his forehead creased. Aleron's cheeks were bright red, his eyes squinting like he had never seen me before. Soon enough his horse stopped right by my feet, his usually gentle hand roughly grabbing for mine.

"Allene, take my hand!" he demanded. *Allene? He told me he didn't want to call me that.* I ignored the odd moment and did as I was told. Aleron grasped my hand tightly, not letting me go. I bent my legs and slowly made my way up. Aleron was staring down at me as my vision was trying to clear, everything around me continuing to blur.

I enjoyed the moment, the moment of feeling safe again, but my thoughts wandered to Hassan. I waited a few moments seeing if Aleron would discuss what had just occurred, doing my best to dismiss the scenes of brutality around us, assuming we were both in a state of shock, but he only continued to stare. I could've done the same but I was tired of waiting. Hassan was hurt and I called it to attention.

"Hassan! Wh-" Aleron looked over my shoulder, then grabbed my elbows, his eyes filled with what I assumed was regret.

"Allene, I'm sorry." It took me a moment to realize he wasn't apologizing about Hassan, he was apologizing to me. Without another thought, something slammed into the back of my skull, sending me to the ground. A gruesome pounding filled my head followed by a painful ringing in my ears. I couldn't gather my thoughts fast enough to realize what had just happened, besides one thing. *Hassan warned me.*

I should've gone back when I had the chance. I was wrong. Somehow I knew that Aleron had let go of me and he had planned to all along.

CHAPTER 25

y eyes peeled open. It was dark and cold, so cold my teeth were chattering the instant I thought of it. A putrid smell of mold and blood was in the air. My head felt like it was pounding and my entire body felt bruised. I looked at my pale skin, noticing blue spots in multiple places accented with goosebumps. My hands were tucked under my body, a blanket draped over my shoulder. My feet showed evidence of being tied up, the marks leftover, burning. My stomach felt empty, my face felt drained of all color, my throat was screaming for water, and my legs implored for movement.

I tried rolling my head to the side, my cheek lying on the stone, stinging my skin in contact. My head jolted up at the feeling, the blood rushing to my head too fast, making me close my eyes while I recovered. My head felt like it would explode, my body felt like it was tilting, like everything was rotating and nothing could stop it, but a simple touch did.

A warm hand wrapped around my cheek, the touch burned, but the feeling of some needed heat was exhilarating, making my senses finally return to normal. I opened my eyes.

Hassan blinked like he couldn't believe what he was seeing. His hair was a mess, blood marks littered his clothes, his cheeks were red, his hands were bruised and there were a few cuts on his arms. He looked like he was in pain, but tried to pull a smile on his face when he saw me staring back into his blank eyes.

He brushed my hair back and lightly laid his hand back on my cheek, his thumb rubbing my skin gently. Slowly, I brought my hand up to my cheek, resting my hand on his, sighing with relief. We sat silently for many moments, staring back at each other, like we hadn't seen each other in ages.

"You're alive," a small whisper escaped his dry lips following a long sigh, his voice filled with exhaustion and relief.

"Hassan–"

His warm finger pressed against my lips. "I'm fine. Are *you* all right?"

I nodded, not mentioning all the pain. Hassan ran his hand up my arm; I shuddered every time his hand brushed my bruises.

His eyes closed. "Allene. . .I'm so sorry."

"Hassan–" He cut me off again, meeting my eyes this time.

"For not warning you," he clarified.

"What do you mean?" I quickly said in my hoarse voice before he could cut me off again.

"Aleron told me his whole plan on the battlefield. Once

you started coming to us, I knew it was too late to warn you. I'm so sorry."

I let my hand drop, pulling away from the moment. "Plan?"

Hassan paused, seemingly happy to tell me the news that would help his point against Aleron, yet saddened he would wound me in the process.

"He isn't what you thought, he used you," Hassan rigidly said.

"Why would you say that?" I asked.

"He made you believe he was someone he never was. He made himself out to be a hero. There was no coincidence in him saving you at the Gala festival. He knew who you were the moment he saw you, Risa was not his only target," he said the words uncomfortably, not pleased to give me the details.

I didn't believe him. I wanted to tell Hassan again that he was wrong, wrong about everything between Aleron and I. It hurt to admit such a thing but I knew Hassan whispered the burning truth. I opened my mouth in shock, flashbacks flaming in my mind. *It couldn't be, could it?* Then I remembered.

The look on Aleron's face as he stared at me on the battle-field. He had apologized and at the time I didn't know why, but now it was all making sense. *How could I have been so wrong?*

Neither of us spoke for many moments. The only noise we could hear was the echo of our breathing. Every cold breath that my mouth released shot back, hitting my face and leaving a deadly chill up my spine. I stared at the stone walls of the cell that Risa had only been in a few weeks prior. I never imagined I would be back in this prison under these circumstances.

I sighed, relinquishing defeat. I knew the truth; it was right in front of me. The difficult part of it all was admitting that it was true and telling my heart that it was wrong. Telling myself that the man I defended so devoutely, betrayed me. My trust and love was taken and manipulated. I felt a flood of embarrassment and pity for myself.

Water was starting to form in my eyes. I was trying my hardest to shield the pain. I attempted to stop the tears, but my shield fell and it all came out. Tears hit the stone floor of the prison and words slurred out after them.

"I am such a *fool*. He's a Praserian. Why did I think anything could change our bad blood? Just because my parents managed to overcome it doesn't mean they were happy! I don't know what I was thinking." I was shaking my head back and forth, trying to comprehend my feelings.

"I'm the whole reason we are in this mess. I can't believe I was that dense to believe the things he said! I risked everyone else's lives for nothing. I can't believe this is happening." I was beginning to panic, the reality of it all consuming me. Before I had time to completely lose my sense of self, I was in Hassan's comforting embrace, the panic vanishing. He stroked my arms with reassurance, holding me close. He didn't need to say any words for me to feel his sympathy. I was fooled, I never saw it coming.

I sighed. *I never saw it coming.* I was disappointed in Aleron and in myself. Eventually my sobs slowed to heavy breathing and then soon faded into a steady flow of air. I had cried for well over an hour, my throat dry and Hassan not letting me go for any reason. Hassan saw I needed water so he spoke to me in the dark, empty room.

"I saved you some food and water. Eat up."

Hassan put his arms behind his back then wrapped them back around, this time holding bread, meat and a cup of water.

"Thank you." I grabbed all of it, shoving it down my throat, my stomach growling in excitement at the unexpected meal. The meat was salted and not cooked very well, but it felt good to have substance in my stomach. The bread was surprisingly softer than expected, but there was no flavoring in it at all. The water brought shivers back into my body, but it relieved my throat from further pain. Once I was done with all the food, I turned to Hassan, shoving the now empty bowls out of the way.

"Hassan, I can't comprehend what I did to deserve your endless kindness." I let my face drop to my chest. I had failed him in every way and I felt terrible.

He sighed. His hand curved under my chin and titled it up.

"Allene, don't rob yourself for a single minute of the kindness you deserve. Need I remind you that you are the victim here? I have never once thought less of you through this process." His words were genuine and I knew that. It was refreshing to realize that I had someone in my life who was being *completely* honest and had no hidden agenda.

I had flashed back to just a few days prior, when we had been in my tent at our camp. He had offered me the possibility of him. Of us. I rejected it as soon as Aleron had appeared the following night.

I came to my knees, ignoring the pain of the bruises that battled me to return to a sitting position. I placed my hands on his cheeks and kissed his forehead. I could taste the salt on my lips from the grim and sweat of his skin, realizing that mine was probably the same.

Hassan laid his hands on my shoulders, letting his forehead fall so that ours were leveled, touching. Despite all we had gone through and the condition we were in, Hassan still looked ruggedly handsome. Then he did something completely unexpected. His head came closer, his lips intending to meet mine.

I abruptly pulled back as I subconsciously found myself thinking about what Aleron would think. I nervously looked at Hassan who was trying not to take offense to my sudden change. *Allene, haven't you hurt him enough?* I was angry with myself for letting Aleron ruin another moment of mine, claiming it to be his, always making his way back in.

"Are you all right?" Hassan asked, confused.

I bit my lip. "I'm sorry I got dizzy for a moment." I tried to laugh to lighten the rejection I had accidently sent his way and to my relief he understood.

"I apologize, I didn't mean to. . ." I gave him a small kiss on the cheek and locked my eyes with his.

"Don't. I wouldn't change a thing." *Well, aside from me thinking of Aleron, I would change that.*

Hassan was smiling at my words and I was grateful to see him happy from something I had said. He deserved every bit of happiness I could give to him.

"How long have we been here?" I asked, trying to change the subject.

"Two days," he replied.

"I've been out cold for two days?" My eyes grew large.

"You took quite the hit; I can see why your body needed time to recover."

I shivered at the realization that I was once again going to have to heal from another battle. Something I never thought would happen to me. I'm a princess, not a soldier, or a prisoner, or so I had thought.

"Did we win?" I croaked as I asked the question. For the first time since hearing about the war, I actually wanted us to be the winner, bitterness had officially settled over me.

"They won't tell me. The guards haven't been very keen on talking," Hassan replied.

I frowned. How long would we be kept in here? Would someone come and get us? Were they all dead? Maybe Praseria wanted to negotiate terms and conditions based on our safe release? I couldn't stand thinking negative thoughts so I thought of happy times.

I thought of my father. Riding horses together, feeding the chickens, reading book after book, singing a sweet tune while we cooked. *I miss him.*

The half of me that he took with his death felt even emptier now that I started thinking of him. Nothing could bring him back to me. I felt half alive, half dead. I was left with half a heart. Is that why I couldn't bring myself to focus on Hassan? Did Aleron take the last part of my heart I had to give? *Stop thinking Allene, for once, just stop thinking.*

Many hours passed. It grew colder and the silence made

me restless. One guard stood at the end of the hall, watching me like a hawk. Even though Hassan couldn't get answers from them, maybe I could.

I grasped the bars, tired of the floor and stood up, looking back at him.

"Excuse me, sir." I looked at Hassan who was asleep, snoring over my words. I was glad he wasn't awake to hear me speak.

The guard didn't even acknowledge that I had spoken, he had completely ignored me, fueling my fury.

"Excuse me, sir. I am a princess *and* a lady, not some petty criminal. I believe I deserve that you at least look at me and acknowledge that I've been heard," I proclaimed, my temper getting the best of me.

The guard tilted his head and nodded.

I growled. "Is the war still ongoing?" I asked, holding out hope that he would give me an answer. I was sorely disappointed when he again ignored me. Maybe I can try a different subject.

"Ezra, I need to speak to him," I demanded, trying to control my request.

"No," was his one word response, his voice low and cruel.

"Why not?" I asked, irritated.

This time he hissed. "Prisoners cannot ask for visitors and visitors cannot see you! Now *princess,* hush up and go to sleep, you're making me angry," he huffed.

"That makes two of us. Ezra is my friend and I need to speak to him. Until I see him I will not *hush up!*"

The guard grinned. "Trust me princess, that can be arranged. It's not like I haven't hushed you before and I promise I have no problem whatsoever doing it again." He gave me a menacing grin as I made the connection that he had been the one to hurt me during the battle. I gasped and sunk deep into the floor. *Barbarian!* And that was the last time I tried to negotiate with the guard.

CHAPTER 26

A week had passed, or so we guessed. Time wasn't convenient to track in a place that never displayed sunlight. No one came. My hopes that someone would come to my rescue, disappeared. The possibility that we had lost the war hung over me, fearful that Hassan and I were the only ones that made it out alive. My heart sank. This was all my fault. I could've stopped this from the beginning. I wish I would have gone back to Valteria with Risa and Damien when I had my chance. Staying in Praseria, fighting for something that never even existed. . . it made me the fool. A fool to let love get in my way, a love that I didn't actually understand. I would never make that mistake again.

If I have learned anything through all of this, it's that love is dangerous. It will blind you from reality. You believe that whoever you love is trustworthy and whoever says they love you is always truthful. It breaks you. When it's gone, you're empty, numb.

Hassan was silent in the corner, eating his food slowly. Maybe he was thinking the same thing I was. Maybe he was still trying to find hope in our situation, that maybe we would be freed eventually. I sighed and moved over to him. I reached my hand out to touch his arm but he didn't move. His eyes were like stone, staring blankly at the tile. I shook him.

"Hassan?" He didn't respond. "Hassan!" I pleaded again.

His eyes didn't move, nothing did, except his lips. "I can't help but wonder what my mother, sister and Damien are doing. Worrying? Do they even suspect that I am alive? Are *they* alive? Who knows if the Praserian army defeated our own. If they did, they could have marched on Valteria by now, rampaging the city. Will I ever see my family again? I feel lost without knowing, I cannot help but wonder." He finally turned to look at me.

I squeezed his arm. "I've wondered the same thing about my family, but it doesn't help us to be worried. We have to look at the bright side." I was trying to channel Risa, respond how she would probably respond to me so I smiled, but he didn't, his face was serious.

"What is the bright side of this? Nothing! We are trapped in a Praserian prison with no idea what fate they have in store for us. We are cold, hungry, tired, and clueless about the outside world. We are sitting ducks!" Hassan got up, throwing his plate of food on the ground as he got up and pounded the wall in frustration. His sudden outburst caused him to whimper, his hand quickly holding his arm.

Blood started seeping through his shirt. My eyes widened and my stomach became queasy, not having realized that

Hassan was more seriously injured than just the bruises and scrapes I could see.

"Hassan, why didn't you say you were hurt? Sit down." I placed my hand on his shoulder, forcing him to sit on the ground. The blood was bright red that was now staining his beige shirt. Hassan winced, clenching his teeth as he tried to not seem bothered by the gash.

"I didn't say anything because it was almost healed. Don't worry, it isn't as bad as it seems," Hassan chuckled in frustration.

I shook my head, not convinced. "There is no way a wound that size would heal in a week," I pointed out.

"It hasn't been a week. It's been almost two months actually." Hassan's eyes were full of heartache. I was confused. Two months ago? Hassan could see me struggling to process the timeline.

"It's the same wound from the Gala festival, from the arrow that got my arm. It split when I was fighting and the impact of hitting the wall. . . I wasn't thinking about it, it was stupid of me." Hassan was irritated, placing his good hand on his forehead as he rubbed it aggressively.

I had nearly forgotten about the attack at the Gala Festival. An impending amount of accountability for Hassan's injuries took over me. He was a resilient man and a committed friend. He was someone I didn't deserve.

"We need to stop the bleeding," I stated the obvious, however, I had never seen a wound like this and had to take care of it myself. I also didn't have any supplies. I considered asking the guard for help, to get Ezra, but I knew how that request went last time. Besides, he was sleeping quite a ways off, waking him would only anger him and Hassan was already suffering.

I took a deep breath, trying to think what I had seen Ezra do for me. *Bandage. We need a bandage.*

"Hassan, I need your shirt," I commanded. Hassan bit his lip, holding back his pain. He tried to give me a weak smile.

"I promise I'm fine, Allene. I just need a minute, the bleeding should stop soon," Hassan protested.

I rolled my eyes, ignoring his objection. "I need something to tie off the wound," I explained.

"I know why you asked. I just don't want to make you uncomfortable." Hassan gave a small twitch of his lips, trying to hide his uneasiness. I gawked at his reasoning. *He thinks I would be uncomfortable?* I couldn't decide if it was sweet or humiliating that he thought I would be uncomfortable seeing him shirtless, or if it was conceited on his part. Maybe a little of all of it.

"I think I'll manage just fine," I persisted. Hassan smirked as he bit his lip again, holding back a groan.

"Suit yourself. I need to hold the wound closed while you pull the shirt over my head," he said collectedly. I nodded at his command. We were both quiet as I grabbed the hem of his shirt. Hassan had turned his head to the side, grimacing and shutting his eyes as I slowly pulled his shirt to his neck, pausing while he got into position to grab his arm as soon as I lifted it over his head.

Hassan's stomach and chest were peppered in small light bruises. I knew Hassan was a strong man, his shirts were always a bit too tight for his body, his bulky figure being difficult to conceal. However, I didn't truly realize how muscular he was until now. Each muscle had defined lines that were raised, making them stand out even in the dim lighting of a dungeon. He had a broad chest and shoulders that seemed to be flexing unintentionally. His breathing was slightly labored as he fought through the pain, his chest heaving and distracting me more than I expected.

My face blushed as Hassan opened his eyes, seeing my dumbfounded expression staring at his body.

He chuckled. "See, I told you I would make you uncomfortable."

I swallowed, my throat had become dry. I tried to pass by his comment.

"I will pull the shirt up and over on the count of three. One. Two. Three." I pulled as gently and quickly as I could. Hassan cringed as he grasped his arm tightly, the blood stopping from his intensely applied pressure.

"Now hold my shirt flat and hold it tight, I will tear it. I should be able to with my teeth," Hassan instructed.

"I can find something else to tear it with." I looked around the cell, trying to see if we still had our fork from dinner the night before. Hassan shook his head at me, his eyes filled with fascination.

"My way is faster." He grinned. I tried not to shudder at the unsanitary action, realizing he was probably right. I pulled the shirt tightly so it was flat and placed it near Hassan's mouth. Hassan grunted as he leaned over and pulled hard on the shirt, rocking me in place, the sound of the fabric ripping was all we could hear. Hassan dropped the fabric in front of me, pushing his head back against the wall as he clenched his teeth in pain again.

"Now I need you to wrap it above my hand and on my command, you will pull it as tightly as you can to tie off the wound," Hassan directed.

I swallowed again, this time because I was starting to feel nauseated. Blood was not something I was used to and I could smell the bit that had made its way onto his shirt. *Be strong Allene, it's just a little blood.* I nodded, unsure I could respond with words without vomiting.

Hassan prepared himself, taking a deep breath. "Now!" Hassan flashed his hand away and I pulled on the fabric quickly, managing to do as he asked. Hassan's hand was now on top of mine, clasping it lightly. His tender brown eyes held mine, gratitude shining through.

"Thank you, I hope that wasn't too intolerable for you." Hassan smiled.

"Not at all, I'm happy I could help," I said honestly. It felt good to finally be helping Hassan instead of him helping me.

"I'm glad you're here, Allene," Hassan said earnestly, his hand pressing against mine. He leaned his head forward, his rugged body tensing into me. My breath was caught in my throat as I realized what he was doing. *He's going to kiss me.*

I panicked at the sudden cognizance of the situation and I quickly kissed his cheek, pulling away. Hassan laughed, not showing any sign of being hurt by my response.

"That was a pleasant surprise but I was reaching for my shirt. It's behind you." I felt relieved and slightly mortified that I assumed he was trying for more.

I couldn't process what I was feeling right now and I wanted to avoid any pressure in having to do so. I was already questioning if the almost kiss from earlier was a mistake. It was too soon, things were still too complicated.

I timidly reached behind me and placed the shirt in his lap. Hassan kept smiling as he pulled the shirt over his head, letting out a loud groan as he shoved his injured arm back through the sleeve. The garment was still primarily intact, only a small gap at the bottom of his shirt was torn where the hem line should be, which was his makeshift bandage. Now that the tattered remains of his shirt were back on, I felt like I could finally look at him without it being strange.

Hassan seemed exhausted as he slouched deeper into the wall, letting his eyes close. I made my way next to Hassan, the cold wall sending chills through my body. I placed my head on his firm shoulder, which was still much softer than the floor. I stared into the darkness in front of me as I listened to Hassan's even breathing, the rhythmic sound sending me into a trance that passed the never ending loop of time we were caught in.

~

A loud cry echoed through the stone walls of the dungeon. Another day had passed and from what we had noticed, we were the only captives down here. The hair stood up on the back of my neck as I jumped back, hugging the corner of our small cell. I cradled myself, wondering what was going on. Hassan and I exchanged glances as we heard shouting and fighting. I tried to pick out the voices. One man was shouting the loudest, but I could not understand his words. *What was going on? Is someone here to finish us off?*

Hassan came to my side, stroking my arm for comfort, but soon I didn't need it as I tried to escape in what had brought me comfort the last few weeks.

I was remembering my first kiss with Aleron, those three important words he spoke to me, his warm embrace, the garden, the painting, his enchanting eyes. . . he did the worst possible thing any man could ever do to me, yet I held this hope that his love was always true. It was proven that it wasn't, why did I lie to myself and claim it was? It was those same enchanting eyes that looked at me as he watched me be captured and clobbered.

Despite all the ways he had wronged me, I still wanted to have faith in Aleron. I wanted to keep that image of him as my hero, someone that would never harm me. I pushed past that and focused on my last memory of him, the anger quickly returned to bring me back to reality, the shame for letting those memories bring me comfort in the first place came flooding in.

The fighting continued for a few minutes. It appeared that it was coming from outside the prison, inside the castle. Soon the fighting became just an echo in the back of my mind, not even noticeable, but one thing brought it all back to my attention.

I heard loud footsteps thundering down the stairs, orders being shouted for someone to halt. I moved toward the bars, all sense of fear and reservation gone as I poked my ear out to attempt to understand what was being said, but soon enough I didn't have too. The door to the dungeon was opened, making a large beam of blinding light enter the dark, cold room. In the midst of the light was a man standing bravely and breathing heavily. *Aleron.*

Aleron was panting, but managed a few words to the guard. For as out of breath as he was, his words were loud and strong.

"Where is she?" he demanded. The guard made no response as he leaned back in his chair, acting like Aleron wasn't even there. *Seems it's not just us that he ignores.*

Aleron growled, aggressively pushing him to the ground and picking up the chair he sat in. Moving faster than the guard could react, Aleron lifted up the chair, swinging it down, the wood meeting the guards head. The guard didn't get back up, unconscious from the blow. Aleron stepped over the motionless body, frantically looking in every cell. I scooted to the back trying to hide myself. Was he going to hurt me again? I cringed. Hassan was now covering me for protection, his hands clenched.

Aleron quickly found our holding cell, seeing Hassan trying to obscure me from his view.

"Amelia!" he gasped in relief, his tone sounding urgent and concerned. Hassan and I were both confused, Hassan especially was not falling for it. Hassan stepped closer to the bars, leaving me in the corner.

Aleron reached into the pocket of his trousers, searching for something. Hassan was on edge and immediately thought the worst. Hassan shot his hand through the bars, catching Aleron's arm, gripping it firmly.

"I'd reconsider whatever you have planned by coming down here. There may only be bars separating us but don't think for a second that I couldn't kill you with whatever weapon you have in your pocket. May I remind you that you only got away from me the first time because you had help. I'd love a fair rematch," Hassan said.

Aleron laughed, finding humor in Hassan's threat and challenge.

"Down dog, it's not what you think. I come in peace," Aleron said sweetly. My stomach churned. *More lies.* Hassan seemed to think the same, not budging.

"Right. . . here's the thing, I don't believe you. I don't trust you and I don't like you," Hassan replied, gripping Aleron tighter.

Aleron rolled his eyes. "Fine, see for yourself." Aleron motioned to his pocket, inviting Hassan to grab whatever it contained. Hassan didn't hesitate at the offer. Without his sight shifting from Aleron, he retrieved the item in Aleron's pocket with ease. Keys.

"Trust me now?" Aleron asked.

"No," Hassan said curtly.

Aleron rolled his eyes again. "Well I think it's obvious I don't intend to cause you any harm with those *deadly* keys. I plan to use them to unlock this cell door, if you would hand them back to me that is." Aleron tried to move his arms, irritated by the back and forth but Hassan kept his grip firm. Hassan stared at Aleron, not believing anything for a second. Who could blame him? We both saw what Aleron did with our own eyes.

Silence overtook the three of us, empty stares being exchanged. My stomach churned at the sight of the shell that stood in front of me that was supposedly Aleron.

If Aleron wanted to kill us both, he would do it anyway. If there is a chance of getting out, are you foolish enough not to take it? Can't be any more foolish than everything else you've done the last few weeks.

I approached Hassan, placing a hand on his shoulder. "Give him the keys," I said.

Hassan finally broke his eyes away from Aleron, looking at me in shock and disappointment. "Are you joking?" he scoffed.

I shook my head. "You may not trust him, but do you trust me?" I asked him. I saw the hesitation in Hassan's face.

"Don't play that card, Allene. I am protecting us both from being blindsided again. I am protecting *you*," Hassan insisited.

Aleron was silent as he watched our exchange, his teal eyes reflecting something I hadn't seen before. Jealousy? *No, that's an emotion he would only have if he had feelings for me.*

I didn't want to argue with Hassan. We had an opportunity and I wouldn't make the same mistake twice. I have already seen the result of not taking an offer of escape, this was not up for discussion.

I reached for Hassan's hand that held the keys. He gripped them tighter, not wanting to let go. I cupped both my hands around his calloused knuckles, gently trying to soften his grip. His eyes locked with mine, both of us silently pleading with the other.

"You're certain you want to do this?" Hassan asked me disappointedly.

"It's better than our current circumstances, isn't it?" I shrugged. Hassan paused for a moment to consider my words. He slowly opened his hand to place the keys firmly in mine, the metal warm from his tightened hand. I knew I couldn't reach the lock from inside the cell, Aleron had to be the one to unlock the door.

I turned to face Aleron, trying to gain the courage to stare at him straight on without feeling any emotion, other than anger. *I wanted to feel anger.* Without batting an eye, I reached my arm through the bar to drop the keys in Aleron's outstretched hand.

"You've already fooled me once, Aleron. Don't let my small sliver of trust in you be something to be ashamed," I remarked snidely as a warning. I turned back around to be alone in the corner, as far away from him as possible. Aleron didn't reply to my comment. He quickly unlocked the cell and came in without a word. He paused and took one look at me, ignoring Hassan's burning stare.

In his eyes there was pain. He seemed to be searching over my bruises, my filthy dress, my smudged face and my heavy eyes. I heard his footsteps come closer to me but soon he halted.

"What do you think you are doing? Step any closer and I promise I will knock you flat on the ground, *right now.*" Hassan was stern and it was obvious he wasn't playing any games. Aleron didn't move, he just stared at me, unfazed by Hassan's second threat for today.

Hassan became irritated. "You've hurt her just like you wanted to. If you are truly trying to help, you'll leave and let us be on our way," Hassan growled every word. I looked up, amazed that his voice could sound so cruel. Aleron did not seem affected by Hassan's words but locked his eyes on me and spoke.

"I can explain everything if you will just give me the

chance," he said this to me, not Hassan, but of course Hassan responded.

"She doesn't want to hear your lies. Go." Hassan pointed in the direction of the door.

"No, I will not. Amelia, I want you to know the truth. I never lied to you and I can prove it. I understand this must be confusing and I don't blame you for not trusting me, but please give me the opportunity to make things right. I haven't let you down." Aleron's voice softened.

I shook my head, consumed with bitterness, taking the liberty to respond this time.

"No." Courage grew inside of me, the shock of Aleron bursting through the dungeon subsided and my thoughts became words.

"You hurt me. You *loved* me? You told me that I was your *everything*, I trusted you! I risked my life for you and in return you gave me false hope. You lied to me, you're deceitful in every sense of the word. I thought I understood you, I can honestly say I don't know who you are." My voice became a whisper toward the end, a furious wave that became a light current.

Aleron's face cringed at my harsh words, but no pain came to me. It was all true and for what he put me through, the least I could do was show him what he had done.

I expected Aleron to slam the cell door shut, lock it and leave us, but he patiently stayed. He held his ground and looked at me with agony flooding his expression.

"You only know half of the story. I cannot go on living without knowing that you know why this all happened. I've fought too hard to lose you now," he pleaded.

"You didn't fight for me, you fought to kill me," I spat back.

"That's not true, believe me, Lia! Give me the chance and I will change your perspective. All that has gone through my mind ever since you left Praseria is all of our memories." His eyes stared into mine with seemingly pure intent and passion, trying to play on my emotions.

He continued. "I have a hunch that I've been the only thing on your mind too. Good thoughts and bad. We both made mistakes, Amelia, I forgave yours. I'm asking for a chance to explain myself. I am asking for one last opportunity to make this right. After that, the decision for how you feel toward me, I will accept. At least then I know it will come from an honest place because you will know the truth." The words slammed me hard, so hard that I forgot to breathe, my chest becoming tight with anxiety.

I gasped for air, my mind racing. He had forgiven me, I had spoiled everything for us, many times. The least I could do was listen.

He was right, he had been the only thing on my mind. Maybe he could see right through me, see my thoughts and play puppeteer, or maybe he really had been thinking of me. Either way, I could at least give him a chance. In a way, I wanted to hear that he was innocent; I wanted to say my heart had been right all along.

"Please?" Aleron whispered.

Memories of the visit in my tent came flooding back. I faltered to answer and Hassan took the chance to fill in the blank.

"I think this conversation is finished." Hassan stepped forward, knocking Aleron out of the cell and into another.

Anger flared from Hassan and it was only headed in one direction.

Aleron groaned from the unexpected swipe. Hassan took another step toward him and it fueled me with the motivation I was searching for. I jumped up and ran in front of Aleron, blocking what would have been Hassan's blow.

Hassan pursued forward, not thinking much of my gesture.

"Allene, move," he warned. I knew he was serious; his eyes had a wild look to them.

Aleron grasped the cell door as I stood in front of him without hesitation.

"If you want to strike him, you can strike me too," I said bravely.

Hassan stopped, gaping. The look of fire in his eyes disappeared to complete devastation.

"Allene, are you crazy? This man tried to kill you! Have you lost your mind?" he shouted.

I paused. Maybe I was crazy. I didn't know why he was here. If anything, he could be trying to kill me once and for all, but for some reason I didn't care. I'd rather listen to him than be locked up in this dungeon and even if he did kill me, it was better than being here forever with no answer.

"What will it hurt to listen to him?" I asked.

"You believed him once and look where it got you. Who's to say you won't believe him again?" Hassan argued.

"So what if I do? Hassan, please, let's just listen to what he has to say! If we don't like it, the door is right there." I pointed in the direction of our possible escape. Hassan sunk, his face showed he felt betrayal. He crossed his arms, slowly backing away from us. I had to look away from him, the shame of defending Aleron once again taking over my confidence. Looking away from Hassan forced me to look in Aleron's direction. Aleron's face was full of joy. He seemed to try to reach for my hand but I shook it away.

"Just say what you have to say and be done with it," I said. Aleron took my words very seriously.

"This isn't the correct setting, I need to take you somewhere." My eyes turned into slits.

"We are not going anywhere with you. You said you were helping us, the only place we are going is out that door to freedom," I inisited.

Aleron sighed. "I'm sorry Lia, this won't do." In mere seconds he picked me up, threw me over his shoulder and started for the door.

"Put her down!" Hassan yelled, already on Aleron's heels. Aleron didn't stop walking but talked over his shoulder.

"My people are also waiting for an explanation, they are all gathered in the ballroom. We are going to get your answers. Follow me," he said smoothly.

"I will not." Hassan ran in front of Aleron, blocking his way. Aleron slowly lowered me to the ground and whispered in my ear, pretending he was quiet enough for Hassan not to hear.

"I am letting you go. Please, don't allow his pride to get the best of him." My mind didn't want to listen to Aleron. He could be lying, it could be another trick. Whatever it was, I knew it couldn't be much worse than the situation we were already in.

I looked into Hassan's eyes. Was he right? Would I listen to

Aleron again? I didn't know what to do; it all seemed too good to be true. He tried killing me and now he's setting me free? He has the solution to all this chaos? But one simple thing made my decision. My heart told me he was telling the truth. I knew my heart had lied to me more than I could count, but this time, I felt like I could absolutely rely on it.

I walked to Hassan and offered my hand. Hassan looked away now, not accepting the invitation.

I sighed. "Hassan, come with me. We have been through so much and as selfish as I am to say it, I *need you* to help me get through this too." That was all it took. I knew it was wrong to say that, to persuade him in such a way, but I hadn't the faintest idea of any other way to relinquish his stubborn nature. Hassan smiled at me.

"You need me?" he cooed, obviously trying to get me to say it again. Aleron grunted in the background, which only made Hassan's flattered demeanor worse. I could tell he was soaking in the satisfaction of Aleron being uncomfortable. I rolled my eyes at his attempt to make Aleron jealous.

"Yes, I need you," I said quietly, trying to display what little respect I still felt for Aleron by not speaking too loudly.

"Okay, I'll go with you. On two conditions," Hassan said, placing his hand under his chin as if he was thinking really hard.

"What are your conditions?" I asked.

"First, I need to hear you say that you no longer have feelings for Aleron."

Aleron's head snapped up, fury dancing behind his eyes at the suggestion.

"That's a ridiculous and meaningless condition," Aleron

defended, staring Hassan down as he spoke. Hassan didn't falter, his stance still steady and his words smooth as ever.

"It's not. Your emotional control over her caused her to be misguided, her feelings for you caused a weakness in her judgement. I won't stand to see it happen again. If I know her feelings no longer exist, then I know you are no longer a threat to her decision making." Hassan had made a valid point. I could see why he asked for the condition. He was a man of logic and a logical man is led by their head and not their heart. It was a characteristic I struggled with so I understood his request for evidence that I could be rational too. I had to do whatever was necessary to get Hassan to trust me. Without turning to see Aleron's face, I gave into Hassan's request.

"I no longer have feelings for Aleron," I whispered. Each word cut me deeper than I expected, my heart practically aching at a claim I knew was false. Hassan folded his arms, satisfied with his first condition.

"Good. Second condition, you have to kiss me," he said intemperately. This time it wasn't Aleron who had to be quick to reply, the shock of his request lit a fire inside of me.

"That's not requisite for this situation, Hassan." I tried to keep my voice controlled, the instant unravelling I felt inside managing to be contained.

"It absolutely is." He spoke with determination, pressing himself closer to me. Aleron stepped in front of me now, pushing Hassan back.

"You bogging, twisted brute. That is an inappropriate, preposterous *condition* that you have no right to ask of her."

Aleron was furious, his arms shaking with rage as he spoke through clenched teeth.

"You heard her didn't you? She no longer has feelings for you, *prince*. If that's true, then a harmless kiss to a man she apparently *needs* shouldn't bother her at all," Hassan said the words with confidence, proving his way again by arguing with logic.

Why does he have to be right? If I said I don't have feelings for Aleron, it shouldn't bother me to kiss Hassan. *It's just a kiss Allene, it doesn't have to mean anything. You can't let Hassan go. He has given you more reasons to trust him than Aleron has. Are you really going to jeopardize another friendship for Aleron?*

"It's meaningless. You are pressuring her into something that doesn't prove anything." Aleron took the liberty to continue to speak for me, his temper boiling over.

"I can speak for myself, Aleron," I said sternly. I was tired of others' influence over my decisions. Earlier, I had been tempted to kiss Hassan when the opportunity arose, but I stopped myself because of my unwavering loyalty to Aleron.

Aleron turned to me, his eyes full of hurt. His shaking stopped as his labored breathing became more restrained. The room had fallen completely silent. Hassan looked disinterested by Aleron's misery and Aleron looked at me with despondency.

I swallowed, trying to get the necessary boldness to do what had to be done. I walked around Aleron, my legs as heavy as they were when I found myself battling the oceans current. I came in front of Hassan, his eyes soft at my approach, his arms bulging as his body tensed while waiting for my answer.

No words needed to be said. I wrapped my arms around Hassan's neck, pulling myself up on my tip toes as I tried to meet his towering height. Giving me a helping hand, Hassan wrapped his good arm around my waist, pulling me off the ground. I leaned in to give Hassan a light kiss, trying to make it as painless for Aleron as possible.

I could almost hear Aleron cringing behind me, his breathing stopped. Hassan had cupped my face, holding onto me tightly as he held the kiss for as long as he could, finally pulling away with an obvious look of satisfaction.

"If you hadn't been so taken aback at the appearance of me shirtless yesterday, I would have done that sooner." Hassan was smiling proudly at his way of informing Aleron of our indecent moment together. I felt my face flush to an unbearable extent as Hassan continued to speak to Aleron in the most pestering tone he could muster.

"All right, *your majesty*, lead the way." He placed me back safely on the ground, motioning with his arms to the door.

Aleron seemed to be in shock, I couldn't understand his facial expression. I could tell he was trying to not be affected by Hassan's display of affection; to act like it didn't bother him, but the envy soon showed. Hassan was overly smug as Aleron stared him down, all of us uncertain how to proceed.

Aleron broke the silence, gently placing his hand on my arm and pulling me in the direction he wanted me to follow.

"Very well, this way," he said, his voice lacked any type of tone, doing his best to stay composed.

We followed Aleron into the hall. No one was guarding the prison anymore, as the two poor fellows that were at their post seemed to receive the same fate as the guard inside the prison. Two bulkier men that I didn't recognize were slumped on the floor, appearing peaceful despite the circumstance of their slumber. If Aleron had done this, hurting his own men, he had to be telling the truth.

Aleron didn't walk near us, he let Hassan and I fall behind him as he led the way. I was amazed that he trusted me enough that I wouldn't run, as tempting as it was, or maybe he knew I was too curious not to receive an answer to this madness before leaving it all behind. Who could blame me for wanting everything to be made clear?

I memorized every inch of the castle as we walked, reality setting in that it may be my last time I walked through the castle. As bad as everything was, the list of wonderful memories I held here could not be taken away. I wanted to be able to look back on those memories and relive every detail, have it remain familiar. It seemed I hadn't been here in ages.

Hassan walked next to me, intentionally brushing his arm against mine. He was on high alert, searching out every corner we passed to ensure we weren't being followed or ambushed. I appreciated having a second set of eyes.

Aleron quickened his pace, not checking to see if we were keeping up. It forced my steps to be faster and my strides longer. I must've gotten distracted by looking around at the castle that I had grown so fond of, because we had arrived at the towering doors of the ballroom sooner than I had expected.

Aleron turned to us, double checking that we had followed. He seemed nervous. I watched him as he anxiously rubbed his palms together; sweat forming at his perfectly trimmed hairline, his curls tucked behind his ears. He was biting down hard on his ruby lips. . . *Stop it, Allene. Focus.* Aleron rocked back on his heels and looked at me.

"I hope this changes things," he said, almost as an encouragement for himself rather than me.

I nodded, still questioning if I was making a mistake. We had no idea what we were walking into and I wouldn't be able to live with myself if something else happened to Hassan because of his loyalty and trust in me. *Trust yourself Allene, it will be okay. It has to be okay.*

Aleron took my hand with courage and this time I didn't shake it off. He ignored Hassan as he glared at the sight. Hassan grabbed my other hand in reply. At that moment we entered the ballroom all together, hand in hand, ready to hear what was supposedly the truth.

CHAPTER 27

J had tried to think of different scenarios that we could be walking into. I started by assuming we might be meeting with a handful of people or that Aleron had some letter or evidence to plead his case. I don't know what I was expecting to be honest, but it definitely wasn't this.

The ballroom was full of people dressed for an evening very similar to my first formal date with Aleron. Women in beautiful dresses, men wearing the best trousers and coats they owned, symbolizing a celebration. There were many individuals I didn't recognize, but I tried to pick out familiar faces anyway. Everyone in the room seemed shocked to see me. *Trust me, I am just as confused as all of you.* I heard a loud gasp and turned my head in that direction.

Noni stood with her fiancé Simon, hand in hand, a large gape on her face. She saw me gaze at her and she quickly waved in return. I smiled, relieved to feel she was still my friend after all of this, but Noni's eyes flickered to something else and it brought my attention in the same direction.

Three people sat at the front of the room. I noticed King Vincent sitting uncomfortably at the center, holding tightly to his wife's hand. Queen Eveline looked sick as she stared at her bracelet as it was catching the light, afraid to look up. I then noticed a new face sitting comfortably in Aleron's chair.

A man, wearing a black tunic and boots, about the same age as Hassan, with thick, black hair and dark blue crystals for eyes. He was staring at Aleron with a disgusted expression. The unsettling part is that they wore the *same* expression. Actually, almost *every* feature was the same, they were practically identical.

I did a double take as I looked back and forth between the two individuals. . . or the same? I was in shock, I must be imagining things. I eventually put together the phenomenon of two Aleron's existing couldn't be possible. I soon settled with a much more reliable and accurate explanation. The one wearing Aleron's crown, sitting in Aleron's chair, looking like he had nothing to offer but turmoil, was Killian, Aleron's older brother.

The resemblance was implausible. I could recognize why Aleron would feel Killian was his greatest competition. If my sister and I were that similar, it would be infuriating having very little that made you different, only having attributes that made the other seem better.

I heard the queen make an indiscernible noise. Eveline was holding back tears as she stared in desperation at both of her sons. I could only imagine what was going through her mind as her sons exchanged such silent hatred between one another.

Everyone else in the room didn't understand what was going on. They all stared at who they assumed was Aleron by my side, waiting to see what would happen next from this turn of events.

Too soon, Aleron stopped my gazing and made his way to the middle of the room, his hand still bonded with mine, pulling Hassan's away. He made his final steps into the center of the crowd and silence fell over the room. He took the time to acknowledge each face, taking time reading their expressions, silently calming everyone's anxious minds. He let out a long sigh when he came to meet the eyes of his long lost brother. Aleron nodded his head in his brother's direction, acknowledging his ominous presence.

"Killian, what an unfortunate surprise it is to see you." Aleron's voice practically shook the room, despite his voice being barely louder than a whisper.

Killian scoffed as he stood, casually placing his arm on the headrest of his chair.

"Don't flatter me little brother, you'll make me vain. The pleasure is all mine, it has been much too long. And Allene, it is wonderful to see you again." Killian raised his eyebrows, as he gave me a wicked wink, challenging Aleron to try and say more words that would do nothing to harm his insolent presence.

My heart practically stopped in my chest. The realization of his statement hit me hard. Flashbacks rushed through my mind of the unexpected obligation the king and queen had the night of the ball, to the fight between Aleron and Vincent

I overheard, the battlefield when Aleron addressed me as Allene, of not being able to see clearly, the unfamiliar demeanor between the two of us. . . it all made sense. Aleron wasn't on the battlefield at all, it was Killian.

A hundred different emotions and thoughts flooded my mind at once, overwhelming my senses. I couldn't pick out where it all had gone wrong or what had happened. To my comforting surprise, Aleron never hurt me at all. I don't know the extent of the entire story. How Aleron was replaced by his brother in so little time, where he had been since then, and many more questions sent me into a panic. All I could grasp was that Aleron hadn't betrayed my trust, he was innocent, a victim as well, in whatever this awful situation was.

My heart felt like it would burst as I immediately felt shame for not having more faith in him. I wanted to fix all the wrongs, to make everything between us whole again.

Killian took it upon himself to continue, interrupting my displaced thoughts.

"I am afraid we are in quite the humiliating state, wouldn't you say, brother?"

I felt the nerves in my stomach clench at the sight of Killian's disinterested stare, making me equally as sick as the queen appeared to be.

"Pardon my brusque response, but I am not particularly interested in indulging your overpowering sense of self at the moment," Aleron spoke with an intense tone, the words flowing out so steadily that I was in awe at his witty reply.

Killian's eyes narrowed, making his vicious stare even more intolerable than before. "That is just even more humiliating and sad brother. That is no way to speak to your future king." Killian beamed with pride.

"Once again, we evidently don't see eye to eye. I have nothing to be humiliated about," Aleron responded without hesitation, taking control of the conversation again.

Killian shook his head back and forth, plainly peeved by Aleron's response.

"Now, now, you are being modest and dense. If I was in your position I would be *mortified*. You have a destined responsibility to this family. The matter has been brought to my attention that it isn't a responsibility you can manage. The fact that father had to seek me out to fulfill your future duties to this kingdom is quite. . . despairing, wouldn't you agree?" Killian's words irked me to the point of outrage as I watched him laugh to himself. Aleron's jaw went slack as he now turned his scrutiny to his father.

"Killian, I almost feel pity for you. You are a hypocrite. You speak of my role as if it hasn't been fulfilled. I stayed when you collapsed under the pressure of our duty to our parents, to our throne, to our people. I sacrificed all I could for the better of Praseria." Aleron made sure his response was loud and clear for everyone to understand. I could feel his dedication to his people, his hope that we would have compassion and sympathy for what he was saying. I squeezed his hand, encouraging him to hold his ground.

Killian let out the deafening bellow of his awful laugh. I could feel all the hairs stand up on the back of my neck. The similarity in their voices made the entire conversation confusing to listen to. If I hadn't been staring at them directly I would have gotten lost as to who was speaking, the only distinction being how uncivil Killian was when it came to his behavior.

It had gotten to the point that I could no longer look at Killian, as feelings of hatred came pouring out toward him. My emotions were confused, like it was Aleron that I was feeling displeased with.

"Exactly, you have sacrificed all you *could,* but not all that you *should.* You still are convinced that you are doing all you can with your responsibility as the heir to the throne? You still have yet to sacrifice the one thing that would ruin this entire kingdom. If you can let go of the pathetic, clinging girl at your side then by all means, the throne is yours." Killian's words were like daggers to my heart. I didn't want to let him get to me and let him have the satisfaction. Aleron however couldn't hold back any longer, his brother's comment sending him over the edge.

Aleron's hand went straight to his sword which had been lying at his side. Killian became amused by the sudden entertainment. Before another action could be taken, the queen had miraculously broken free from her silence.

"That is enough!" her humble voice rang throughout the room, sending a quiet fear into everyone's souls. Queen Eveline had suddenly gained an unquestionable amount of power in her position, stopping the tension that had quickly risen, but it wouldn't last long, as the king couldn't seem to stand that she was capturing everyone's attention.

"Aleron, I will not entertain anymore of your nonsense!" Everyone cringed at the booming voice of the king, his presence having been overshadowed during the dramatic scene.

Aleron's father started for us, everyone moving out of his way in fear.

I looked up at Aleron, pleading for him to tell me what I could do. As the king approached us, Hassan took it upon himself to come by my side. Aleron pushed me behind him, Hassan taking my spot by Aleron's side.

As the king closed the distance and was only a few feet away, eyes full of rage, Aleron swiftly took out his sword and pointed it at his father's throat.

Everyone in the room held their breath. King Vincent was frozen and the queen was almost in tears. Aleron was growing tired of all of this, the anticipation to put an end to this chaos taking control. Without flinching, he addressed the queen.

"Mother, don't let them do this. We can still turn all of this around, for the sake of us all." Aleron took the chance of engaging his mother, trying to communicate what he assumed was obvious.

Queen Eveline refused to make eye contact with Aleron, leaving him to stand alone. Every member of his family had turned away from him, robbing him of what was rightfully his.

"I don't understand. . ." Aleron shook his head, trying to get his mother to look his way. Killian took her silence as his opportunity to snake his way back into the conversation.

"Of course you don't. Let me speak, plain and simple. I am the new heir to the throne, you have been stripped of your title. Under fathers command, you have been exiled from Praseria, guilty of treason and attempted murder of our king. I don't see how you assumed there would be no consequences to your actions, brother." Killian hissed, making my skin crawl at the sound.

Aleron had no words. He scanned the room, observing the long faces of his people as they tried to find refuge in the king and queen. Aleron waited patiently, the silence dragging on as his father stared at his optimistic son and his mother unable to meet his eyes. Aleron was waiting for them to interject and set things right.

King Vincent sighed, bravely nodding to Killian under Aleron's sword, ignoring Aleron's pleading eyes. Killian smiled at the gesture, recognizing his newly developed power, seizing the moment.

"I believe I speak for all, Aleron, when I say you are ruining the party and I have had quite enough of it. Lower your sword. We will let you off with a warning this time, considering what title you once held here." Killian spoke so each word would rub deeper into Aleron's mind of what was actually happening.

Aleron looked at Hassan, each of them letting their guard down, not wanting to escalate the situation. Aleron did as he was told, lowering his sword, letting his arms fall to his side. His father slowly backed away, returning to his place by the queen, holding her lightly as she kept herself turned away from her son. *Cowards.*

"Guards, see my brother and his friends out, immediately." Killian gave another wicked smile and gave one wave in our direction, signaling our dismissal.

Before the guards could get to us, Aleron and Hassan had formed a barrier between me, protecting me from all sides. Swords were quickly drawn on us, showing just how quickly allegiance could be swayed in people. These were guards I have no doubt Aleron had trained beside, even led, and here they were, no loyalty to offer him in his time of need. Hassan's hands were held into fists and Aleron didn't flinch at the new threat. I bit my lip hard to keep my thoughts to myself.

"We are capable of escorting ourselves out," Aleron said calmly, trying to halt the situation. Vincent hesitated at the response but Eveline gestured for the guards to stand down, undermining his authority as he slipped back to his throne.

Without a second to spare, Aleron had grasped my hand once again, leading Hassan and I back the way we came. The urgency to leave was evident and I shared Aleron's pain as the people we loved watched as we were dismissed from their lives, from our home. I tried not to think of what was going through their minds. What would Ezra think? How would Noni react? How could the king and queen do this to their own son?

Hassan led the way through the door, pulling me behind. I felt Aleron break free from my grasp, stopping in the doorway. Hassan pulled me to him, almost desperate to be near me.

"Are you okay?" he whispered. I nodded. I wasn't worried about myself, I was worried about Aleron.

Aleron's hand had signaled us to stop, to give him this last moment. Aleron made one last promise to his brother, soaking in his last words.

"Enjoy your freedom now, big brother. When I am finished with you, you will regret this very moment. I promise I will be back and when I am, you will beg for mercy on your rueful soul." Aleron's words sent chills up my spine, the essence of them striking trepidation into his brother.

Killian put up a strong front, pretending it was amusing by supplementing a bitter laugh. "Until then."

The doors closed behind us. The air was still. Any tension between Aleron, Hassan, and I had disappeared. An uneasy sense of entitlement had taken its place. I could only clearly discern one emotion that was overtaking me. Vengeance.

I turned to Aleron, my hands resting on his cheeks, my eyes imploring for his courage to not falter. I understood precisely what he was going through. Distress, betrayal, doubt, misplaced and irreparable feelings were translating across his handsome face. I wanted to take it all away, free him from his pain.

I knew at that moment we had an uncertain future lying ahead. I knew in my heart, no matter what the future contained, I wouldn't allow another moment of it to be away from Aleron. I was going to make things right between us; I was going to make our lives whole once again.

I embraced him, trying to absorb the invisible weight off of his shoulders as best as I could. I could feel the tears on his cheeks as they fell onto mine. The first words I could form through all the commotion finally slipped through my lips as I whispered in his ear.

"Aleron, this is *not* the end. I promise, this is only the beginning."

The End of Book One

PRONUNCIATION GUIDE

Allene Amena – Uh-leen Uh-men-uh

Risa Amena – Rih-zuh Uh-men-uh

Laerina Davore (Amena) – Luh-ray-nuh Duh-vor Uh-men-uh

Praseria – Pra-sehr-e-uh

Praserian – Pra-sehr-e-ihn

Valteria – Val-tehr-e-uh

Valterian – Val-tehr-e-ihn

Hassan Durand – Haa-sihn Der-and

Damien Durand – Day-me-ihn Der-and

Freira Durand – Fur-ehr-uh Der-and

Aleron Hadway – Al-uh-ron Had-way

Vincent Hadway – Vin-cent Had-way

Killian Hadway – Kill-e-ehn Had-way

Eveline Demese (Hadway) – Ehv-eh-lin Deh-meese Had-way

Ezra – Ez-ruh

Noni – No-nee

Terris – Tare-is

Ajax – Uh-jax

Modesta – Moh-des-tuh

ACKNOWLEDGEMENTS

I want to express my gratitude for my family. Without them, Praserian would not have been possible. To my dad, Brent, thank you for creating my beautiful cover and map. You made the images in my head come to life with your amazing artistic talent. To my mom, Macquel, thank you for being the first person ever to read my book. You made me feel proud and capable of being an author. My sister, Kendra, I couldn't have done any of this without you. Your guidance, support, book knowledge, and brainstorming sessions with me were exactly what I needed to push Praserian further than I ever thought possible. You inspire me every day to accomplish more and you are an amazing example to follow as a self-published author. I am so grateful to have your support through this journey. To my husband, Chasen, for believing in me. For helping me feel confident enough to share my work with others. To my son Nash, thank you for motivating me every day to be the best person I can be. Lastly, thank you to every beta reader and supporter of Praserian in the early stages. I wouldn't be where I am today without your feedback and excitement towards the series. I love you all!

ABOUT THE AUTHOR

Kaydrie grew up in Mapleton, Utah and currently lives in Utah with her husband and little boy. She loves baking, traveling, all things Disney, and spending time with family and friends. She has had a love for literature since she was a little girl. Some of her fondest memories are bonding over books with her father and mother. She has been writing since she was 12 years old. Her books are creations of what she wanted to read as a teenager. These books that were once exclusively hers to enjoy are now available for the teen and young adults across the nation.

CHAPTER 1 & 2 PREVIEW OF BOOK TWO

VALTERIAN

CHAPTER 1

$\mathcal{I}$ was facing Killian once again. His mischievous smile was stirring the fear that was prominent in my gut. He had such an invasive power over me that made me feel utterly hopeless. Despite my best efforts, it was like he knew the effect he had on me and it fueled his cruelty. He could practically strip away any happiness I ever felt, taking pleasure in my misery.

Aleron was helpless, barely able to hold his body weight as he kneeled in surrender to his brother. As I pleaded with Killian, I had never felt such disgust for anyone before. I still felt myself shiver as he spoke, the echo and familiarity of Killian's voice to Aleron's making my head spin as it always did. It abused Aleron's innocence having to be associated with such a despicable, sadistic person and my heart felt conflicted each time.

I could hardly hear the panic in my voice as Killian reached for the hilt of his sword, his hesitation unwavering despite my desperate attempts of negotiation and under-standing. Before I could scream the cries I could feel ready to explode, a violent shaking overcame me.

"Allene! Allene! Ugh, please wake up Allene!"

I slowly managed to lift my heavy eyelids, surprised to no longer be confronted with the bone-chilling face of Killian, but rather a bewildered Risa. Instant relief overcame her as she realized her attempt to wake me had worked. She reached her arm underneath my shoulders, pulling up to embrace me. My cries had somehow made their way out and filled my quiet room. Risa was patient as she tried to soothe me. The warmth that radiated from her quickly made the sobbing subside and unflattering sniffles took their place. *It was just a dream Allene, it wasn't real.*

I felt Risa's hand smooth back a piece of hair that had gotten stuck to my cheek from my tears, the gesture comforting.

"It happened again, didn't it?" Risa asked, the sadness in her voice weighing heavily in the air. I nodded in reply then let my head hang low to my chest, my neck unwilling to bear the strain of my emotions.

"Allene, you have hardly slept since your return. Your body isn't going to be able to keep up much longer if you don't get proper rest." She stated the obvious but provided me no solution on how to fix it.

"I will get plenty of rest once this is all sorted out," I insisted, my stubbornness taking over the need to sleep.

"You can't keep doing this. I know you feel a responsibility to make things right, but there is only so much you can do at this moment. You have done everything you can, that needs to be enough," Risa pleaded with me.

"It's not enough. Nothing has changed. It has been five weeks and we have made no progress." I stated, the weight of reality making me *almost* wish I was dreaming again, but Killian's face crept into my memory, reminding me that reality was only slightly better.

Hassan, Aleron and I had arrived back to Valteria five weeks ago. The journey home was difficult but it was incredibly short lived. Search parties had been ongoing since my capture on the battlefield. We had only been walking for half a day when a soldier had stumbled upon us. I shuddered at the reminder of the awkward silence that we exchanged on our way back to Valteria, hardly any words being passed between the three of us. To add to the bleak atmosphere, the soldier had informed us of the heavy loss we suffered in the battle. Fortunately, the Praserian's retreated soon after my capture, but it still left an astounding number of injured soldiers and many more among the dead.

None of us could quite find the words to address what had happened, and addressing anything else before that seemed inappropriate. Aleron was dispirited, Hassan was cumbersome and I was indignant. We were dealing with a flurry of emotions and all for different reasons. I had never felt so overwhelmed.

On our arrival, Aleron was quickly ushered into the palace, my mother trying to avoid a scene. I wasn't sure what I thought would happen once we got to Valteria, but I definitely wasn't planning on the immediate separation from Aleron. My mother was still unwilling to indulge our relationship and she wanted time to know how to best approach the "unfortunate" situation.

I had immediately regretted the lack of communication that I could have had earlier with Aleron. He was now locked away in a room on the first floor, far from my reach and I could hardly bear not knowing how he was coping. If I was this bad, I could only imagine how it was affecting him.

I had been burdened with nightmares every night since I had returned. Killian was the dreadful focus of each one, his primal sneer perpetually haunting me. The amount of sleep I was receiving was close to none. The lack of rest had made me consistently woozy and irritable. I tried drinking tea before bed, stretching, exerting all my energy, and many other useless tactics to exhaust me into a submission of sleep, while holding out hope that the nightmares would miraculously disappear. As a last resort, I asked Risa to stay with me, hoping her cheery presence would help. None of the attempted remedies seemed to be effective.

Up to this point I had missed my father dearly, but the *need* for him had never felt so pressing. It hurt me knowing he couldn't help me in the most difficult situation I had been faced with. I knew he would be on my side, I knew he would've found a solution, I knew he could've made it better.

My mother had refused to see me until she felt she could be unbiased in her decision making process going forward. Damien, along with the other soldiers, were working over-time, trying to prepare for whatever Praseria and their new prince, Killian, may throw our way. Hassan had requested to go home for a little while. His mother and sister had been worried about him, considering the news of him being captured as well. With him gone, it left me with only Risa to turn to.

"Allene, it pains me to see you this way. You are even more upset than when father passed. There must be something I can do."

My heart sunk as I noticed the dark circles that surrounded Risa's eyes from the sleepless nights she had willingly endured with me. I felt guilty for dragging her through the same hopeless feelings I had been battling. She didn't deserve it and I wanted her to feel like her efforts were useful.

"Risa, why don't you go to your room for the rest of the night? I appreciate your unwavering determination that I get better, but I would be lying if I said I had the slightest idea of anything you could do." I felt my shoulders shrug, too tired to pretend for anyone's sake.

Risa pulled together her abnormal amount of positivity with one final effort to make me happy.

"If that is what you wish. I'm sure mother will come to a decision soon and you will be able to speak with Aleron. Until then, Hassan returns to the castle tomorrow, maybe he can offer some insight into what you are feeling," she suggested, hoping the news would lift my spirits while also trying to be subtle in how appealing the offer was to sleep in her own bed. Her exhaustion must've been equal to mine given how submissive she was toward the suggestion.

I hadn't told Risa about the recent development of complicated feelings between Hassan and I. There was already too much going on. I hadn't shown it, but I was secretly grateful he had decided to go home. It had spared me from an awkward conversation and feelings I wasn't ready to address.

I knew Risa was coming from an innocent place so I faked an excited smile, wanting her to feel somewhat triumphant.

"You might be right, Risa." I felt my cheeks hurt from the lack of energy that I was somehow forcing into my grin.

Risa sighed; relieved something had seemed to get through to me. "Wonderful, now try to get some rest and sleep in if you can. Sweet dreams." Risa had squeezed my hand as she gracefully stood from my bed and left the room.

I tossed and turned for a while, the pressure of how late it was getting made the challenge of sleep seem even more impossible. It had to have been past midnight.

I rolled over to my side, staring out my window as the moon crawled it's way across the vacant sky. My mind found its way to Aleron. I wondered if he was having nightmares too, I wondered if they were treating him well. I knew he was in a room similar to my own, but the idea that he had no one here, or in Praseria, made my heart ache.

Aleron had family, friends and his people that adored him. In a single day, it was all taken from him. He lost everything. I could relate to the feeling, having gone through a similar experience when I arrived in Praseria. However, I was relieved to get away from Valteria when that happened and the choice to stay in Praseria was entirely my own. Aleron was abandoned by the people he thought loved him – people he thought would always be loyal to him. I couldn't imagine the anguish he must be feeling. It was a different kind of loss that no one could comprehend. It was betrayal. Ruthless, stinging, unkind betrayal.

I tried to picture him only a few floors below me, wondering if he was thinking about me too. I could almost feel my arms wrap around his waist as we would hold each other in a comforting silence, knowing at least we had each other. Then it hit me. *Do we have each other?* We still hadn't had a proper conversation regarding where we stood in one another's lives. Because the complications in our relationship were attributed to Killian, did that mean Aleron and I would go back to how things were before the war? Was it right of me to disregard the conversations I had with Hassan and the feelings it had evoked? They weren't the same feelings I had for Aleron but maybe that was a sign? If it was a sign, I wasn't sure how to interpret it.

My thoughts drifted to Hassan now. I tried to find a sliver of fortitude from the idea that I could mentally prepare myself for what was to come; playing scenarios in my head that I may face with him tomorrow. It didn't matter how many I invented, they all were cumbersome and I was dreading it.

Somehow overcoming the stress of Hassan and the longing for Aleron, I managed to fall asleep, and once again, Killian found another way to haunt my dreams.

~

I did exactly as Risa instructed. When the sun rose, I made my body believe it was a mistake and that it wasn't time to get up. I closed my eyes a good majority of the morning, attempting to fall asleep but knowing I couldn't with the brightness kissing every corner of my room.

I eventually gave up once my stomach started to growl from hunger. I groaned as I used every bit of energy I had left to heave my body off my sunk in bed. Risa had begged me to allow a handmaid to help me with daily tasks, realizing I wasn't doing a good job at taking care of myself as of late. At first, I didn't want to listen. I had always been independent here and I didn't want to seem weak by accepting the extra help. Risa understood I was too prideful and forced it upon me, saying it was by her instructions. I was thankful to her for sparing me any additional humiliation.

I fumbled with the door handle and opened it to find my handmaid, Sonora, standing patiently for my invitation to enter. She graciously broke the barrier between us, her soft smile a joy to see.

Sonora slightly towered over me, her short blonde hair was situated neatly under her cap and her uniform was pressed to the point that I didn't think a wrinkle would ever appear again. She had glistening olive eyes that were not afraid to look at yours directly. She was bold, yet subtle, and I began to enjoy her presence more than I thought I would. I didn't know much about her yet, but I could tell that we were becoming close friends.

"Rough night again, your majesty?" she asked, concerned, aware of my inability to sleep, but too kind to ask why.

"It's that obvious, is it?" I tried to giggle but a short sigh was all that could be heard.

"Princess Risa informed me of your guest that will be arriving soon. We will finally be getting you ready today to actually be *seen*! I can have you cleaned up in no time and I will make sure you don't display even a speck of exhaustion." She gave a firm nod, confident in her abilities to hide the sleepiness that was plastered onto my face.

I felt uneasy at the mention of Hassan again, but I ignored the comment and let her get to work. Sonora was purely elegant as she managed to twist my hair into a low bun and place additional curls perfectly to frame my face. She hummed a song as she applied my makeup, bragging about the makeup's magical capabilities to make any infirmity disappear. I would need to ask her one day where she got it. I had a feeling I would be needing a lot of it if my sleeping patterns didn't improve soon.

Sonora slipped me into a long gown that was lightweight and airy. It was cream in color and feathered at the short sleeves. After slipping on some heeled boots, she let out a long, content sigh. She clapped her hands quickly in anticipation for me to see the final product of her hard work.

Just as she promised, my face appeared completely rested and alive. She somehow hid the puffy dark bags that hung underneath my eyes and even managed to make my eyes look bigger. My cheeks were rosy, rather than drained of color, and my lips that were cracked had been smoothed over in a beautiful shade of pink. With my hair being so neatly done I looked like I had it all together. It was a miraculous façade that I hoped I could pull off.

"You are incredibly talented, Sonora. I could never have done this myself," I complimented her, completely sure of my statement.

Sonora shrugged off my praise. "You make my work easy, your majesty, I hardly had to do a thing. However, I am delighted that you approve." She was beaming as we both stared in the mirror at my image.

Sonora looked upon me like I meant the world to her. It

had been so long since one of my people admired me the way she did. It was refreshing and all at the same time, confusing. I wasn't sure how to respond to her kindness.

At first, I thought it was an act. As I have spent time with her every day, I realized how genuine she is towards me. It is such a relief to have someone display kindness to me despite all that has happened, and I appreciated her for it.

I turned and faced Sonora, holding one of her hands in mine. "I want to thank you for being pleasant towards me. I can't recall being treated this way by anyone in the castle, aside from my sister and Damien. I don't know what makes you treat me differently, but I am grateful for it," I whispered my appreciation, hoping she could understand how much it really meant to me.

Sonora's eyes seemed astonished and sad as she swiftly responded. "Princess Allene, you deserve respect and adoration. I have to admit, many people would assume your character to be unjust from your appearance, I feel awful to admit that at one point in time, I was one of them. It is wrong for anyone to judge you. I can hardly imagine the things you have gone through recently. I believe I would be practically traumatized, maybe even gone slightly insane. I am part of the people and I can honestly tell you there has been a change since the war. All that fear and hatred towards you has dissipated. Your stay in Praseria, it has turned out for the better. Rumors of your sacrifice for Aleron on the battlefield circulated and your selflessness for the people you love has become obvious to everyone. I feel deeply ashamed I ever thought otherwise. I know many people are sensing a new hope for Valteria. I know I do. After your father's passing, not everyone held the confidence in your mother to lead us on her own. I'm confident that the new hope we are all sensing is coming from you. If you can love the enemy in such an altruistic way, I can't imagine the proclivity and things you would do for your people."

I could feel my face begin to blush as Sonora told me words I only dreamed I would one day hear. *The people were truly having a change of heart?* Was my reign as a failure coming to an end, to bring a new beginning?

I had been searching for a place to feel like home and I found that in Praseria. Could it be possible that I could now finally make my true home, *home*? Was this a chance to change my past and build a better future? Despite all the heartache and confusion, could it actually change?

I knew I wasn't able to communicate yet with Aleron but I instinctively knew he would be looking to me now more than ever. I was the only thing that stayed consistent as his life got turned upside down. He had been my support and constant when I needed one and now it was my turn to be that for him. This was my opportunity to change our path.

"It is difficult for me to comprehend anyone having a change of heart towards me, but I really do hope your words ring true," I assured her.

"You have been hiding yourself away in this room ever since you've returned. I promise, once you venture outside these walls, you will see the difference, " Sonora whispered, patting my shoulder.

"Thank you," I said, not knowing any other words that could convey my gratitude.

"My pleasure. I am supporting you, a lot of us are. We

want to see you pull through this, to bring Valteria peace once again," she said softly.

I could feel a spark of hope as well, a hope that things would be better. Sonora's words had given me the shred of confidence I needed these last five weeks. I found a new determination kindled inside of me as I pictured the idea of what could be my new future. I wanted to be that princess the people were now seeing. I wanted to be someone they could rely on, to be their advocate. I wanted to be as my father had been, a new era of peace, love and acceptance.

I was done having nightmares. I was done being scared and pitied. I was done having to be taken care of. I was done having people walk all over me, especially my mother.

For the first time in my life, I realized the word princess before my name actually meant something. I'd been Allene and I'd been Amelia, but I had never embraced the title of princess. It gave me power, a power that few could ever have. I felt foolish realizing it took me this long to take that title seriously, to wield it to my advantage. I had to hit rock bottom before I actually would do something about it. I was the only thing that had been holding me back and now I was going to make sure that didn't happen. Not ever again.

CHAPTER 2

Sonora escorted me to the study. As we walked the halls, arm in arm, I did notice a change. Soldiers, maids, butlers, chefs, everyone was taking the time to acknowledge me with a curtsy or a bow. These interactions felt incredibly strange and at first, made me more uncomfortable than flattered.

As it happened more and more, I began to feel a sense of pride take control, almost fueling my determination even more to finally see a change. In return, I responded with a smile and nod, hoping that would be an appropriate reaction to their gestures.

The palace hadn't changed since I had been gone. Since my return, I hadn't roamed any farther than the floor my bedroom was on. I did this primarily out of spite and slightly out of fear of running into my mother. I was stubborn, exhausted, and the thought of unwelcoming stares had deterred me from venturing out of my comfort zone. Had I known this was the response I would have received, I would have left my room much sooner.

We arrived at the large cherry wood doors that led into my father's old study. I took a deep breath as I observed a scuff mark at the right hinge. The memory of Risa and I running through the palace with one of the chef's cart played through my mind. We managed to run into the corner of the door, knocking Risa off the cart. I remember Risa instantly crying, afraid father would be upset. Father had been sitting in his study at the time of the incident. He skeptically observed the new accessory we had created for the door. As he pushed our cart inside the study, we prepared for the worst. He took us by surprise, throwing Risa on the top shelf of the cart, me on the bottom, and pushing us around his study. I remember being amazed that he hadn't displayed any anger towards our rambixous shenanigans. Like any good parent should, he cared more about our wellbeing and happiness than his perfectly crafted decorative door. There wasn't a single memory I could recall of my father that ever made me feel anything less than loved and extraordinary. I missed him dearly.

I pushed back the tears that had come to my eyes. Sonora could tell I needed a moment to myself, and as always, was very tactful in how she handled the situation.

"I hope you enjoy your company, your majesty. I will see you before dinner," she spoke very softly, trying to be inconspicuous.

"Thank you for the company and for helping me find. . . new motivation. See you soon." I thanked her in the same reverent manner she had spoken to me. She curtseyed and walked away in the opposite direction.

I had requested to meet Hassan in the study, hoping it would give me the necessary comfort and knowledge that my father always used to provide. What if he was still angry at me for the choice I made in Praseria? We hadn't discussed anything since then and the anticipation of our conversation was making me practically sick.

I tried to clear my foggy thoughts from my lack of sleep as I opened the door to the study. *Remember, princess. Not Amelia, not Allene, be a princess.*

Hassan was fiddling mindlessly with one of father's old dictionaries, opening and closing the cover. I couldn't help but wonder if it was from boredom or from nerves. I could at least relate to one of those at the moment.

Hassan stopped, his eyes struggling to get only a quick glance at me. I chuckled at his efforts to not stare, trying to ignore his awed expression.

Hassan looked very different since I last saw him. I could smell him from across the room. Being primarily in unhygienic circumstances with one another, I assumed he only smelled of dirt, sweat and grim. I realized, he was probably thinking the same thing about me. Hassan being cleaned up however was entrancing, bringing back the initial attraction I felt towards him at the Gala festival. Even being many feet apart, I could smell his cedarwood scent, the pleasantness of it making me want to move a little closer. His hair had been neatly trimmed to weigh more heavily on the top as it spilled over the sides while his eyes held a lighter tint of brown. His eyelashes seemed to have grown and his skin had been kissed by the sun, giving him a warm glow. After only five weeks, he no longer showed any signs of bruising or injury.

He stood a little taller as he gave me a swift wink. I was captivated by this new poise and courage that seemed to surge through him. I could feel myself getting lost in him and a princess shouldn't let that happen. I took control of the situation as soon as I could.

"Hassan, it's a pleasure to see you are well. I must admit, I am surprised you came back to the palace," I stated, trying to hide the flurry of emotions I could feel brewing in my stomach.

Hassan took a step around the desk, casually leaning back on his hands and propping a leg against the desk for support, acting like he owned the room. *Where was this coming from?*

"Why are you surprised? Did you honestly think I would leave something so important to me behind?" He gave me a half smile, appearing to joke for amusement, but I knew his comment contained the slightest amount of seriousness to see what I would say. His flirting was definitely more than what my exhausted mind could handle, but I made an effort nonetheless.

"I didn't realize you had anything to leave," I played along, curious to see where his new confidence would take the conversation.

"I am no coward, nor am I a fool, I sensed you were hurting. I wanted to stay and be here for you, but I know you prefer being alone. . . in situations like this." He stared into my eyes, holding me there until I acknowledged his selfless observance of my character when I was feeling low.

What he said was the truth, I did tend to sulk if I was

depressed and I preferred to be alone until I could escape it. It was exhausting enough being upset, having to pretend to be happy or a better version of myself when I was low, it only made me feel worse. It was easier for me to be left alone in moments like that, saving me from being fake.

I gave him a tender smile. "How keen of you. I have a difficult time believing that I am the only reason that you left however," I challenged him, folding my arms as we stared each other down from across the room.

Hassan chuckled, holding his hands up in defense, his hair swaying to the side as he moved. "You caught me. Don't get me wrong, I did it for you, but I also did it for my family. I had been gone far too long. Plus, I thought a little separation might be good for us. To be honest. . . I hoped that, *maybe*, you'd even miss me." Hassan had grown shy towards the end of his sentence, the innocence in his voice flattering me beyond what I thought he could.

"Did you miss *me*?" I fired back, amused by our little game. It was invigorating talking to someone other than Sonora or Risa. I almost forgot how much I enjoyed Hassan's company. It made me remember why he caught my eye the night of the Gala, and more importantly, why he made my love life seem so unclear at times.

Hassan chuckled, taking a few steps forward until he was standing firmly a foot away. His scent was even stronger now and I was quickly reminded how training to be a soldier had graciously toned his chest and arms. *Stop it, Allene, pull it together. It's just Hassan. You are simply tired. Aleron is just a few floors below your very feet.*

"I did miss you. *Very* much." Hassan swept one of my curls

behind my ear, the sheer touch of his fingertips electrifying my delicate skin.

I knew I held affection for Hassan but it wasn't the same affection I had for Aleron. I wasn't sure what the reason for this newly discovered excitement I was feeling, but I was sure it didn't mean anything. I swallowed hard, suppressing any emotion that was trying to take over my princess moment.

"I can certainly say I missed you more than I realized," I replied. That was the truth. I didn't realize that I had missed him the way I did.

I instantly regretted those short words as I had let my guard down. *So much for my strong princess moment.*

Hassan's eyes were dancing as he seemed to memorize my face, delighted to hear my honest thoughts.

"Allene, pardon my bluntness; you are incredibly alluring at this moment," Hassan whispered in a deep tone, sending chills up my neck that I was hoping he wouldn't notice. Obviously he did, his laughter confirming that he was well aware of the effect he was having on me.

I rolled my shoulders, shaking off the goosebumps. I held a serious face, refusing to amuse him any longer. "You look pretty sharp yourself. The difference of a good washing can be alarming," I snickered, discounting the intention he had for a flirtatious comment as I walked past him to take a seat at my father's chair. I knew there I could feel comfortable and in control.

"I wasn't stating that you looked clean, Allene. I mean, you do, but that is not what I was implying. I was trying to convey that you look stunning." He willingly gave me another compliment, waiting for me to crack under the pressure of his flattery.

"Thank you, Hassan," I said abruptly, hoping the back and forth would come to an end. Gratefully, it worked.

"Allene, one day . . ." Hassan shook his head as he held back a laugh. I felt my eyebrows furrow, suddenly taken back by his lack of disappointment that our gander had ended.

"One day what?" I pressed, leaning forward in my father's chair.

"You'll see. Anyhow, it's been five weeks. Would you like to update me on what's going on?" he asked.

I could tell Hassan wasn't one to budge. It was no use trying to lure out an explanation.

"*If* I have anything to update you on. What would you like to know?" I inquired.

"To start, how are you holding up?"

I sat up a little taller in my chair, my eyes level with his as his face grew concerned. I tried not to falter in my confidence at the sudden question.

"I am doing well, no reason to be concerned about me. Are you doing all right?" I asked, trying to take the spotlight off myself.

Hassan shook his head, disappointment showing on his face. "I know you want to put up a strong front, but you don't have to pretend with me. Damien mentioned he hasn't seen much of you since our return. In fact, rumor has it; I am one of the first people you've actually talked to," he said, confirming that he did more digging than I was aware of, alluding to me that I couldn't hide.

I sighed, not wanting to talk about my feelings. However,

Hassan being concerned and offering a listening ear was too tempting not to take.

"I recognize I have been a little. . . distant. Granted, I haven't had the opportunity to see Aleron and when I am not worrying myself sick about him all day, I am being haunted in my sleep by his brother." I didn't tiptoe around my concerns for Aleron and Hassan accepted my feelings without a tinge of envy, his poise being another characteristic to admire. *Or maybe it was the deliberate kiss he was able to achieve five weeks ago that took away his envy.* I tried not to blush at the sudden thought.

Hassan nodded like he understood exactly what I was going through, leaving me to process how to acknowledge his sympathy.

"I may not be on the best terms with Aleron. However, I recognize what he has lost. That day keeps playing in my head, over and over again. I regret the moments that I could have done things differently, possibly changed the outcomes for everyone's sake." Hassan had begun talking to himself, sharing his thoughts out loud for me to hear. Understanding he hadn't acknowledged my problem, he continued.

"I wish I had a solution to your nightmares. It sounds like half your problem is not being able to speak to Aleron, correct?" Hassan asked, trying not to seem bothered by it. I nodded.

"Fortunate for you, isn't he here? Your problems could be solved by descending a few flights of stairs. What's stopping you?" he asked, confounded by my lack of authority in my own home. I became slightly offended, shifting my elbows so they rested on the desk, leaning in his direction.

"My mother has strict instructions to not let me speak to him until she decides how to approach the situation further. I actually plan to speak with her this evening, to straighten things out," I confirmed, proud of my progress. Hassan let out his beautiful laugh, making me automatically feel a little happier.

"Since you've broken almost all the rules the last few months, why do you think you need your mother's permission now?" Hassan snickered at his own comment.

I was baffled at Hassan's insistiance for me to see Aleron. Was he not just helplessly flirting with me a few minutes ago? I addressed the observation immediately.

"I am confused. You are incredibly flirtatious one moment and practically pushing me into another man's arms the next," I accused, not necessarily bothered, but definitely bemused.

Hassan shook his head back and forth, approaching the desk and slightly sitting on the edge with ease. He gracefully placed his hand on mine, that electric feeling pulsing between us once again.

"By no means am I pushing. I am playing fair. I am free to roam the palace; he is confined to a room. Currently, I have the upper hand. However, I only find it equitable for us to be honest with each other. We can't move forward if you still have feelings to work out with Aleron. I have come to accept that as I have been away," he pointed out, saying each word courtesy.

I could feel the color drain from my face as Hassan was speaking, the nerves almost restraining my mouth from moving. I stared down at his hands that were now holding mine. His skin was immensely soft and his touch was warm, he was making me dizzy. I tried to pretend the wobbly sensation was from being overly exhausted; to my dismay, I knew the cause was something much more frightening all together.

"Hassan, I have to stop you before you get ahead. I can't comprehend where this is all coming from. If I have given you any indication that–"

Hassan immediately interrupted me, not acknowledging his negligent manners.

"That's just it, you *haven't* given me anything. One dance, one kiss, and a few conversations. I can't speak for you, but the few moments we have been graced with, they are some of the best moments I've had in a long time. You haven't given me proper consideration and you are not bound to Aleron. You still have opportunities for your life to take another direction. I am one of those opportunities," Hassan paused, his optimism advancing through his tender smile.

"Allene, if given an equal chance, I am confident you will see exactly what I see. I refuse to waste anymore of our time together. If I want to prove that we have something, something as real as you think you have with Aleron, I want to do it right. You may have feelings for both of us, and that's all right for now, there will only be one of us in the end. Go talk with him, I will see you at dinner," he said with certainty.

"Dinner?" I asked, perplexed.

Hassan's eyes danced with amusement. "You didn't hear? I have been invited by the queen herself," Hassan replied. *Why would my mother invite Hassan to dinner?* Hassan kissed my hand lightly and turned towards the door, not allowing a single word to escape my lips.

The door had quickly shut, the opportunity to discuss the

oddness of what had just occurred, sent to a halt. Hassan's little speech had left me dumbstruck. I had no idea how to respond to his words of affirmation, which I believed was his objective. He had taken me off guard, my attempt at preparation for our discussion had been useless. I had wanted to ask about his mother and sister, how he was handling everything, what he planned to do now that he had returned, but all those questions somehow got swept away and would need to be addressed later. Dinner was apparently going to be that opportunity.

I laughed quietly to myself. I couldn't wrap my exasperated brain around a few of his statements. Did I actually have feelings for both of them, or was that just Hassan assuming things? Would I actually consider him, *us*, as a possibility? What would Aleron say? I couldn't disrupt anything between him and I right now, not when everything was so delicate. I knew my feelings for Aleron with absolute surety and I saw no value in exploring anything else. I had already tried denying my feelings for him once and knew how difficult it had been. The news of Killian being the real target to spew my hatred towards alleviated any contempt I had for Aleron, the knowledge resolving my feelings back to where they had been before the war. But what if Hassan was right? What if he was someone I could be happy with but hadn't given him the chance?

I needed to shake this odd feeling that was bubbling out of me. I needed to talk to Aleron – probably more than I ever needed to before.

I had no time to twiddle my thumbs and try to manage my thoughts. Dinner was approaching rapidly and I was pressed for time – or so I was telling myself that was why I was in a hurry to get to Aleron's room.

The real reason, *the possibility of considering that I had feelings for Hassan, and the risk of if I considered it one moment longer, that I may actually believe it,* I was completely ignoring. By trying to control my tempted thoughts, I had overlooked the problem I would soon face – getting to Aleron.

I rounded one last corner to find myself at the end of the corridor that led to Aleron's room. As I had hoped, one guard stood alone, protecting the entry to his room. To my relief, I noticed it was Marshal. It couldn't be more perfect.

I approached him slowly, his delayed reaction to my footsteps quite amusing. He regained his posture and seemed a little taller, and rather than seeming bored from his work, his eyes had developed an instant façade of concentration.

"Princess Allene." He bowed deeply, still trying to convince me of his earnest attitude.

I chuckled to myself, breaking the tension. "Marshal, lovely to see you."

Marshal had done a sweep of the area to ensure we were alone. His eyes grew shy and his voice a mere whisper as he approached a subject I wasn't expecting.

"Princess, I have been meaning to apologize to you for the scene that you witnessed before we left the castle. I am deeply humiliated to have been seen under such private circumstances that were highly inappropriate. I want to assure you, I am abiding by the utmost standards of being a perfect gentleman and have distanced myself from Princess Risa." I could hear the restlessness in his voice as he spoke. He was only trying to be comforting and I appreciated that he was unsettled at the idea of offending me by being with my sister.

I graciously placed a hand on his shoulder, staring into his caramel eyes as I tried to suppress a laugh. "I am not the least bit worried about what is going on between you two. I have never seen her so giddy! She has impeccable judgement of character and I would not doubt the goodness of any man she deems worthy to be with her. All I ask is that you spend time with her. To hear that you avoided her because of our incident makes me sad. She has been working incredibly hard to make me happy these last few weeks, please do the same for her," I pleaded, acknowledging my acceptance in every way I could.

Marshal hung onto every word I said, his smile growing between each sentence. I stepped away, being proud of the joy I was able to bring to him. He was kind and extremely handsome; I hoped Risa could truly find love with Marshal. She would be with a courageous knight, someone who could always protect her purity and decency. I could not ask for her to be in better hands.

"I promise you have my full support and my secrecy," I whispered the last words.

"I am in your debt, Princess Allene," he said softly. *Here is my opportunity.*

"Actually, I may ask for that debt to be paid sooner rather than later." I bit my lip, the guiltiness exposing my intentions. Marshal raised an eyebrow, uncertain of what he had just promised. I proceeded before he could take back his offer.

"I came to *secretly* see Aleron. I have no doubt that he is being well taken care of, however, I have many things I need to discuss with him. Would you let me in to see him for a few minutes?" I tried to muster up as much distraught in my voice that I could, stressing how much it meant to me.

I could see Marshal was hesitating, trying to figure how to handle the situation best. He wiped his palms on his pants after rushing his fingers through his hair to distract himself from his new nerves. Part of me felt bad for asking it of him, but the other part of me knew it was necessary.

"Ten minutes. That's the most I can give you. Supper will be coming soon and I cannot risk you being seen by one of the maids," he whispered, trying to be discrete.

I nodded my head, a smile instantly coming to my face. "Marshal, you cannot comprehend how much this means to me, thank you! Ten minutes is all I need," I assured him, making my way to the door.

Marshal staggered to find the key to open the three inch thick door, the only thing keeping me from Aleron. Each second that went by felt like an eternity. I could hear my pulse as it echoed in my ears, my heartbeat racing fast. As the knob turned, a streak of light cracked through the small opening. Without a moment to stall, Marshal ushered me in, locking the door behind me, the reality that I couldn't turn back now hitting me in a rush. I wished I had given more thought of what to say when I got the chance to see Aleron. I was beginning to regret my last minute decision for not preparing mentally the way I had when I expected to see Hassan. *Not that the preparation with Hassan had done me good anyways.*

Then I noted the difference between the two men. I hadn't

prepared because with Aleron I didn't need to. A sudden new feeling flooded my gut. Not anticipation, not fear, not uncertainty. I knew the feeling instantly. It was the comforting warmth that I felt when I was near Aleron.

My excitement grew as my eyes fell upon an elegant figure in the corner of the room. He was sitting on a chair, his right leg being held close to his body as his chin rested neatly on his knee. His startled expression melted into one of longing, as his ice blue eyes captured mine. I searched every inch of him, noticing the extended length in his hair, the beard on his face that was thick and full, and the flawless complexion that was masked behind it all.

Not a mark or a scratch was found on his body from what I could see. I noticed his muscular arms, exposed from wearing only his undershirt, were flexed just slightly from the position they were in, and I could feel my heart sink just a little more. To add to it all, he had to show off his remarkable smile, the stark whiteness of his teeth dazzling me. How could I – even for a second – think that I could have feelings for someone else? All I needed was to see Aleron to know what we had.

Right when I thought it couldn't become more of a dream, I was put into a state of pure fantasy. Aleron only needed to say a few words in his velvet voice with his enticing lips to make me question my grip on reality.

"Hello, my angel. I knew you would come."